Murder Among Strangers

Books by Jonnie Jacobs

The Kate Austen Mysteries

MURDER AMONG NEIGHBORS
MURDER AMONG FRIENDS
MURDER AMONG US
MURDER AMONG STRANGERS

The Kali O'Brien Mysteries

SHADOW OF DOUBT
EVIDENCE OF GUILT
MOTION TO DISMISS

Published by Kensington Publishing Corp.

Murder Among Strangers

A Kate Austen Mystery

JONNIE JACOBS

KENSINGTON BOOKS
http://www.kensingtonbooks.com

M
c.1

KENSINGTON BOOKS are published by

Kensington Publishing Corp.
850 Third Avenue
New York, NY 10022

Library of Congress Card Catalogue Number: 99-066831
ISBN 1-57566-540-9

First Printing: March, 2000
10   9   8   7   6   5   4   3   2   1

Printed in the United States of America

For Helen, Judith, Martha, Pam, Pru and Sandy
Through triumphs and sorrows

Acknowledgments

I am grateful to Leila Laurence for giving me a glimpse of behind-the-scenes police work, and to the sharp-eyed members of my critique group—Margaret Lucke, Lynn MacDonald, and Penny Warner—for their feedback on the manuscript. Their insights and comments were, as always, invaluable. My thanks, as well, to Lee Harris, Lora Roberts, and Valerie Wolzien, for encouragement and camaraderie along the way. A final thanks to my editor, John Scognamiglio, for his continued support.

I

At the tender age of six, my daughter Anna has already learned that it's hard to tell the good guys from the bad. The saints from the sinners, friends from foes.

She's standing at the window, her eye on the cable-television truck parked across the street.

"Is it them, again?" she asks hesitantly, afraid that this time the answer will be yes.

I run my hand over the top of her head. Her honey brown hair is fine and silky under my palm. "No. That's over. Remember?"

"For how long?"

"For good. It's not something we need to worry about anymore."

"Libby says—"

Anna's words are cut short by the appearance of Libby herself, who sashays into the room in a whirlwind of teenage energy.

"Have you seen my yellow sweater?" she asks without preamble. It sounds like an accusation, but I'm reasonably sure that's not what she intends.

Libby is a foster child of sorts—the daughter of a friend who was killed last year. While we've had our disagreements, the absence of a blood tie seems somehow to cut us more slack with one another.

"I haven't," I tell her. "Did you check your backpack?"

"Backpack. Closet. The car. Everywhere."

"It's in my room," Anna exclaims, as though she's just scored in *Jeopardy*. "You took it off when we were doing our exercises."

Libby slaps her forehead with the heel of her palm. "Right. I remember now."

The two of them head for Anna's room, the specter of bad tidings forgotten.

I sink down in the armchair near the window and find my eyes drawn, as Anna's were, to the van across the street. My mind, though, is filled with images from the night it all began. Like the opening credits on the big screen, they unfold in my mind.

It was January—cold, wet, and ugly. People think it doesn't rain in California, but it does. That night, it was raining heavily. The kind of downpour that makes you think God has opened a faucet over your head. Even at the fastest speed, my windshield wipers couldn't keep up with the deluge. The wind howled, dropping limbs and blowing debris across the roadway.

I was headed home, hugging the winding, two-lane road like a safety line in the night. In this unincorporated part of the county, houses were few and far between. Streetlights were nonexistent.

It was later than I'd expected, which would irritate Michael. But then, he was already irritated, although about what I couldn't say. That, in turn, made me peevish. We'd been snapping at each other for weeks, then compounding the problem by ignoring it.

I squinted into the darkness, cursing the ineffectual wiper blades he'd promised to replace. The rain pounded loudly against the car roof, threatening to drown out the radio. I was concentrating so hard on the parallel ribbons of yellow at the center of the roadway that at first I didn't see the car with its lights off stopped near the shoulder on the other side. It was an older model turquoise sedan, long and wide. And it blocked enough of the lane that anyone coming the other direction would have to swerve across the double line to avoid hitting it.

As I went by, my gaze caught the face of a woman in the driver's seat. Young, with an expression so petulant it was almost comic. Her eyes met mine briefly; then she looked away. I'd passed before it all registered.

I thought of simply driving on. She hadn't flagged me down, after all. Nor did she appear to be injured. She would have managed, I told myself, if I hadn't happened by. Couldn't she manage just as well if I passed and didn't stop?

Sure. Is that what you'd want if the situation were reversed? Or if it were Libby stranded there on a deserted road in the middle of the night?

I found a wide spot in the pavement and managed, with considerable effort and some deft maneuvering, to turn the car around without getting stuck in the mud. I headed back in the direction I'd come and pulled in behind the car.

Okay, Ms. Good Samaritan. What if she's out here on purpose, studying the effects of rain on asphalt or some such thing. You'll inconvenience yourself for nothing and wind up looking like a fool.

It wouldn't be the first time, I told myself.

With the illumination of my headlights, however, I saw

immediately what the problem was. The car's right rear wheel was missing.

I parked on the shoulder, behind the stranded car, and felt a moment's satisfaction at doing something which would undoubtedly irk Michael if he knew.

Grabbing my umbrella, I climbed out. The woman rolled down her window when I approached.

"You need help?" I asked.

She shook her head. Straw blond curls shimmied with the movement. "No. I mean, I don't think so."

She was attractive in a hardened kind of way. Without the dark lip liner and heavy shadow she might even have been pretty. She looked to be in her early twenties, although between the makeup and the darkness of night, it was hard to tell. She sounded about twelve.

"I can give you a lift somewhere, if you'd like."

"No, I . . ." She was shivering so hard she had trouble talking. "My . . . friend went for help. Only I thought he'd be back before now."

"How long has it been?"

"I don't know. Over an hour."

"You sure he's coming back tonight?"

"This is his car." She hugged her arms across her chest in an effort to keep warm.

"Why don't you at least turn on the engine and stay warm?"

"The tank's almost empty."

"Look," I told her, holding the umbrella tight against a gust of wind. "You're freezing cold. Besides, with the car jutting out into the road the way it is, you could get hit. Why don't you let me take you into town? You can leave a note for your friend."

She shook her head. "No, really. Bobby wouldn't like that."

To hell with Bobby, I thought. What kind of friend leaves a young woman alone on a night like this, without even enough gas to keep the engine running?

"What's your name?" I asked her. "The least I can do is call Bobby when I get home and make sure he hasn't forgotten you."

"It's Sheryl Ann. But I wouldn't know where to have you call. He was going to get the tire fixed. I'll be okay, really." She was putting up a brave front, but I could hear the doubt in her voice.

"Maybe there's a blanket in the trunk," I said. "And some flares."

"I don't . . ."

My patience was wearing thin. I was cold and wet and anxious to be on my way. But Sheryl Ann seemed incapable of helping herself. I was afraid that if I simply walked away, I'd be reading about her demise in the news: *Young woman freezes to death in winter storm.*

I reached through the open window for the keys. "Let's take a look and see. Okay?"

"No," she said, more firmly this time. "I'm fine. Really."

But I'd already grabbed the keys. I was used to dealing with recalcitrant children, which was how I was beginning to think of Sheryl Ann. I found the lock and opened the trunk.

Sheryl Ann was out of the car now, without an umbrella or a jacket. "I'm fine," she said again, tugging on my arm. "You really don't need to—"

"See, there is a blanket," I told her. "Now that you're wet, you'll really need it."

I grabbed a corner of the blanket and pulled, uncovering a man's shoe. Tugging harder, I saw that it wasn't just a shoe. There was a foot inside. Attached to a leg. Which, given the futility of my tugging, I felt certain was connected to a body.

It took a moment for these realizations to sink in, and when they did, they hit me like a lead ball in the chest. Fear sucked the air from my lungs.

"It's not the way it looks," Sheryl Ann said.

That was often the case. But unless this body in the blanket was something other than flesh and bone, it didn't look good.

"Is he dead?"

She nodded.

"Who is he?"

"Tully."

"Tully," I repeated, simply for something to say.

"My husband," she added.

I didn't try to sort it out, not just then. All I wanted was to get away from there as quickly as possible. I started to back up, heading for my car.

"I know what you're thinking," she said, following me.

"Look, whatever's between you and your husband, I guess it doesn't really concern me, right? So I'll just . . ."

A flash of headlights around the bend, a screech of tires as a car skidded to a stop on the opposite side of the street.

Fear prickled my skin and sent a tremor down my spine.

I should never had stopped.

Squinting into the glare, I saw a man emerge from the passenger side. As he began rolling a tire up the road toward us, the car took off again with another squeal of rubber on wet pavement.

"Bobby!" Sheryl Ann's voice was flooded with relief.

I, on the other hand, felt nothing of the sort.

Bobby couldn't have been far out of his teens, if that. But he was big, built like a linebacker. His hair was cropped close to his scalp, and he sported a silver ring through his left eyebrow.

"Jesus Christ, Sheryl Ann." He let the tire fall flat at our feet as he inspected the open trunk. "What the fuck do you think you're doing?"

"I didn't . . . I mean, she just stopped to help."

"And you opened the goddamn trunk for her? Now what are we going to do?"

I started backing up again.

Bobby stepped forward. "Where do you think you're going?"

"Well, now that you two are set I'll just be heading on—" My heart was pounding so loudly, I was sure he could hear it.

Bobby grabbed my arm, roughly. "You're not going nowhere, lady. You think we're *that* stupid?"

No, I was the one who was stupid. Utterly, totally stupid. Why hadn't I just driven on? Why did I feel this need to offer a hand to anyone who looked the least bit needy?

His fingers dug into my flesh, bringing tears to my eyes.

"What are you going to do with her?" asked Sheryl Ann.

Bobby shook his head. "We can't let her go. She'll head straight for police." He kicked the tire in disgust. "Fuck. We'll have to get rid of her, I guess."

Bile rose in my throat. "I won't say a word to anyone," I stammered. "Honest."

Bobby spat on the ground.

"You mean you're going to kill her?" The awe in Sheryl Ann's words wasn't comforting.

"You got a better idea?"

She shook her head slowly. "No, I guess not."

Panic filled my head like a blinding white light. I screamed and managed to pull free. I started to run. Bobby's hand grabbed my wrist; his other arm circled my neck. I could feel his breath on my face.

With one quick movement, he released his grasp on my wrist and reached into his pocket. Out of the corner of my eye, I saw him raise a hand. Something dark and shiny glimmered in his fist.

Then red-hot pain shot through my body. I sank into merciful nothingness.

2

I was cold. Chilled to the bone. Maybe even *through* the bone. With a throbbing lump at the back of my skull and a headache so terrible I didn't dare open my eyes.

"Michael?" My lips had trouble forming the word. I struggled to say his name louder, but all that came out was a low moan. I tried again, leaning slightly toward the pressure of his body. He needed to take out the garbage. It smelled something terrible.

So cold. My muscles knotted against the frigid air. The bedcovers must have slipped off during the night. Carefully, shifting only my right arm, I tried reaching for the comforter. But my arm wouldn't move. Nor would my left. Or my feet.

Then I remembered the flash of metal, the burst of searing pain. And Bobby. It all came back to me in sudden, bold relief, and turned my stomach inside out.

I'd never given much thought to the journey from life to death. Never spent much time wondering whether it entailed a passage through pearly gates, a white light beckoning at the end of a dark tunnel, rivers of smoldering embers, or simply a fading of consciousness. But I was pretty sure none of us made the trip by garbage truck, rattling around in pitch-black, breathing gasoline fumes.

I took this as a positive sign. I wasn't dead. But I had a gut-wrenching headache, and my mouth tasted of blood. With a searing jolt of consciousness, I realized that the body pressing against my back wasn't Michael but a dead man named Tully.

Panic gripped me. Tears burned the corners of my eyes. I tried moving my arms again. They were bound. As were my feet. And it wasn't a garbage truck, I determined with growing lucidity, but the trunk of a car.

Me and Tully.

One dead, one on her way.

Again I felt the white swell of terror. My heart pounded in my ears. I couldn't breathe. They were going to kill me.

Kill. Me.

Gradually, panic gave way to overwhelming grief. I'd never see Anna again. Never feel the soft warmth of her slender body in my arms. Never hear the *I love you* that accompanied our ritual good night kisses, or experience the utter joy of a spontaneous and unexpected hug. Never again. Hot tears snaked down my cheek.

Anna was only six. Two months shy of her seventh birthday. Would she even remember me in the years to come? I tried to recall if we had any good photos of me. If we had any photos of me at all, since I was usually the one behind the camera. Would Andy, who was my former husband and Anna's father, fill her head with verbal pictures that were wrong? Would he let Michael see her? Anna was fond of Michael. If she lost him along with me . . .

Anna, Michael, and Libby. Andy, too. For all his faults,

I cared about him. A wave of sadness rolled over me—
a desperate longing so powerful I thought it might kill
me before Bobby had a chance.

Kill me. There it was again. My own death staring me
in the face.

Looking at the situation from Bobby's point of view, I
could understand the logic of it. They'd already killed
poor Tully. What did they have to lose by doing away
with me, too? They couldn't very well let me go. Not
when I'd seen the body in their trunk. Even I could
understand that. So what choice did they really have?

I wondered how they'd do it. Would it be over quickly?
Would it hurt?

And why hadn't they done it already?

The car turned sharply, and I rolled against Tully. His
flesh was stiff and unyielding. Colder even than my own.

We turned again and stopped so abruptly I thought
for a moment we'd hit something. Then into reverse. We
backed up, turned, and came to standstill again.

Car doors opened, then slammed shut. Footsteps,
voices. Where were we? Would someone hear me if I
yelled for help?

I managed to lift my bound fists against the inside of
the hood. There wasn't much room for leverage, but I
pounded as hard as I could. The sound was muffled, not
nearly as loud as I'd have liked.

"Help," I screamed at the top of my voice. "Help me.
Anyone, please. I'm in the trunk."

Hurried steps, a muttered *shit*, and the trunk sprang
open. Bobby towered above me, a shadowy giant barely
discernible against the dark sky.

A blue neon sign, dim with dust and age, flickered in
my peripheral vision. I felt a surge of hope. We'd stopped

near a business. Surely, there were people here who could summon help, if only I could find a way to alert them.

"I thought I told you to fucking gag her," Bobby said to Sheryl Ann.

"The handkerchief was too small. I couldn't tie it. Besides, she was out like a light."

"Yeah, well she's not now." He looked to his right in the direction of the neon sign, then back at me. "We're lucky we didn't stop at one of those busy places right off the freeway."

"Please," I said. "I'm cold."

"You're going to be a lot colder before long." He turned to Sheryl Ann. "Give me that handkerchief."

"I have to go to the bathroom," I pleaded.

Ignoring me, Bobby began folding the handkerchief.

Sheryl Ann stopped him. "C'mon, Bobby, have a heart. Let her go the bathroom. You want her to pee all over your trunk?"

"Don't see how it matters. We're going to have to wash it real good anyway."

"You ought to let her ride in the car, too. Where it's warm and not so, so . . ." Sheryl Ann stopped and took a breath. "Where she doesn't have to lie next to Tully."

"What?" Bobby's voice exploded like gunfire. "We running a bus service or something?"

Sheryl Ann pressed her body against his, ran a hand down his cheek to his lips. "C'mon, what's she ever done to you?"

"That's not the point. I explained to you what we gotta do."

"Yeah, I know. You gotta get rid of her. I understand that. But we don't have to treat her mean beforehand, do we?"

Bobby kissed Sheryl Ann's finger. Then he pulled her close and kissed her hard on the mouth. "You're a hell of a lot of trouble, woman." But he leaned over and untied me.

"You try anything, lady, and it's all over. You got that?" He patted his jacket pocket revealing a gunlike bulge. "I'll walk the two of you to the rest room door. Sheryl Ann, you keep a good eye on her inside."

My head throbbed when I stood up, and I felt the sour taste of nausea in my throat. I looked for someone to signal for help.

"Come on, lady." Bobby shoved me ahead of him. "We ain't got all day."

We'd stopped at a small, old-fashioned gas station somewhere well off the beaten path. Except for the station attendant, who was inside a spartan cubicle off the service bay talking on the phone, we were the only people around. At least the rain had stopped.

The rest rooms were located on the side of the building, and locked.

"Go get the key," Bobby barked to Sheryl Ann. He kept his right hand in his pocket, calling attention to the gunlike bulge. "I shoulda killed you straight off," he muttered when we were alone.

I didn't tempt fate by asking why he hadn't.

Sheryl Ann returned with the key and opened the bathroom door. Bobby nudged me forward, then did the same to Sheryl Ann. "Go on."

"It's a single," she protested. "Just a toilet and sink." "So?"

"Bobby, I don't want—"

"Either you stand watch over her, or I will."

Sheryl Ann looked at him, started to say something, then changed her mind. "Okay. I'll do it."

Joining me in the tiny, far-from-clean bathroom, she seemed no happier about the situation than I was. As I crossed the sticky floor to the toilet, she turned to face the aqua-tiled wall, giving me the semblance of privacy.

What I really wanted was the chance to scrawl a message, to somehow indicate that I needed help. The illusion of privacy wasn't enough for that. Although, to be honest, I wasn't at all sure anyone would have noticed. The walls were covered with several generations of graffiti.

And there was no window. No way out but the door where Bobby stood watch.

"What's your name?" Sheryl Ann asked, still facing the wall.

"Kate."

"You married?"

"I was. My divorce was final last month."

"He run out on you?"

"Not exactly." Andy had left me, but he'd come back. Not with his tail between his legs, exactly, but willing to pick up where we'd left off. Trouble was, where we'd left off wasn't all that great, even from my perspective. And in the interim I'd met Michael.

"Did he hurt you?"

Andy made me feel insignificant. Generic woman rather than cherished one. And he was a first person singular pronoun guy—*I* and *me* instead of *we* and *us*. But I didn't think that was the sort of hurt she was talking about.

"It was a mutual decision," I told her. "We're still friends."

"That's good." Sheryl Ann giggled, a thin sound edged with nervousness. "Better than killing the guy," she added in a whisper.

"Is that what you did?" I asked, washing my hands in the thin trickle of available water. My whisper matched her own. "Did you kill your husband?"

"Poor Tully," was all she said.

"Why'd you do it?"

She looked at me. "Do you miss him?"

"Who?"

"Your husband. Or are you seeing someone?"

I felt a stab of anguish when I thought of Michael.

Before I could answer, there was a banging on the door from outside. "You about finished in there?" Bobby yelled.

"Yeah, she's coming," Sheryl Ann shot back. "But then I gotta go."

"Send her out first."

"Yeah, yeah." She opened the door.

"We'll meet you at the car," Bobby snapped. "Don't take all day, either."

As we headed back, I tried to catch the attendant's eye. He looked our way once, briefly. I mouthed, "Help," with as much exaggeration as I could muster. The man must have misread my plea for a yawn because he yawned himself several times in succession and showed no interest at all in me or the jacket pocket Bobby kept pointed in my direction.

Traveling in the backseat instead of the trunk was definitely warmer, but only marginally more comfortable. Bobby had again bound my hands and feet with rough, itchy rope, told me to lie flat, then wrapped me in the scratchy, smelly blanket that had formerly covered Tully. I could hear Bobby and Sheryl Ann in the front, munching on potato chips. The beat of rap from the radio pounded in my head.

"You sure this is a good idea?" Sheryl Ann asked after a while.

"Sure what's a good idea?"

"Taking him to Idaho."

"What else were we gonna do with him? Couldn't leave him at the house where someone would find him. No body, no crime."

I bit my tongue to keep from correcting him.

"I don't know," Sheryl Anne mumbled. "It doesn't seem right somehow."

"Wasn't right the way he treated you, either."

"Could have been worse."

Bobby gave a throaty laugh. "Is that why you took up with me, 'cause you were so in love with Tully? Don't go making the guy into a saint just 'cause he's dead."

"I didn't mean that."

"Besides, what's done is done. It's ourselves we've got to worry about now."

Silence, then Sheryl Ann giggled.

"Not here, Bobby. Kate's back there, don't forget."

"So?"

"Bobby, stop it. Please."

He laughed. "Kate, huh? You two seem to have gotten chummy real fast."

"You spend time with someone, you got to know their name."

"Why?"

"Because."

"Because, why?" Bobby's tone vacillated between teasing and peevish.

"Because it's only right."

"*Only right*," he mimicked. "Sweetheart, you aren't by any chance a preacher's daughter, are you? You seem awfully interested in remembering what's right."

"My father wasn't any preacher, for sure."

Bobby gave a few grunts in time to the music. "Let me have another handful of chips."

The rattle of cellophane. "How much longer?" Sheryl Ann asked.

"Tonight? We'll stop pretty soon. It's almost two o'clock, and I'm about done in."

Two o'clock. What would Michael be thinking? He'd be worried by now. Past the anger on which we'd parted, past the irritation at my being late, past the point of trying to convince himself that everything was okay.

I tried to remember if I'd left the number of my evening appointment. I'd been late getting out of the house, busy leaving instructions for Libby and Anna. But the name and number were in my appointment book. Certainly Michael would think to check. As a policeman, he knows his way around trouble as well as anyone.

But what good would it do? He'd talk to Donna, find out that we'd discussed various options—watercolor, oils, tapestry. That we'd looked at slides, set a date for me to come back with selections, and that I'd left before nine. Someone would eventually find my car. And then what?

It wasn't hard to imagine.

Kate Austen, last seen leaving the office of a client she was visiting in connection with her art consultant business, did not return home last night. Her car, an older model Volvo wagon, was found early this morning along a deserted stretch of road in the Diablo Canyon area. Although foul play is suspected, there were no signs that she left her car under duress. Friends and family have no clue as to her whereabouts.

And they might never know, I thought, swallowing against the lump in my throat. Me and Tully buried in some far-off corner of Idaho.

No body, no crime. Not true in the strictest sense, but it sure made solving a crime more difficult.

3

Outside the rain lashed against the windows and pummeled the roof. Inside, the house was quiet, the predawn stillness almost palpable. Michael could feel it graze his skin, hear it ringing in his ears. He filled the kettle with water and set it to boil. More coffee was the last thing he needed. But he wasn't going to be sleeping tonight, anyway. This morning, he corrected himself. It was already half past three.

He'd waited until midnight before calling the highway patrol and the Walnut Hills Police Department, where he himself was a lieutenant. Kate didn't like him breathing down her neck. He needed to give her room, she said. And she had told him, rather curtly, that she wasn't sure what time she'd be home, certainly not before ten.

It wasn't like Kate to be late without calling, but he hadn't been too worried at first, despite the rain. An undercurrent of tension had settled between them the past few weeks, and he figured that Kate was simply flexing some muscle. Putting him on notice that she wasn't to be trifled with.

It was his fault, he knew. Or mostly his fault, anyway. He would be the first to admit he'd been difficult to live with, snapping when he shouldn't have, withdrawing when Kate asked him what was wrong. But with what was going on at work, well, he was worried. And it didn't help matters any that he felt uncomfortable talking about it with Kate.

When he'd checked at midnight, there'd been no reports of an accident involving a Volvo wagon. By twelve-thirty, no longer able to ignore the uneasiness at the back of his mind, he'd called Kate's evening appointment, a woman by the name of Donna Saxon, apologizing profusely for waking her.

Kate had left her place a little before nine, Donna said, and no, she hadn't mentioned plans to go elsewhere. Not that she would have necessarily. Michael had called Kate's friend Sharon Covington next, again with apologies. The things women knew about their friends, and their friends' lives, always astounded him. He'd been hoping Sharon would laugh at his worry and remind him that Kate had a midnight PTA meeting or some such thing. Sharon hadn't been able to help, though, and her apprehension about Kate's absence only compounded his own.

Michael had intended to wait another two hours before calling work again. But by one o'clock he was frantic. He'd picked up the phone and sent a couple of cars out to look for her. He would have gone himself except that Libby and Anna were asleep, and he wanted to be home in case Kate called.

And then there'd been nothing more he could do but pace the house, watch the clock, and listen for the sound of Kate's car pulling into the driveway. That's what he'd been doing for the past two and a half hours.

When the kettle came to a boil, Michael spooned coffee

into the Melitta cone and poured the water through. He'd taken one of the chipped mugs. Kate hated using them, but he didn't mind. He'd never even considered it an issue before meeting Kate. Of course, his ex-wife wouldn't have kept a chipped dish in the house, so maybe he'd never had a chance to consider it.

Michael took his coffee to the small eating area off the kitchen and sat watching the rain splatter against the window. He was past the initial waiting, past the growing anxiety that came with the knowledge something wasn't right. Now, he was scared. The news, when it came, was going to be bad. The only question was how bad.

4

"This place must be at least fifty years old," Sheryl Ann said as the car slowed to a stop. "Makes Motel 6 look like a four-star resort."

"It'll do," Bobby replied.

"I hope it's clean. I'm not sleeping where there's bugs."

"I'll shake out the bedding for you. How's that?"

"If there's bugs," she grumbled, "shaking them loose isn't going to make it better."

I was glad we were stopping, no matter how bad the place was. My body felt cramped from lying in one position unable to move. More importantly, it might give me another chance to summon help. And anything was better than the cold dread that had paralyzed me the last few hours.

"Go get us a room," Bobby told Sheryl Ann. "Don't give them your real name, either. Here's sixty dollars, Kate's treat, but the room better be a whole lot cheaper than that."

Sheryl Ann hesitated. "What are we going to do about Kate?"

"She can spend the night in the trunk."

"We can't do that," Sheryl Ann protested, taking the words right out of my mouth. Not that I could have spoken them anyway, with the gag binding my flesh.

"Can't leave her in the car. She might attract attention."

"We've got to let her come inside, Bobby. It's cold out here, and she probably needs to use the rest room again."

I grunted agreement. I didn't like them talking about me like I wasn't there.

Bobby gave a humorless laugh. "You're missing the point here, baby. She's no guest or nothin'. She's a witness to a fucking crime. *Our* crime."

"Only 'cause she was trying to help me."

"Doesn't matter *why*, Sheryl Ann. Fact remains, she's a danger. She opens her yap, and we go to jail."

The car door opened. "Bobby Lake, you've got a heart of stone." And then it slammed shut.

"Lady," he muttered, presumably addressing me, "you're nothing but a heap of trouble. I can't wait to be rid of you."

Why didn't he kill me then? Not that I wanted to encourage that line of action, but it was a thought that passed my mind with alarming frequency.

"Nothing personal," Bobby added.

As if that made any difference.

Fear churned inside me, making it difficult to breathe. I didn't want to die. Especially not like this.

I didn't want to spend the night in the trunk, either, lying next to a stinking dead man. Frustration mixed with the fear. Tears again filled my eyes.

I was *not* going to spend the night in the trunk. It was cold outside. Close to freezing probably, based on the icy chill that swept the car when Sheryl Ann opened the door. My muscles were sore, my wrists burned from trying to work free of the restraints, and my throat tickled from the cloth gagging my mouth. My whole body screamed in protest.

Sheryl Ann returned a few minutes later. "We're in 3B," she said.

We drove a few hundred feet, parked, and the two of them got out without exchanging another word.

Alone, I began working myself free of the blanket. I wasn't sure how long I had before Bobby returned to stuff me into the trunk, but I wasn't about to let opportunity pass me by. Certainly we couldn't be the only people at the motel, however old and seedy it was. If I could just catch sight of another human being, I'd hit the horn if I could reach it, or pound the car window with my fists.

I'd barely managed to extricate my head from the scratchy wool shroud when I heard Bobby coming toward the car. My optimism dissipated like a puff of smoke. But the charge of energy that had accompanied it remained. I wasn't going back into the trunk without a fight. I tensed, ready to start thrashing the minute he touched me.

Bobby opened the backseat door with an angry tug. "Come on. You're sleeping inside tonight." He leaned in and untied my feet.

I struggled to slide out of the car—something that's not easy when your hands are tied.

"Any funny business," Bobby warned, "and you'll wish I'd left you in the trunk. That understood?" He removed the gag.

"Thank you."

"It wasn't my doing."

Looking around, I could appreciate Sheryl Ann's concern about the quality of the accommodations. The motel consisted of six tiny concrete-block bungalows. The tar-paper roofs didn't look strong enough to keep out the night air much less the rain. There wasn't one single car in the lot besides Bobby's.

We went through the bathroom routine again, with Sheryl Ann's back keeping me company while my mind raced through possible scenarios of escape. Then Bobby retied my feet and replaced the gag. I spent the night on the floor of the closet, but thanks to Sheryl Ann I had both a blanket and a pillow.

What I needed was a plan for escape, and that I didn't have. My hands and feet were tied tightly. No matter how much I twisted and tugged, the rope wouldn't give. Besides, I'd heard Bobby moving furniture. I was sure he'd managed to pen me in so that I couldn't break free without alerting him.

I tried to stay calm. I knew that was important. Tried not to think about how desperately I missed Anna and Libby and Michael. How much I wanted to see them again.

My wrists were raw from trying to work the ties loose. My shoulder and hip pressed uncomfortably against the hard floor, and my right foot had developed a painful cramp. But it was my heart that hurt most.

Tears welled in my eyes. I cried silently, choked with despair.

The sudden glare of the overhead light woke me.

"You gotta get up," Sheryl Ann said. "It's morning."

I didn't want morning. I wanted to climb back into the world of my dream. A world with Michael and Anna and Libby. A comforting world, the memory of which again brought tears to my eyes.

"Bobby went to get some donuts and stuff," Sheryl Ann explained. "He won't be gone long. If you want a shower, you need to do it now." She removed the gag, and untied my feet and hands. "I've got the gun. Don't make me use it, okay?"

I nodded. Sheryl Ann was a strange mix of compassion and callousness. I had no doubt that she'd shoot me if she had to.

"There's toothpaste near the sink if you want to rub some on your teeth. And you can use some of my body lotion if you want. Only you've got to be quick about it."

My head still thick with sleep, I stumbled into the tiny, worn bathroom.

"I'll give you privacy," Sheryl Ann said. "Just leave the door cracked a fraction."

The tub was pitted and rust-stained, and the surrounding tile was edged with mold, but the hot water soothed my aching muscles. I closed my eyes for a moment and let the spray massage my shoulders and back. I used the time to think. There was no window, no visible weapon. Could I leave a secret message of distress?

No, I decided, I couldn't. There was no way. I had nothing to write with and no place to write that wouldn't be evident to my captors.

And then I remembered the toothpaste. Not as good as lipstick, but better than nothing.

I stepped out of the shower, squeezed a half inch of Crest gel onto my finger and climbed back into the tub. Several fingers of toothpaste later, my message was scrawled on the tiles above the spigot. *Help. Kidnapped. Call police.* And then Michael's phone number. My fervent hope was that whoever cleaned the room would be both observant and able to read English.

Stepping from the shower, I pulled the curtain closed across the end where I'd left my message.

I was buttoning my blouse a minute later when I heard Bobby return.

"What's she doing in there alone?" he screamed at Sheryl Ann. "I told you to keep your eye on her."

"I am."

"Only she's in there, and you're out here."

"She can't go anywhere, Bobby. There's not even a window."

He yanked open the bathroom door and glared at me. "Come on. You're finished in there whether you like it or not."

I held my breath as I slid past him. *Don't let him check the tub. Please.*

Bobby gave the bathroom a cursory glance, then stepped back and tossed the plastic bag of groceries onto the bed. He tied my hands again while Sheryl Ann reached for the bag and began plowing through it.

She gave him an impish grin. "Good, you got some with chocolate frosting."

He lifted her chin and kissed her on the mouth. "You know I'd do anything for you."

She paused. "Guess you just about have, Bobby."

"Yeah," he said, suddenly serious, "guess I have." He pulled his shirt over his head. "I'm going to take a quick shower myself, and then we're outta here."

My apprehension returned with the suddenness of a summer storm. I felt bile rise into my throat. Felt my limbs go cold. Bobby would see the message I'd scrawled on the tile. Any minute now he'd come thundering through the door in a rage. God knew what he'd do.

I was sitting in the chair, my hands tied in front of me this time instead of behind me. The gun was at Sheryl Ann's side on the bed opposite from where I was sitting. If she turned toward the door when Bobby emerged, I might have time to grab it.

"You got any kids?" Sheryl Ann asked, breaking a chocolate donut in half.

I jumped, as though she might have read my thoughts. "A daughter."

"How old?"

"Six, almost seven." I kept my ear on the sounds from the bathroom. I could hear the water running in the tub, and then the shower.

"Little girl would be nice. I'd like to have a little girl someday. Tully didn't much care for children."

"Well, now that Tully's no longer in the picture . . ." My words trailed off while I concentrated on the sounds of Bobby in the shower. The words I'd traced in toothpaste would be lower than eye level for him, but he'd be bound to see them eventually. I was surprised he hadn't already.

"Your husband a good father?"

I turned my attention back to Sheryl Ann. "My husband?"

"Your ex. Does he treat her nice?"

"Yes, he does. The two of them get along very well."

She nodded toward the box of donuts. "Aren't you going to eat anything?"

Until Bobby announced his intention to shower, I'd been starving. Now the thought of food made me nauseated. I shook my head.

"May be your last chance for a while. Bobby doesn't like stopping once he's on the road. Doesn't believe much in regular meals in any case." She licked the chocolate frosting from her fingers. "Guess that's how he keeps the super body."

I nodded absently, my heart pounding in my chest. If he started his shower with his back to the spray, would the lettering wash away before he turned around? I sent a silent prayer that it would.

"And he *does* have a body, doesn't he?"

"Excuse me?"

"Bobby. He's a real hunk—don't you think?"

He was big. Beyond that I hadn't noticed.

Sheryl brushed a loose strand of hair from her face. "I swear, the minute I laid eyes on him I knew we'd end up together."

"Except that you were married to Tully."

She shrugged.

"Is that why you killed him?"

"Wasn't me. It was Bobby."

The water from the shower stopped. I froze, expecting Bobby to burst through the door any minute. A trickle of sweat worked its way down the back of my neck.

"Sheryl Ann," I said after a moment, "if you didn't kill him, you've nothing to worry about. Why did you let Bobby drag you into it?"

"He didn't drag me."

"Why did you let yourself get involved, then? You want to go to jail for something you didn't do?"

"We're not going to jail. Bobby's got it figured out."

My eyes darted to the bathroom door. I lowered my voice. "You'll live your life on the run, always looking over your shoulder. Is that what you want? And eventually the cops will catch up with you.''

"No, that's not—''

I cut her off. "Killing me is only going to make it worse. You *will* be a party to that.''

"He doesn't want to kill you, you know, or he'd have done it by now. It's not like he's a bad person or anything.''

That was a point we could argue forever. "You've got the gun," I told her. "You don't have to do what Bobby says.''

Sheryl Ann sucked on her cheeks.

"When you check us out of here, tell the guy at the desk to call the police. I'll tell them that it was Bobby who forced me into the car, that you've tried to help me.''

She shook her head. "That wouldn't be fair to Bobby.''

"What about *me?* You think you're being fair to me?''

Her chin jutted forward. "Nobody asked you to get involved.''

"You're in big trouble, Sheryl Ann. Don't make it worse. You should—''

Suddenly the bathroom door opened, and Bobby loomed against the light like a giant at sunrise. I tensed, ready for his unleashed anger. I kept my eye on the gun.

"You leave any donuts for me?" he said, toweling his dark hair.

"Practically the whole box. Kate's not hungry.''

He grabbed a sugar donut and ate it in two bites. "Just let me get my contacts in, and then we'll hit the road.''

Contacts.

Bobby wore contacts. Without them he'd obviously

been unable to tell my toothpaste lettering from soap smudges. The words were probably washed away by now, but suddenly that no longer mattered. My insurrection had gone undetected.

I found myself giddy with relief.

5

The call came at 6:07, before the light of day. Out of habit, Michael checked the clock and mentally noted the time.

"We've found her car," Frank said, not mincing words. "But no sign of Kate."

"Where'd you find it?"

"Huckleberry Drive, headed east."

"East? You sure about that?" She'd have been heading west coming home, Michael thought.

"East," Frank said. "She pulled off onto the shoulder. No sign of an accident and the car works fine. We checked to see if she'd had engine trouble."

Michael hesitated. He wasn't sure he was ready to hear the answer to his next question. "Any indication of a struggle?"

"None that was obvious. We'll pull the car in if you'd like and run some tests."

Of course he'd like. "The sooner the better," Michael said, irritated that the issue had been in question. Nonetheless, Frank's words brought a tenuous thread of hope. If Kate hadn't put up a struggle . . .

"Looks like she left the car voluntarily," Frank continued, as if reading Michael's thoughts. "Least that's how it appears on first impression."

"What about her purse?"

"No sign of it."

Michael rolled his shoulders, fighting the tension that wouldn't let up. "That doesn't make sense. Where would she have gone?"

"Got me."

"Any indication of other cars parked in the area last night?"

"Nope. But any footprints or tire tracks would be washed away by now. Last night's storm dropped a lot of water." Frank paused. "I've called in men to comb the area on foot. It will be slow going in the rain, but it's something we should check."

A minor stroke? Some sort of sudden illness that impaired her thinking? "What about the hospitals?" Michael asked. "You should check those."

"Did that first thing."

They were on top of it, Michael reminded himself. They knew the drill and they worked efficiently. Because he was a fellow officer, they'd be even more diligent than usual. Under normal circumstances the department wouldn't even be involved at this point.

"Keep me posted," Michael said. He hung up phone and dropped his head to his hands.

Another hour and the girls would be up. What would he tell them?

"Kate's not stupid," Libby said in exasperation. "She wouldn't stop on a deserted road in the middle of the night unless she had to."

Michael nodded numbly. Libby wasn't stupid either.

She'd known immediately, even before he'd had a chance to tell her. "Something's happened to Kate, hasn't it?" she'd said as she entered the kitchen. Not a question, not even a statement seeking affirmation, but an acknowledgment of the obvious.

At sixteen, Libby had known more loss than most people twice her age. Her mother and two high school friends in a period of only two years. She'd developed a sort of sixth sense for adversity and misfortune but not the toughness for shielding herself from the hurt. Michael wasn't as close to Libby as Kate was, but he was close enough that her pain and confusion underscored his own.

Anna had been easier. Six-year-olds, even smart ones, had a worldview colored by simple immediacy. He'd explained that Kate had gotten lost on her way home last night. They didn't know where she was, but there were a lot of people looking for her. Not a lie really, but it didn't begin to touch the terror Michael felt in his heart.

Libby stood up, fists clenched, and pounded the kitchen counter. "If Kate was okay, she'd have called us by now."

"You're probably right."

Maybe she'd been expecting an argument from him, or a bland "everything's going to be okay," because she looked at him expectantly, and then her face crumpled.

He put an arm around her shoulder and hugged her silently.

By the time Michael arrived at the spot on Huckleberry Road where Kate's car had been discovered, the rain had stopped and shifting spots of blue appeared sporadically in the sky.

"Nothing's turned up," Frank said by way of greeting. "Nothing new at any of the local hospitals, either." Frank Bowen's shoes were thick with mud, his thinning hair damp and flat against his head.

Michael opened the door of the old Volvo and looked inside. The parking brake was set and the key was gone. Kate's notebook and canvas tote were on the passenger seat where she usually set them, along with a half-eaten apple. The projector and slides she used in her business were in the back. Nothing to indicate where she'd gone or why.

He turned to Frank. "Was the car locked when you found it?"

"The back doors were locked, but neither of the two front doors."

Michael's eyes scanned the area around where they were standing. There was a narrow dirt shoulder, but no sidewalk or path. The terrain sloped up on the side where the car was parked, down on the other side. Not an area conducive to walking. He headed up the road anyway. Frank followed.

"Gina saw the missing person's report," Frank remarked. "She said to tell you anything she can do, just call."

He paused, waiting for Michael's response, which wasn't forthcoming. "She wanted to make sure you got the message."

Michael nodded.

"Something going on between the two of you? Something I'm missing?"

"No. Absolutely not." The words were clipped and emphatic.

Frank raised an eyebrow. "Just asking."

Michael drove to the station under the cloud of his last conversation with Kate. The one where she'd asked him about Gina.

"She's one of the work-study students," he'd told her, referring to the internship program the department offered to criminal justice students at the local college. "Why?"

"You used her name just now when you meant Libby."

Michael had been sure she was mistaken. He didn't think he'd have been careless enough to drop Gina's name inadvertently. But it seemed odd that Kate would have come up with the name on her own. It was another wrinkle in the fabric of their relationship.

He didn't know why he felt uneasy about telling Kate. Maybe because he'd never shared much with Barbara, and wasn't used to it. Of course, his relationship with Barbara had been a disaster from the beginning. He was surprised their marriage had lasted as long as it did. Probably he hadn't told Kate because he was afraid of testing their relationship. Or maybe he wasn't sure, himself, what was going on.

At the station, he poured himself a cup of coffee on his way through the lounge, then settled at his desk and began reviewing police reports for the last twenty-four hours, looking for a clue that might lead him to Kate.

Half an hour later Janet buzzed him from the front desk.

"There's a woman here to talk to one of the detectives."

"Can't someone else take it?" he said irritably.

"No one else is here. We've put everyone available on Kate's trail."

Michael pushed the stack of police reports aside. He sighed. "I'll be right out."

The woman, whose name was Heidi Harrington, appeared to be in her mid-forties. She was a bottle blonde, with one of those coiffed, every-hair-in-place styles that a breeze couldn't touch. Her skin was smooth and tight, most likely helped along by a surgeon's scalpel, but her eyes were puffy.

She took the chair Michael indicated and launched into the reason for her visit.

"I'm afraid something terrible has happened to my son."

"How old is he?" Michael's stomach clenched. He hated cases where children were the victims. He couldn't handle it, not now.

"Twenty."

The knot in his gut loosened. Twenty wasn't exactly a child. "What makes you think something's happened?"

"He didn't come home last night, and he didn't show up for work, either. Robert buses tables evenings at the Hideaway."

"He lives at home?"

"In the apartment over the garage, actually. He'd like a place of his own but Rudy, my husband, refuses to give him a cent. Robert stays in the apartment because it's free. If Rudy had his way, he'd charge him rent for that, too."

"I gather Robert and his father don't get along."

"Rudy is Robert's stepfather and, no, they don't get along."

"Maybe Robert decided to take a trip, or stay with a friend."

She shook her head. "He had a photo shoot this morning. When he didn't show up, they called the house looking for him."

"He's a fashion model?" Michael imagined Robert as a younger, male version of his mother.

"Model, yes. But primarily sporting equipment and fast food. He's trying to break into the business. He wouldn't have blown an assignment like that."

"It hasn't even been twenty-four hours, Mrs. Harrington. Robert is an adult—"

"I'm his mother," she said forcefully. "I *know* when something's not right."

Michael pressed his fingertips together. A boy of twenty with a stepfather who treated him like scum and a mother who kept close tabs on his life. Michael had seen it many times before. The boy ties one on and loses track of the days. He meets a woman and suddenly nothing else matters. Or he decides he's had enough and takes off on his own for parts unknown. But with Kate missing, the standard explanations rang hollow.

"When did you last see him?" Michael asked.

"Yesterday afternoon about two."

"He give you any idea about his plans for the day?"

"We didn't talk. But I saw him drive off."

"You've checked with his friends?"

She licked her lips. "A few of them. I'm not really privy to his social life."

Michael pulled out a report form and took down the boy's name, age, physical description. "What kind of car does he drive?"

"An '86 Chevy Caprice."

"Color?"

"Blue."

"License number?" He wrote as she talked. "I'll let you know if we hear anything," he said. "Most of the time, though, these things have a way of working themselves out without our help."

Heidi Harrington held out a hand. "Thank you, Lieutenant. You can't imagine how worried I've been."

Unfortunately, he could imagine only too well.

6

"I'm hungry." Sheryl Ann's voice had the plaintive drawl of a child pushed to her limits.

"Eat an Oreo," Bobby told her.

"I've been eating Oreos all day. I want some *real* food. I bet Kate's hungry, too." She twisted to face me in the backseat. "You're hungry, aren't you, Kate?"

No way was I going to take sides. "Whatever you two decide is fine by me."

With the exception of one very quick break to refuel and use the rest room, we'd been traveling nonstop since leaving the motel that morning. Bobby and Sheryl Ann in the front seat, me lying on my side in the back, still bound at the ankles and wrists but no longer gagged or wrapped in the foul-smelling blanket. My relief at having my hastily scrawled message escape Bobby's detection had left me feeling oddly complacent. And the small kindness of being able to see and speak made me almost grateful. At times, it seemed almost that we were pals headed off on a merry adventure.

But we weren't, and the weight of that thought was like an iron chain around my heart.

"It's not healthy to live on cookies," Sheryl Ann grumbled.

"We'll stop in a bit."

"That's what you promised an hour ago."

"Next town we come to, I swear."

"Swear on what?" Her tone had turned playful.

"My prized hubcap collection?"

Sheryl Ann leaned over his direction and tickled him in the ribs. "Next town, or else."

Bobby laughed, and the car swerved. "Okay, I got the point. Now cut it out, or we'll never make it to the next town."

He draped an arm around Sheryl Ann's shoulder, pulling her closer. She snuggled against him. Quiet once again reigned from the front.

I looked up through the window at the pale gray sky, unbroken as it had been most of the day except for an occasional telephone pole or tree. The vista was not particularly interesting, or enlightening. I wondered where we were, where we were headed.

And how much longer I had.

"This isn't going to work," I said, hoping Bobby's playfulness would leave him open to discussion. Although I would rather have made my points face-to-face, I was worried I might never get the chance.

"Seems to me it's working just fine."

"Somebody's going to notice that Tully's missing."

"He was a creep," Bobby said. "Nobody's going to miss him, except maybe Sheryl Ann here. And she's not exactly weeping her eyes out over him."

"He wasn't all bad," Sheryl Ann insisted.

"Didn't say he was."

"He stuck by me."

"Stuck by your paycheck, more like it."

"And he was a good drummer."

Bobby's laugh was harsh. "Yeah. Too bad he practiced on your body."

"He beat you?" I asked. Whatever sympathy I'd had for Tully was rapidly fading.

"He didn't mean to," Sheryl Ann said, sounding almost defensive. "And it was only a couple of times."

"There are shelters, you know. Places to go for help."

Sheryl Ann snorted. "It's a little late for that now."

Right. There I was, Ms. Fixit again. "Why didn't you leave him?"

She hesitated. "I was trying to."

"Only Tully didn't like the idea," Bobby explained.

So they'd killed him. I kept that comment to myself. No point being contentious. "Eventually, someone's bound to notice he's gone. You'll be the first person they come looking for, Sheryl Ann."

"But they aren't going to find a body," Bobby said. "No crime in a grown man going missing."

"He was traveling a lot," Sheryl Ann added. "It'll be a long time before anyone even figures he's not around anymore."

Were these two really that naive? "What are you planning to do, drive around forever with Tully in the trunk?"

Bobby shook his head. "We're going to bury him where no one will ever look."

"Bobby's friend's uncle has an old cabin in—"

"Zip it," Bobby said, cutting her off. "The less she knows, the better."

"I don't see why it matters." Sheryl Ann turned sideways. Her features were drawn in a pout.

Bobby raised his eyes, framed me in the rearview mirror. "You in the backseat, you zip it, too. And don't waste your sympathy on Tully, 'cause you're going to be joining him before long."

Sheryl Ann was quiet a minute. "Do we have to?"

"Have to what?"

"You know . . ." She dropped to a whisper. "Get rid of Kate."

"You got a better idea?"

She gave it some thought. "No, I guess not." Her voice was small, like a child's.

"I don't like it any better than you do," Bobby said softly. "It wasn't supposed to happen this way. None of it."

"I know. And I feel bad you're in this mess on account of me."

"On account of *us*, Sheryl Ann. I'm crazy about you— you know that. I just want us to be together."

Sheryl Ann leaned her head against his shoulder. "You're the nicest thing ever happened to me, Bobby Lake."

"Don't you go forgetting it, neither."

I tried again. "Look, whatever took place, I'm sure you had your reasons. Maybe Tully deserved what he got. But killing me isn't going to help. It's going to make things worse. You're getting yourselves in trouble for—"

"We're already in trouble," Bobby said.

"Well, you're going to be in worse trouble," I said, exasperated. "Maybe you're right that no one will miss Tully, but they'll miss me. You can't get away with it."

"Shut up," Bobby snapped. "I've listened to enough of this crap."

"It's true. Let me go and—"

He pulled his arm from Sheryl Ann's shoulder and turned to give me a menacing glare. His face was flushed with exasperation. "I told you, shut the fuck up."

So much for trying to sway them with reason. It wasn't going to work.

Silence descended. Sheryl Ann cuddled against Bobby. I passed the time looking out my window to the world and trying to come up with a plan.

Every avenue was a dead end.

More gray sky, but lighter now. I could see a faint outline of the sun behind the clouds and calculated that we were headed east. Or mostly east. Assuming I wasn't completely turned around. NEWS: north, east, west, south. That was the way I'd learned map reading back in grade school. I still used the device to orient myself, even though, as Anna pointed out, it made you zigzag across the country. As the product of a modern education, she preferred the more logical Never-Eat-Soggy-Waffles.

Anna. The surrealistic quality of the day suddenly evaporated as I felt anew the despair of my predicament. Anna and Libby and Michael. My heart ached at the thought I might never again be with them. My mind filled with all the things I should have said, and didn't. All the things I shouldn't have said, and did. Sadness enveloped me like a thick, suffocating fog.

"Hey, look at that," Sheryl Ann said, bouncing in her seat. "It's a Hogan's."

"What's a Hogan's?"

"I don't know, but I bet it sells food. We're going to stop, aren't we?"

Bobby grumbled. "Yeah, sure."

He pulled off the road and parked. I could see the faded orange lettering from Hogan's billboard across the gray canvas of the car's window.

"What do you want?" he asked Sheryl Ann.

"I got to see what they have, first."

"I'll take a turkey sandwich," I said, with strained joviality. "And a diet cola."

"You'll take what we bring you," Bobby growled. "And stay out of sight, or you won't get anything. Got that? We'll be keeping an eye on you."

"We're going to leave her here?" Sheryl Ann asked.

"We sure the hell aren't going to drag her inside."

The door slammed, and I was alone. No gun pointed at my chest, no muscle-bound stallion breathing down my neck. This was my chance. Maybe my last chance.

I'd been trying all morning to loosen the rope that bound my wrists behind my back. It was a lost cause. But now that no one was watching, I tried to reach the cord wrapped around my ankles. Twisting, I arched my back and flexed with all the determination I could muster. The knot that secured my feet remained a frustrating few inches out of reach.

Tears of defeat wet my eyes. So close, and yet so far. I wasn't going to be able to free myself.

Slowly, I raised my head to the point where I could just see out. We were parked at the side of the building—an old-fashioned quick stop of the sort that lined the roadsides forty years ago. I could see Bobby and Sheryl Ann at the counter, talking. A family with two young children hovered nearby, probably waiting for their orders. Otherwise, the place appeared empty.

And then I saw the telephone booth, not twenty feet from the car. My heart kicked into overdrive.

I pulled myself to a sitting position. Another glance at the checkout counter. Bobby and Sheryl Ann were still talking. With silent thanks for a car of prealarm vintage,

I slid sideways so my back was close to the door, grabbed the handle and eased it open. I slithered out feetfirst.

Crouching behind the car's bulk in order to keep out of sight, I inched forward on hobbled feet. It wasn't easy going. When I reached the open stretch between the car and the phone booth, I glanced again at Bobby and Sheryl Ann. They had their backs to me. Heart pounding, I did a quick, mincing shuffle across the unprotected length of asphalt. By the time I made it to the phone booth, my skin was clammy in spite of the frigid outside temperature.

The booth's interior was grimy and smelled of stale french fries, but I'd never in my life been so grateful for a phone. With my hands tied behind my back, I was forced to use my chin to lift the receiver. In the process, it dropped, clanging loudly against the side of the phone booth. I used my nose to punch in 9-1-1, then dropped to my knees to talk into the dangling receiver.

"Emergency response." The voice was female, and clipped.

"I've been kidnapped," I said, too softly.

"What? You'll have to speak up."

"Help me, please. I've been kidnapped."

"Where are you?"

"I'm not sure." I wasn't even clear on the state. "At Hogan's."

"Which Hogan's?"

"I . . . I don't know. It's got an orange sign."

"They all do."

Hysteria worked its way into my voice. "I don't know where I am. I was kidnapped in California. The unincorporated area near Walnut Hills. Don't you have a system that pinpoints the call?"

She ignored the question. "This better not be another prank."

"This isn't a prank. I—"

"Stay on the line. I'll alert the sheriff."

"How long before he gets here?"

"Depends. Definitely within the hour."

The hour? We'd be sixty miles away by then.

I stood up, disconnected with my chin, and hit O with my nose to summon the operator. From the vantage point of the phone booth, I could no longer see inside the restaurant, but I knew that Bobby and Sheryl Ann wouldn't be there much longer. Panic swelled inside me as the minutes ticked by. Finally, I managed to reach the Walnut Hills Police Department.

"This is Kate Austen," I said without preliminaries. "I've been kidnapped."

"Kate! We've been so worried." Janet, the dispatcher, had a daughter in Anna's class. "Half the department has been looking for you. Where are you?"

"I don't know. A roadside place called Hogan's. I don't think we're in California. They're going to kill me. They've already killed a man. Someone by the name of Tully." The words poured out in a wave of hysteria.

"Who? Who's kidnapped you?"

"Tully's wife and her boyfriend, Bobby." Why hadn't I thought to check the license of the car? "Her name is Sher—"

Suddenly, Bobby was behind me. I hadn't heard him come up. He yanked me roughly to me feet and punched me hard in the side of my face.

"Bitch."

The pain was sharp, but it paled beside the raw-edged

despair that cut through me like a knife. Help wasn't going to come in time.

Bobby hung up the phone, then hit me again for good measure. "You little bitch. We're in there buying food for you, and you sneak off and pull a stunt like that."

"Let me go, please." I was surprised to find that I was sobbing hysterically. "You're only getting yourself into deeper trouble."

He grabbed a fistful of my hair and held it tight. "Listen to me, and listen good. I'm *not* going to jail. I had it all worked out until you came along. You're the one who screwed things up."

I started yelling, wildly. "Help. Someone help." I looked in the direction of the diner, but the family with two kids was nowhere to be seen.

Bobby yanked me by the shoulder and half dragged me back to the car, where Sheryl Ann was waiting. He opened the trunk. The rank odor from inside was over-powering.

Sheryl Ann gave me a reproachful look. "You shouldn't have done that, Kate. It's stupid to make Bobby mad."

"You won't get away with this," I screamed. "The police are on their way."

"Shut up." Bobby shoved me headfirst into the trunk and slammed it shut, enclosing me in cold, damp darkness.

My face stung from Bobby's punch, my shoulder was bruised, and my hip hurt where it had scraped against the metal edge of the trunk. The inert mass of Tully's corpse pressed against my clothing. I pulled myself into a ball to avoid touching him.

My tenuous grasp on hope had all but slipped away. I felt as though I were already in my grave.

7

"Move it," Bobby said, shoving me roughly from behind. "It's fucking freezing out here."

Even before he'd opened the trunk to let me out, I knew we'd entered snow country. The air had a bite to it that went beyond mere cold.

"I'm moving as fast as I can," I told him. My ankles were no longer tied, but I was having trouble walking because of the icy ground and the encroaching dusk. Not to mention my cramped muscles.

"You give me any trouble and you'll be spending the night in the car. You hear? I'm just looking for an excuse."

"Where are we?"

"Shut up and walk."

We slogged the remaining hundred or so yards to the cabin in silence. The snow on the ground wasn't deep, only a couple of inches in most spots, and it crunched underfoot. Except for the pale light coming from the cabin, there were no signs of human habitation. Wherever we were, we were alone.

Sheryl Ann was inside already, kneeling at the hearth

and blowing on a feeble, isolated flame. "The damn wood is wet and half-frozen," she said.

"Well, it's the only wood we've got."

"You should have warned me this place didn't have heat."

"It's got a fireplace."

"It's a dump."

"It's fine. Just hasn't been used in a while is all."

Bobby nudged me into an upholstered chair, sending a puff of dust into the air. Sheryl Ann glared at him as the flame flickered out.

"You do it," she said, shoving the book of matches into his hand.

Bobby was right in that it appeared the place had not been used for some time. Sheryl Ann was right, too. It was a dump.

The furniture was old and stained, the curtains torn. Shredded tissue and fluffs of cotton were strewn about like confetti. It took only a moment for me to recognize the telltale signs of mice.

Bobby took the matches and worked on the fire while Sheryl Ann explored the rest of the cabin. I coughed to clear my throat of the dust and grit I'd inhaled when I'd landed in the chair.

"It's a good thing we stopped for provisions on the way," Sheryl Ann said, returning with two cans of beer. "There's nothing here but tuna and beans."

Bobby took a beer. "We're not going to be staying long.

"You want any beer?" Sheryl Ann asked, addressing me.

Bobby spoke up before I could answer. "No way. This isn't some bed-and-breakfast we're running here."

"Never hurts to be nice." Sheryl Ann stood with her back to the fireplace, drawing meager heat from the log Bobby had finally coaxed into flame.

"What now?" she asked Bobby.

"Tonight, nothing. Tomorrow I'll dig the graves, and then we're out of here."

Graves. Plural.

An eddy of dread swirled in my chest, like vertigo of the soul. I swallowed the saliva gathering in my mouth.

"Where are you going to put them?" she asked.

"I don't know yet." Bobby was sprawled on the sofa, slugging his beer like it was water. "Most anyplace will do. No one's going to come looking for them way out here."

"Isn't the snow going to make it hard?"

I could tell from the look on Bobby's face that he hadn't thought of that aspect. He tossed back the rest of his beer and stood. "I'll manage."

"Men," Sheryl Ann muttered when Bobby left to retrieve another can of beer.

"Don't throw your life away," I whispered to her when we were along. "He's not worth it."

"I already made a mess of my life."

"You're young, Sheryl Ann. It's not too late to turn it around."

She stepped away from the fire, which had grown to a sizable blaze. "You sure you don't want some beer?"

"Sheryl Ann, listen to me. What happened with Tully— there were extenuating circumstances. You kill me and it's cold-blooded, premeditated murder."

"Bobby's the one—"

"You can still be convicted of murder, Sheryl Ann, even if it's Bobby who pulls the trigger."

She shook her head. "He's got it all figured out."

"Got what figured out?" Bobby returned from the other room, balancing two cans of beer and a tub of fried chicken. He set them on a dusty table near the sofa. The aroma of food filled my nostrils and caused my stomach to dance.

"Nothing," Sheryl Ann said quickly. "We were just talking."

"You're always talking. Beats me why you never run out of things to say." He kissed Sheryl Ann on the mouth, then flopped onto the sofa again, pulling her with him.

"Don't you think—"

He slipped a hand under her sweater and silenced her with another forceful kiss.

Sheryl Ann squirmed and made a halfhearted effort to pull away. Bobby persisted and she stopped struggling. They moaned and groaned and kissed for what seemed, from my uncomfortable vantage point, like an eternity but was probably no more than a minute.

When Sheryl Ann came up for air, Bobby leaned back and let loose with a piercing coyotelike howl. "Sheryl Ann," he said, "you are one hell of a woman."

She started to laugh, then glanced my direction. "All depends, I suppose."

Bobby draped one arm across her shoulder and reached for a fresh beer with the other. "Guess we'd better eat by the fire. It gets cold when you're away from it for long."

He offered Sheryl Ann a piece of chicken, then reached for one himself and bit into it hungrily. Bobby licked his lips and grinned. "Damned if this isn't mighty fine fried rat."

Sheryl Ann poked him. "Yuk. Don't even joke about that."

"Sorry, babe." The apology was offered with a glint of amusement.

"Don't forget about Kate. You've got to undo her before she can eat."

I should have been thinking about escape, but I was ravenous. I realized I'd eaten nothing all day.

Bobby wiped his mouth with the back of his hand. "Feeding her is a waste."

"She's got to eat," Sheryl Ann argued.

"Why?" It was a smart-ass remark delivered for full effect.

Sheryl Ann leapt to her feet. "Go ahead and kill her then if that's what you've got to do. But do it now and quit dragging it out."

"Why me?" Bobby's eyes flashed with sudden anger. "I did Tully."

She brushed the air with her hand. "By accident."

"For you. I did it for you." Bobby threw his half-eaten piece of chicken back into the bucket and stood. He grabbed Sheryl Ann by the arm. "I've got myself into a real mess because of you, so cut the crap, okay."

"Bobby, I just—"

"You think I *like* killing people?"

She shook her head silently.

"Because I don't." He was still gripping her arm, his face only inches from her own. "It's all for you."

Sheryl Ann tried to free her arm.

"And the reason we've got to do Kate is because of you, too."

She stopped fighting. "What do you mean?"

"You were the one who was stupid enough to let her find Tully."

"I didn't think—"

"Right, you didn't think at all." He shoved her aside in disgust. "And now it's *me* who's got to deal with it."

"I'm sorry, Bobby." Sheryl Ann's head was bowed. She addressed her thumbs; her voice was small and soft. "Really, I am."

For a moment, he didn't move. Then he pulled her close, pressing her head against his chest, and stroked her hair. "As long as we're together," he whispered, "that's all that matters."

When they finished eating, Bobby and Sheryl Ann went off to bed, leaving me with the couch and a moth-eaten blanket. Not that I had any intention of sleeping.

I'd worked the ties at my wrists until the skin was raw, but I hadn't succeeded in loosening them. I didn't see anything I could use to fray them, either.

Still, I couldn't let myself give up hope. Every time I'd catch a mental glimpse of what surely lay ahead, the black vacuum of despair would descend, sucking the air from my lungs. I was certain the anguish was more painful than a bullet would ever be.

I clung to the knowledge that I'd managed to reach Janet. Within minutes of being cut off, she'd have the resources of the Walnut Hills Police Department pursuing every avenue available. I didn't know if it was possible to trace an out-of-state number. And I couldn't recall if I'd had a chance to give her Bobby's name. I knew I hadn't given her a description of the car, which would have been the wisest choice. In fact, it wasn't clear to me how anyone, even with the best police work in the country, would be able find me. But like a stranded swimmer grasping for a twig from shore, I clung to the thought that they might.

The embers in the fireplace were still glowing faintly when I heard the creak of a floorboard from the other room. Then a shuffling sound.

I tensed. My heart stopped momentarily, then kicked into overdrive. I sat up.

Bobby? Had he finally decided to kill me and be done with it? My whole body trembled with fear.

Dark upon dark, a shadowy form moved stealthily across the room. Another squeaky board.

"You awake, Kate?" Sheryl Ann's voice was just above a whisper. "I didn't think you'd be asleep."

I hadn't answered, but that didn't seem to deter her. She lit a single propane light.

"Are you warm enough?" She'd wrapped herself in a blanket, Indian style.

"I've been warmer."

"Me too. I'm going to make some hot tea. Would you like a cup?"

"Yes, please." If only to free my hands.

"I think there's some chicken left, too."

No doubt teeming with salmonella by this point. But what did it matter? I was going to die anyway. "Thanks."

She went into the kitchen and returned a few minutes later with chicken and two camp-issue metal cups. "Be careful. It's hot." She set a cup on the table for me, then frowned. "I guess you can't drink that with your hands tied behind your back."

"No, I can't."

She untied my hands, but left my feet bound. "Don't

try anything funny like you did this afternoon. Bobby's right in the other room.'' She gave an incongruous laugh. "Even if he is snoring up a storm."

I flexed my wrists. The movement was painful at first, but wonderful all the same. I arched my back and stretched. Then I bit hungrily into the chicken.

"Bobby was really pissed about what you did," she said.

"I'm sure he'd so the same thing if the situation were reversed."

Sheryl Ann settled in the chair across from me. She nodded toward the cup of tea. "I added sugar. I hope you don't mind."

I sipped my tea. "It's good. Thanks." For once, I wasn't worried about calories.

"Bobby is actually a pretty decent guy," she said after a minute.

"Could have fooled me."

Her expression grew thoughtful. "He treats me better than anyone I've ever known."

"He's planning to kill me," I said, looking her in the eye. "That doesn't sound like a kind and decent person to me."

She studied her cup. "Things weren't supposed to happen this way. Bobby's right. It's my fault."

"Don't let him fool you with that I-did-it-for-you stuff, Sheryl Ann. The only way you're at fault is by letting this go on."

She shook her head.

"Nobody forced him to kill Tully. No one forced him to run off with the body, and no one's forcing him to kill me."

"Things got out of hand."

"You can stop them from getting worse," I said.

Another small shake of her head.

"Are you afraid of Bobby? Is that it?"

She raised her eyes. "Bobby loves me."

"If he loved you, he wouldn't have sucked you into killing two people."

"It's my fault. All of it. Tully didn't deserve to die."

I held my cup in both hands, warming them. Trying to read this woman.

"Tell me about him," I said.

"We met when I was seventeen. We got married a couple of months later."

"How old are you now?"

There was a flicker of a smile. "Twenty-one last month."

She was younger than I'd imagined. Only a few years older than Libby. "What did your parents think?"

She straightened and tossed her head. "My parents are dead."

"I'm sorry."

"It's not important." She brushed the air with her hand. "Tully was older than me. Twenty-five when I met him. He was real nice at first. Treated me like I was special. I thought it was cool, him being a drummer and all. And being older. But really he only cared about himself."

A familiar story. It wasn't all that different, in essence, from my marriage to Andy. Once the initial passion fades, it's a rude shock to discover you're married to someone who's already married to himself.

"And Bobby?" I asked.

"His stepdad owns the club where Tully's band played. Bobby helps out some nights, clearing tables and stuff.

That's how I met him. I used to hang out waiting for Tully to finish playing for the evening."

"So you were going to leave Tully for Bobby?"

She shifted in her seat. "I don't know, really. I was thinking about it. Then Tully came home early from a trip and found us together. He and Bobby got into a fight, and Bobby punched him hard." She paused. "Hard enough that it killed him."

Suddenly, I saw a ray of hope. "That's how Tully died? From a fist punch?"

She nodded. "Either that or hitting his head when he fell."

"If Bobby didn't mean to kill Tully, it's not murder." I wasn't certain about that, but I wasn't about to let details dissuade me. "He doesn't have to worry."

"What do you mean it's not murder?"

"It's manslaughter. It might not even be that. Accident maybe. Bobby needs to talk to a lawyer."

"But he'd still spend time in jail, wouldn't he?"

"Maybe. Maybe not."

Sheryl Ann shook her head vigorously. "He won't do it."

"Then you need to talk to one yourself. Legally you're as guilty as Bobby." Again, I didn't let my ignorance of the law get in my way.

"Maybe that's what we should have done," Sheryl Ann said emphatically, "but we didn't." She stood up. "Now we have to go through with the plan."

"No, you don't. It's not too late." The words burned in my throat. This was my life we were talking about. "There's still a choice to be made. Don't let Bobby take you down with him."

Sheryl Ann hugged the blanket tight around herself.

"I'm going back to bed. Put your hands behind your back so I can tie them again."

I made a quick calculation. If I tried to fight, how much time did I have before Bobby appeared? And did I stand even the slightest chance against a woman who was younger and had free use of her legs and feet?

"Don't try it, Kate. You'll just make Bobby mad again."

Reluctantly, I held my hands behind my back.

Sheryl Ann bound my wrists, not as tightly as Bobby had, but securely enough that my raw skin burned in protest. She pulled my blanket over me, then as an afterthought, added the one she'd been using as well.

At the doorway, she turned. "Your little girl—what's her name?"

I didn't want Anna to be any part of this. I thought about lying, but somehow that seemed wrong, too. As if my daughter herself would be obliterated with her name. "Anna," I said at last.

Sheryl Ann smiled. "That's a nice name. Kind of like mine."

8

Michael woke with a start, and out of habit stretched his arm to Kate's side of the bed.

Empty.

The awful truth, muted for a few hours by sleep, slammed against his chest anew. Rolling onto the expanse of cold sheet on her side of the bed, he allowed himself to succumb to the terrible dread he spent most of his waking hours seeking to thwart.

Finally, he opened his eyes to the gray light of morning. When he'd checked the clock last it had been three-thirty and now here it was almost six. A whopping two and a half hours of sleep, but at least it had been peaceful, which was more than he could say for wakefulness.

In the twenty-odd hours since Kate's call, he'd been riding a roller coaster of emotions. The relief at knowing Kate was alive—or had been alive—was quickly replaced by worry about the fate she would suffer as the minutes ticked by. He'd listened to the tape of her call to Janet. Over and over he'd listened, hoping to find a crumb of useful information.

A man by the name of Tully had been murdered by his wife and her boyfriend. What did that have to do with

Kate? Michael racked his brain trying to remember if Kate had ever mentioned anyone named Tully, or anyone married to a man by that name. He was almost certain she hadn't.

Mentally, he played the tape again, cringing as he always did when he came to the male voice in the background.

Bitch. And then Kate's sharp intake of breath and anguished cry.

He could tell nothing from the voice, nothing from the few seconds of commotion that followed. Kate had managed to get to the phone once, he reminded himself. Maybe she could do it again.

Except Michael knew that the first time was always the easiest. After that, she would be watched more carefully.

He extracted himself from the bed, but not the memories. They followed him everywhere, like gnats. In the bathroom, Michael splashed water on his face. Kate's brush and lotions were spread on the counter in their usual disarray. A tube of lipstick sat beside the sink. She'd applied it hurriedly before leaving for her appointment the night she disappeared, complaining because she thought the orange tones were wrong for her coloring. But it had come as a free sample, and Kate was loath to pass up a bargain.

Michael found an odd comfort in having Kate's things there on the counter. As though Kate's presence could somehow be channeled through something as mundane as lipstick and hand lotion.

He shaved, brushed his teeth, and took a quick shower, then headed into the kitchen to make himself a cup of coffee. Max trailed at his heels, his customary canine enthusiasm subdued somewhat by the change in routine

and household configuration. This morning there were
just the two of them since Anna was with her father and
Libby had sought the comfort of a friend.

The house was quiet without the girls. Empty. Their
absence on top of Kate's left him feeling untethered,
gave his mind too much room to roam.

It had surprised him to discover how much comfort
he found in domestic life. Married to Barbara he'd never
felt this way. What he'd felt then was tension, and the
constant struggle between them for control. Kate was
made of steel, but softer on outside. And softer in the
heart, where it mattered most.

Michael leaned over to scratch Max's furry brown head.
"It's okay, boy," he said, but he realized that it wasn't.
That it might never be okay again.

Michael drank half his coffee, scanned the morning
paper then called the station, asking to be patched
through to Frank. The captain had assigned Kate's case
to Frank with the explanation that Michael was too emotionally involved to handle it himself.

"Any new developments?" Michael asked.

"Nothing of substance. The sheriff's department in
Idaho has talked with the staff at that fast-food joint where
Kate made the call. No one there remembers seeing
her. They got some coverage in the newspaper, but no
response so far."

"She was talking on the phone, for Christ's sake. Someone has to have seen something."

"The phone's outside, away from the business area.
And I gather it's not exactly a bustling sort of place in
any event."

"What about customers they *do* remember?" Michael

asked. "Her kidnappers must have bought food, used the rest room, whatever. Maybe someone saw them."

"I imagine so. Unfortunately, they weren't wearing T-shirts with the word 'kidnapper' stamped across the front."

"I'm not in the mood for humor."

"I wasn't trying to be funny."

The last person Michael wanted to alienate at the moment was Frank Bowen. He backed off. "No one saw anything at all?"

"Just the usual mix of truck drivers and travelers. But the guy at a service station nearby remembers seeing a car with California plates. It was an older model sedan. Turquoise. He noticed because it looked, in his words, very California."

"What about the occupants?"

"He can't remember."

"I don't suppose he got the plate?"

"No, but it shouldn't be hard to spot. The sheriff has put the word out."

Michael felt a tightening in his chest. He wasn't sure if it was hope or anxiety. Maybe both.

"Could be nothing," Frank said. "There've got to be a number of cars with California plates driving around Idaho. And we aren't even sure that Kate's captors are local."

Michael's muscles ached with the tension of doing nothing. Of sitting on the periphery. Abruptly, he leapt to his feet. "I'm going out there."

"What good will it do?"

"I feel useless sitting here."

"The sheriff seems to know his business. And he's

willing to work with us. It's not every division that would
take a possible adult abduction as seriously."

"Possible?" Michael couldn't contain his irritation.

"You know what I mean."

Michael recalled the willingness with which he'd been
ready to dismiss Mrs. Harrington's concern about her
missing son. What Frank said was true: Police often viewed
missing-adult cases with skepticism. And there'd been
plenty of instances proving them right.

"Anyway," Frank continued, "he's got officers keeping
an eye out for the car. There's nothing you can add by
being on the scene."

Logic told him Frank was right, but Michael found
little comfort in logic.

It bothered him that they didn't know why the kidnappers had nabbed Kate. There were plenty of sickos running around. Sexual perverts, psychotics, people who
enjoyed inflicting pain. People who killed for sheer plea-
sure. His gut twisted into a knot thinking about the possibilities.

"What about the dead man, Tully?" he asked.

"What do you mean?"

"Do we have any leads on his identity?"

"Unfortunately not. No reports of a missing person by
that name or anything close. Twenty-three listings for the
last name in the greater Bay Area, all of them accounted
for. And the DMV can't run a check by first names."

Frustration pounded in Michael's chest. How many
people with the given name of Tully could there be?

At Libby's suggestion they'd spent hours yesterday
searching the Web. Most search-engine white pages
required a last name. Those that didn't required a city

and then incorporated every listing beginning with T. It was an exercise in futility.

"Can you get a registration list for cars like the one spotted at the gas station?"

"We don't have year or model." Frank's tone was vaguely patronizing.

"There can't be that many older model turquoise sedans."

"This," Frank said with a snort of disgust, "is why the captain didn't want you working on the case. Trust me, I'm doing everything I can."

It was probably true, Michael thought. But the uncomfortable fact remained that he didn't find Frank Bowen entirely competent.

By the time Michael sat down at his desk, the morning bustle had quieted. The station was largely empty of other officers, and he was glad he didn't have to respond to their inquiries and condolences. He appreciated their show of support, but the sentiments required a response on his part that he wasn't up to.

Popping a breath mint into his mouth, Michael pulled the files of his open cases. A convenience-store robbery, an ATM holdup, an assault. One open homicide, going nowhere fast. Michael read over his recent notes.

Li Chen, a man in his late sixties, had been shot to death in his own kitchen with his own gun. No break-in, nothing taken. Michael had come onto the case a couple of weeks into the investigation when the detective in charge had required emergency bypass surgery. Michael suspected Chen's nephew, who was the sole beneficiary of his uncle's will, but the kid had an alibi and witnesses to back him up.

Michael sighed. He was having trouble locking into the excitement and urgency he usually felt about his cases.

And then there was the missing young man, Robert Lake. Michael checked the night's messages. No word on him or the car. It had been three days now, and although he still felt it likely that the boy had taken off for some personal space, he knew only too well the anxiety the mother must be feeling. He'd experienced it during the last three days himself.

Michael had leaned back to toss a waded sheet of paper into the trash bin when the congruity struck him between the eyes like a well-aimed pellet. Three days for both of them. Kate and Robert.

Robert, Bobby. Blue, turquoise. An '86 Chevy would qualify as an older-model sedan.

Michael's throat constricted. Were his emotions playing with his mind? Had he gone completely around the bend?

He grabbed his jacket and headed for the lounge to dump his lukewarm coffee. As he was hanging his cup on the hook, Gina Nelson appeared behind him.

"I've been wanting to talk to you," she said, softly.

He turned abruptly. "About what?"

"Just to let you know that I'm here for you." A half smile, worried and at the same time beguiling. "You know, if you need anything."

"Thanks." Michael moved toward the door.

"I know it must be uncomfortable for you right now."

"Excuse me?"

"I can understand that." She licked her lips. A full mouth glossed in a deep, rich red that reminded him of good port. "Anything," she said. "Just call."

Michael felt a nervous flutter in chest as though a butterfly were trapped there. He didn't need this, not now. Gina was a problem that would have to wait.

"Thanks," he said without meeting her gaze, then left.

Heidi Harrington greeted him at the door. She was wearing navy slacks and a white silk blouse. Not your everyday at-home attire.

She ushered him inside, her expression pinched with alarm. "Do you have news? Have you found Robert?"

"No. There's nothing to report. I thought I'd see if I could fill in some details that might help us in our search."

The look of alarm faded, but tension in her features remained. "Would you like some soda? Or some coffee?"

"No, thanks. I'm fine."

They sat in a sunroom at the rear of the house. The floor was terra-cotta tile spread with Oriental carpets. The authentic kind.

"I take it you haven't heard from him?" Michael asked.

"Nothing."

Michael adjusted the floral-print throw pillow at his elbow. "Tell me about the car your son drives. You said it was a blue '86 Chevy Caprice."

She nodded.

"Is it dark blue?"

"No, it's a light blue. Almost a greenish blue, I'd say."

"Could it be described at turquoise?"

She frowned. "Turquoise? Well, yes, I guess you could call it that."

Michael felt a tingle at the back of his neck. "Mrs. Harrington, does your son Robert ever use a nickname?"

Once again, alarm sprang into her expression. "His

father," she said tentatively, "his natural father, calls him Bobby. So do his friends. Why?"

What could he tell her that wasn't pure conjecture? Someone by the name of Bobby had abducted a local woman and killed a man. There was reason to believe he was in Idaho, where a gas station attendant had spotted an older model turquoise sedan with California plates. Coincidence? Maybe. Far-fetched? Definitely.

But not without merit. Michael could feel the excitement of discovery in his veins. A sixth sense that he was right. Or maybe simply desperate.

"Where does Robert's natural father live?" Michael asked, hoping she might say *Idaho.*

"Chicago," Mrs. Harrington said. "I called him. He hasn't heard from Bobby for weeks."

"What about family or friends out of state?"

Mrs. Harrington shook her head. "I've called everyone I could think of. No word of him."

"Does he know anyone in Idaho?"

Again, she shook her head. "You have reason to believe he's in Idaho?"

"I don't know where he is. I'm just trying to see if I can't piece together enough information to give us somewhere to start."

Heidi Harrington closed her eyes for a moment, took a deep breath. "What if he's never located? That happens sometimes, doesn't it? A person disappears, and that's the end of it. You never know why or how. Never know if they're alive or dead."

The very thoughts Michael himself had been wrestling with for days. He pushed them aside.

"What about girls?" He knew that by twenty they were

no longer girls, but it was the word that had come to mind. "Does Robert have a girlfriend?"

She hesitated. "For a while there he was seeing a girl named Kim Romano. But I haven't heard him mention her in a couple of months. She called here about a week ago looking for him."

"Do you have an address for Kim?"

"I'm sorry, I don't. But I know she lives in Danville."

"How about other friends? Can you give me names?"

Mrs. Harrington pushed a loose strand of hair off her face. "As I told you other day, I'm not really privy to his social life. I know he kept in touch with a few of the guys from high school, though. I've checked with them already myself, but I'll give you their names if you'd like."

Michael nodded. He wasn't convinced that they'd be any more forthcoming with a policeman than a mother. But they would know things about Robert that might give him some idea where to look.

Mrs. Harrington went into the other room and returned with a slip of paper. "I wrote down the names and phone numbers of the boys he was closest too."

"Thanks."

As he was about to leave, she stopped him at the door. "Something's come up, hasn't it?"

"What do you mean?"

"The other day you were barely interested. A twenty-year-old man goes off on his own a few days—nothing to worry about. Now you're here asking about his friends, his car, whether he knows anyone in Idaho."

Michael gave her his official, noncommittal smile. "Just checking."

"What was it, an accident? A"—she swallowed—"a body without identification?"

The look on her face was painful to observe. He understood all too well what she must be feeling. "No," he said. "Nothing like that."

Her expression relaxed.

"Does the name Tully ring a bell with you?" he asked.

"It doesn't sound familiar. Do you think the two of them are together?"

"I'm grasping at straws," he told her. "But I'll tell you when I know something for sure."

9

Michael clicked his pen while Kim Romano twisted a lock of hair around her index finger.

"You sure you don't want a Coke?" she asked a second time, taking a long drink from her own can.

"I'm sure."

Michael's eyes made another sweep of the small apartment. They were sitting in the living area of a room that mutated to dining area and then kitchen at the other end. The sofa was covered in some sort of vinyl and had emitted a rush of air when Michael sat down. He'd been there ten minutes and already filled two pages with notes.

Kim Romano lived with three roommates—two women and a man. She worked the afternoon shift at the Wells Fargo check-processing center and took classes at Cal State Hayward. She was majoring in business with a minor in French—which, she'd told him, was totally impractical and should have been Spanish or Japanese, but she'd started with French in high school because the teacher was male, and cute. Kim was home this morning because she was waiting for the landlord to show him that the shower did, in fact, drain much too slowly. Yes, she'd been dating Bobby Lake, but he hadn't called in weeks, and no, she didn't know where he was.

She'd told Michael all of this while alternating between nervous giggles and exclamations of concern over Bobby's disappearance. He'd wondered at first if she was high on something, then determined that it was simply her style.

"Last time I talked to Bobby was right after Christmas. No fight, no 'hey, this isn't working.' Nothing. Just like that, out of the blue, he stops calling. Doesn't return my calls either." She brushed her forehead with the back of her hand. "Takes a real prick to dump a girl without saying good-bye."

Michael nodded sympathetically.

"Or even a letter. How hard can that be?"

Michael shifted in his seat, slowly so as to avoid another rush of air. "Do you remember him ever talking about Idaho, or maybe someone he knows there?"

"Idaho? Like the state?"

Michael nodded. He'd given up on the idea that Kim might be the girlfriend who'd helped Bobby abduct Kate. What he was hoping for now was information.

"Idaho's in the middle of nowhere, isn't it?"

"North of Nevada, between Oregon and Wyoming."

"Doesn't sound like a place Bobby would have much to do with. He likes being where the action is. Bright lights, people, energy. I could picture him in Los Angeles or New York. Maybe even Miami or someplace like that. But not Idaho."

Still, Michael was reasonably convinced that's where Bobby was. "Tell me about Bobby. What's he like?"

Kim shrugged. "Fun, nice, kind of stuck on himself. He doesn't talk a lot."

"Is he violent?"

"Violent?"

He could tell from the tone of her response that he'd missed the mark. Maybe violent was too strong a word. "Does he have a temper?"

Kim tapped the floor with her foot. "Not that I've seen. I mean, he has his moods and all. But he's no worse than the rest of us. Why? You think he's gotten himself into trouble?"

"It's one possibility I'm exploring."

"Geez, I hope not." She finished the soda and burped. "He was in trouble with the law once before. Did you know that?"

Michael felt the rush of her words in his chest. He leaned forward. "When?"

"In high school. Robbery. Bobby says it was his friend who did it, not him. But the cops arrested them both. He'd been picked up before for shoplifting. A couple of candy bars, but still, they had him on one of those security cameras."

Punk trouble or the first steps of a hardened criminal?

"The second time," Kim continued, "they locked him up. It made him crazy. I know it scared him."

Not enough to keep him clear of bigger trouble apparently. "Do you have a picture of him?" Michael asked, thinking he should have asked the question of Mrs. Harrington, earlier.

"I've got one of his portfolio shots." Kim rose, went into one of the bedrooms, and returned a few minutes later with an eight-by-ten black-and-white head shot. "Bobby's real tough on the outside, or he likes to think he is anyway. But there's a soft side to him, too. I think that's why he makes a good model."

Michael took the photograph from her and moved closer to the window where the light was better. Bobby Lake wasn't handsome. Michael wasn't even sure most people would consider him good-looking. But something about him caught your attention. He had a square jaw, a broad, slightly flattened nose, and eyes that sparked with the promise of untold secrets.

Was his the face of a killer? It was foolish to think you could judge a man's character by his appearance. Michael knew that. But in this instance, he couldn't help trying.

"Can I keep this for a while?" he asked Kim.

"It's kind of special." She was reluctant to hand it over.

"I'll get it back to you as soon as I have copies made. It shouldn't take long."

"Okay. I guess."

Michael slid the photo into his case file. "If Bobby was seeing someone new, any idea who it might be?"

Kim's eyes narrowed. "If I did, I'd certainly set her straight about what a shit the guy is."

Michael could feel the heat of her anger. "Does the name Tully ring any bells with you?"

Her nose wrinkled in protest. "Funny name. You think he's with her?"

"No, this is a man I'm asking about."

She rolled her eyes. "A man? I don't think so, not Bobby."

"I'm thinking Tully might be the husband of someone Bobby's involved with."

"Oh. Sorry." She looked embarrassed.

"The name mean anything to you?"

Kim started to shake her head, then snapped around to look directly at him. "I should have known."

"Known what?"

"It was clear she was coming on to him. All that 'poor me' stuff she laid on Bobby. I could see that he was falling for it."

"Who?"

"Dimwit by the name of Sheryl Ann. She's married to a drummer named Tully."

"Do you have a last name?"

"Martin. Sheryl Ann Martin."

By three o'clock that afternoon, Michael had determined that Tully and Sheryl Ann Martin were out of town. According to the manager at the insurance claims office where Sheryl Ann was employed, the couple had left on an unexpected trip the previous Monday. The same day that both Kate and Bobby disappeared. The timing fit perfectly.

Michael left a detailed message, including copies of Bobby's photo, for both Frank and the captain, then made arrangements for Libby and Anna and caught a six o'clock flight to Boise. Maybe there wasn't anything he could contribute by being in Idaho, but waiting by the telephone was out of the question.

10

Like an inmate awaiting dawn on execution day, I watched with dread as the night sky slowly softened from black to gray. The bare tree limbs outside the window emerged as distinct shapes instead of undefined slashes of shadow. A lone bird trilled, and others joined him, signaling dawn. My heart grew heavier by the minute.

I was sure that if I were smarter, stronger, more clearheaded, I might have found a way to escape. But my mind was befuddled with a wildly escalating sense of panic. There was no way anyone was going to find me. Not in time. I'd been a fool to think otherwise.

Soon I'd be just another statistic. One more short-lived story in the headlines. A lifetime of emotions and memories would simply cease to exist.

Bobby got up first. He muttered something to Sheryl Ann, pulled a heavy jacket from the pegs by the door, and stomped outside. Sheryl Ann was still in bed when he returned about half an hour later, looking half-frozen.

"It's fucking snowing again," he called out to her, heading past me on his way to the bedroom. "Between the frozen ground and the snow that fell last night, digging is impossible.''

"I knew this wasn't going to work." Sheryl Ann's voice sounded agitated. "What are we going to do?"

I heard the springs creak as Bobby sat down on the bed. "We don't have to bury them, I guess."

"But you said no body—"

Bobby snapped at her. "I know what I said. And I'm not suggesting we just leave them out in the open. There's other ways to hide a body."

"But it's got to be where no one will find them."

"Go make some coffee and see what you can put together for breakfast. I have an idea."

Bobby headed out again, and Sheryl Ann shuffled into the kitchen, ignoring me as if I were a piece of furniture. The protective barrier of silence and denial. I could understand why she'd want to distance herself from my fate—and it underscored for me the certainty of what was coming next. The cold terror I felt in my chest was almost unbearable.

"Sheryl Ann," I called to her in a whisper so Bobby wouldn't hear me. When she didn't answer, I tried again, more loudly. "Sheryl Ann, don't let him do this."

She came to the doorway. "Shut up." Then she turned and went back to measuring out the coffee.

When Bobby returned, they ate breakfast in the kitchen. Neither of them so much as looked in my direction.

"I think I found a place," Bobby said.

"Where?"

"There's an old root cellar beyond that clump of trees there in front. Hasn't been used in years. All we've got to do is pry the boards loose from the top and then nail them back again. A whole lot easier than digging.''

My terror of dark, small places reared its ugly head. It was almost a relief to know that I'd be dead by the time I was there. Or would I? A new wave of panic filled my lungs.

"I'm going to go get started on the boards," Bobby said after a while. "I could use your help with Tully, though."

"Okay."

"We'll take care of him first, and then deal with Kate."

"Fine."

Did I imagine it or was there a flicker of hesitation in Sheryl Ann's voice?

Bobby must have heard it, too, because he pushed his chair away from the table with an abrupt flash of anger. "We don't have a choice, Sheryl Ann. It's her or us. She knows about Tully."

"We could say it was self-defense. They can't put you in jail for that, can they?"

"It wasn't though. Not really. The police have a way of knowing that stuff."

"What about temporary insanity or something? Lots of people commit crimes and don't end up behind bars." The pitch of Sheryl Ann's voice rose.

"Once the law gets a hold on you, you're screwed. Even innocent people get the shaft. No way am I going to do that."

"But—"

"Besides, we've already moved Tully's body and forced Kate to come with us. It's too late to turn back."

She let her breath out slowly. "I guess you're right." She didn't sound convinced.

"After all I've done for you," Bobby said angrily, "don't you turn on me. I'm getting good and pissed with all your moaning and groaning. You hear me?"

She must have nodded, because his voice softened. "I don't like it either. It's not something I want to do. But it's got to be done. Now get some more clothes on and come help me move Tully."

Bobby slipped on his jacket and left. Slipping on a heavy parka, Sheryl Ann followed a few minutes later. She walked past me twice without acknowledging my presence in any way.

When she was gone, I managed to hop to the window. The ground was a blanket of soft white. Snow was still falling. In the distance, I could see Sheryl Ann and Bobby pulling something dark and heavy from trunk of the car. Tully.

A spasm of nausea worked its way into my throat. I choked on the sourness. Frantically working at my hands, I hopped toward the kitchen in search of a knife to cut myself free.

Halfway there, I stumbled and toppled forward onto the hard floor. For a moment, I lay there unable to move. Unable to do anything but ride the wave of pain from my unbroken fall. I had to remind myself to breathe.

I tried getting up, but without my hands to brace me it was an impossible task. I arched my back, flung myself from side to side, got as far as sitting up but no further. Finally, I was able to roll facedown on the floor and bring my knees under me. But I still couldn't get to my feet.

I inched forward on my knees, making slow but steady progress. When I reached the wall, I pressed my back against it and was finally able to pull myself to my feet.

Struggling to keep my balance, I hobbled to the kitchen. They'd left a knife on the counter by the sink.

I sidled up with my back to it and bent forward slightly so my arms could reach the counter. With my hands tied behind me, I had to work by feel. I managed to curl my fingers around the knife handle, but I couldn't angle the blade properly to cut the rope.

Despite the cold, perspiration beaded on my forehead and along the back of my neck. I shifted the knife to my other hand and felt it connect solidly with rope. Slowly moving it back and forth, I sawed a strand of fiber at a time.

I was making progress! I could feel the knife working against the taut cord. When my fingers tired, I tried switching hands again—and dropped the knife. It clattered on the grimy linoleum floor.

No, please. I was so close. Tears of frustration stung my eyes. I kneeled, reached behind me for the knife.

And then I heard the sound of footsteps on the porch.

Sheryl Ann opened the door. She was alone.

She stared at me in silence, then walked past to the bedroom and returned with the gun.

"God, no." My voice was pitched with terror. "Please, Sheryl Ann. Don't do this."

"Shut up for a minute, would you?" She sounded impatient. "Now listen to me because we don't have a lot of time. I'm going to untie you, and then I want you get out of here. I've got the gun, and I'll shoot you if try to take me on. You understand?"

I nodded in stunned silence.

"Just get out. Get away fast."

I could feel my heart pounding in my ears. "What about Bobby?"

"He'll probably go looking for you. That's why you need to go now." She was already working on my feet.

"I meant, what will you tell him?"

"That you were gone when I got back here."

"Don't you think he'll figure out what happened?"

"He might suspect, but he won't know for sure."

She untied my hands, then held the gun, aiming it at my chest.

"Come with me, Sheryl Ann. Don't leave yourself alone with Bobby."

"I can handle him."

"He's going to be angry."

"You better get going."

I backed away toward the door, hesitated for a moment, then decided it wasn't my job to convince her to leave. "Thank you," I whispered. "You've got a good heart."

"Take my jacket," she said, grabbing it from the chair where it was draped and handing it to me. "It's cold out there."

She kept the gun aimed at me as I stepped out the door and into the frozen world beyond.

As the plane descended, Michael stared out the window at the blanket of white below. He'd been told it wasn't a heavy storm, but the stark contrast to the green hills of California was a powerful reminder how different a world he'd entered.

Passengers disembarked slowly, and Michael, seated near the rear, was ready to burst with impatience at the delay. He'd managed to hold his anxiety at bay during the flight, but now that he was on the ground, he felt an unbridled urgency. The paperwork on his rental car—a Ford Explorer with snow tires—produced further delay, and by the time he finally got on the road, over an hour had elapsed since the plane's scheduled arrival.

Leaving Boise, Michael headed north, climbing gradually higher into the mountains. The majestic Sawtooth National Forest was to the east and the Boise Wilderness to the west. The road followed a creek, winding through forested slopes and open glens of downy white. Snow was falling intermittently, light flakes as tiny as powdered ash. If he were here on almost any other mission, he'd have been captivated by the pristine beauty of his surroundings. As it was, his only thought was how easily the vast unpopulated landscape could swallow up the trail of someone who wanted to remain hidden.

Before leaving California, Michael had spoken with the sheriff handling the investigation in Idaho, a slow-speaking, ratchety-voiced man by the name of Gus Olson. Michael had been hoping that armed with the make, model, and license plate of Robert Lake's car, Olson would waste little time bringing the man into custody. One look at the stretch of rugged country around him had been enough to send those hopes crashing.

It was after eight when Michael reached Elk Grove and pulled into the small, bungalow-style motel Olson had said would be his best bet. His only bet, Olson had said, if he wanted to stay close by. The room was small, Spartan, and stuffy, the walls water-marked and the carpet frayed. Accommodations of the most basic sort, but they were clean and, most important, not far from the roadside phone Kate had used to call.

Michael dumped his overnight bag at the foot of the bed, plopped himself down on the faded brown spread, and put in a call to Olson.

"You made it, then?" Olson said.

"Just got in a few minutes ago."

"Did you eat?"

Michael tried to remember. He'd had half of a dry turkey sandwich on the plane and a package of M&Ms during the drive. "Not really," he said.

"I'll meet you at the Hitching Post in fifteen minutes. Won't be any of that California gourmet stuff you're probably used to, but it's good food." He gave Michael directions and hung up.

The Hitching Post wasn't hard to find. Neither was

Olson. He was the only customer in the place. He rose as Michael entered the room.

Olson was a bit older than Michael, maybe forty-five, with a barrel chest and nonexistent hips. His skin was weathered, from exposure or a lifelong tobacco habit. Michael couldn't tell.

After the barest of introductions, they sat. Olson ground out his cigarette. "See you found it okay."

"Good directions," Michael said. The town was only two blocks long, so he'd have managed, even without the detailed instructions.

The waitress brought menus and joked briefly with Olson.

"The meat loaf and mashed potatoes are first-rate," Olson told him. "Fried chicken isn't bad either."

Michael hadn't eaten meat loaf since he was in grade school, but he ordered it anyway. And a beer. In truth, there weren't a lot of options.

Olson had coffee and cherry pie. "I already ate dinner," he explained, pouring a heavy dose of cream into his mug. He stirred it with his finger. "You been a cop long?"

"Fifteen years," Michael told him. "How about you?"

"Twenty-five years this fall. My dad and uncle were both cops, and I sort of fell into step behind them." He paused to taste his coffee. "Hell of a life, ain't it? Every day, face-to-face with humankind at its worst. I'm looking forward to early retirement and nothing more stressful than fly-fishing."

"Hope it works out for you."

Olson cut a piece of pie. "So what drew you to the profession?"

Michael swallowed a mouthful of meat loaf. The truth

was that he'd fallen into police work by accident. Two years into graduate school, just when he'd been on the verge of knuckling down to serious work on his thesis, his father had died. With two younger siblings in college, Michael felt he needed to make a contribution. Besides, he'd begun to realize that a life studying and teaching classics might not be what he wanted after all.

But he hadn't come all this way to swap personal histories with the local sheriff. By way of an answer, he shrugged. "You got the information I faxed this morning on Robert Lake?"

Olson nodded. "Photo and license plate number. I sent the description out over the wire. Nothing's come back."

"Did you show the photo to the gas station attendant?"

"Not yet." Before Michael could frame a protest, Olson leaned back in his chair with arms crossed. "This missing woman is a friend of yours, right?"

More than a friend. But Michael wasn't about to get into his relationship with Kate. "Right."

"Does she do this sort of thing often?"

It took a moment for the words to register, and then Michael rocked forward, halving the distance between them. He resisted the urge to grab the man by his collar. "What the hell is that supposed to mean?"

Olson shrugged. "Simple question, that's all. A woman disappears, ostensibly kidnapped—"

"Ostensibly?" Anger hardened the word more than he'd intended. "She was kidnapped, period."

Olson studied him a moment. "I'm not trying to cast aspersions on your friend, merely trying to get a clear understanding of the situation."

"Seems fairly clear to me," Michael snapped.

"You and she didn't happen to have a fight right before all this happened, did you?"

Michael started counting to ten, made it only to four. "I don't know what kind of game you're playing here, but I didn't come—"

Olson leaned back in his chair. "You have any idea how many missing-persons cases turn out to be something other than that?"

Just what he needed. Some backwoods, know-it-all cop running the show. Michael took a sip of water to calm himself. "This isn't like that," he said, with an edge of irritation. "This is the real thing."

"Okay, let's say it is." Olson tapped his fork on the tabletop. "Why'd they bring her here?"

"If I had a clue, you can be sure I'd have told you by now."

"So this is what we have? You found her car, abandoned. No witnesses. And now you've got the name of someone you say is her abductor. Name, description of car, and license number." Olson's voice exhibited skepticism.

"Two people actually. Robert Lake and Sheryl Ann Martin. But it's Robert's car they're driving."

Olson scratched his cheek. "How sure are you that these are the people who've got your friend?"

"Not one hundred percent," Michael conceded. "But close." The swell of anger had subsided, and he was working hard to keep it that way. The sheriff was only doing what any good law-enforcement officer would do— endeavoring to separate speculation from fact.

Michael pushed his plate aside and told Olson the full story from the beginning. He was sure that most of the pertinent facts had been communicated already, but hearing it again, one-on-one, was bound to cast the situation in a different light.

Olson listened without interrupting, then asked, "Any idea *why* they've taken her?"

"None whatsoever."

"Could be as retribution for something you've done, you know."

"I've thought of that. But as best I can tell, I've never had any dealings with either of them. Besides, there's the dead man, Tully. He was Sheryl Ann's husband."

"A love triangle."

"Looks that way."

Olson sucked on his lower lip. "And you don't think your friend knew any of them?"

Michael didn't know for sure. Kate had so many contacts—people she knew through her art-consulting business or through Anna's school or various community activities. Grocery clerks, the vet's assistant, the tree trimmer. When the two of them were out about town, Kate would occasionally run into people she knew, and when Michael asked afterward who it was, she'd tell him *the librarian*, or *the woman who has the flower stand near the bakery*. Kate's life incorporated a web of connections Michael had trouble fathoming. He envied the ease with which she related to people.

"I never heard her mention any of them," Michael said. "I checked with a couple of Kate's friends. They weren't aware of a connection, either."

A pause. "What are your plans now that you're here?"

"I don't know exactly." Aside from the fact that he was desperate to find Kate and didn't trust the locals to put much energy into it. "I guess I'll start by talking to people at the fast-food place where she made the call."

Olson's expression softened. "We did that already, but I can understand how you want to try again, yourself."

Michael nodded.

"We hit most of the main stops along the highway, too. Haven't found a soul who saw anything, aside from the guy at the gas station. You're welcome to look at our files."

"Thanks."

Olson ran a finger along the edge of his plate. "My first wife was killed by a hit-and-run driver. I tore the state apart looking for the guy, double-checked every lead the police had, interviewed everyone who'd been within miles of the incident. I made sure her name stayed in the papers, too."

Michael looked up, surprised by a vulnerability in Olson he hadn't seen before. "Did you find him?"

"No. It's still an open case."

"I'm sorry."

"Anyway, I understand what you're going through."

The motel sheets were cold when Michael slid between them, and the thin blanket provided little warmth. He was sure he spent the night fully awake, shivering and tossing from side to side, but when he heard a car engine rev outside his window and saw morning light, he was surprised to discover that he'd been asleep, and it was now almost nine o'clock. Snow continued to fall lightly.

Still groggy, Michael stepped into the small shower stall and adjusted the water temperature. The spray was warm enough, but very thin. It left him with the feeling he'd taken a sponge bath rather than a shower.

He stopped by the motel office for his complimentary

sweet roll, served cold, and cup of coffee, more lukewarm than hot. They landed in his stomach like cement.

His plan was to start with the employees at the Hogan's where Kate had placed her call and then move on to the gas station attendant who'd seen a car with California plates. From there, he wasn't sure what his next step would be.

Twenty minutes from the motel, Michael pulled into the Hogan's parking lot. His eyes were drawn immediately to the phone booth at the side of the building. Unbidden, a vision of Kate filled his mind and tugged at his chest.

Kate, scared and miserable, trying desperately to reach someone who could help her. Bobby yanking the phone from her hand, following up with a forceful punch. And then what?

Pushing the images from his mind, Michael slid out of the car and into the bitter cold. The pavement was layered with several inches of snow, and he walked gingerly to avoid slipping.

As he'd expected, two of the people he wanted to talk with weren't working that morning, and no one he did talk to recognized Robert's picture or remembered seeing anything unusual.

With an eerie sense of incongruity, Michael stepped back outside to the phone booth—the very phone Kate had used to call for help—and tried to reach the remaining two employees. A busy signal and no answer. He called the Walnut Hills station next. Janet read him his messages. Nothing that couldn't wait, Michael decided, except for a call from Heidi Harrington.

"Did she say what it was about?" he asked, feeling his pulse quicken.

"No, only that she wanted you to call her."

Michael jotted down the number, cleared the line and dialed.

"You asked about Idaho," Mrs. Harrington said, getting right to the point. "At first nothing registered, but then last evening I remembered that Robert has a friend whose uncle owns a place there. A hunting and fishing cabin, I believe. Robert and his friend used it a couple of times during summers."

Michael felt a rush of adrenaline. "Do you have a location for the cabin?"

"Not exactly. The closest town is Whitehall. That's the address we used for mail."

"What's the friend's name?"

"Ted Thornton. As I recall, the uncle's last name was the same. I tried calling Ted this morning, but I didn't reach him. Would you like me to try again?"

"Let me do it," Michael said. He took down Ted Thornton's number. "Thanks," Michael said. "This may help."

"Do you think that's where Bobby is? You think he simply took a trip without telling us?" Her voice registered both confusion and hope.

Robert Lake was in Idaho. Michael was sure of that. Sadly, there was nothing simple about it.

12

The cold was biting, even without the wind. But the snow cave helped. It wasn't really a cave. Just the well surrounding a large pine that I'd managed to enlarge on one side and partially line with branches. I huddled there with my back to packed snow. My feet were solid blocks of ice and my face so numb it no longer stung. The gray sky had darkened, muting the greens and browns of the landscape.

Night was falling, and I was lost.

Lost. Alone. And filled with the bleakest sorrow I'd ever known.

I hugged Sheryl Ann's jacket across my chest, tucking my chin into the upturned collar and burying my fingers in the sleeves. Though I wanted to sleep, I knew that wasn't a good idea. I'd read about hypothermia, the slow decline of strength and will. I needed to keep moving, keep the blood circulating and the muscles limber.

But it was so much work.

Five minutes, I told myself. Five minutes, and then I'd climb out into the wind again, wave my arms, and stomp my feet.

Not that it would make any difference. I was going to

die anyway, frozen to death in the godforsaken wilds. My bones would be picked clean by spring.

Me. Bones. That's all that would be left.

In its own way, death was almost enticing. A long, comfortable sleep. An easy slide into restfulness.

Better not to think like that. Better to focus on finding a way out of there.

Only I had no idea anymore which direction to head. I'd run from the cabin in a blind panic, sure that Bobby was only seconds behind me. Slipping and stumbling, I'd bolted for the nearest clump of trees, and then for the next. By the time I stopped to catch my breath, I was half-frozen and totally disoriented. I tried retracing my steps, but the falling snow covered my tracks and made it impossible.

All day I'd forged on, or maybe wandered in circles. Trees and rocks blanketed with snow were the only landmarks. After a while they all looked the same.

I needed to get up and move. I knew that, but I didn't do it.

Five more minutes, I told myself groggily. Five minutes for sure.

Mommy, get up.

Anna's voice was soft. It drifted through the mists of my mind as though she were playing in a nearby room.

Sweet Anna. So innocent and trusting. So full of fire when she had her mind set. The rosebud mouth tweaked at the corners. Her button nose wrinkled.

Mommy! You have to get up.

I snapped awake.

Night had fallen. I tried to stand, and couldn't.

Brute terror clutched at my heart. I pulled a vision of Anna into my mind and held on to it. I wasn't going to leave her. I wasn't going to die. No way was I going to let that happen.

Somehow, I managed to get to my feet. My limbs were stiff and without sensation, my balance uneven. Though I could barely stand, I swung my arms, shifted my weight from side to side. Cried silently.

And then in the distance, I saw a light. It was visible for a few seconds before disappearing. It reappeared a moment later further to the right.

Headlights!

I felt a surge of elation. My heart danced in my chest.

Slowly and painstakingly, I plodded on wooden legs toward the spot where I'd seen the light. The darkness confused me. I fell numerous times, had increasing difficulty getting to my feet. Anna's voice in my head urged me on.

It was slow going, and the distance was farther than it looked. The road wasn't heavily traveled. Only three lights after the first one. Without a beacon to guide me, I headed off course repeatedly, only to correct myself when another light appeared.

Then, finally, I was at the top of a rise. The road was below me.

And on the other side of a rushing creek.

I wailed silently.

Defeat hovered. I ignored it.

Blindly, I pushed on, not even stopping to test the depth of the water. My eyes were on the lonely strip of blacktop ahead. It beckoned like the proverbial light at the end of a tunnel.

My last memory was the sight of an approaching car.

13

Michael placed a hand on the car's dash to steady himself as Olson took a sharp left turn off the main road onto a narrow lane. The terrain wasn't steep, but it was rugged with large boulders and thick vegetation. Craggy mountain peaks loomed in the horizon.

"Shouldn't be too far now," the sheriff said.

Whatever the distance, the time it would take them stretched like an eternity. The two-hour drive into a neighboring county had crept by so slowly that Michael had felt each second as a lifetime unto itself.

"Shouldn't they have called by now?" Michael asked.

Olson shrugged. "It's a territorial thing. Especially with Foley. He wouldn't waste the breath it took to share information."

On learning the location of the fishing cabin, Olson had muttered a curse. "That's Foley's turf. He's going to do it his way. You'd best accept that right off."

"And what's his way?"

"He's going to call the shots, and he's going to resent any kind of interest or involvement from outside."

Michael knew the type. Whether they were power-hungry, imbued with an inflated ego, or simply distrustful of others, these were the cops who lived the myth of single-handed justice. Some of them were good at what they did, and some were total jackasses, but they all made team effort impossible.

As the car slid on a patch of ice, Michael again gripped the dash. "Foley *did* say he'd let us know if Kate was there."

Olson snorted in response. "He didn't say *when* he'd let us know. I wouldn't go holding my breath if I were you."

Involuntarily, Michael took a fresh gulp of air. He tried playing through the scene in his mind. If the cabin was empty, would Foley be in any hurry to call? Maybe not. But if Kate was there, surely he'd have let them know.

Unless she was dead.

The harder Michael tried to ignore that awful possibility, the larger it loomed in his mind. He could feel the pressure in his chest building. "Maybe we should try calling Foley ourselves," he said.

Olson shook his head. "We'd only get dispatch."

They drove several minutes in silence, then slowed to a crawl as they forded a creek bed. The exertion of waiting bore down on Michael like a lead weight. "You sure we're on the right road?" he asked.

"Unless Foley misled me on purpose."

"You think he'd do that?"

Olson chewed on his lip. "I wouldn't put it past him, but I don't think in this instance he did."

Another, longer round of silence. Finally, they came to a fork in the road. To the left, an unblemished dusting of white powder still covered the roadway. The route to the right showed tire tracks. A short distance ahead,

Michael could see three official vehicles—two patrol cars and a van—parked diagonally at the side of the road.

"I think we're there," Olson said, pulling in next to one of the cars.

The tiny, dilapidated cabin was set back about fifty yards from the area where they'd parked. A front door and single window were visible from the road. There was no light inside, no smoke coming from the chimney. But Michael could feel a buzz in the air the minute Olson pulled to a stop. He couldn't have said exactly what it was—the posture of the two deputies standing on the porch, the way a third man crouched, examining the ground—but Michael knew with certainty that they'd found something.

He bolted from the car, then stopped to steady himself on the slippery surface. In his haste to leave California, he hadn't thought to bring boots.

One of the officers from the porch started toward them and again Michael felt the charge in the air. He was still ten yards from the cabin when he saw the spots of darkened snow near where the third man crouched.

Blood.

Michael felt his chest collapse as if the air had been sucked by force from his lungs. He tried to speak but couldn't.

The approaching officer wasn't as tall as Michael, but he was built like a bulldog.

"That's Foley," Olson whispered.

"Do you think they've—"

"We'll know soon enough." A moment later, he greeted Foley by name, then asked, "What have you got?"

"A body. Gunshot wound."

The words faded in and out of Michael's hearing. *A body.* Living people were not bodies.

Finally, he found his voice. "Is it Kate? Is it the woman who was abducted?"

Foley seemed to see him for first time. Olson made a quick introduction, followed by an equally quick explanation.

"No ID yet," Foley said, "but the body's male."

The wave of relief that rolled over Michael was so great it almost knocked him over. Someone was dead. But not Kate. Thank God, not Kate.

He followed Olson and Foley into the cabin. More blood, toppled furniture, a shattered mirror. Michael could imagine the rage that had been party to such destruction.

The body lay on the floor, faceup. Michael stepped closer to get a better look.

"Recognize him?"

Michael nodded. Even with an expression frozen by death, there was no mistaking him. "His name is Lake. Robert Lake, also known as Bobby. I've never met him, but he looks like his picture."

Although he'd done this countless times on other occasions, Michael felt his gut twist in a way it never had before. It struck him that the quiet desperation he'd felt himself only moments earlier would very soon be visited upon Heidi Harrington.

Only in her case, there would be no reprieve.

14

What I remember most vividly is the white light. Pure, radiant light that filled my mind with such intensity all other images faded to near nothingness. I was drifting effortlessly, like a wisp of cloud on a summer's afternoon. Tranquil, serene, absorbed only in the moment.

Then, suddenly, it was gone, and there was only shadow.

I heard a whimpering sound. Heard it first, then felt it in my throat. I struggled to speak, but my mouth was made of cotton.

A hand touched my shoulder. "Hey, darlin'. You awake?" The voice was female and not familiar.

My eyes opened long enough to take in a black face, a white uniform.

"Page Dr. Singer," the voice said. "She's coming around."

Wakefulness came slowly at first, then in a torrent as the memories flooded my mind. Sheryl Ann's watchful eyes as I slipped away from the cabin; the unexpected, last-minute hug she'd given me at the door. The biting cold, my toes and fingers so numb they were beyond pain. Trudging over the rough terrain, dazed and disoriented, until I'd reached the road just minutes before a car that passed me by as though I were invisible. And then the terrible, all-consuming suspicion that perhaps I was.

How long had it been—minutes, hours, days? And then another car. A man with a red muffler and curly white hair, like one of Santa's elves. "Lady, are you all right? My God, you're half-frozen."

Again, a hand touched my shoulder. "Ma'am?" A different voice this time. I opened my eyes and saw a doctor. He was dressed like a doctor, in any event. And he had a plastic name tag that identified him as Isaac Singer, MD. But he looked about seventeen. "Ma'am," he said again. "Can you hear me?"

My mouth was too dry for words, but I nodded.

"Do you know where you are?"

The nurse brought ice chips. They were cool and wet against my parched mouth. Slowly my voice returned.

"Hospital?"

He smiled, like the pleased parent of a precocious three-year-old. "Do you remember how you got here?"

"A man. White hair like an elf."

"He found you wandering, half-coherent, alongside the road."

"There was a creek," I mumbled.

Dr. Singer's eyes were a soft, liquid brown, like chocolate. They watched me closely. "Can you tell me your name?" he asked.

"Kate."

"Kate what?"

I felt a sudden urgency. "What day is it?" The words came out as though I were talking with a mouthful of marbles.

"Tuesday," Dr. Singer replied.

"Still January?"

Another smile. "Still January. Can you tell me your full name?"

"Austen. It's Kate Austen. I live in California. Walnut Hills. I was kidnapped."

"Kidnapped?" Dr. Singer sat up straighter.

My eyes filled with tears of joy. I was free. Alive and free. I would hold Anna again, be held by Michael. I'd see Libby, and the first blooms of spring. My terrible ordeal was finally over. I wiped away the tears with a bandaged hand.

"What's the matter?" Dr. Singer asked.

"I've got to call my daughter. I've got to talk to Michael, let them know I'm okay." I sat up and immediately felt a swell of nausea rise into my throat.

"Easy now." The nurse helped me back onto the pillow. "You can't go leapin' around just yet. You need to rest."

"No, I need to reach my daughter."

"You gotta take care of yourself, darlin'."

"But my daughter—"

"You were kidnapped?" Dr. Singer asked again.

"Yes. Call Michael Stone, Walnut Hills Police Department. California." I could feel hysteria creeping up on me. "Let him know where I am. Please."

Dr. Singer placed a hand on my arm. "We'll notify the police, and your family. You need to rest now. Understand?"

He lifted his eyes to the nurse and mumbled something I couldn't make out. The last thing I remember is her short black fingers fiddling with a butterfly valve on the IV.

*   *   *

When I woke again, it was evening. Different doctor, different nurse. And a third man who introduced himself as Sheriff Foley. He had the ramrod-straight posture, closely cropped hair, and unsmiling countenance of an ex-Marine.

"You feel up to talking, Mrs. Austen?"

"Yes. Please."

The nurse handed me a glass of water.

Foley pulled up a chair. "You want to tell me what happened?"

"I was kidnapped. A man and a woman. There's a third man, too. Only he's dead." The words poured forth before I had time to organize my thoughts.

The doctor checked his watch. "Ten minutes," he said. "She needs her rest."

"What I need is to make a call," I told him, but he and the nurse were already heading out the door.

I turned to the sheriff. "Michael Stone. He's a police lieutenant in California where I live. He's my . . ." I faltered as I searched for the right word.

Foley saved me the effort of labeling my relationship with Michael. "He's here."

"Here?"

"Not at the hospital, but in the area."

"Does he know I'm okay?"

Foley sucked on his cheek. "Not yet, but I'll let him know."

My head throbbed. I rubbed the area between my eyes. "What's he doing here?"

Ignoring the question, Foley pulled out a notebook. "Why don't you tell me what happened, from the beginning?"

Okay, I thought, we'll play it his way. Statement first, and then maybe I'd get some answers.

I took it more slowly this time, trying hard to recount the events in sequence. Coherent witness testimony makes for a more efficient investigation. Michael had told me that often enough.

"This woman Sheryl Ann," Foley said when I'd finished, "she let you go free, just like that? For no reason?"

"She knew Bobby was going to kill me." That seemed like reason enough.

"She'd known that for several days."

"This time it was different, though. This time he was *really* going to do it." I shut my eyes, willing my mind to work more clearly. "It's hard to explain, but we'd developed a sort of bond."

"You and the woman who kidnapped you?"

I nodded. "I know she committed a crime, but Bobby Lake is the one who's responsible. Sheryl Ann was kind to me. She didn't like what was happening."

Foley frowned. "But she went along willingly until, out of the blue, she changed her mind?"

I didn't like Foley's tone, but the core of the statement was accurate.

"And the dead man. You say he was Sheryl Ann's husband?"

I nodded and felt a thrust of pain at my temples. "Bobby apparently killed him. I don't think he meant to, though." I was surprised to find myself defending Bobby as well as Sheryl Ann.

"Why'd they run, then?"

"I think they were scared."

"And you'd never seen either of them before that evening you stopped to help?"

"Right."

Foley leaned back in his chair and gave me an appraising look. "You want to tell me where Sheryl Ann is now?"

"There's a cabin. It's somewhere near where I was picked up. I think I might be able to find it again with a little help."

"We've been there," he said tersely.

I was surprised. "How?"

"Lake's mother tipped us off."

Bobby's mother? I looked at Foley, confused. His face showed nothing.

He wasn't telling me the whole story. Even in my befuddled state, I could tell that much. But I was trying to stay focused on what I *did* know. "You found the cabin?"

He nodded, expressionless.

"Bobby and Sheryl Ann were gone?" Not that I really expected them to stick around.

Foley rocked forward. "We found Bobby Lake, but Sheryl Ann wasn't there."

Good for her, I thought. She'd decided to leave Bobby after all. "What did he tell you?"

"Bobby Lake isn't talking. He's dead."

"Dead?" I felt as though I'd had the wind knocked out of me.

Foley pressed his fingertips together and nodded.

"How?"

"He was shot."

My mind was reeling. "And there was no sign of Sheryl Ann?"

"No body, if that's what you mean."

I felt a wave of relief. Sheryl Ann was alive.

Maybe.

And then another thought struck me. Had Bobby gotten angry at Sheryl Ann for letting me go? Had she been forced to kill him in self-defense?

"Bobby was alive when you left the cabin?" Foley asked.

"Yes, of course." Then the unspoken question behind his words hit me. "You don't think *I* had anything to do with his death, do you?"

The muscle in Foley's jaw twitched. "Did you?"

The pounding in my head became a roar. "You can't be serious?"

"Why not?" His voice was cool.

Indignation bubbled in my chest. I'd been abducted, my life threatened—first by man, then by nature. And I hadn't heard one word of sympathy or concern.

"What if I had?" I cried. "They kidnapped me, held me prisoner. They were going to kill me."

"So you've said."

It was like a slap in the face. "You don't believe me?"

"I'm merely trying to find out what really happened."

"I *told* you what happened."

Foley cracked a knuckle and gave me a steely look.

"Get out," I told him, no longer able to contain my anger. "I'm through talking to you."

"Your call." He rose and headed for the door, then stopped. "From what you've told me, it's likely to be justifiable homicide. But I need you to level with me."

I didn't dignify the comment with a response.

I was still fuming half an hour later when the door to my room opened again. I saw the flowers first, and then Michael.

Even with the dark circles under his eyes and a sallow tint to his skin, Michael looked wonderful. At the mere sight of him, the weight of my troubles seemed lighter.

"I'm so glad you're here." The lump in my throat caused my voice to waver.

"Likewise." Michael set the flowers, a large and colorful mixed bouquet, on the bed next to me. He touched my face with his fingers, tracing the hollow of my cheek. "You're the most beautiful sight in the world."

I brushed away tears. "I was so scared. I was sure I was going to die. I was terrified."

He nodded. His gaze was soft, a mixture of love, joy, and utter exhaustion. He kissed my forehead as though he were afraid I might break. I slipped my arms around his neck, and he hugged me tight against his chest.

"Jesus, Kate. I've been so worried."

"I know. I thought I'd never see you again."

Gingerly, he touched the patch of raw skin by my left eye. "Did they hurt you?"

"A few scrapes and bruises. Nothing bad."

He examined my bandaged hands. "The doctor says you were lucky with the frostbite. You'll probably keep all your fingers and toes."

I was grateful, though a finger seemed a small price to pay for my life.

"How are you feeling?" Michael asked.

"Overwhelmed, I guess. Happy to be alive."

He tucked a loose strand of hair behind my ear. "You're safe. It's behind you, now. Try to remember that. You're going to be okay."

"What about Anna and Libby? Do they know I'm here?"

"I called them as soon as I heard. Anna's with Andy, and Libby is with her friend Erin. They both send their love and want you to hurry home."

I lay back against the pillows, suddenly exhausted. It

was a relief to feel that I no longer had to carry the burden of my ordeal single-handedly.

"I can't believe you're really here," I told him. "I didn't think that stupid sheriff would tell you."

"Foley? He didn't tell me. I found out on my own."

Michael explained how his search for Robert Lake had led him to Idaho. And ultimately to me, thanks to the hospital, which had sent word of an unidentified and incoherent woman to a number of local law-enforcement agencies.

My eyes drifted to the window and the darkened sky outside. I could see our reflection in the glass. It felt good to be someplace warm and safe.

I turned back to Michael. "The sheriff says Bobby Lake is dead."

Michael nodded.

"He thinks I might have had something to do with it."

Michael patted the mound of gauze that was my hand. "He's just doing his job, Kate. It will sort out in the end."

"It's all so awful. Why would he suspect *me?*"

"He doesn't know you, honey. All he's got right now is your story and a dead body. There's no shortage of people who've claimed to have been kidnapped in order to cover up a crime."

"That's true, I guess." Although without Sheryl Ann to back me up, I didn't see how my story would become more credible.

"He'll get to the bottom of it," Michael said. "You don't have to worry."

"He said Bobby was shot."

"Right. Several times in the chest, at close range."

"I hope Sheryl Ann is okay." Even though Michael didn't push for details, I told him what had happened.

It helped to talk through the experience, to share the memory with someone who was concerned and sympathetic. Someone who never once pointed out how stupidly I'd gotten myself involved in a situation that didn't concern me. For that, I was more grateful than he'd ever know.

"Bobby must have gotten angry with Sheryl Ann for letting me go," I said, coming back to the matter that was troubling me most. "She wouldn't have killed him except in self-defense. It happened because of me."

"Nothing she did is your fault, Kate."

"I can't help feeling somehow responsible, though."

"You've been through an ordeal, honey. Irrational fear, feelings of guilt, a sense of hopelessness—that's all normal. It will fade with time."

Michael was silent a moment, lost in thought. "Tell me again about Tully."

"He was Sheryl Ann's husband. Bobby killed him, not intentionally, I think. They were bringing the body to the cabin here to bury him. No body, no crime."

"That's not—"

"I know. But it's what Bobby thought. Only the ground was frozen, and Bobby couldn't dig a grave."

"You're sure they put the body in the root cellar?"

"I saw them do it. Why?"

He paused. "It's not there. Foley's men searched the whole area. There was only one body anywhere in the vicinity, and that was Robert Lake's."

15

The crime scene at the cabin was still cordoned off when Michael revisited it two days later. He wasn't sure, really, why he'd come. Clearly not with the expectation he'd find telltale evidence the local cops had missed. Foley might not win any congeniality awards, but he knew how to process a crime scene. Michael could only hope he was as thorough about running an investigation. His pegging Kate as a suspect, while it made some sense in the abstract, was going to hinder progress in closing the case.

Michael walked the area surrounding the cabin. By now there were so many footprints and tire tracks it was impossible to get a sense of how things had looked initially. Even then, there'd been little to go on. The recent snowfall had covered the existing prints, making them virtually useless. Aside from Kate's account of her kidnapping and escape, there was no indication that Sheryl Ann Martin had been anywhere in the area.

Slipping under the yellow plastic tape, Michael took a look at the root cellar where, according to Kate, Tully's body had been deposited. Angled wooden doors covered the entrance. Inside was a narrow and flat cavelike structure. Empty. The packed-dirt floor showed signs of foot traffic but it was hard to tell if the markings were recent.

Was it possible that Kate only *thought* she saw them dump the body? She'd been in a panic, afraid Bobby was going to kill her as soon as he'd finished hiding Tully's body. It made sense that she might be confused about what she'd seen.

Michael checked his watch. He wanted to reach Foley this morning if possible. Taking a last look at the cabin, he thought of Kate's terror at being brought here. Her determination to stay alive. And her incredible luck at finding her way to safety.

"Foley here." The sheriff's voice was clipped.

"This is Michael Stone." He leaned a shoulder against the brick wall by the pay phone. He was standing outside Harry's General Store on the main street of Whitehall. The only street of Whitehall, as far as Michael had been able to determine. And it was one block long in its entirety.

"You back in California?" Foley asked.

"Still here in Idaho. The doctor says Kate should be able to travel in a day or two. I thought I'd wait and head back with her."

A pause. "Might be better if she stuck around for a while."

Michael felt a sliver of apprehension lodge in his chest. "What do you mean?"

"Might be better is all. She's involved in a violent crime." He paused again. "As a witness at the very least."

The unspoken words were the ones that registered. "You don't seriously see her as a suspect, do you?"

"Put yourself in my position. What would you think?"

Foley's tone was reasonable but his message grated nonetheless.'' For God's sake,'' Michael snapped,'' she's the victim of a kidnapping. Or do you doubt that, too?''

''I don't leap to conclusions before all the evidence is in,'' Foley said, not unkindly. ''I'm sure that usually you don't either.''

Michael bit back his irritation. ''Any word on Sheryl Ann Martin?''

''Nope. We've put the license and her description out over the wire. Also a warning that she's probably armed. That ratchets it up a level, so we ought to get a better response.'' A phone rang in the background. ''I've got a call on the other line. Keep in touch.''

Michael hung up, rolled his neck and shoulders to release the tension. As soon as Kate was well enough to travel, they were out of there. Let Foley try to detain her. He could posture all he wanted, but when push came to shove, he didn't have one solid piece of evidence against Kate.

The door to the store opened, bringing with it a rush of warm air. Michael waited for the customer to exit, then went inside himself. It was a small store, but the shelves were tightly packed. Everything from apples to fishing worms, ant poison to tar paper.

He bought a can of ginger ale and a pack of cherry Lifesavers from the man behind the counter.

''I bet you're one of the law-enforcement guys,'' the man said. He reached into his own pocket for the extra penny needed to make change. ''Town's been crawling with them last coupla days. Not that I'm complaining, mind you. It's good for business. Most excitement we've had in years.''

''Pretty quiet around here generally?''

"Winter's so quiet we'd all be better off hibernating. Rest of the year we get people who come up for the hunting and fishing. Occasionally there'll be folks passing through, usually on account of they've taken a wrong turn."

"So a turquoise car with California plates would stand out?"

"Like a sore thumb. I told the other fellow coupla days ago I hadn't seen it. By now the gal's gotta be long gone anyway."

Michael nodded. There he was again, back to the sticky point: All Foley actually had was a corpse and Kate. The rest was high drama but totally without substantiation.

16

Pain comes in many colors. Mine was gray. Not the sleek silver-gray of pounded steel or the soft, dove-gray of summer dawn, but a flat, unyielding shade of darkness. In the four days since my return home I'd tried hard to go on with life as usual, to slip back into my routine the way I would after a short trip away.

I did the laundry and the vacuuming, gave Max a flea bath, read Anna her bedtime story. With all my heart I yearned for normal, and at the same time felt that nothing would ever feel normal again.

I went through the motions, but that's all they were. Foley's suspicions and my own fears shadowed me.

When Michael and I had stepped off the plane onto California soil, I'd naively thought the whole mess was behind me. I was safe, and I was home. But the experience had left an indelible mark on my psyche. It felt like a stranger was inside my skin.

The experience had, in fact, touched all of us. Anna's burst of exuberance when I first walked through the door had been supplanted with whiny, clinging demands for attention. Libby's anxiety surfaced as cool indifference, and Michael . . . well, I wasn't sure what he was feeling.

Maybe, like me, he wasn't so sure himself. The difference was, I wanted to talk about it, and he didn't.

It was my friend Sharon Covington who listened to my ramblings and commiserated without trying to sweep the experience under the rug. When she appeared at my door Thursday morning armed with chocolate brownies and a box of PTA flyers that needed folding, I was delighted.

"We don't have to do the flyers," she said, brushing dark, windswept curls from her eyes. "They're more a prop than anything."

"I'd like to help." And more than that, I was eager to embrace the comfort of routine. "Just let me wipe up the remnants of Anna's breakfast. Do you want some coffee?"

Sharon followed me into the kitchen and dumped the box of flyers on the counter. "You making your famous cappuccino?"

"Sure." Country-mouse cappuccino was a more apt description. A good substitute for those of us without exotic gadgets and steamers. But the end product was almost as good as the stuff Sharon made with her four-hundred-dollar Italian import.

While I put the kettle on the stove and warmed a saucepan of milk, Sharon unwrapped the brownies. Max padded into the kitchen to join us. He has an appreciation for the crinkle of plastic wrap, and the knowledge that food usually follows.

"Health food," I said, reaching for a brownie.

"Don't laugh. I read the other day where chocolate has the same good-for-the-heart stuff as red wine."

"Not everyone considers red wine a health food."

"Besides," Sharon said, ignoring the jab, "these are

low-fat." She twisted to face me, elbows on the table. "But I guess healthy eating isn't a top priority at the moment."

"Right."

She hesitated. "Any news?"

"About Sheryl Ann, you mean?" That seemed to be the main thread of every conversation.

"About her, you—that shit Foley."

"Nothing I'm aware of. But then, I'm not the first person they'd rush to tell, either."

Sharon sighed in disgust. "He can't honestly believe you're lying about the whole thing."

I poured the warmed milk into the food processor and flipped the switch. The whir of the motor made conversation momentarily impossible.

"I'm not sure that lying is the right word," I said when the noise had stopped. "But Foley definitely views my story with skepticism."

So much so that I'd been afraid he wouldn't allow me to leave the state. It was Michael who finally convinced him that he didn't have enough evidence to hold me.

I reached for the mugs. "The truth is, I can understand where Foley's coming from. Sheryl Ann is nowhere to be found, and neither is Tully's body."

"But there *was* a body. You know that."

With a renewed appreciation for domestic ritual, I poured coffee into the mugs, then added the warm, frothy milk and a touch of powdered cocoa. "I *think* I know that."

"Don't let them play with your mind, Kate. You're one of the most sensible people I know. If you say there was a body, there was a body."

"Then where is it?"

"That's a different issue." Sharon broke off a piece of brownie and fed it to Max.

"He'll never leave if you feed him," I told her. "Besides it's not good for him."

"He's not going to leave anyway, not unless you shove him outside. And a little bit won't hurt him. You've told me so yourself."

Max is seventy pounds of boundless energy, limitless appetite, and steely canine determination. Unfortunately, obedience is not one of his strong suits.

"More to the point," I said, pushing Max away from the table, "I don't know for sure that it was Tully's body."

"Why would Sheryl Ann tell you it was, if it wasn't?"

I shook my head. Michael and I had tried out every scenario we could come up with. None of them made sense.

"Maybe he wasn't dead," Sharon said. "Only stunned."

"I thought of that. But comatose people aren't totally inert, and they don't smell."

She grinned. "See, you *do* know there was a body."

I conceded the point with a wave of my hand.

"At least the news stories have died down," Sharon said. "You're no longer a front-page headline."

"Thank God. I've had enough being in the spotlight to last a lifetime. Unfortunately, interest hasn't died down completely."

Although phone calls from the media were less frequent than they had been, the calls continued to come. And while the stream of gawkers driving slowly past the house had lessened, it hadn't stopped. People still parked by the curb and waited, hoping for a glimpse of notoriety in the flesh. I couldn't decide if the attraction was *Abducted Mom* or *Prime Suspect.*

"I'm still more newsworthy than I want to be," I said.

Sharon nodded. "When I pulled up, I thought that panel truck might have been a reporter. I was ready to do battle."

"What truck?"

"The one parked across the street. I'm glad it had nothing to do with you."

"I saw a van there the other day. My reaction was the same as yours." I reached for the box of flyers. "We may as well get started on these."

Sharon took part of the stack. "This mess will all settle and fade in time. Just remember that. I know it's hard right now, but they won't get far trying to make you out to be a killer."

"How about a lunatic?"

She smiled. "That either."

We sipped our coffee in silence for a moment. "Where would you go," I asked, "if you wanted to hide out?"

Sharon hesitated, then put a hand on my arm and looked me in the eye. "Running away won't make it better, Kate."

"Not me. I'm thinking of Sheryl Ann."

Sharon's face registered surprise. "Aren't Foley and his band of merry men looking for her?"

"Presumably. But they haven't found her." I wasn't even sure how hard they were looking.

"And you'd like to be the one who does?"

I folded a flyer and ran my thumb along the crease, taking a moment to consider my answer. "Foley isn't convinced she was even there. Until this gets straightened out, the police are going to regard me with suspicion.

Or worse. Every time the doorbell rings, I half suspect it's Foley, come to arrest me.''

"I realize it's hard having something like that hanging over your head, but—''

"It's more than that. I worry about her, too. I feel responsible.''

"For what?'' Sharon's voice took on a shrill edge.

"Sheryl Ann saved my life. There's no doubt in my mind that if she hadn't helped me escape, I'd be dead.''

Sharon hugged her arms across her chest. The look on her face was hard to read.

"Bobby was going to kill me,'' I said. The words came easily, disguising the sheer terror that haunted me. "Sheryl Ann took a risk. For me. And now she's in trouble.''

"She may have helped you escape, Kate. But don't forget she also helped kidnap you. I'm having trouble working up much sympathy for the woman.''

"That's what Michael says. But neither of you know her. I do.'' I knew that she wouldn't have killed Bobby except in self-defense. And Bobby wouldn't have turned on her if she hadn't let me escape.

I could see Sharon measuring her words. "If I may be blunt, Kate, you don't know her worth beans. Sure, you spent some time with her—under very peculiar circumstances, I might add—but that's not the same as knowing a person.''

"I realize that. I can't really explain how I feel because I don't understand it either. But it's there, like a shadow over my shoulder. She's in my dreams. I catch strains of her voice when I least expect it. I try to put her out of my mind, but it doesn't work. For my own peace of mind, I need to find her, to know that she's okay.''

"And if she isn't?"

That was one of the visions that kept me awake at night. I pushed it away. "At least I'll know."

"Maybe you just need a little more time."

"No, that's exactly what I don't need. The longer this hangs over my head, the worse it is. I'm afraid that if I don't do something, I'll be living with regret the rest of my life."

Sharon was quiet, looking at me intently; then she reached out and touched my hand. "Okay, I guess I still don't understand. But it's *you* I care about, and if you feel it's important, that's enough for me."

"Only I'm not sure where to begin."

Sharon sat back, drumming her fingers against the tabletop. "If I were going to hide from the law . . . I don't know where I'd go. Maybe you could start by looking into Sheryl Ann's background and habits."

"I already called her office. They're being very tight-lipped." Michael had given me the name of the insurance agency where Sheryl Ann answered phones and did filing. The police had apparently gotten little more information than I had.

"What about her family?" Sharon asked.

"Her parents are dead."

"Brothers or sisters?"

I shook my head. "She's an only child, raised in foster homes."

Sharon rolled her eyes with dramatic flair. "Sheryl Ann sure picked the right woman to kidnap, didn't she? You've got a real soft spot for lost souls and strays."

"Sheryl Ann didn't pick me," I said testily. "I was the one who stopped and insisted on getting involved."

"Geez, it was just an offhand remark."

"Sorry. I shouldn't have snapped at you." I offered an apologetic smile. "I'm going over to her house this afternoon with Frank Bowen."

Frank was in charge of the case locally. It wasn't clear to me how he and Foley had divvied up responsibility, but I was much happier dealing with Frank than Foley.

"You're going to the house?" Sharon's eyes widened. "That's kosher?"

"I'm not sure. Frank's not much of a stickler for rules, but I must admit I was surprised when he agreed." I couldn't tell if he was hoping to gather dirt on me as a suspect, or if he was simply trying to one-up Foley by locating Sheryl Ann himself.

"What does Michael say about it?" Sharon asked.

I have her a sideways glance. "Michael doesn't know."

She raised an eyebrow.

"I asked him first, and he said no."

"Oh my." She was wise enough to keep her tone neutral.

"He's been . . . distracted lately," I explained. "I know he was scared and worried when I was missing. I think now he's reacting to his own fears. He tries to pretend the whole thing never happened."

"He doesn't want you involved, in other words."

"That, too." I broke off a piece of brownie and popped it into my mouth. Rich wonderful chocolate that didn't taste the least bit low-fat. "Besides, there's some kind of tension between him and Frank."

"He's bound to find out, isn't he?"

"We'll cross that bridge when we get to it."

Frank was waiting for me when I pulled up in front of the one-story clapboard bungalow that Sheryl Ann and

Tully had been renting. It was in the old section of town, where the homes had been built originally as summer cottages. A tiny house on a narrow lot with an overgrown apple tree in front. The white picket fence was missing a number of boards and badly in need of paint.

Frank inserted the key into the lock and pushed open the door, then led the way inside.

"I've gone through everything myself," he said, combing his mustache with his fingers, "but you're welcome to look for yourself."

"What should I be looking for?"

"Anything that jogs your memory. Maybe she said something about a place she'd visited or a town she used to live in. Most people on the run don't pick a spot out of the blue."

"Do you have any leads at all?"

"None that have proved productive."

The house consisted of a main room with a kitchen at one end and two tiny bedrooms. The sofa and single armchair were draped with blue cotton fabric, a sort of home-fashioned slipcover. The coffee table, painted a glossy lime green, was stacked with old issues of *True Confessions*, a couple of tabloids, and an assortment of music magazines. A sound system and television lined one wall, and a vase of tulips, long past their prime, perched on a nearby shelf along with a collection of Tully's bowling trophies.

From the looks of things, neither of them was much of a housekeeper, but they'd made an effort to make the place look homey and cheerful.

Frank sat on the edge of the sofa and watched as I made my way gingerly around the room. I wondered again if he really thought I might come up with something useful, or if he was merely sizing me up as Sheryl Ann's coconspirator.

Or maybe he was simply trying to be nice. Despite the fact that he and Michael tended to get their backs up around each other, Frank had never been anything but gracious to me.

"What do you think of Foley?" I asked after a moment.

Frank shrugged. "Seemed decent enough on the phone."

"I get the feeling he doesn't think I'm telling the truth about what happened."

There was no rush on Frank's part to reassure me.

I hesitated. "You believe me, don't you?"

"It's not really my call."

"Sheryl Ann was there," I insisted. "I didn't make it all up. You at least believe that, don't you?"

"I don't see why you'd say she was, if she wasn't."

It was as much as I was going to get. I went back to my search. I peered inside drawers and cupboards, read the shopping list next to the television. Although I wanted desperately to locate Sheryl Ann, I did not like being in her home. It reminded me of the time I'd caught sight of my high school history teacher hanging her underwear on the backyard clothesline to dry. I'd felt as though I were peeking into a part of her life that didn't concern me.

"Did the two of you talk much?" Frank asked suddenly.

"What?" My mind had been elsewhere.

"You and Sheryl Ann. Did she tell you much about herself?"

"A little."

"I guess she must have talked about her husband, too."

I nodded. "She sounded almost protective of him, even though she was carrying on with Bobby."

Frank ran his fingers through his mustache again, and said nothing. With his slight build, fair complexion, and receding hairline, Frank looked nothing like Michael. I sometimes wondered if the physical difference was what first set them at odds.

His eyes followed me as I moved into the cramped kitchen. There were stains on the Formica and dirty dishes stacked in a plastic tub next to the sink. A thin line of ants worked its way down the wall above the counter and into the tub.

"What about her husband?" Frank called out. "Do you think they were telling the truth about Tully's death being an accident?"

"I don't think they planned on killing him, if that's what you mean." I pried a magnetized picture frame from the refrigerator door. Sheryl Ann and a shaggy-haired man with dark eyes and a thin, unsmiling mouth.

I retraced my steps to the living room and showed Frank the picture. "Is this him?"

"That's him." He paused a moment then asked, "You never saw the body then?"

"I never got a look at his face."

"So you don't know for sure that it was Tully."

"Why would Bobby and Sheryl Ann lie about that?"

Another shrug. Frank tapped his foot against the floor. "And you got the impression the fight between Bobby and Tully was over Sheryl Ann?"

"I don't know whether it was *over* her exactly. It was triggered by Tully's coming home unexpectedly and finding Bobby here."

"That's all?"

His question struck me as odd. "Seems to me that's enough."

Frank laughed. "Yeah, I guess so."

When I went into the bedroom, he followed and leaned against the door. "Did Sheryl Ann say why Tully had come home unexpectedly?"

I shook my head. "Only that he'd been on a trip."

The bed was unmade, and I wondered if that's where Bobby and Sheryl Ann had been when Tully barged in on them. It was an unpleasant thought all the way around, and I fought to block it from my mind.

"Before the two men got into a fight, was there any conversation?"

His questions had nothing to do with finding Sheryl Ann, and they were beginning to annoy me. "I wasn't there," I said a bit testily. "I only know what she told me, and it wasn't a whole lot."

"And you don't know where she is now?"

I shot him an angry look. "If I did, do you think I'd be here looking for some clue about where she might be? You sound like Foley."

Frank held up a hand in apology. "Sorry." He watched my search for another couple of minutes in silence. "You find anything yet?"

"I'm afraid not. But I've really only scratched the surface. She must have papers somewhere, photo albums, that sort of thing."

"I've had men go through the place with a fine-tooth comb already." He checked his watch. "Ten more minutes. Then we've got to split."

"That's barely enough time to get started."

"If nothing hits you straight off, it's not going to." His

mood had shifted. No longer chatty, he was now impatient to be off.

While Frank leafed through *DrumBeat* in the main room, I poked around closets and bureau drawers. A limited amount of clothing, both male and female, most of it casual and funky. Sheryl Ann's jewelry was largely of the street-fair variety—fun and inexpensive. The one exception was an heirloom necklace of what looked to me like real emeralds. Sliding it carefully back into its tissue wrapping, I marveled again at what a strange mix Sheryl Ann was.

By the time I'd finished looking through the bedroom, I'd found a postcard of Hearst Castle sent nearly a year ago by someone named Jane, some Spanish language tapes, and a paperback of *Murder Mile High* by Lora Roberts. I couldn't recall Sheryl Ann's mentioning any of the locales, but it was the best I could do.

"San Simeon, Mexico, or Denver," I told Frank, explaining the connections. "But I wouldn't put my money on any of them."

He stood and stretched. "Well, it was a long shot anyway."

"I'm sorry I couldn't find anything specific. Maybe if I had more time—"

"Not a problem." He locked the door and pocketed the key. His pace slowed as we reached the sidewalk. "Michael seem okay to you?" he asked in a tone that was intended to appear offhand.

I hesitated. "He seems fine. Why?"

Frank shrugged. "Nothing. Just idle conversation."

But I had the sense that it wasn't.

17

I was still weighing Frank's parting remark when his cream-colored Lexus pulled away from the curb. He waved at me over his shoulder and tooted the horn.

As I headed to my own car, a small brown-and-white terrier bounded down the steps next door and scurried around the hedge into the Martins' yard.

"Scampy, come here." Scampy's owner, an elderly gentleman in bedroom slippers, pushed his walker onto the porch and called again. "Come on, Scamp. Be a good boy and come home."

Scampy showed no signs of having heard the summons. This is a canine behavior that Max has perfected. He can hear the refrigerator open from the other end of the house and the postman when he's two houses away, but call his name when he's got better things to do and you might as well be talking to a turnip.

"Scampy." The elderly gentleman raised his voice. "Come on now."

Scampy lifted his leg on a camellia bush, then headed down the Martins' driveway. I crouched down and called to the dog. "Hey, Scampy. Come here, boy."

He looked up at the sound of an unfamiliar voice.

When I called again, Scampy darted toward me, tail wagging. I grabbed his collar and walked him next door.

"Thank you," the man said. "I don't think I could have managed on my own."

"Terriers are headstrong. I have one of my own."

"It's my son's dog. He's headstrong, too. Probably why they're such a good match." The man chuckled at his own cleverness.

A woman appeared at the doorway. "Henry, are you talking to yourself again?"

"The damn dog got out. This lady was kind enough to ambush him for me." He turned to address me. "Are you a friend of the Martins? I saw you coming from the house."

I shook my head, glad that he hadn't connected my face with the news photos. "I've met Sheryl Ann. The man I was with is a detective with the Walnut Hills Police Force."

By now the woman had joined us with the dog's leash. She was about her husband's age, but more agile. With the easy movement of experience, she snapped the leash onto Scampy's collar.

"Policemen, reporters, lookey-loos." She gestured with her free hand. "This neighborhood has never seen such excitement. Not in the thirty-five years we've lived here—I can tell you that."

"Thirty-six years, Betty."

"No, Henry, it's thirty-five. Won't be thirty-six years until June."

"Do you know the Martins well?" I asked, not eager to listen to a detailed account of their move to the neighborhood.

"They seemed like nice enough people," the woman

answered. "Of course, they're much younger than we are so we didn't have a lot in common. It was Sheryl Ann I talked to mostly. Fence talk was what it was. 'Looks like more rain'—that sort of thing."

"Husband's a strange one, if you ask me," Henry said. "Didn't go off to a regular job like most folks."

"He was a musician," Betty explained, addressing her husband. "I've told you that's why he was around so much during the day."

"Kept to himself, too. Couldn't hardly get two sentences out of him."

Betty glanced next door. "We had no complaints about either of them."

"Imagine, him getting killed right next door, and we didn't suspect a thing. Until that story ran in the paper, we just thought they'd gone away for a few days."

"Where did you think they'd gone?" I asked.

"Oh, we wouldn't have any idea about that," Betty said. "And we don't know where Sheryl Ann is, either. Though if I had a dollar for everyone who's asked, I'd be rich."

Henry chuckled. "One of them was actually going to pay you. More than a dollar. That tall, skinny man—remember him?"

"Clay Potter. The name struck me as funny because a potter works with clay." Betty tightened her grip on the leash. "I wonder if his parents did it on purpose."

"He's a detective?" I asked. The name didn't ring a bell.

"Said he was her brother," Betty explained. "But I suspect he's a reporter. Probably for one of the tabloids given his manner. He was very insistent." Her voice trailed off as she studied me for a moment. "You know, you look familiar. Aren't you the other woman involved in this? The one who was kidnapped?''

Reluctantly, I nodded. Maybe it was time for a change of hairstyle, or even some flattering cosmetic surgery.

"Sorry I didn't recognize you sooner," Betty continued. "I hope we didn't upset you talking on the way we did."

"You didn't upset me," I assured her. "I'm trying to learn more about Sheryl Ann. This man, Clay Potter, said he was her brother?"

"Isn't that what he told us, Henry?"

"That's what I recall. Seemed like he knew her anyway. We've got his phone number somewhere if we didn't toss the danged thing out. Where'd you stick it, Betty?"

"Probably in one of the desk drawers." She turned to me. "You want me to call you if I find it?"

"Yes, please."

Sheryl Ann didn't have a brother. Or so she'd said. So who was Clay Potter?

Libby was having dinner with a friend, an invitation I'd persuaded her to accept. Since my return, she'd taken to hanging around the house in a misguided effort to show support. And Anna had filled up on so many cookies after school that she wasn't interested in eating. I read her a story and put her to bed early.

That left Michael and me free to have a quiet, romantic evening to ourselves. Unfortunately, neither of us was in the mood.

We were eating at the dining table, with candles (my idea) and a bottle of wine (Michael's suggestion). But instead of gazing with rapture into each other's eyes, we were walking a conversational tightrope.

"How was your day?" I asked, cutting into a piece of chicken.

"Same old stuff."

Normally, Michael's answer would have been rounded out with anecdotes and personal observations. Hearing about Michael's day was something I looked forward to, not only for the stories, which were generally intriguing, but also for the sharing itself. I liked being part of Michael's work life.

Of late, the pattern had changed. Certainly since we'd returned from Idaho. Probably before that, but I had trouble remembering. It was nothing I could put my finger on, really. He wasn't short-tempered or angry, but there was a definite shift in mood. I thought again of Frank's question—*Does Michael seem okay to you?*—and wondered if others had noticed a change in him, as well.

Michael swallowed a forkful of salad. "I told you about the surprise party for the captain, didn't I?"

"I've got it on the calendar."

"It'll probably give the old guy a heart attack, but it's his wife's show, so I guess she knows what she's doing."

"Maybe. Or maybe *she's* the one who likes surprises."

"And parties. I never pegged the captain for much of a social animal." Michael gave me one of his quirky grins, the kind that reaches to the eyes and lights up his whole face. "Promise me you'll never surprise me like that, no matter how old I get."

"As long as you'll promise me the same."

"Deal." His hand touched mine and lingered there. Then he grew suddenly serious. "I sometimes have trouble believing that you're really back home, safe and sound."

"Me too." Although I wasn't so sure about the sound

part. I sometimes wondered if I would ever again feel a spring in my step or a smile in my heart. "I wish I could count on it staying that way."

"Everything's going to be fine, Kate. Foley doesn't have enough to arrest you."

"It's not just—"

"He doesn't now, and he won't ever." Michael's tone was gruff. I couldn't tell if it was me he was trying to convince or himself.

"There's Sheryl Ann, too," I said.

Michael gestured with his hand, brushing my concerns aside. "Foley's got troopers looking for the car. And her photograph has gone out over the wire, identified as someone who's armed and dangerous."

"Armed and—"

"You don't have to worry. They'll find her."

But that was exactly what did worry me, or more accurately, unsettled me. And it was something Michael didn't understand at all.

"Has there been any news?" I asked after a moment.

Michael hesitated, ran a hand over his chin. I could see the internal debate played out in his expression.

My heart had picked up its pace. "Do they know where she is?"

"There's been some activity on their bank account. Two ATM withdrawals in the last two days. Both in Nevada."

She was alive then. I felt the weight on my shoulders ease ever so slightly.

"When did that come in? Frank never said a—" I caught myself, but it was too late.

"Frank?" A shadow crossed Michael's face. "When were you talking to him?"

"This afternoon."

"He called?"

I gave fleeting thought to an elaborate lie, but in the end I opted for the truth. "I visited the Martins' place with him."

Heavy silence fell between us.

"Leave it alone, Kate."

"Frank thought it was a good idea."

Michael pushed his chair back from the table. "He shouldn't have taken you there."

"He thought I might see something that would give us a hint where Sheryl Ann had gone."

Michael threw up his hands. "There's no *us* about this, Kate."

"When somebody saves your life you can't just walk away."

"Did it ever occur to you," Michael said coolly, "that you should worry about Sheryl Ann in a different way?"

"What do you mean?"

"She might be looking for you." His tone underscored his meaning.

"She wouldn't—"

"You're the only person who can put her at the scene. Kidnapping and murder aren't charges to be taken lightly."

"She saved me," I cried. "Don't you understand that?"

"It's over, Kate. Put your energy into other things. Spend time with Libby and Anna. Get back to your clients. Start painting again. But leave it alone."

"I've tried putting it behind me."

He touched my cheek. "Give it time. Eventually, the memory will fade."

Later than night, under the covers, we nested like two

spoons. Michael's arm was draped over my hips, and I could feel his breath on the nape of my neck. He fell asleep instantly while I stayed awake listening to the wind in the trees outside.

Maybe Michael was right, I told myself. Maybe if I didn't let myself dwell on what had happened, didn't let myself think about the risk Sheryl Ann had taken for me or the trouble she was now in, I would eventually be able to put it out of mind. All it took on my part was determination.

Maybe.

18

Checking his watch, Michael made a quick calculation. Forty minutes until Bobby Lake's funeral. Not optimal, but time enough.

A neighbor's son-in-law had had his new BMW stolen the day before. Auto theft wasn't Michael's detail, but the neighbor had requested his help and Michael had promised he'd follow up. His involvement wouldn't make one iota of difference to the outcome—with car theft, that was invariably more chance than detection—but it would make people feel better. Sometimes that's what the job came down to.

Looking a bit embarrassed, Adam O'Neil adjusted his tie and thanked Michael for coming out to see him. They were standing on the front steps, and O'Neil clutched a cell phone in one hand.

"My in-laws," he said, rolling his eyes. "They have to be involved in everything. I'm sure they wonder how I got through the first twenty-six years of my life without their help."

"I don't mind," Michael said, "though I doubt I'll be able to add much. You've filed a police report?"

"Yesterday morning, as soon as I discovered the car was gone."

"Parked on the street?"

O'Neil nodded. "The garage was converted to a den before we bought the place."

Michael took the necessary information again, said he'd check to see if any abandoned vehicles had slipped through the system unnoticed.

"What are the chances of having the car returned?"

"Hard to say. If it was taken by some kids looking for a joyride, then it might show up soon and pretty much intact. On the other hand, it might have been in a chop shop fifteen minutes after leaving here, and you'll never see it again."

O'Neil looked pained. "That's the first new car I ever bought. Doesn't even have five thousand miles on it."

Michael offered a murmur of sympathy. Not that he'd ever be able to afford an expensive new car himself.

Why he was going to Lake's funeral wasn't entirely clear to Michael. True, he'd been the one to speak with Mrs. Harrington when she first reported her son missing, and the department encouraged follow-up contact in the name of good public relations. But it was more than that.

Officially, Michael wasn't working the case. In fact, he'd been told stay clear of it. But the stakes were too high. He'd be damned if he was going to let that asshole Foley try to pin anything on Kate.

Michael walked past the guest registry in the outer lobby of the church and took a seat in the last row, closest to the door. The room was about half-filled. There were a number of people in their twenties, but the bulk of the mourners were the age of Bobby Lake's parents.

And no sign of Kate. That was a relief. He'd been afraid that she might show up, though they'd agreed it was better she stay away. He didn't understand why she'd want to attend the funeral in the first place, but it was hard to understand Kate's thinking sometimes.

Michael's gaze settled on the casket near the front of the church. It rested on a raised platform surrounded by flowers. Next to it was an enlarged photograph of Bobby Lake and an altar of memorabilia. Ordinary items like a basketball, a Walkman, and a pair of dark glasses. It was an odd juxtaposition: this personal side of Bobby with the image in Michael's head. He felt a moment's regret at coming. Better that Bobby should remain the cruel and heartless thug he'd pictured.

He shifted in the hard pew. Funerals always made him uncomfortable, but this one felt particularly awkward. Michael hadn't known the deceased, or the family. And what he did know of Lake filled him with rage. Mourning was out of the question.

A hushed silence fell over the room as Heidi Harrington walked in on the arm of a thickly built man Michael took to be her husband. Head lowered, eyes focused on the carpet at her feet, she appeared years older than she had two weeks earlier. They were followed by a young woman who looked to be about Bobby's age. She was on the pudgy side, her brown hair held by a barrette at the nape of her neck

"Who's the girl?" Michael whispered to the woman seated next to him.

She scowled, but gave him an answer. "Marcia Harrington, Rudy's daughter by his first marriage."

The preacher talked of young Lake's energy and youth, his concern for family and friends. It was a generic sort

of eulogy. Clearly, Bobby hadn't been inside the church
in years.

When the service was over Michael stepped outside,
carefully observing those who stayed at the fringes. Sheryl
Ann wasn't likely to show up, but you never knew.

A wave of mourners passed in front of him, and he
caught sight of Kim Romano, Bobby's girlfriend. Ex-girl-
friend, he corrected himself.

Michael followed the crowd into the reception hall,
then moved around the room listening to snippets of
conversation. Finally, he stopped near Kim and the
woman he now knew to be Bobby's stepsister. Ducking
behind the foliage of a large potted plant, he was able
to listen without being easily seen. Neither woman so
much as looked his direction in any event.

"I don't even know why I'm here," Kim was saying.
She blew her nose, tossed the wadded tissue into her
purse, and pulled out another.

"You were still in love with him. That's why."

"Fat lot of good it did me. Two years of being there
whenever he needed me, and then boom, suddenly he's
not interested anymore. Only to find out he's dumped
me for some woman who is married. Married and older
than him!"

"In time, you'd have gotten back together again."

Kim gave her companion a look of disgust. "He was
never going to come back to me. He probably never
cared about me in the first place."

Marcia played with the button of her sweater. "It's
really ironic that *she's* the one who wound up getting him
killed."

"Yeah. I'd say it served him right except that I miss
him so much." Kim looked as if she might start crying

again, but she managed to fight back the tears. "They haven't found her, have they?"

"Not yet."

Three women ambled past just then, intent on comparing bed-and-breakfast accommodations in the Napa Valley, and Michael missed Kim's next comment. He inched closer and strained to hear.

"Sounds lame to me," Marcia was saying. "Besides, if Bobby was all hot for Sheryl Ann, why would she kill him?"

Kim nodded. "What are the police saying?"

"Not much. Heidi thinks they're a bunch of morons. My dad keeps explaining that they're doing what they can, but you know how Heidi was about Bobby—she thought he was Mr. Perfect."

"She certainly did. I like her, though. She's always been nice to me." Kim paused. "Nicer than your dad."

Marcia snorted. "Don't take it personally. My dad thinks everyone is a jerk."

"So true." Kim laughed. "Remember the time he brought live lobster for dinner and Bobby set the things to crawling around the floor? I thought your dad was going to blow a gasket."

Bobby as a prankster? It never ceased to amaze Michael, this filling in of the pieces. Kate had told him little about Bobby Lake except that he was selfish and callous, but, she thought, a reluctant villain. Heidi Harrington, of course, had presented a different picture. Now a third perspective had been added. It was like one of Kate's sketches. At first there were only sweeping lines and shaded forms. Gradually, the details were added that brought it into focus and made it vivid.

Not that any of it changed Michael's underlying animosity toward the man. Lake had abducted Kate and been on the verge of killing her. That was not something Michael could forget.

Kim and Marcia moved toward the tables of food. Michael continued his tour of the room. When the line of mourners offering condolences had dwindled, Michael approached the Harringtons. They were talking with a thin, dark-haired man he'd seen seated next to them during the service.

"Detective." Heidi greeted him with a nod. She looked ragged and emotionally spent. "This is my husband, Rudy, and a family friend, Carlo Rossi."

"Thank you for coming," Rudy said, extending a stubby hand. "We appreciate it." He was only a few inches taller than his wife, built like a barrel. His suit fit as though it had been hand-tailored.

"A mother should never have to bury her child," Heidi said tearfully.

Michael nodded. "I'm sorry things turned out the way they did." Despite his own feelings about Lake, he sympathized with her grief.

"It's a real tragedy," Rossi said. His voice held the hint of a boyhood in Brooklyn.

"The press is making Robert out to be someone he wasn't. All their talk about abducting that woman, hiding a body—that's . . . that's not Robert."

Her husband placed an arm around her shoulder. "Honey, you know he had problems."

"But he wasn't bad, not like they're saying."

"He was a good son, honey. No one says any different."

"A fine young man," Rossi added. He slouched in his suit, shoulders drooped.

Heidi Harrington's eyes filled with a fresh round of

tears. "Excuse me," she said, turning to leave. "I think I need some time alone."

"Nice meeting you," Rossi said with a nod to Michael. He followed after Heidi, leaving behind him a trail of heavy aftershave.

Rudy Harrington ran a hand along the back of his neck. "She has a blind spot where Robert is concerned."

"Comes with the territory of being a mother, I think."

"The boy was always a poor judge of character. And impulsive. Getting mixed up with Sheryl Ann is just the sort of lamebrain stunt you'd expect from him."

Michael was surprised by the vehemence in the man's voice. Even without knowing Robert, Michael could see how having Harrington as a stepfather might not be easy.

Michael rocked back on his heels. "Maybe now isn't the right time, but I'd like to talk with you about Tully and Sheryl Ann."

Harrington hesitated. "Isn't another detective handling the case?"

"If you don't mind, though, I've got a few questions of my own."

"Well, okay." He cleared his throat. "I guess now is as good a time as any."

They moved toward a corner, away from the crowd. "I gather Robert and Sheryl Ann met through the bar you own?"

Harrington took offense. "It's a nightspot, not a bar. The Hideaway—you must have heard of it."

Until recently, Michael hadn't. But that didn't mean much. He wasn't a nightlife kind of guy.

"It's an upscale establishment, lots of young professionals," Harrington continued. "We get headliner groups sometimes, big names. But we have a regular band, too. Tully was the drummer. Sheryl Ann would come along and hang out while they played.''

"What kind of work did Robert do for you?"

"Busboy, general cleanup. I thought I was doing him a favor, giving him a real job. Let him see that work is more than smiling at the camera. What kind of man wants to be a model, anyway?"

Michael stuck a hand in his pocket. "There's good money in it, I hear."

"For some. Robert wasn't in that class." Harrington made no attempt to hide his contempt.

"How long ago did he and Sheryl Ann meet?"

"He started at the club just before Thanksgiving, so that's been about two months. Right from the start, he was like a puppy dog, all eyes for her. And she clearly got a kick out of it. I suspected it was more than flirtation, but I didn't know for sure. Whenever Robert took his break, Sheryl Ann would disappear, too. Once or twice I saw them together sitting in his car."

"Do you think Tully realized what was going on?"

"Couldn't say. He was a hard one to read."

"Do you have any idea where Sheryl Ann might be right now?"

"Not the foggiest." Harrington was jiggling the change in his pocket, whether out of habit or distaste for the conversation, Michael couldn't tell.

"What's Sheryl Ann like?"

Harrington grew quiet, dropped into thought for a moment. "Sex and trouble," he said. "It was written all over her in neon."

19

Michael pulled into the Chevron station and waited impatiently for the vehicle in front to finish refueling. It was a Suburban that seemed to be drinking up an infinite amount of gasoline. He tapped the steering wheel, conscious of the tension across his shoulders and in his jaw.

He didn't like being out of the investigative loop. It was frustrating beyond belief. Frank wasn't saying much, and Foley hadn't returned either of his most recent calls. If only Michael had a clearer picture of what was going on, and how seriously they were looking at Kate as a potential suspect. But he was having a damned hard time finding out.

He wasn't happy about Kate's self-imposed feelings of responsibility either. She didn't owe Sheryl Ann a thing. The sooner Kate realized that, the better.

Kate was a pushover for anyone in need. An endearing quality in small doses, but it had a way of ushering in trouble. That's what had gotten Kate into this mess to begin with.

Finally, Michael inched the car forward and began

filling up. He crinked his neck while he waited, stretching against the stiffness.

It wasn't really Kate's fault, he conceded. She hadn't done anything wrong. But neither could he ignore the prickle of irritation he felt. Irritation he didn't fully understand. Maybe it wasn't so much what she'd done initially in stopping as her unwillingness to let go of it.

Michael hooked the gas nozzle back on the pump and waited for the machine to spit out his receipt. Kate had thought that Sheryl Ann needed help that rainy night when this all started. Now she was convinced that Sheryl Ann needed help again.

She seemed determined to ignore the more likely possibility that Sheryl Ann was, herself, a threat. Sure, the woman might be able to verify Kate's account of events, but Michael couldn't imagine why she would. It was far more probable that she'd deny everything. In fact, he wouldn't be surprised if she wanted Kate silenced for good.

Sheryl Ann was a loose cannon. Who knew where she was, what she was up to?

Sex and trouble was how Bobby's father had characterized Sheryl Ann. Michael sensed that trouble was rolling their way, gathering speed as it came.

"Good morning, Janet," Michael said as he passed the dispatch station.

"It's afternoon."

"Right, it is."

"Frank was looking for you."

"Did he say why?"

She smiled. "You think he'd tell *me*? Anyway, he

stepped out about ten minutes ago. Said he wouldn't be gone long.''

Michael nodded. He could use a word with Frank himself. What he really wanted was to punch Frank in the nose for letting Kate search the Martins' place. Half the time he wanted to punch Frank in the nose just for being Frank.

Risking the captain's wrath, Michael retrieved the file on Lake's homicide. The case was Idaho's, and more specifically, Foley's, but they were happy enough to have Walnut Hills fill in background whenever possible. In this instance, however, Walnut Hills meant anyone but Michael.

He sat down at his desk, pulled out the turkey and Swiss on rye he'd made that morning, and opened a can of Coke to go with it. Then he got down to work.

Unfortunately, there was very little to work with. Foley had faxed the crime-scene report, the coroner's report, and summaries of the statements from both Kate and the driver who'd taken her to the hospital. Locally, detectives in Walnut Hills had interviewed people who knew the parties involved, including Kate. A copy of Michael's own notes regarding Bobby's disappearance was included as well.

Michael tried putting himself in Foley's shoes. The one solid starting point was Bobby Lake's body. Kate's account of being kidnapped, even the phone call she'd made from a pay phone, could conceivably be viewed with suspicion. Not by anyone who knew Kate, of course, but on a purely objective basis. And the gas station attendant who'd seen a car with California plates had been able to identify Lake from his photo, but claimed he'd never seen Sheryl Ann.

So, objectively, there was no saying that Sheryl Ann and Tully were even involved. Sheryl Ann had called work and explained that she and Tully were taking a short vacation. Foley couldn't completely discredit that. And if Sheryl Ann *was* involved, it stood to reason, again from a purely objective vantage point, that Kate might have killed her, as well as Bobby. Or maybe that Kate and Sheryl Ann had plotted the whole thing together.

Michael pushed the sandwich aside, barely touched, and stretched his shoulders and neck in an attempt to ease the strain. None of the scenarios made any sense. But it didn't make a lot of sense, either, that Sheryl Ann would voluntarily let Kate escape.

Michael heard footsteps and looked up as Gina entered the room.

"Hi." She tugged at a springy blond curl, pulling it forward toward her mouth, then letting it bounce back to her temple. "You look tired."

"Guess I am."

"That's understandable."

He willed her to leave. Instead, she took a step closer.

"We need to talk," she said.

"About?"

A slight pause. "Us."

The word slammed against his chest. He stiffened. "There is nothing to discuss."

Gina smiled, a knowing smile that lingered on her lips. "But there is," she said softly, then stepped behind him and began slowly kneading his shoulders. "I feel it. You feel it too, but you're afraid to admit it."

The only thing he felt was increasingly uncomfortable. "Gina, I'm flattered by the attention, but you're missing the boat here."

"I remember the way you looked at me, the way you held me."

Michael tried pulling away from her touch, but Gina had him pinned between herself and the desk.

"You know what I'm talking about. You know you do."

He knew the night she was talking about. And he was willing to admit, if only to himself, that there'd been a charge in the air. He'd sensed it, even relished it in a moment of private fantasy. But the holding and the cuddling was something different. An attempt to comfort, nothing more. Of that, he was sure.

They'd gone out after work, four of them. It was something Michael rarely did, but Kate and Anna were away, and Gina wanted to question some detectives for the criminology paper she was writing. Dan and Frank, in a hurry to be off, gave her bare-bones answers. Michael, feeling benevolent, stayed to give a more detailed response. Somewhere over the second or third glass of wine, their conversation had turned personal. Gina told him of an abusive father, a cold and distant mother, an unplanned pregnancy at sixteen. Her tears had moved him to slip a sympathetic arm around her shoulder. The same way he would with Anna or Libby.

It was Gina who had pressed herself against him and buried her face against his shirt, catching him by surprise. Sure, he'd been tempted, just for a second. But more than anything, she made him uneasy. Maybe he hadn't been quick enough, or forceful enough, in resisting. Maybe he'd inadvertently sent the wrong signals. Or maybe she was seeing only what she wanted to see.

"I'm sorry," he said now. "Sorry if you got the wrong impression, but . . ."

She slipped a hand over his shoulder to his chest. "Listen to your heart, Michael."

He didn't have to listen. He could feel it pounding in his chest. Not with passion but with anxiety.

"I know this isn't the time, what with all that's going on for you already, but I can't ignore my feelings. Some things are simply meant to be."

Michael pushed her hands from his chest and forcibly extracted himself from his chair. "Listen to me. Please. I am not interested in having a relationship. You're a lovely young woman, but there is nothing between us. There never was, and there never will be."

There was that smile again, faint and lingering. Gina reached for his hand and clasped it to her breast. Her soft flesh was warm beneath her sweater.

"That's where you're wrong," she said. "There *is* something between us whether you realize it yet or not."

At the same moment, Frank pushed open the door, knocking as he entered. Michael hadn't even realized that Gina had closed it behind her when she came in.

"Uh, sorry." Frank looked less shocked than amused. "I didn't know I was disturbing something."

"You're not," Michael growled, pulling his arm free from Gina's grasp.

Gina glanced briefly at Frank; then her eyes slid back to Michael. "We'll continue our conversation some other time."

When she'd left, Frank cleared his throat. "Guess I should have knocked louder."

"It's not what you're thinking," Michael said.

"Of course not." There was a glimmer of sarcasm in Frank's tone.

"She's got some kind of foolish notion."

"Ah."

"A crush."

"That's a tough one." Frank managed to sound both supportive and doubting at the same time.

Michael returned to his seat with a disgusted sigh. "You wanted to see me?"

"Yeah." Frank slid into the chair opposite Michael's and took his time getting comfortable.

"Something new about Sheryl Ann?" Michael asked.

Frank shook his head. "Not a word."

"You've checked with friends?"

"No one has a clue where she might have gone."

"Assuming she's even alive."

"Right."

An awkward moment of silence passed between them. Finally, Frank again cleared throat. "I thought you might want to know that Foley is flying in."

Michael experienced a spike of alarm. "When?"

"Tomorrow morning."

"There's been a new development?"

Frank looked uncomfortable. "The clothing Kate was wearing when she arrived at the hospital . . . there was blood on it."

"Blood?"

"Bobby Lake's blood."

The words hung in the air a moment. "A lot?" Michael asked finally. He wasn't sure why.

"I don't know any more than I've told you. I probably shouldn't even have said anything, but . . ."

"I appreciate it."

"If I can help in any way . . ." He let the sentence trail off without finishing it.

"Thanks." Michael waited for Frank to leave. He

wanted to process this latest information in private. He needed space for the jumble of thoughts that filled his brain.

"I guess this thing has kind of driven a wedge between you and Kate."

Michael looked up. "Why do you say that?"

"Just an impression."

"Did she tell you it had?"

Frank appeared to bite back his first response. Instead, he shrugged and picked at an invisible speck on his lower lip.

He's enjoying this, Michael thought. That bastard is getting a kick out of watching me squirm.

Michael leaned back in his chair. "What were you doing anyway, taking her to the Martins' place?"

"She asked."

"That doesn't mean—"

"You said no. I said yes. It was my call."

Goddamn Frank and his smarmy, condescending attitude. "I don't want Kate involved in this."

"I got news for you. She *is* involved." Without another word, he pushed back his chair and departed.

20

I looked at Michael in dismay. "What do you mean they found Bobby's blood on my clothing?"

"I'm just telling you what Frank told me."

"They couldn't have."

Michael had been unusually quiet and tense during dinner. Now I understood why. What I didn't know was whether the tension reflected worry or doubt.

"Frank talked to Foley himself," he said.

I turned off the kitchen faucet and leaned back against the sink. "There must be some mistake."

"I don't think that's very likely."

"It's the only explanation that makes sense."

Michael didn't say anything.

My head was spinning. Would Foley have planted evidence in order to make me look guilty?

"They couldn't have," I said again.

Michael touched my shoulder. "You were being held prisoner, Kate. You were under tremendous stress. Maybe you don't remember clearly everything that happened."

"But I do. That part, at least." My memory of the hours spent wandering the frozen countryside was fuzzy—nothing beyond being numb with cold and near hysteria. But the events leading up to it were so vivid I couldn't forget them even when I tried.

"You'd be surprised what tricks the mind can play."

I shook my head. "My mind isn't playing tricks."

"But that's the whole point. You wouldn't remember."

"I remember very clearly."

Michael ran his tongue over his lower lip. When he spoke, his voice was gentle. "It would have been justified, Kate. You—"

The impact of what he was saying broadsided me. I twisted free from his touch. "Are you implying that I might have killed Bobby and blocked it from my mind?"

"I'm trying to suggest an explanation."

"That's not what happened."

Michael's tone grew even softer. "You have to look at the evidence, honey. Bobby Lake's blood was on your clothing."

"That's not possible."

"Foley ran it through the lab."

"You're taking their word against mine?" Rage coursed through my veins.

"It's not simply their *word*, Kate."

I was having trouble breathing. The ground beneath my feet felt unsteady, the way it does during an earthquake. "How can you? How can you even *think* such a thing?"

A deep furrow formed over Michael's eyes. He rubbed his cheek. "You're taking this the wrong way."

"The wrong way! You stand there accusing me of murder and I'm *taking it the wrong way*?"

"I'm not accusing you."

"No?"

"And it wouldn't be murder. That's the whole point."

Hurt and anger fed on one another, swirling through me like a small windstorm.

"I'm trying to help," Michael said. He reached for my hand, but I pulled it free.

"Help?" I screamed at him. "You're a goddamn Judas. One stupid lab report, and you're ready to throw me to the sharks."

"I'm not throwing you anywhere. I'm on your side, Kate. I want what's best for you."

"You've got a funny way of showing it."

Michael let his arms drop to his sides. "Like it or not, police operate by looking at evidence. And they're particularly fond of physical evidence."

"And you, being a hotshot policeman, choose to believe the so-called evidence rather than me."

"It's not a question of belief, Kate."

"No?"

"Evidence is evidence."

I turned back to the sink and began scouring the rice pot with such force I sent water sloshing over the countertop.

"You're being unreasonable," he said.

"Unreasonable? Maybe you weren't listening to what you just said."

Michael threw the dishtowel down on the counter in a gesture of disgust. "Forget unreasonable. You're downright pigheaded."

"Me?"

"You've flown off the handle without thinking about what I'm saying. I'm through talking to you until you've regained some sense."

A heavy silence fell between us. I kept my eyes focused

on the globs of gluey, soapy rice. With shaking hands, I scrubbed the same spot again and again.

Then I heard the floorboards creak, and turned to find Anna standing at the doorway.

"Why are you guys yelling?" she asked unevenly.

"We're not," I snapped.

Anna tugged at the hem of her shirt. "You're having a fight, aren't you?"

Michael sat in one of the kitchen chairs and beckoned to her. Anna hesitated briefly, then sidled up next to him so that she was half-sitting on his lap.

"I could hear you in the other room," she said, clearly upset.

"You're right," Michael told her. "We were yelling a bit. But we aren't fighting."

Oh, yes we are, I thought.

"Sometimes when people discuss things that are very important to them," he continued, "they get excited and speak louder than they mean to. Louder and more emotionally."

Anna looked to me for confirmation. I relented.

"Sometimes, too," I explained, "you can be angry without actually fighting."

We'd crossed that line, but the last thing Anna needed was something more to worry about. Ever since I'd returned home she seemed intent on searching out reasons to fret. She slept with the light on, didn't want to go to school, checked on me constantly. My usually ebullient daughter was becoming a nervous wreck.

"Why are you mad?" she asked me, pointedly ignoring Michael's explanation.

"I'm not sure." To some degree, that was the truth. I

was mad at Michael, but I had the feeling it went beyond that.

She wound a finger through a lock of hair. "I don't like it when you get angry."

"We're not mad at you, sweetie. Remember that."

Anna looked at Michael, and he nodded. "Absolutely," he said.

I dried my hands on the blue striped dishtowel Michael had tossed down in a fit of anger moments earlier. I touched Anna's shoulder. "You ready for some ice cream?"

Ice cream was an all-purpose cure where Anna was concerned. She slid off Michael's lap and came to give me a hug. "Give me lots. I'll go tell Libby."

Michael leaned forward, crossing his arms on the table. "You can't simply ignore evidence, Kate."

Silently, I scooped Rocky Road into glass bowls with the same determination I'd used on the gluey rice pot, never once letting my gaze shift his direction.

"You have to face facts."

He waited a moment, then without another word, picked up Max's leash and took him for a walk.

Later, after ice cream and Anna's bedtime story, I took a long, hot bath. When I got out, Michael was already in bed. I crawled in quietly, careful to stay on my own side. After a moment I felt his hand slide gently along the ridge of my back.

"It's not that I doubt you, Kate. Honestly." When I didn't respond, he continued. "It's that I love you. And I'm scared."

Foley insisted on questioning me alone, without Michael in the room.

"We should call an attorney," Michael said.

"That makes it look like I've got something to hide."

"Screw how it looks."

"Foley wants to talk to me now. I'd like to get it over with."

"Don't be a fool, Kate." His tone showed his displeasure.

I rubbed my arms, fending off both the winter chill and my nervousness. We'd smoothed over our differences last night in bed, but I had a feeling the peace was a fragile one. There were simply too many raw emotions on both sides.

Michael tried a gentler approach. "He can't force you to meet with him."

"It'll be okay." I wanted desperately to believe that myself.

"Kate, it's silly—"

I snapped. "Back off. This is my decision."

It was an ongoing point of contention between us. Michael relented. "Remember, don't answer any question you don't want to. And don't volunteer explanations."

Curious advice coming from a police officer who'd been known to rant about uncooperative witnesses and sneaky legal maneuvering. It made me realize how worried he was.

The interview took place in the conference room rather than the tiny, windowless chamber where suspects were usually questioned. The floor was carpeted, the chairs padded. Small details, but I was grateful.

My hands were shaking so I folded them together in my lap, away from Foley's watchful eyes. He'd trimmed his dark hair since I'd last seen him, but the burlap skin and hooded eyes brought back memories of an ordeal I longed to put behind me.

He offered me a soda, which I declined, then pulled a chair up at right angles to mine. He rested an arm on the laminate conference table.

"You're looking healthier than the last time I saw you," Foley said congenially. "How are you feeling?"

"Better than I was then."

"Good." He flipped on the tape recorder. "You don't mind, do you?"

I shook my head. Actually, I did mind, but I was afraid he'd see my discomfort with the tape as a sign that I wasn't going to be truthful.

Foley's lips parted in a smile. "Why don't you tell me again how you happened to escape from the cabin?"

"I'm not sure *escape* is the right word. Sheryl Ann let me go."

"Just like that?"

"It was down to the wire. Bobby was ready to kill me." My voice trembled from nervousness, rendering my response less forceful than I'd hoped.

Foley popped a stick of clove gum into his mouth. "How'd you convince her?"

"I didn't."

He raised a brow.

"I mean, I don't think it was anything I did. I'd told her all along that she was only getting herself into deeper trouble by sticking with Bobby. She'd never listened to me before, but I think she realized time was running out."

"Or maybe you sweetened the idea somehow. A promise? A reward?" His tone was casual, but there was a snide edge to it that made me uncomfortable.

"What do you mean?"

He ignored my question. "Or perhaps the two of you decided it would be easiest simply to get rid of Bobby."

"Rid?"

His face was expressionless. "To kill him."

I shifted my position and the chair squeaked. "We never even talked about such a thing. I tried to get Sheryl Ann to leave Bobby and come with me. That's it."

"To run away with you?"

I nodded.

Foley looked surprised. "This woman who'd been instrumental in holding you prisoner? Why would you want her to go with you?" It was apparently a rhetorical question because he moved on without waiting for me to elaborate. "Where was Bobby during all this?"

"Outside. Trying to bury Tully."

Foley leaned back, twisting a paper clip with his fingers. "You expect me to believe that suddenly, for no apparent reason, Sheryl Ann just up and tells you to leave? The same woman who had been guarding you at gunpoint for several days said you were free to go?" The skepticism in his voice was thick as molasses.

"It's what happened."

He was silent a moment. "I should think Sheryl Ann would have been worried about Bobby and what he might do when he found out she'd let you escape."

"That's why I wanted her to come with me."

Foley spat his gum into the foil wrapper and twisted it into a ball before tossing it into the waste can. He leveled his gaze. "So you didn't have any contact with Bobby that morning?"

"None. In fact, I didn't have much contact with him at all once we got to the cabin."

Foley drummed the table with his fingertips. His gaze was sharklike. "You want to explain to me how Bobby Lake's blood ended up on your clothing?"

"I don't see how it could have." My voice sounded tight. "There's got to be a mistake."

"Or how your prints ended up on a rather nasty-looking knife we found near the body."

"Knife?"

Heat prickled the back of my neck, and I felt a wash of nausea. I flashed on that terrible morning in the cabin. The knife, and my struggle to cut free from the ropes binding me. Until now, we'd been so focused on what happened after, that it never occurred to me to mention the details of my captivity.

I swallowed hard, trying to keep my tone neutral. "I thought Bobby was shot."

"He died from gunshot wounds. But he was cut up a bit first."

My breathing was shallow. I was finding it hard to get enough air. "I did touch the knife," I said, weighing my words. "At least, I touched *a* knife. In the kitchen. I was trying to cut the ropes around my hands and feet."

"When was this?"

"Earlier that morning, when Sheryl Ann and Bobby were both outside."

Foley squinted, as if trying to visualize the scene. "So while no one was looking you walked into the kitchen and—"

"No, I didn't walk. My feet were tied. I hobbled. And jumped."

"And they didn't see or hear you?"

"Right." It was more a choking sound than a word.

He frowned. "Why didn't you leave right then, once you'd freed yourself?"

I was beginning to understand why suspects being questioned by the police sometimes twisted the facts. Straight truth left too much room for creative interpretation.

"I wasn't able to free myself," I explained, looking him in the eye. "I tried cutting the rope on my hands, but I dropped the knife and wasn't able to pick it up again."

"Why is that?"

Idiot. "I was tied up—that's why."

Foley ran a hand over the table's surface. "You know, if you'd just cooperate with me, I'm sure we could work something out."

"I *am* cooperating. I'm telling you the truth."

"And the problem I'm having is that I'm unable to verify anything you say."

I crossed my arms. "You really think I'm making this up?"

"Whatever I *think*, I'm reserving judgment until all the evidence is in." He rocked forward, closing the space between us. "Thing is, what I have so far has your name on it. You're the only link I have to a dead body."

With great effort I held my posture and didn't shrink back. "Are you going to arrest me?"

Foley's eyes were serious, his voice surprisingly benign. "Not yet," he said.

I was living a nightmare. Caught in a world turned inside out. Unfortunately, I wasn't going to escape it by waking up.

To make matters worse, it was a nightmare partially of my own making. I played over in my mind that pivotal moment when I made the U-turn and went to help a defenseless young woman in a malfunctioning car. That one moment, a split-second decision that wasn't even a conscious choice. It had indelibly colored my life, bathing it in peril.

"Well?" Michael said, pulling me aside as soon as I stepped out of the conference room.

"He's not ready to arrest me just yet." I tried for a veneer of humor.

"This isn't funny, Kate."

"I know." The full force of Foley's questioning was still sinking in. "There's more than we thought." I told him about the knife.

"Jesus, why didn't you mention that before?"

"I guess I didn't think it was important."

"Not important?" His face was a mosaic of emotions.

"I wasn't intentionally keeping quiet about it. It's just that my mind was on Sheryl Ann and what happened after."

He closed his eyes a moment and took a deep breath. "It's going to be okay, Kate. It's going to work out."

It was, I thought, more a mantra than a statement of certainty.

21

Sharon was getting out of her car when I arrived at school that afternoon. It was an early-dismissal day, and the parking lot was jammed.

"You look terrible," she told me by way of greeting, then immediately clarified the remark. "I mean, you don't look happy. Like an emissary from the living dead or something."

"That's about how I feel."

"What happened?"

I told her briefly about my conversation with Foley.

"He can't be serious?"

But he was. A fresh wave of apprehension washed over me. "I don't want to talk about it, okay? It's more than I can deal with right now."

Sharon squeezed my arm. "I know it's hard, but try not to worry. They can't get you for something you didn't do."

"Says who?"

A gust of wind blew up, scattering leaves and debris into the air. We turned our backs to protect our faces.

"Do you know that guy?" Sharon asked, nodding at a

wiry man in a blue windbreaker standing off to one side. "I don't recognize him."

I didn't either. It was usually the mothers and au pairs who showed up to accompany the children home. The sprinkling of househusbands were as conspicuous as a giraffe in a kindergarten class.

"Must be some dad with a day off," I said.

"Or with a working wife who's finally said 'your turn' and made it stick." Sharon brushed the windswept hair from her eyes.

The bell rang, and in a nanosecond the breezeway was filled with shrieks, giggles, and a steady stream of frenzied energy.

"I've got to get Kyle to the dentist," Sharon said. "But call me if you want to talk. There's got to be something we can do to get Foley off your back."

Usually when Sharon says *we*, she's roping me into some activity I haven't actually agreed to, like helping her sell raffle tickets at the annual fund-raiser. But this time I took comfort in the word. It was awfully nice to feel I had someone solidly in my camp.

Anna had a bowl of Apple Jacks and went off to watch television. In the hopes of settling the nervousness in my stomach, I pulled out my charcoals and sketch pad, and settled into a comfortable chair by the back window. On good days I can lose myself completely in my work. Even when I can't, I still find solace in the simple activity of drawing or painting.

Today the magic eluded me. I found myself staring at the blank paper, waiting for inspiration while my stomach continued to churn. Foley didn't trust me. Frank didn't

really care. Even Michael had his doubts, though he pro-
fessed otherwise. I felt terribly alone.

Finally, I began sketching the image that dominated
my mind—Sheryl Ann. She knew the truth. She could
set it right.

Page after page, I tried for a likeness. Several of my
efforts were close, but none captured the spirit so readily
apparent in the flesh. The funny thing was, I could see
Sheryl Ann clearly in my mind. Feel her presence, as
though she were hovering just beyond the range of consciousness.

Ours was a kinship as complex as it was troublesome.

I owed Sheryl Ann my life. I worried about her. In
helping me, she'd placed herself at risk. But I was angry,
too. It was *me* Foley had his eye on.

If only she had run away with me.

At the time she hadn't seemed worried about Bobby's
reaction. *I can handle him,* Sheryl Ann had told me. Certainly she hadn't meant that she was going to kill him,
had she?

Exasperated, I closed the sketchbook and pushed back
my chair. Sheryl Ann's coworkers had not been particularly helpful when I'd reached them by phone. Maybe
they'd be less reluctant in person.

Before I had a chance to work through my plans, the
phone rang. The voice at the other end was female and
familiar, but the name meant nothing to me. It wasn't
until she said, "The Martins' neighbors," that I remembered Betty. Her husband had been attempting to call
the dog when I left Sheryl Ann's place the other day.

"I couldn't find the number," Betty told me. "I looked
everywhere. Henry thinks we must have tossed it out."

My mind worked to fill in the missing pieces. "Are you

talking about that reporter's phone number? The one who claimed to be her brother?"

"Right. I promised I'd let you know if I found it, and I didn't want you to be thinking I forgot."

"I appreciate that." Promises made on the fly rarely meant much, so I'd never counted on this one panning out.

"But I told you his name, didn't I?" Betty continued. "Clay Potter."

"Right. I'll check the phone book."

"Oh, he wasn't from around here. It was one of those Central Valley cities. Modesto or Fresno. Or maybe Bakersfield."

"I wonder why a reporter from that far away would be looking into the story of Sheryl Ann's disappearance."

"We thought it was strange, too. And to be offering money. None of the others did that."

I thanked Betty, hung up the phone, then pulled out the phone book and a map of California. The possibilities were daunting—and clearly more extensive than I had time for right then. Clay Potter would have to wait.

I found Anna in the den, watching a cartoon program. "How about going out for a frozen yogurt?" I asked. As soon I was out from under Foley's cloud of suspicion I was going to enter a twelve-step program for parental bribery.

Anna, however, was captivated by the plight of a baby dragon crying real tears, and wasn't interested in taking a drive with me. Even for a large-sized frozen yogurt with sprinkles and Gummi Bears. I debated forcing her, but dragging a reluctant six-year-old anywhere is only inviting trouble.

I could wait until Libby got home.

"No problem," Libby replied when I asked if she'd watch Anna while I went out. "I've got a test to study for, so I'm not going anywhere."

She opened the fridge and pulled out a Coke and the jar of salsa. From the cupboard she grabbed a bag of tortilla chips. Libby eats like a junk-food commercial and never gains an ounce. Some days it's the aspect of youth I envy most.

"I won't be long," I told her.

"Stay away as long as you like. I'm desperate for money. Brian's birthday is next month, and I want buy him something nice."

"Maybe you can talk Michael into letting you mow the lawn this weekend."

Libby groaned. "I'm not that desperate."

I had an idea. "I've got a job for you. I need the phone number for a man named Clay Potter. I'm not sure about the area code or the city, so it might take a while to find him. Only I can't pay you very much because all those information calls are going to add up."

Libby gave me the look that bespoke teenage superiority. "You're such a dinosaur, Kate."

"What do you mean?"

"I'll do it on the Web. For free. Leave me a list of the possible cities." She scooped salsa onto a chip and handed it to me. "It'll be done by the time you get back."

Sheryl Ann worked in the accounts-payable department of a medical-insurance company in Danville. The drive, which would have been only fifteen minutes at midday, took twice that with heavy afternoon traffic. At least the parking was easy.

The receptionist was young, no more than nineteen

or twenty if I had to guess, and as peppy as a high school cheerleader, which might have been her training.

She greeted me with a high-wattage smile and a cheery, "Good afternoon."

"I'm looking for accounts payable."

"Who do you wish to see?"

I hesitated. "I'm here about Sheryl Ann Martin."

The smile remained fixed between apple cheeks, but I saw a dimming in her eyes. "Ms. Martin is not here this afternoon. Perhaps someone else can help you."

I nodded. "Actually, I'd like to talk with people who know her. Maybe you could give me the names of some of her coworkers."

"Sorry, but we've been instructed not to talk to the press. It's company policy."

"I'm not a reporter."

The smile turned quizzical. "Then why do you want to talk to Sheryl Ann's coworkers?"

"I'm hoping one of them might know something that could help me find her."

"Are you with the police?"

"Not exactly."

The young woman's eyes grew wide. "You're a PI, right? I've read a couple of books by that alphabet lady—you know, the one who writes mysteries. Being a private investigator sounds so exciting."

I debated the wisdom of a lie. The PI persona might work with Ms. Smiles, but I had the feeling it wouldn't get me much further.

I shook my head. "I'm a friend of Sheryl Ann's."

"Oh." The woman's expression deflated. "Maybe you should talk to Ms. Richardson then."

"She knows Sheryl Ann?"

"Probably, a little. She's in charge of the department."

The receptionist picked up the phone and buzzed Ms. Richardson, who wasn't, it appeared, any too happy about being bothered. But peppiness has its uses, and I was finally granted an audience.

Maybe because the dean of girls at my high school had also been named Miss Richardson, I was expecting a gray-haired woman with a heavy bosom and jowls. My image was definitely off the mark.

Ms. Alexandra Richardson of CalHealth was tall and slender with honey blond hair stylishly cut to chin length. She wore a power suit of blue wool gabardine, diamond earrings, and an expression of authority. This was a woman who was going to break through the glass ceiling if she had to use a pickax.

"I'm afraid it's our policy not to give out information about employees," she told me when we were seated in her office.

Her chair was leather, with a high back and padded arms. I sat on the other side of her wide teak desk in a chair that was much smaller and less imposing.

"I'm not asking for anything confidential," I explained. "I merely want to talk with coworkers, anyone she was close to."

"We've already given a statement to the police. Sheryl Ann called and left a message that there'd been a death in the family. She said she would be gone for a few days. We don't know any more than that."

There'd been a death in the family all right. But Sheryl Ann gave the expression new meaning. "I was hoping someone here might have an idea where she is now."

"If that were so," Ms. Richardson said with a flash of

white teeth, "you can be sure the police would have been notified."

I tried again. "I don't mean know with certainty, but, like, in conversation. Sheryl Ann might have mentioned something in passing."

Ms. Richardson blinked at me. Her eyes were such a bright blue, I decided she had to be wearing tinted contacts. "If you're a friend of hers, you know as much as anyone, probably more."

"But I don't know where she is." I was growing exasperated, as much with myself as the woman across from me. It had been a waste of my time to come here. "I take it you don't know Sheryl Ann yourself," I said.

"I am the division vice president," Ms. Richardson said in a tone that could only be described as haughty. "I know her the way I know all of those under my supervision. But no, I did not exchange rumors and recipes with her at the watercooler, if that's what you're asking."

I had the feeling Ms. Richardson did not have much use for either rumors or recipes in any form. "How long has Sheryl Ann worked here?" I asked.

"I thought you were a friend of hers."

"A recent friend."

Mr. Richardson frowned. "Roughly three years. She does her job well and doesn't cause any trouble. Until this recent incident, she's been a model employee."

"So you're surprised by what happened."

Ms. Richardson favored me with a tight smile. "After twelve years in this business, I am no longer surprised by anything." She rose from her desk, signaling an end to our conversation.

I pushed back my chair as well. "Thank you for taking the time to speak with me." I made it sound more heartfelt than it was. As I was leaving, I turned back. "Is there a rest room I can use?"

"Down the hallway on your left. You'll pass it on your way out."

The rest room was empty. I didn't know how long I could linger there without raising suspicion, but I figured ten minutes or so wouldn't be unreasonable.

After washing my hands, I took ample time combing my hair and freshening my lipstick. I straightened my blouse, then turned to reading the fine print on the paper-towel dispenser.

I'd about decided to leave—it was a nice enough rest room but not an exciting place to hang out—when two women came in, midconversation. They continued to chat while using facilities, verbally moving from Laura's baby shower to the selection of shoes at Macy's. I washed my hands again and applied more lipstick.

Emerging from the stall, the dark-haired woman smiled at me. She was about my age, with a wide mouth and freckled skin. "Four o'clock," she said. "Nearing the finish line."

I returned the smile. "I'm ready."

"Amen to that. Are you new? You don't look familiar."

I hesitated. "Actually, I'm trying to find someone who knows Sheryl Ann Martin. I'm worried about her."

"I think we're all a little worried about her."

"So impetuous," said her friend, a short, athletic-looking blonde. "Jumps first, thinks later. You'd think she'd learn."

"You both know her?"

"Sure, this is a friendly place—though you wouldn't know it by looking. Corporate blech."

I dropped my lipstick back into my purse. "Do you have any idea where she is?"

"None. We've talked about it plenty, too. Haven't we, Jane?" The dark-haired woman nodded to her friend. "It's not every day something like this happens."

Jane removed the barrettes from her blond hair and began brushing it back from her face. "Were you a friend of Tully's too," she asked me, "or just Sheryl Ann?"

"Just Sheryl Ann."

"I only met Tully once. He seemed like a nice guy. Quiet, but sincere. This whole thing is so crazy, even for Sheryl Ann."

I nodded agreement. "Do you know who her closest friends are?"

"No one at work, if that's what you're asking."

Jane twisted the hair away from her face and reclipped the barrettes. "She mentioned Darla a lot. Works as a manicurist at the mall. Her boyfriend is in Tully's band."

Just then the door opened and Ms. Richardson walked in. My companions gave her a perfunctory nod and beat a hasty retreat.

"You still here?" she asked me pointedly.

"Just leaving." I gave my hair a one last finger-fluffing, then made my own swift exit.

22

Michael pulled to a stop as the light at the intersection turned red. He reached into his pocket for the pack of cherry Lifesavers and popped one into his mouth. The coffee at the station, barely palatable as usual, had left an unpleasant aftertaste. So had this afternoon's conversation with Foley. As far as Michael could tell, nobody was looking to anyone but Kate as a possible suspect.

Foley had viewed her story with skepticism from the start. In his more rational moments, Michael couldn't entirely blame him. Taking events at face value, he found that Kate's explanation left a lot of holes. She'd been traumatized by the kidnapping, and he suspected she might not be remembering things as clearly as she thought she was.

Frank wasn't much help, either. Despite the fact that he knew Kate wasn't some flake with a loose grip on reality or a penchant for cockamamy adventures. He should have been busting his butt trying to get to the bottom of the Martin case.

The driver behind him tooted his horn. Michael saw that the light had turned green and pulled through the intersection. Tonight he'd try reasoning with Kate again.

He'd explain that while he wanted to believe her, did in fact believe her, the evidence pointed to a different chain of events. They couldn't simply ignore evidence. He'd lay it out for her, point by point, and then they'd figure out how to handle it. Together.

Meanwhile, he was going to do what Frank should have been doing all along.

Michael turned left on Magnolia and checked the street numbers. Four blocks farther north he pulled into the parking lot of the Hideaway.

Nightclub, lounge, tavern, cabaret—whatever fancy name you gave it, it was still a bar. A single building with fake Tudor trim and windows of machine-fabricated stained glass. The slightly tattered awning over the front door proclaimed MUSIC NIGHTLY, and a glass frame near the entrance listed the month's entertainment attractions.

Stepping inside, Michael was immediately seized with disquieting memories of Jake's and the part-time job that supported him in grad school. Long, tedious nights where the loneliness gnawed at his gut like a hungry animal. Thank God those days were behind him.

Michael pushed the memories aside and surveyed the room. A balding man sat at the bar with his laptop and a beer. Two women sitting at one of the nearby tables sipped white wine and flirted with a gaunt-faced, stoop-shouldered man in an apron who Michael recognized from Bobby's funeral. Carlo Rossi, family friend.

Seeing Michael approach, Rossi moved back behind the bar. His cologne mixed with the scent of beer and stale cigarette smoke.

"Harrington around?" Michael asked.

"Not until tonight." Rossi's gaze was flat, the sort that looked right through you.

Michael introduced himself. "We met at the funeral."

"Right." Rossi's lips parted slightly, and his eyes grew alert. As was often the case, the word *detective* had had a visible, and not entirely comforting, impact.

"Do you work here nights?" Michael asked.

"Except for Sunday and Monday."

"You must know Sheryl Ann and Tully Martin then."

"In passing." Rossi wiped the bar counter with a damp rag, making it clear that he wasn't going to stop everything to talk with Michael.

"What was your impression of them?"

A shrug. "Neither one of them was a rocket scientist."

"Did you know about Sheryl Ann and Bobby?"

A veil of wariness fell over Rossi's face. "You investigating Bobby's murder?"

Michael nodded.

Rossi hesitated. "There was a different cop here before."

"We've got a number of officers on it."

Another shrug. "I'd see Bobby and Sheryl Ann together, sure. I didn't feel it was any of my business."

"Except that you're a family friend."

"Rudy Harrington and I go way back," Rossi explained. He tossed the rag into the sink. "But Rudy only married Heidi five years ago. Bobby is her son, not his."

It was an explanation that apparently made sense to Rossi. To Michael, however, it was most telling for what it implied about Harrington's relationship with Bobby.

Rossi pulled on his earlobe and gave Michael a questioning look. "Has there been a new development in Bobby's murder?"

Michael shook his head. "I'm here looking for members of the band. Would you happen to have names and phone numbers?"

"You're in luck. Jack Clevenger is our main contact. He's here now with one of the other band members, setting up for tonight. You want to talk to him?"

Rossi led the way past the bar and through a folding door to a room at the other side. "Hey, Clevenger." He yelled in order to be heard over a high-pitched hum. "Someone to see you." Without another word to Michael, or even a glance in his direction, Rossi was gone.

On the raised stage at the far side of the room, two men were working on the sound system. The taller of the two stopped what he was doing and looked up. He was clean-shaven with dishwater blond hair pulled back into a ponytail.

"What can I do for you?"

Michael held out his badge. "I'm looking for information about Sheryl Ann Martin."

Clevenger turned back to his tinkering. "I don't know where she is or anything about what happened."

Michael looked at the other man. "You in the band, too?"

He nodded. "Dick Arnold, sax."

"When did you last see her?" Michael addressed the question to both men.

Arnold answered. "Couple of nights before this whole thing started. She usually hangs around when we play here," he explained. "But she's in the audience. It's not like we interact much."

"What about when you're not playing? Do you get together socially?"

"Some."

"You knew about her involvement with Bobby Lake?"

Clevenger tapped the mike, which emitted another shrill electronic squeal. "Don't believe everything you hear. Sheryl Ann is a flirt, but no way she'd run away with Bobby."

"Why's that?"

"She just wouldn't."

The angry undercurrent in his tone caught Michael by surprise. Maybe Sheryl Ann had something going with Clevenger, as well.

Michael turned to Arnold.

"Don't look at me," Arnold said. "I make no claim to understand anything at all about women."

"How long were Sheryl Ann and Tully married?" Michael asked.

"Long as we've been playing together."

"How long is that?"

"Almost five years." Clevenger pulled a screwdriver from his pocket and connected a lead. "The gigs were sporadic back then. Not enough to live on."

Arnold snorted. "Still isn't, for most of us." He turned to Michael to explain. "Except for our fearless leader here, the rest of us work on the side."

"Tully, too?"

"Yeah, till he got laid off."

"When was that?"

"About six months ago. Worked for a yard-maintenance service that went belly-up."

A wisp of a comment Kate had made floated through Michael's mind. He took a moment to pull it back. Travel. Tully had found Bobby and Sheryl Ann in bed together when he'd returned unexpectedly from a trip. That was what had precipitated the whole bizarre course of events.

"I understand that Tully had been out of town," Michael said.

Arnold laughed. "You talking about his trips to Reno?"

"I don't know, maybe. I got the feeling it was related to business."

"He was interested in cutting a record," Clevenger said, without looking up from his work. "He made a couple of trips to LA to meet with some people there."

"Wasn't going to happen," Arnold added. "You know that, Clev. Tully was big on dreams but short on follow-through."

The comment triggered something else that had been bothering Michael. "Wasn't the band worried when Tully didn't show up to play?"

"Pissed is more like it," Arnold said. "Especially when Clev called the place where Sheryl Ann works and found out her and Tully had taken off without telling us. That's what we thought at the time anyway."

Clevenger muttered under his breath.

"What?"

"Nothin'."

"Do you have any idea where Sheryl Ann might be hiding?"

Clevenger was silent.

Arnold shook his head. "Last any of us heard was when she called from Idaho."

Michael wasn't sure he'd heard right. "You talked to her?"

"Not me, my girlfriend, Darla. Sheryl Ann called and asked if Darla would run over to the house occasionally and pick up the mail and newspapers."

Michael felt a surge of excitement. This was something positive. Not much, but something. A witness besides Kate who could place Sheryl Ann in the area of the murder. "When did she call?"

"I'm not sure of the date. A couple of days before we learned what had happened."

"And you're sure it was Idaho?"

"Yeah. A small town. Something Mills. Darla had to call back because Sheryl Ann didn't have enough change. So typical."

Even better, there would be a record of the call. Just maybe, this was a lead that would go somewhere.

23

Libby greeted me with a piece of computer-printed paper and an impish grin. "Look what five minutes on the Internet can do."

"Mommy," Anna said at the same time, "look at Max." She'd balanced a baseball cap on his head.

"Cute." I slipped off my jacket and turned my attention to Libby. "You found a listing for Clay Potter?"

"Three of them. Bakersfield, Carmel, and Glendale. There were a couple of others too, but they lived farther north."

"Amazing," I said, with genuine awe. Although my natural inclination was to fight technology, I was slowly coming to appreciate the wonders of cyberspace.

"Nothing to it," Libby said. She handed me the print-out, gave Anna a thumbs-up, and headed back down the hallway to her room.

"Look at him now," Anna commanded. She'd added a red bandanna, tied around his neck.

"Honey, I'm busy."

Since only Bakersfield could be considered a "Central Valley city," I tried that number first—and got an answering machine. The greeting was one of those maddeningly cryptic, machine-generated voices that simply asked you to leave a message, and told you nothing at all about the person you were calling. I left my name and number but no details.

For good measure I tried the other two numbers as well. The name Sheryl Ann Martin meant nothing to either of the gentlemen I reached, nor did the mention of Walnut Hills.

By the time I'd gotten off the phone, Anna was trying to squeeze Max's front legs through the arms of one of my sweaters.

"Anna, enough. Leave the poor guy alone."

"He likes it. Can we get cable TV?"

I wasn't sure if there was a connection there or not, but the answer was the same. "I've told you before, it's expensive."

"Some people down the street are getting it. I saw the truck there this afternoon. I saw it yesterday, too. Maybe they're having a special."

"Maybe, but the answer is still no."

As I began cutting vegetables for dinner, I tried to ignore the trepidation that had been churning inside me since talking to Foley. But I couldn't. The way he saw it, I was a killer. His efforts were going into assembling the case against me—and he would arrange the pieces however he could to fit the picture in his mind.

Even Michael, who knew and cared about me, had his doubts. He wouldn't admit them. Certainly not out loud, and maybe not even to himself, but I could read the hesitation in his eyes.

There was only one answer—find Sheryl Ann. Assuming she was still alive. What if she wasn't? Or what if she never turned up? What then?

I pushed the thought from my mind. That wasn't going to happen. I would find her. Somehow, I would find her.

Michael arrived home earlier than usual, and with none of his customary good cheer.

"Rough day?" I asked, carefully tearing the butter lettuce into bite-size pieces.

"You might say that."

He loosened his tie and kissed me on the forehead just as the phone rang. I dried my hands and reached for it.

"Kate Austen?" The voice was female, with a touch of Texas drawl.

"Yes."

"I'm Mrs. Potter." Emphasis on the *Mrs.* "You were trying to reach my husband?"

"Right."

A pause. "May I ask why?"

"He asked me to call," I replied, stretching the truth. He'd asked Sheryl Ann's neighbors to call, presumably he'd have asked me, too, if our paths had crossed. Of course, he'd asked them to call if they heard from her and I clearly hadn't.

Mrs. Potter wasn't easily dissuaded. "Concerning?" she asked.

"He was looking for information." I waited for her to speak, and when she didn't I continued. "Information about a young woman by the name of Sheryl Ann Martin."

There was a moment's pause. "He gave you *this* number?"

"I'm not sure what the number was. I lost it. But I remembered his name and town. Maybe I should have called the newspaper. I'm sorry to have bothered him at home but—"

"I'm afraid you've made a mistake." Her voice had inched up a notch in pitch, and the words were close and tight. "There's no one here who can help you."

"If you could give me his work—"

She hung up abruptly before I'd finished.

"What was that about?" Michael asked, pulling a handful of pretzels from the cupboard.

He wasn't going to like the answer, no matter how carefully I presented it. I gave a quick and cursory synopsis.

Silence stretched between us for a minute. When Michael finally spoke, his voice was agitated. "I thought you were going to forget about looking for Sheryl Ann."

"How can I forget about it? Foley is convinced I killed Bobby Lake, and she's the only one who can tell him I didn't."

"Kate, listen to what you're saying." Michael turned to look at me straight on, his expression incredulous. "Do you really think Sheryl Ann is going to support your story when it points to her own guilt?"

"But—"

"You honestly expect her to greet you with open arms?"

"Maybe not open—"

"She's hiding for a reason, Kate."

"She might not be hiding. She might be in trouble."

He gave a disgusted sigh. "She *is* in trouble. And it's because she kidnapped you and killed Bobby Lake."

"It was Bobby who kidnapped me, and she only killed him in self-defense."

"If you go after her, she's likely to kill you, too."

Michael's voice spiraled higher. His facial muscles were taut. "Do you think she wants *you*, the only witness, hanging around to point a finger at her?"

I went back to tearing lettuce leaves. He was giving it the wrong spin because he didn't know Sheryl Ann.

"She tried to help me," I explained, even though we'd been down this road before. "She didn't have to let me escape. She took a risk for my sake."

"She is *not* your friend, Kate. Nor is she the good and kind person you seem to think she is. If she was, she'd never have been involved with Tully's death or your kidnapping."

"Tully's death was an accident."

There was fire in Michael's eyes. "You don't know that for sure. You know only what she told you. And she *was* involved in trying to cover it up."

"That was Bobby's idea. Sheryl Ann stood by him because she thought it was the decent thing to do."

"Kate, listen to me." Michael took the lettuce from me and gripped my upper arms. "No matter how you slice it, she's involved in trying to cover up Tully's death and in your kidnapping."

"Only by default."

"She also killed Bobby. She's facing arrest and prison, maybe the death penalty. Sheryl Ann is *not* going to save you. She might even be out to harm you."

"Harm me how?"

Michael released his hold on my arms. "I don't want to scare you, but if she's killed once already—"

"Stop. You're wrong about her. I owe—"

"You don't owe her at all." Michael's mouth was set in a tight line. "Sheryl Ann worked on your sympathy with that story of being an orphan."

"It wasn't just that. She was kind to me."

"A twisted kindness."

Deep down Sheryl Ann was a decent person. I still believed that. But when push came to shove even decent people put themselves first.

"It's not just you, Kate. It's us. Anna and Libby, too. You aren't going to put Sheryl Ann before us, are you?"

"Of course not." I dropped into a nearby kitchen chair.

Michael pulled out the chair next to mine and sat. "Want to know what I learned today?"

I attempted a smile and a little levity. "Probably not, given your tone."

"Sheryl Ann isn't an orphan," he said, ignoring my attempt to lighten the mood, "and she wasn't raised in foster homes."

I was perplexed. "Her parents aren't dead?"

"Her mother is dead. She died in a suspicious fire when Sheryl Ann was fourteen."

I swiveled to look him in the eye. "What do you mean 'suspicious?' "

"There was talk of arson."

"Are you suggesting that Sheryl Ann murdered her mother?"

"I'm saying there was speculation to that effect. Nothing was ever proven. Her father is still alive."

Had she lied as a bid for sympathy? "Does her father know where she is?"

"He says he doesn't. Apparently, they aren't close."

"From what you've just said to me, that doesn't surprise me."

"She left home at fifteen," Michael said. "Her father

hasn't seen her since. Or talked to her, though he'd like to. He's dying of cancer."

Maybe Sheryl Ann considered herself an orphan in spirit. "Where does he live?" I asked.

"Bakersfield."

I rocked back. "Clay Potter?"

Michael gave me a puzzled look. "No, the name's Cy Lipcott. Why?"

"That man Potter, the one whose wife phoned a bit ago, he's from Bakersfield."

"You said he was a reporter? Maybe he's after the hometown angle. In any case, finding her isn't going to resolve anything. That's what I've been trying to tell you."

I stood and rubbed my hands over my upper arms to ward off the chill. "If finding Sheryl Ann isn't the answer, what is?"

Michael shook his head, indicating the lack of a simple answer. "I had a talk with Foley this afternoon."

"And?"

He took a breath. "I was going to wait until after dinner, but since we're on the subject . . ." He paused. "I don't know where he's going with this, Kate, but it's taking on a shape I don't like."

"I'm not any too happy with it myself."

"You need a lawyer," Michael said. He stood and reached into his shirt pocket. "I got a couple of names from the DA. Attorneys who specialize in criminal defense work. This guy Horvath is supposed to be one of the best. I can tell you from personal experience, he's dynamite on cross."

Criminal defense. The words echoed in the silence between us. I felt suddenly sick.

Police scrutiny is one thing, but hiring a criminal

defense attorney is a measure of a different magnitude altogether. The very thought brought a sour taste to my mouth.

I shook my head. "We can't afford—"

"We can't afford not to," he said emphatically. "Believe me, I know all too well how these things play. It's easy to inadvertently lock yourself into a version of events that will eventually hang you out to dry."

I could feel the rush of heat to my face. "Version of events? What about the truth? That's the only version I've ever told."

Michael rubbed his forehead irritably. "Like the knife you *forgot* about handling?"

"You don't believe me?" I felt a terrible burning in my chest.

"I do believe you." His voice was gentle, but his answer was a beat slow in coming, like he'd had to think first.

I stepped back. "You don't, do you?"

"I love you, Kate. Of course I believe you."

It was not, I thought, an unequivocal endorsement of faith. "That's not the same as really believing me."

Michael put his hands on my shoulders. "The real issue is whether Foley believes you. And ultimately, whether a jury does."

"All I was doing was trying to free myself, to cut the ropes binding my hands and feet. They can't arrest me based on that."

Michael looked at me, thin-lipped and grim. "It's not just the knife," he reminded me. "There's the jacket, too."

I raised my head. "What jacket?"

"The one with Bobby Lake's blood on it, remember?"

"It was a jacket?"

Michael nodded.

I laughed, suddenly giddy. "His blood was on the jacket?"

Michael gave me a funny look. "Mostly on the right sleeve. Some on the collar."

It was as if someone had opened the windows in a dark and stuffy room. All at once, I could breathe again. "It's not my jacket," I told him. "Sheryl Ann gave it to me as I was leaving."

"What do you mean, *gave it to you?*"

"She told me to take it. She was worried about the cold."

"It's her jacket?"

"I don't know whose it is. She was wearing it. She gave it to me. Bobby's blood must have already been on it."

Michael tapped his lips with his fingers. He looked at me, his gray eyes narrowed. "Do you see what this means? The jacket was a setup. She wanted it to look like you killed Bobby."

"No." I shook my head. "That's not what happened. Sheryl Ann was trying to be nice. She was concerned about me." But even as I said it, I felt the first stirrings of doubt.

24

It had to have been a setup, Michael told himself for probably the hundredth time in the last two days. Sheryl Ann wanted Kate to take the blame for Bobby's death, so she'd orchestrated the escape and offered Kate the jacket. Even Kate was beginning to see that.

Unfortunately, Foley remained skeptical. Even after Michael had told him about the phone call placing Sheryl Ann in Wyoming.

Michael couldn't entirely blame him. At moments, Michael himself had trouble buying into the theory. It wasn't that he didn't want to believe Kate's account, but he'd been trained to look at the evidence. And it was hard to refute bloodstains. *Evidence is evidence.* How many times had he heard that over the years in police work?

That brought him full circle. It had to have been a setup.

If only he could take the case himself and run with it. But the captain had made it clear—Michael's personal involvement prevented that. Prevented him from working on the case at all. Emotions colored one's thinking, the captain explained. They clouded reason.

Of course they did, Michael thought with disgust. But

reason only got you so far. And sometimes it gave you the wrong slant entirely. Foley's so-called reasoning had him so he couldn't tell up from down.

With an inward groan, Michael opened the file on his desk. His official cases had become an annoying distraction, demanding energy and time he would rather devote to clearing Kate. At least he'd finally managed to convince her to drop her own search for Sheryl Ann.

Again, he found his thoughts heading off in the direction of Bobby's murder, and forced them back to the assignment at hand—the Li Chen homicide. The investigation was going nowhere and the mayor was vocal in his criticism. But now a neighbor had come forward to report hearing a fight between Chen and his nephew a couple of days before his death. Lots of yelling, the neighbor said. She couldn't hear what they were saying, but the tone was angry, the voices loud. She knew it was the nephew because she saw him leave, kicking his uncle's door as he departed. Yes, she was sure it was the nephew. She recognized him because he often visited his uncle.

Unfortunately, the nephew had an alibi for the night of the murder, and five friends who would attest to being with him. That didn't mean he couldn't have killed his uncle, only that they'd have a hard time convincing a jury.

Frank, who'd handled the initial interviewing on the case, had noted that the alibi was solid. Michael closed the file and crossed the room to Frank's desk.

"Got a minute?"

Frank looked up. "Sure."

"It's about the Li Chen case. You talked to the nephew, Jason Liao, right?"

"Yeah."

"What did you think?"

Frank made a face, like what did it matter. "He was partying with some friends the night of the murder."

"What about the friends? Did you talk with them?"

"It all checked."

"You're sure?"

"Yes, I'm sure. Neighbors called the police complaining about a loud party. One of the uniformed officers spoke to Liao himself." Frank's tone was testy. "Are you suggesting I wasn't thorough?"

Michael shook his head. "Just trying to make sure we aren't missing the obvious. He's the one who inherits, you know."

"You're going to have to take a different direction. Liao didn't do it." Frank leaned back in his chair, causing it to squeak. He stroked his chin. "You're all wound up, Michael. It's not healthy. Not effective in terms of getting the job done, either."

Talk about the pot calling the kettle black. Even wound up he was more effective than Frank. "I'm handling my work just fine."

"Hey, that was friendly advice, not criticism. I know this stuff with Kate has got to be weighing on you."

Why did even a simple comment from Frank rub him the wrong way? He wasn't sure, but it did. "The jacket wasn't hers. Sheryl Ann gave it to her."

Frank nodded. "I heard that." His smile said he didn't necessarily believe it.

Alibi or not, Jason Liao looked better than anyone else as a suspect in his uncle's death. Michael checked Liao's work address—a wheel shop on the northern end of town. There was certainly no harm in paying a visit.

"I'll get him for you," the manager said. "For safety reasons we don't allow the public in the work area." He picked up the phone and paged Liao. "Someone here to see you."

Much better than *a detective here to see you.* Still, Liao took his own sweet time about coming to the front of the shop. He sauntered in and looked at the manager, who nodded toward Michael.

"You want to see me?" Liao asked. He was shorter than Michael, with small dark eyes and a partially shaved head. He sported a scraggly goatee and a diamond lip stud.

Michael introduced himself. The word *detective* had surprisingly little impact.

"This about my uncle?"

"A neighbor heard the two of you arguing a couple of days before your uncle was killed."

Liao shrugged. "We argued a lot. He had opinions about everything."

"What was this argument about?"

Liao shoved his hands into his pockets. "How should I know?"

"You were there."

Another shrug.

"What did you usually argue about?"

"All kinds of stuff."

"Money? Jobs? Girls? Drugs?"

"Look, I don't remember what we argued about, okay? Mostly it was just little stuff. But if you think I woulda killed him, you're full of crap."

"Did I say that's what I thought?"

"Don't know why else you'd be here."

Michael leaned an arm on the candy machine. It was

one of those that offered you a handful for a quarter. Chocolate-covered raisins. "That a real diamond in your lip?" he asked.

Liao gave him a funny look. "What if it is?"

"Nothing. Kind of a big expense, is all."

"I earn it. I can spend it where I want."

"Now that your uncle is dead, you'll come into some money from him."

Liao scoffed. "Twenty grand maybe."

"What's wrong with that?"

"It's a waste—that's what. My uncle, he saved his whole life for that. Scrimp here, scrimp there."

"And now it's yours."

"I don't need my uncle's money."

"Maybe not, but it's always nice to have a little extra."

"I can make it on my own."

"Working on tires and wheels?"

Liao's face tensed. "This is a country of opportunity, right? That's what my uncle always told me." He shifted his weight. "Look, I got an alibi for the night he was killed."

Michael nodded. "A party at your house. With friends. Third time in as many nights according to the cops who came out. You guys got something to celebrate?"

"Wasn't celebrating—just some guys having fun. Anything else? I got to get back to work."

Michael watched him swagger back through doorway into the work bay beyond. The kid gave off vibes. Anger, cockiness, but also a sense of vigilance. Could be that he was lying, or could be that he was simply a nineteen-year-old with an attitude. Hard to tell.

And the worst part was, Michael's heart wasn't in it. Not like it usually was. All he could think about was Kate.

25

My picture was in the paper again Thursday morning. Second page this time instead of headline news, but prominently positioned in the upper left corner.

Foley had held a press conference the previous afternoon. While he stopped short of calling me the prime suspect, anyone with half a brain could figure out that's what he meant. Apparently, my explanation of the jacket hadn't swayed him. To his credit, he did ask that anyone with information about Sheryl Ann contact him.

I wasn't banking on it.

Coursing through my veins was the fear that Foley would swoop down on my doorstep unannounced, arrange for any arrest and haul me off to Idaho. Every time the phone rang or there was a knock on the door, my breath would catch, and my stomach turn to scrambled eggs.

Michael was worried, too, though he tried to pretend otherwise. And if he still had doubts about my role in Bobby's death, he kept them to himself.

I spent Thursday and Friday close to home, away from public scrutiny. By the weekend, however, the uncertainty had begun to settle, like dust after a storm, so that it no longer filled my lungs with every breath. Determined to reclaim my life, I set up client appointments, took Anna shopping, and started on a collage I'd been thinking about for months.

And I stopped focusing on Sheryl Ann. I couldn't stop thinking about her entirely, though I tried, but I didn't let myself dwell on the doubts and conjecture. What's more, I gave up trying to make sense of it. Whether the jacket had been a setup or not—and most of the time I was inclined to think it hadn't been—there was nothing I could do about it now. I was determined to move on.

Early the next week, Sharon and I, with Max in tow, took an afternoon walk around the Walnut Hills Reservoir. The three-mile perimeter path is paved and mostly level though the parklands surrounding it are hilly. An oasis of pastoral quiet in the midst of an area burgeoning with new development.

Dark clouds were building, but the sky broke with occasional patches of sun, and the temperature was relatively mild. The scent of spring was in the air.

"On days like this, I love the world," Sharon exclaimed.

I nodded. "Even the dreck of day-to-day living seems less taxing."

"God knows, you've had your share of that lately."

A squirrel crossed the path just ahead of us, and Max yanked so hard at his leash I nearly lost my balance. "I think I'm beginning to move beyond it though."

"Foley is off your case? I thought he didn't buy your explanation of the jacket."

"He's certainly skeptical, but Michael thinks if he had anything conclusive, he'd have arrested me by now."

"What was with that piece in the paper the other day

then? He did everything but say, '*We're keeping a close watch on our key suspect, Kate Austen.*'"

"Michael says that Foley is putting on the pressure. He doesn't believe I'm telling the truth, and he's waiting for me to trip myself up." Max lunged in a different direction, apparently captivated by the scent of a dead fish near the water's edge. I reeled in the leash. "Heel, Max."

Sharon laughed. "Don't waste your breath, Kate. Max will trot at your feet when he feels like it." She patted Max's head, as if to assure him she didn't mean to be critical. "You're still a possible suspect then?" she asked me.

"As far as I can tell, the *only* suspect. It's a horrible feeling. And doubly upsetting because there's nothing I can do about it."

A jogger passed us on the left, a young woman with a strong, high stride and an easy rhythm. I suddenly felt old and tired. "I want my life back," I told Sharon. "I'm sick of the incessant worry and second-guessing. I watch people going about their daily lives, and I feel so disconnected. Like I'm half-dead or something."

"You've been through a major trauma, Kate. Things are bound to feel unsettled for a while."

"The unsettled I could deal with. It's the fear and the unfairness of it all that really gets to me. I was a victim, goddamn it. Foley forgets that."

As Sharon and I chugged up the final hill, I channelled my anger at Foley into a fast-paced stride.

"Whoa, you're not going to get even with him by keeling over." Sharon shuffled to keep up with me.

We were winded by the time we neared the parking lot. We stopped at one of the picnic areas by the water and shared an orange. The sky had darkened, but I found the setting exhilarating despite the cool air. It had been months since I'd come to the reservoir. The murder here last fall of a UC Berkeley coed had dampened my enthusiasm for the area. But now, enough time had passed that I could once again focus on the beauty of the setting. I made myself a promise to come back more often.

Sharon elbowed me in the ribs. "See that man over there, stretching?"

I looked toward the reeds where she indicated. A slightly built man was stretching his leg muscles.

"Isn't he the same guy we saw waiting outside school last week?"

"Could be." His face was turned so it was hard to tell. "He's got a similar build, and he's wearing the same sort of blue windbreaker."

"I'm sure it is. Funny that we'd never seen him before, and now it's been twice in a week."

"Seems to happen like that." Still, a twinge of uneasiness lodged in my chest.

"Maybe he's new in town," she continued, still watching the man. "Whatever his story, he clearly doesn't have a nine-to-five job."

I'd taken off my sweatshirt while we were walking. I slipped it back on. "Let's go. There's probably an innocent explanation, but still . . ."

As we passed behind the man on the way to the car, I tried for a better look at his face, but he was bending over, tying his shoe. He seemed to take no notice of us, and I relaxed.

By evening the clouds were thick and low. An icy wind had begun to blow in from the west. I was running late for an appointment with a new client in Danville, and had stopped by the grocery to pick up a few things for dinner.

It was dark by the time I pulled into the driveway, my mind occupied with the size and color requirements my client had dictated regarding art for her new house. I was reaching into the backseat for the grocery bag, when I felt a hand across my mouth and the hulk of a man's body behind me. For a nanosecond I froze, and then panic ripped through me.

Not again. Not just when I'd begun to put the kidnapping behind me. I twisted and kicked, but the more I struggled, the tighter my assailant's grip.

"Don't make me hurt you." His voice was a low growl, and so close I could feel his breath against my ear.

He dragged me away from the car, into the shadows. My heart was high in my throat, pounding like hail on a tin roof. He wrenched my right arm behind my back, sending a spear of pain shooting through my shoulder.

"Please," I begged, but my words were muffled by the gloved hand across my mouth.

As he pulled my head back against his chest, I caught sight of Anna's profile in the window. Dread of a different sort exploded inside me. The girls were home alone. A thousand horrible pictures flashed through my mind.

Would he harm them, too? No. I wouldn't let him. Whatever it took.

The car key was still in my left hand, now pinned at my side. By loosening my grasp, I managed to ease the key between my thumb and forefinger; then suddenly, I jammed it hard against the man's leg. Not enough to really hurt, but it caught him by surprise.

The moment I felt his hold on me slacken, I pulled my arm free and aimed for his eyes with the sharp end of the key. He raised an arm to defend himself. I missed his face, but caught the arm. I could feel the metal tear his skin. He recoiled in surprise. I slashed wildly and again caught flesh.

He cried out. His hands found my neck. He pressed a thumb against my throat so that I couldn't breathe.

The front porch light came on and Libby opened the door.

"Kate? Is that you?"

Purple dots danced before my eyes. I tried with all my might to scream a warning. *Go back. Lock the door. Call the police.* But I couldn't utter a sound.

Libby stepped forward. "Kate?"

The purple dots became a solid sheet. My head felt as though it were filled with helium.

And then, suddenly, my lungs were filling with blessed air. I took rapid, gulping breaths, sucking in oxygen so fast it burned.

"Kate, what happened?" Libby had her arm around me, and I found myself shaking uncontrollably.

"A man. He was hiding in the bushes."

"Are you okay? Should I call an ambulance?" Her voice was pitched with alarm.

"I'm fine." Slowly, my breathing was becoming more regular, my limbs quieting. "Or I will be in a minute."

"You're sure?"

I took another breath. "I wasn't hurt as much as scared. I don't want to think about what would have happened if you hadn't frightened him away."

"I heard your car, but then you never came in. I thought it was odd."

"I was terrified that he'd harm you and Anna." I stopped to pull myself together before we went inside.

"Speaking of Anna, I'd prefer if you didn't mention this to her."

Libby nodded. "I won't say a word."

"Did you get a look at him?" Michael asked. He was firing questions at me in rapid succession. "Any kind of description at all?"

"He was tall. Big but not fat. That's all I can tell you."

Though I was still shaken, my terror had subsided some in the twenty or so minutes since the attack. It was also tempered by the elation of having escaped. Michael, on the other hand, was still reeling from hearing the news. He'd arrived home not ten minutes after I'd called.

He paced the living room, clearly agitated. "Why you? Do you think he was waiting for you?"

"I don't know. He may have been. Or he could have seen me come home and decided to take advantage of the fact that I was alone."

"I'll check to see if there've been any similar attacks in the area recently." Michael turned. "Did he seem drunk or on drugs?"

"I didn't smell alcohol. I don't know about drugs. He wasn't totally spaced-out."

Finally, Michael dropped onto the couch next to me. "I wish I was confident this was a random thing."

"What do you mean?"

Michael rubbed his palms together. "Your name's been in the news. Anybody who wanted would know where to find you."

"But why—"

"Have you noticed anyone unusual around lately?"

"There was a man when I was picking up Anna from

school a few days ago. Sharon and I thought we saw him again today, at the reservoir."

Michael's expression grew alert. "He was following you?"

"No. He was stretching near the parking lot when we finished our walk. But it's not unusual to recognize people at the reservoir. And it couldn't have been the same man who attacked me. The guy tonight was muscular. The man at the reservoir had a wiry build."

Michael slipped an arm around my shoulder. "Still, I don't like it. I'm going to see if I can get out of the trip to Texas later this week."

"The captain was pretty adamant about your going. This probably isn't a good time to make him mad."

"The Li Chen homicide isn't as important to me as you are."

"It's not just the captain, Michael. There are people counting on you."

"I'd hope that you were one of them."

"I am." I touched his cheek. "Most definitely."

26

In the end, Michael left for Texas. Captain's orders. Short of risking his job by refusing, he didn't have a choice.

He was mollified somewhat by the discovery of another attack several weeks earlier. A woman coming home late at night had been knocked to the ground and her car hijacked. The two crimes weren't identical, and the assailants' descriptions differed, but there were enough similarities to offer us both some assurance that my attack was a random event.

A part of me was even happy to have Michael gone for a bit. Happy to be free of his hovering and his second-guessing. We hadn't talked about the murder for a few days, or about Sheryl Ann, and I had the sense it was deliberate on his part. Maybe he found it easier to sidestep the doubts that way.

Anna had a doctor's appointment late in the afternoon. By the time we were through, rain was falling steadily. Wind blew the heavy drops hard against the windshield, darkening the evening twilight. I could tell it was going to be a cold and dreary night.

"You want to get Chinese takeout for dinner?" I asked

Anna. "It's just the two of us. Michael is out of town, and Libby said she'd be home late."

Anna nodded, bouncing in her seat. "With sizzling rice soup," she said. "And lots of fortune cookies."

Because I hadn't phoned in the order ahead of time, we had to wait. I sipped tea while Anna had a soda and told me about her day.

"Look," Anna said with considerable pique as we turned the corner onto our street, "someone else is getting cable." She'd been nagging us for months, pointing out at every opportunity that we were probably the only people on the face of the earth without cable television.

The gray panel truck had a less-than-pristine appearance and no logo. "I don't think that's a cable truck," I told her. "But it wouldn't matter if it were. *We're* not getting cable."

Anna crossed her arms and jutted her chin forward in a pout. "I can't wait until I'm a grown-up so I can do whatever I want with no one to boss me around."

I gave her knee a pat. "Even grown-ups have constraints, honey. But you'll certainly be able to have cable if that's what you want."

"And I can eat Chinese food whenever I want, too."

It was dark outside when I pulled into the driveway, but I saw a light in the kitchen. "Looks like Libby's here," I said. "She must have decided not to stay for the study group after all."

Anna crossed her arms. "I hope we got enough food."

"There'll be plenty. I'm not very hungry."

I unlocked the front door and pushed it open, calling out to let Libby know we were home. Although she'd turned on the light in the kitchen, the rest of the house was dark. I flipped the hallway switch and handed Anna the bag of food.

"Set it on the kitchen table and get some napkins. Ask Libby to pour the milk. I'll be there in a minute. I want to check the answering machine first."

Max, who'd bounded to meet us with an unusually frantic burst of barking, followed Anna into the kitchen, his nose twitching at the array of enticing aromas.

"You can have a cookie," Anna said to him, "*if* we have enough."

I was almost at the bedroom door when Anna's shriek pierced the air. Her cry was followed by a dull thud and the scrape of a chair sliding along the wooden floor. My heart leapt to my throat.

I darted for the kitchen so fast my feet barely touched the floor.

Anna was standing near the doorway, frozen in place, the bag of Chinese food at her feet. Max was already exploring it with his nose. Across the room, at the kitchen table, sat a soggy, bedraggled woman—the sort you see talking to themselves on street corners. She was spreading peanut butter onto crackers with her finger.

Alarm shot through me like a current. Shaking, I pulled Anna close and glared at the woman. "What are you doing in my kitchen?"

"Sorry," she said, looking first to me and then to the mess at Anna's feet. "I guess I startled your little girl."

Her voice had a familiar lilt. I stepped forward.

The hair, which had been a cascade of shoulder-length curls, was now short and unevenly cut, as though she'd done it herself with dull scissors. Her clothes were several sizes too big, and carried with them the odor of someone badly in need of soap and water. But I recognized the face.

"Sheryl Ann?"

"C'est moi." She grinned and stuck another cracker into her mouth.

27

I stared at Sheryl Ann.

For a moment, I was speechless. Then the questions began piling up faster than I could get them out. "Where have you been? What are you doing here? How did you get in?"

Sheryl Ann licked peanut butter from her forefinger. "I had your keys. They were in your purse, remember? I would have waited for you to come home, but it was getting late. I was cold and wet." As if to illustrate the point, she coughed. It was a deep-chested rattle that left her gasping for air.

"Also hungry," she added when she could talk again. "It's been a while since I've eaten." She dipped her finger into the peanut butter jar. "Not that you have much interesting in the fridge. I finished off the chips and salsa. Hope you don't mind."

Anna, who'd gradually turned from stone to flesh again, slid next to me and pressed against my leg. "Who is that woman? Do you know her?"

My heart was racing. As was my mind. Should I call Frank? 9-1-1? Should I grab Anna and bolt from the house?

Michael had warned me again and again about Sheryl
Ann. She could be dangerous, he said. She might try to
kill me.

But if she wanted to harm me, she'd hardly be sitting
at my kitchen table eating peanut butter, would she?
Besides, if I called the police now, that would put an end
to any possibility of securing her help.

Anna tugged at my sweater. "Is she a friend of yours?"

"Sort of," I explained as my pulse slowly returned to
normal, "but it's complicated."

"What is she doing here?"

Good question. "Why don't you go into the other room
and watch TV for a few minutes?"

Anna didn't move, and I couldn't really blame her. It
wasn't every day we found a homeless woman in our
kitchen. Television paled by comparison.

Sheryl Ann held the peanut butter finger aloft, watching me carefully. My own eyes were locked on to hers.
We were like two boxers, vigilant and wary, each waiting
for the other to move.

Keeping myself between Anna and Sheryl Ann, I
nudged Max away from the food and lifted the bag onto
the counter. Juice from one of the takeout containers
had leaked onto the floor. I let him finish lapping it up,
thinking it would serve him right if he got something
spicy. As a guard dog, he was useless.

"Sorry I scared you," Sheryl Ann said, addressing
Anna. "I expected your mama, not you."

"You're lucky it wasn't Michael," I told her.

"Your boyfriend? I did worry about that." Her expression was ever so slightly guarded.

"So what *are* you doing here?" I asked.

Sheryl Ann coughed again. This time, the hollow rattle went on for almost a full minute.

I looked at her, really looked this time. Her skin was dry and chapped, her face flushed. The matted hair around her face was damp with perspiration. Even without a medical degree, I could tell that she was sick.

"I didn't know were else to go," Sheryl Ann said, and coughed again. "Do you have any whiskey in the house? This cough is getting to me."

"How about some cough syrup?"

The flicker of a smile. "I think I'd prefer whiskey."

I poured her a small glass, then another for myself. I needed it as much as she did. Anna continued to hang on to the hem of my sweater.

"Where have you been?" I asked, handing her the glass. I started to sit down, then thought better of it. No point backing myself into a corner where escape would be difficult.

Sheryl Ann took a dainty sip. "Around."

"The police are looking for you."

"I figured they would be. That's why I cut my hair and picked up some clothes at the Goodwill store in Tucson. If you look like a bag lady, you can go anywhere and nobody notices. They don't even fucking *see* you." She glanced at Anna, who was hovering by my side, then back to me. "Sorry about the language."

Max had finished licking the sauce off the floor. He wandered over to his water dish and began noisily slurping.

"I'm confused," I said. "You've been hiding from the police, and yet you came *here*?"

She nodded.

"Why?"

She took a breath. Focused her eyes on the floor. "I was hoping you'd help me."

"Why would I do that?"

Sheryl Ann looked hurt. Her expression clouded. "Because I helped you," she said in a small voice. "Remember? You'd be dead now if it wasn't for me."

"I'd never have gotten tangled in this at all except for you." Anger had seeped into my voice. "I ought to call the police right this minute."

Sheryl Ann eyed me warily. "You'd do that?"

"You kidnapped me, or have you forgotten that part?"

Anna moved closer, hugging my leg. I put an arm around her shoulder to reassure her. I should call the police, I thought. I was going to have to do it sooner or later, and the longer I waited the harder it would be to explain. But I also wanted Sheryl Ann to tell them I had nothing to do with Bobby's death. Throwing her to the wolves hardly seemed the best approach. And it was unlikely she'd stick around to wait for their arrival anyway.

Sheryl Ann began rocking back and forth in the chair. "You said before that you'd vouch for me, that you'd explain it was all Bobby's idea."

"That was before."

"You said you'd tell them how I was nice to you and how I tried to help."

I reminded myself of the blood on the jacket and the mess I was in because of Sheryl Ann. "Things have changed," I told her, reaching for the phone.

"No, please." Her features twisted with alarm. "Please don't call the police. I treated you good, didn't I? I made sure you had food and a warm place to sleep. And a shower. Please, Kate. I feel like sh—" A glance toward Anna. "I feel lousy, and I'm scared."

Against reason, I felt the stirrings of compassion. I hesitated. "Why didn't you run away with me? We'd both be safe now if you had."

"I know," she whimpered. Her skin appeared feverish, her eyes glassy. "I should have."

"Why didn't you then?"

"I'm not sure."

"You were planning on killing Bobby all along, weren't you? You set me up to look like a murderer."

"Set you up?"

"It was a dandy plan. Worked beautifully. The police are breathing down my neck, and most of the people in town treat me with suspicion. Even Michael has his doubts."

"They think *you* killed him?" There was a look in her eyes I couldn't read.

Inside me, the emotional storm gave way to a sudden quiet. I'd blown it for sure. Now that Sheryl Ann knew her scheme had worked, she could tell Foley what he wanted to hear and walk away a free woman. The very thing Michael had warned me about. I took a step toward the door, pulling Anna with me.

"They think *you* killed Bobby?" Sheryl Ann asked again.

"They haven't entirely discounted the possibility," I said, backtracking, "but that doesn't let you off the hook. They're looking for you. They've got police in every state itching to arrest you."

Still rhythmically swaying in her seat, Sheryl Ann wrapped her arms around herself and shivered. A cloud of despair contorted her features. She looked small and helpless.

"Was it self-defense, Sheryl Ann? Did Bobby threaten

you? Or maybe come after you in a rage? If you explain, they'll take that into account.''

She shook her head. "I didn't—" A fit of coughing cut her words short.

"Didn't what? Didn't mean to kill him?''

"I *didn't* kill him.'' She looked me in the eye, suddenly still. "I left the cabin after you did—I knew Bobby was going to be mad, and I wanted time to think about it. I couldn't have been gone more than an hour. But when I got back, he was dead.''

28

"I never thought they'd blame *you*," Sheryl Ann said, pulling the tattered gray sweater across her chest. "Why would they blame you?"

I was still stunned by what she'd said a moment earlier. "If you didn't kill Bobby, who did?"

She shook her head. "Beats me."

I wanted to believe her, if only because it freed me from guilt. I'd spent the last week worrying that I'd put Sheryl Ann in a position where she was forced to kill Bobby. But this pointing a finger at some unknown suspect seemed a bit too convenient.

She must have read my skepticism. "It wasn't me," she said. "I swear."

Anna tugged at my sleeve with impatience. Her interest in the stranger had waned considerably. "Can we eat? I'm starving."

"Go wash your hands," I told her, and began opening the cartons of food.

Anna hesitated until I assured her no one would touch the food until she returned. Then she raced down the hallway like a bolt of lightning.

Still alert to the possibility of a trap, I set the cartons

on the table carefully. "Sheryl Ann, listen to me. Your story doesn't make sense. Who would drive to the middle of nowhere in a snowstorm to commit murder?"

"I told you, I don't know. But it scared the shit out of me. All I could think was that if I'd stayed around, they'd have killed me, too."

"I assumed you set the whole thing up to pin the murder on me," I said.

She frowned. "Why would I do that?"

"To deflect the spotlight from yourself."

"But I didn't kill him." A shadow of dismay crossed her face. "You don't believe me, do you?"

"What about the jacket?"

"What jacket?"

"The one you gave me as I was leaving. So I wouldn't freeze, remember?"

She nodded, stifled another cough. "What about it?"

"The jacket had Bobby's blood on it. That's one of the reasons I'm in hot water with the police right now."

Her expression was troubled; then slowly comprehension dawned. "I never thought . . . Oh, my God, I didn't realize . . ." She paused to look at me. "That's the jacket I was wearing when Tully punched Bobby in the nose. That's what started their fight."

"Bobby was cut?"

"The whole thing was over so quick, I'm not sure exactly what happened. But I remember rushing to Bobby and holding him. There was blood all over his face. He was the one who looked hurt, not Tully."

She was either a damned good actress, or she was telling the truth. I leaned toward the latter.

Doubt must have lingered in my eyes, however, because Sheryl Ann was growing agitated. "I swear, Kate, I was not trying to set you up. I was trying to *help*. Do you think I'd have come back here now if what you say is true?''

Anna breezed into the kitchen just then, hands still damp. She passed over her usual seat at the table and instead pulled out a chair close to mine.

"You want a fork or chopsticks?" I asked Sheryl Ann. She glowered. "What I want is for you to believe me."

There was a moment of uncomfortable silence; then I sighed. "I do. Mostly, anyway. Now what will it be, a fork?"

Sheryl Ann relaxed. "Chopsticks."

Anna glanced my way, gritting her teeth. "She's going to eat dinner with us?"

I nodded. I wasn't thrilled at the prospect myself, but Sheryl Ann and I had unfinished business. And by now I was reasonably sure that she wasn't an immediate threat.

Anna shot me a dirty look, then turned toward Sheryl Ann. "We weren't expecting company, so we didn't get very much. If you're really hungry, you'd better eat somewhere else."

Under other circumstances, I'd have leapt on Anna for being rude. This time I let it pass.

"That's okay. I'll manage." Sheryl Ann was already sniffing appreciatively at the spicy aroma of Chinese food. "If I'm still hungry after dinner, I'll fill up on crackers."

Anna gritted her teeth but otherwise hid her disappointment admirably.

Over dinner we put a halt to our discussion of Bobby's murder and ate in silence. Sheryl Ann stuffed herself with two servings for every one of Anna's, and took the last pot sticker, which was the straw that broke the camel's back. Anna left the table in a huff, taking with her all the fortune cookies but two.

Sheryl Ann continued to be seized with periodic coughing spasms so intense I was afraid I might have to call 9-1-1 for something other than the police.

"You sound terrible," I told her with concern. "How long have you been sick?"

"Coupla days. All I need is a good night's rest."

She licked the last of the rice from her plate with a finger, then reached for a fortune cookie. "'You are about to embark on a new adventure,'" she read. "Sounds good to me." Then she added with a laugh, "As long as it's not jail."

My fortune cookie was empty.

"Uh-oh," Sheryl Ann said dramatically. "Bad luck."

"More like bad quality control." In the back of my mind, though, I wondered if my future held something worse than jail. I felt a shiver of trepidation.

As I started clearing the dishes, Sheryl Ann went into another fit of coughing.

"You ought to see a doctor," I told her.

She shook her head. "I just need to be someplace where it's warm and dry for a change." She paused. "You'll let me stay, won't you?"

"*Stay?*"

"Just for the night."

I should have expected it, but I'd been too busy thinking about when and how to call the authorities. I shook my head in apology. "I'd like to, but I can't."

"I came to you because I trusted you. Because you said you'd help me." Her voice had a pleading quality to it.

"I wish I could."

"Please, Kate. I'm scared."

"It's not just me—"

"I was nice to you, wasn't I? I tried to protect you."

It was a convoluted logic, but I let it pass.

"I saved your life, Kate." Sheryl Ann was whimpering now, growing more and more distraught. She kept breaking off tiny pieces of fortune cookies and letting them fall to the table. "Despite what you think about it being a setup, it wasn't that way. I wanted to *help* you."

I felt my resolve soften. Sheryl Ann was sick and feverish. Another night on the streets might kill her. What harm could there be in one night?

I was ready to agree until I thought of Anna and Libby. I couldn't take a chance where the girls were concerned.

"I'm sorry," I told her again. I stopped rinsing dishes and leaned against the counter. "I'd like to help, but I can't let you stay here."

"What am I going to do?" It wasn't so much a question as a wail. She cradled her head in her hands. "I'm so scared I can't even think straight."

"We're going to have to call the police. You know that, don't you?"

She raised her head and nodded. "But not tonight. Please."

"It might be better to get it over with."

She shook her head, still agitated. "I thought you'd help me. That you'd tell them I treated you well. That it wasn't really my fault. That's what you said you'd do. You said you'd vouch for me."

"That was before Bobby was murdered. Before I became a suspect myself. They're not going to believe me any more than they do you."

Sheryl Ann moaned softly. "They're going to arrest me, aren't they?"

"I don't know. They haven't arrested *me* yet. But they'll probably charge you in connection with the kidnapping."

She sat up. "We could tell them Bobby kidnapped us both."

"That's not true. Besides, I already told them what happened."

She hesitated. "About Tully, too?"

I nodded. "Tell me, is he really dead?"

She gave me a funny look. "Of course he's dead. Did you think he was just napping?"

"His body wasn't in the root cellar when the police checked."

"Bobby moved him?"

"I don't know. The police searched the whole area, and they didn't find any sign of Tully."

Her forehead creased with a frown. "That's really weird."

I nodded.

For a moment, she didn't say anything. Then her eyes welled with tears. "Poor Tully," she said with genuine sorrow. "He didn't deserve this."

"I thought you were leaving him."

"I don't know. These last couple of months Tully got all tense and short-tempered. He wasn't usually like that. Then he came home and found me and Bobby, and he went crazy."

"Is that when he punched Bobby?"

"Yeah, it seemed like he was possessed or something." She paused. "If he hadn't gone so crazy, Bobby would never have shoved him so hard he hit his head and he'd still be alive. It's my fault. I should never have gotten mixed up with Bobby in the first place."

It would certainly have saved everyone a lot of heartache. I handed her a box of tissues. "Let's back up a moment. You left the cabin while Bobby was still outside, and when you came back he was dead."

She nodded.

"And then?"

"And then I got outta there as fast as I could. I didn't think to check about Tully. I just got in the car and drove."

"Where is the car now?"

"New Mexico. At the bottom of a ravine. I thought if I got rid of it . . ." She blew her nose. "I guess I don't know what I thought, except that I was scared."

"How'd you get here?"

"The bus mostly." Her mouth trembled. "None of this was supposed to happen. Bobby and I were just fooling around. It didn't even mean much."

The reign of unintended consequences was one of life's unfortunate constants. "We need to lay this out for the police," I said. "If neither of us killed Bobby, then they need to find whoever did."

"But what if they don't believe us?"

That was the problem in a nutshell. Foley already had his suspicions about me and my alliance with Sheryl Ann. For all I knew, Frank shared them. If I called Frank now, he might decide to hold us both. Even if he didn't, we'd be at the station for hours. He'd arrest Sheryl Ann on the kidnapping charge if nothing else. That would mean I'd have to give a statement. I'd have to wait until Libby got home to watch Anna.

It simply wasn't a workable plan.

I pulled out a chair and sat at the table across from Sheryl Ann. "How about this," I told her. "I can't let you stay here, but I'll pay for a motel for the night."

"I'd rather stay with you."

I shook my head. "That's not possible."

She crossed her arms over her middle, looking at me like she wanted to argue.

"Why don't you take a shower?" I suggested. "I'll give you some clean clothes. We'll have some tea and then I'll drive you to the motel. By then it will almost be time for bed anyway."

"You won't call the police while I'm in the shower?"

"If I was going to call them, I'd have done it already. Besides, I have one particular cop in mind, and he's out of town at the moment."

She raised an eyebrow. "Who's that?"

"The man I'm living with."

Her jaw dropped. "Geesh, you live with a cop? It's a good thing he didn't come home and find me."

"Right." Or maybe it would have been better if he had. Then I wouldn't once again be in the middle of it. "Come on. I'll show you where the bathroom is."

29

While Sheryl Ann was in the shower, I tucked Anna into bed.

"Is that lady staying here?" she asked, nestling close to my side.

"No, she's going to spend the night at a motel."

"Good. I don't like her."

"You don't have to, honey. Anyway, I imagine she won't be back again."

I kissed Anna and promised her two stories the following night for the one we'd skipped tonight. It was the missed story, I suspected, more than the visitor herself that was the root of Anna's displeasure.

Returning to my own room, I set out underwear, a red turtleneck, and a pair of jeans for Sheryl Ann. She was thinner than I was, and a couple of inches shorter, but the difference wasn't enough to matter to anyone but the fashion police. I also packed up a nightgown and sweatshirt, along with some extra toiletries, and stuck them in a paper sack for her. It wasn't Louis Vuitton, but it worked.

I could hear her in the bathroom humming over the pounding shower like a carefree child. When she emerged sometime later, wrapped in my white terry robe and toweling her hair, she looked scrubbed and fresh. The aroma of herbal shampoo wafted from the bathroom along with a cloud of steam.

"That felt so good," Sheryl Ann said.

"I've laid some clothes on the bed. When you're ready, we'll have tea."

Her smile was filled with gratitude. "Thanks."

I went to put the kettle on. A few minutes later she flew into the kitchen, waving a scrap of paper in her hand. "What are you doing with *this?*"

It was the torn sheet on which I'd written Clay Potter's name and number. I'd left it on the bedroom dresser.

"You know him?" I asked. It was obvious from her agitated expression that she did, and that the association wasn't a pleasant one.

"You didn't call him, did you?" Her voice was tight with anxiety. "You didn't tell him I was here?"

"I haven't even talked to him. Who is he?"

Sheryl Ann flopped into a kitchen chair without looking at me.

"Is he involved in what's happened?"

She shook her head, barely moving it from side to side. Another stretch of silence. "He's my stepbrother," she said finally. "What I told you before about being an orphan isn't exactly true."

I handed her a mug. "I know."

Her eyes widened. "You know? You *have* talked to him, then."

"You want sugar?"

"Yes, please."

"I heard the story from the police," I explained, joining her at the table. "How your mother died in a suspicious fire when you were fourteen."

Sheryl Ann made a face. "You bet it was suspicious. I bet Clay set it, too."

"Clay? The police told me that their suspicions focused on you."

"Only because Clay and his gold-digging mother lied." Sheryl Ann paused for another fit of coughing. "I was supposed to be trapped in the fire, too, but I got out in time." She wrapped her fingers around her mug and hugged it to her chest. "Nobody believed me, including my dad."

"How come?"

She tossed her head. "I was fourteen, always in trouble. Clay was twenty-five at the time. And a polished ass-kisser."

I traced a finger along the edge of the table. "After your mother died in the fire, his mother married your dad?"

"Four months later. She'd been his secretary before that. He was probably sleeping with her, too."

"And that didn't raise police suspicions?"

"Not in Bakersfield," she said bitterly. "Not when my father, who happens to run one of the biggest companies in town, went out of his way to tell them I'd been nothing but trouble my whole life."

The truth, or a convenient deception? "Clay Potter was at your house not long ago," I said. "He was looking for you."

"How'd he know where I live?"

"I don't know. Your neighbors thought he was a reporter. I tried to reach him because I wanted to find you, and I thought he could help."

"But you didn't talk to him?"

I shook my head. "I left a message. It was his wife who called back, and more or less chewed me out for calling her husband."

"Geesh, just what I need—more trouble."

"What do you think he wanted?"

"I can't imagine, and I don't care. I haven't talked to any of them in six years. In my own mind I don't even have a family."

When Libby arrived home, I introduced Sheryl Ann without elaboration. I knew I'd have to fill in the particulars later, especially because Anna was sure to recount the story of finding a homeless woman in our kitchen. Then we left for the motel.

"Can we stop on the way for rations?" Sheryl Ann asked, as we pulled out of the driveway. The shower had lifted her spirits, and she sounded almost excited, the way Anna does when we head off on an excursion.

"Rations?" I asked.

"Sure. You can't stay at a motel without rations. Soda, chips—that sort of thing."

Like a slumber party, I thought. We made a quick stop at the store while she loaded up—at my expense.

"This is it?" Sheryl Ann asked when I pulled into the parking lot of the Snuggle Inn. Her voice was steeped with disappointment.

"You were expecting the Four Seasons?"

"No. Not exactly."

The Snuggle Inn wasn't fancy, but it was clean, convenient and affordable. A two-story L-shaped building with interior corridors, a meeting room, and a pool. Continental breakfast was included.

I handed the man behind the desk my credit card while Sheryl Ann explored the lobby.

"I'll call you in the morning," I told her, handing her the key. "About nine?"

"Okay." She took an uneven breath. "Guess I should enjoy this night since I might be spending the rest of them in jail."

"I'll tell the police how you were kind to me, how you saved my life. That's got to count in your favor."

Impulsively, she leaned over and hugged me. "Thanks, Kate. I don't know what I'd have done without you."

I didn't point out that without me, she wouldn't be in the mess she was.

I'd barely walked in door at home when the phone rang.

"I wanted to thank you," Sheryl Ann said.

"You already did."

"But I really mean it." A siren wailed in the background, growing fainter as it passed.

"You're welcome."

A moment's silence. "Also, I thought of something."

"What's that?"

"You know how a smell can bring back memories, sometimes even memories you didn't know you had?"

"Right." I shifted the phone to my other ear. I'd about had enough of Sheryl Ann for one night.

"Well, when I came back to the cabin and found Bobby dead . . ." She spoke slowly as if evoking the memory as she went. "I . . . I was in a panic and wasn't thinking clearly, but there was this sense I had . . . this sense of something familiar. And I realized just now that it was the smell of ginger."

"Ginger?"

"Maybe it's not really ginger, but it's kind of got a zip to it. More like ginger ale, I guess. It's a smell that I know. I just can't remember where I know it from."

"Memory is funny business," I told her. "Sleep on it, and something might come to you."

"Good night, Kate. See you in the morning."

I was awake for what seemed like the entire night, although I know I must have dozed off intermittently because several times I snapped to awareness with a start, drenched in sweat. What if Sheryl Ann wasn't telling the truth about Bobby? Or what if she was, and no one believed her but me? What if I'd made things worse by not calling the police the instant I found her at my house?

At five I gave up on sleep and got out of bed. The house was cold and dark. The morning paper hadn't come yet. Despite the rain, which had now turned to a steady drizzle, I pulled on a sweatshirt and running shoes and took Max for a jog. We moved at a slower-than-normal pace because I have trouble seeing in the dark, and Max, wonderful beast that he is, is no guide dog.

The neighborhood was quiet. Only a few houses showed signs of life. Max and I had the roads to ourselves except for an occasional early commuter and delivery van.

I made waffles for breakfast, an unheard-of weekday treat that pleased both girls as well as Max; then I drove Anna to school. The minutes until nine o'clock ticked by very slowly.

Precisely on the hour, I called the motel and asked to be connected to Sheryl Ann's room. The phone rang fifteen times before switching back to the front desk. No,

I told the man who picked up, I didn't want to leave a message. I'd try back later.

When there was no answer at nine-thirty or ten, I grew worried. Finally, at ten-fifteen I left a message. Sheryl Ann might have been in the shower one of the times I called, and maybe in the lounge getting her complimentary coffee and sweet roll another time—but it seemed unlikely. Besides, she was expecting my call.

With growing anxiety, I climbed into the car and drove to the motel. My knock on the door went unanswered. I tried the knob and found it locked. I rapped harder and called her name until a man stuck his head out of a neighboring room and told me to quiet down.

The day clerk was reluctant to open the door for me until I showed him that it was my credit card paying for the room. "I'll have to accompany you," he said, rubbing a hand across his chin. He was in his mid-twenties but hadn't yet outgrown the scourge of teenage acne.

"Fine. I just want to make sure she's okay." By now I was in a panic, my head filled with visions of accidental falls, blocked windpipes, fever-induced coma, even slashed wrists.

I experienced a moment's relief when we opened the door. There was no body on the floor.

But there was no Sheryl Ann either. The nightgown I'd given her had been tossed onto the floor. The bed hadn't been slept in.

"She must have stepped out," the clerk said. "See, there's nothing to worry about."

If only that were the case. "Did she make any calls? Did anyone see her leave?"

"I wouldn't know." My young escort was already at the door, yawning in boredom.

Back in the lobby, I asked the question again, posing it this time to the assistant manager.

"I'm not at liberty—"

"Something has happened to her," I snapped, although I wasn't entirely convinced that was the case. Maybe she'd simply decided that turning herself in to the police wasn't such an appealing choice after all.

"You can help me determine if there's an innocent explanation," I said hotly, "or you can deal with the police and the media."

His brows creased in an annoyed scowl, but he finally checked the records. "Your friend made two calls," he said. "Both last night. One was at ten. The other twenty minutes later."

The first had been her call to me. Who else had she called?

"Do you know the numbers?"

"Only that they were local."

"What about incoming calls?"

"Four of them. All this morning."

Again, my calls.

"Did anyone see her leave? Or talk to her at all?" I addressed both the clerk and the assistant manager.

Both shook their heads.

"We just came on this morning," the clerk said. "You might have better luck asking the night manager."

"How do I reach him?"

"He'll be on duty starting at five."

Most likely, I told myself, Sheryl Ann had changed her mind. But once again the voice of worry wouldn't be silenced. Sick and exhausted as she was, wouldn't she at least have spent the night in a warm, comfortable bed before taking off?

30

For the second time in less than two weeks, Michael found himself driving a rental car along an unfamiliar highway. This time, at least, there was no snow and heavy wind. Gone, too, was the frantic, gut-gripping fear that had shadowed him during the trip to Idaho.

He still worried about Kate, especially after she'd been attacked the other night. But it was a worry that gnawed quietly in the recesses of his mind. No easier in the long run, maybe, but not nearly as draining in the moment.

Once he left Houston city limits, the traffic thinned to almost nothing. The road was wide and flat, as were the open plains beyond. Michael had allowed himself three hours for the drive to see Li Chen's brother, but it looked now as though the trip wouldn't take more than two. He hoped the younger Mr. Chen could accommodate his early arrival. Frittering away time in some podunk part of Texas wasn't high on his list of ways to pass the morning. Given his worries about Kate, he wouldn't have come at all if the captain hadn't insisted.

To his left, a hawk circled overhead. The horizon was otherwise unbroken. Michael reached to turn on the radio and felt again the stiffness of folded paper in his pocket.

Gina's note.

He'd found the ornately penned page among his papers when he arrived at the airport last evening. Purple prose and sophomoric passion. In a different context, he might have found it amusing, flattering even. Instead the note filled him with dread. The situation was fast reeling out of control.

Michael had been hoping the whole thing would defuse on its own. Hoping that if he simply ignored her, she'd let the matter drop. But that was apparently not going to happen. He'd make one more attempt to help Gina understand, and then he was going to have to report it to the captain.

The hawk made a low swoop and dropped momentarily out of view. When it passed over the freeway again, it clutched a small animal in its talons.

An involuntary shudder spread across Michael's shoulders as he thought of his troubles circling in the distance like the hawk.

Mr. Quon Chen lived with his wife in a well-maintained trailer park on the outskirts of town. Under the green awning that served as a porch, pots of yellow flowers bloomed in profusion. The interior space, though dark and stuffy, was less cramped than Michael expected.

"You found your way okay?" Mr. Chen asked. "Here, please have a seat." He gestured toward an orange-and-red floral couch.

"The directions were excellent."

"Good. Still, a long way to come when there is nothing I can tell you. I did not see my brother very often."

"But you visited him a couple of weeks before his death."

Mr. Chen nodded. "My wife was going to Florida with some women from the church. I decided it would be a good time for me to see Li." He paused and looked down at his hands. "He was getting old. I felt the opportunities for us to be together were running out. But I never expected that he would die as he did. To be murdered in one's own home is unthinkable."

"It's painful to lose someone to violence."

"Li was a quiet man, with only goodness in his heart. What happened to him isn't right."

"No, it isn't. That's why we're working hard to catch his killer. But we don't have a lot to go on."

"And you think I can help?"

"I don't know whether you can or not," Michael explained, "but we've reached an impasse in the investigation. Since you were with him recently, we were hoping you might have seen or heard something that could give us some direction."

"Li was a kind man. His kindness was repaid by the kindness of those around him. Who would want to harm an old man?"

Michael pressed his palms together. Might as well get the tough questions over with first. He leaned forward. "Tell me about your nephew, Jason Liao."

Mr. Chen looked up. "What does Jason have to do with my brother's death?"

"Maybe nothing. A neighbor heard Li Chen arguing with him the day before the murder."

"You're saying Jason killed him?"

Michael shook his head. "Jason says he was with a friend the night your brother was killed."

Chen lowered his gaze. "Jason is my sister's boy. She

died five years ago, when Jason was fourteen. She was many years younger than me and Li, much too young to die." Chen paused. "Li tried to be a good influence on the boy, but it has not been easy."

"What about Jason's father?"

Chen made a dismissive gesture, brushing the air with his hand. "My sister's husband left her before Jason was born. He has not been a father in any sense."

"So Li acted as a sort of surrogate father?"

Chen nodded. "Li had no family of his own. He watched over our sister and Jason, and helped them financially. He wanted to pay for college, but Jason wasn't interested. Jason is too much influenced by his friends and what he sees on TV. He wants it all, without work."

The curse of the younger generation, Michael thought.

"But Jason wouldn't hurt Li. He wouldn't do that."

"Not even for money?"

"Jason wouldn't hurt Li," Chen said again. This time, though, it sounded as though he were trying to convince himself of that fact.

Michael leaned forward. "Were there bad feelings between your brother and Jason?"

Chen considered the question before answering. "Not bad feelings, but differences. Although Li was an uncle, he was almost two generations older. And he was born in China. Jason has been raised in America. This is the land of opportunity, but there are also many temptations, especially for young people."

Michael pressed Chen for details of his brother's life, finances, friends, and habits. But what he learned only reinforced the picture already in his mind. Li Chen was a quiet man who kept to himself and tried his best to help a nephew who adamantly rejected everything about the life Li Chen embraced.

In Michael's mind, Jason Liao remained a key suspect, but there was still no supporting evidence.

31

With Sheryl Ann's disappearance, I was in a real mess. If I called the police, they'd want to know why I hadn't contacted them yesterday. But if I did nothing, they'd never learn what she knew about Bobby's death. More than that, I had the discomfiting feeling that Sheryl Ann was in trouble.

If only I knew how to reach Michael. He'd have checked out of the hotel by now, and his destination "somewhere near Houston" didn't narrow the field much. Finally, I used the pay phone in the motel lobby to call the station.

"I don't have a way to contact him," Janet said, "but I can relay a message if he calls in. He's flying back this afternoon anyway, isn't he?"

"Yeah. I guess it can wait." I hesitated. In the ten seconds of silence, I went back and forth a dozen times. Finally, without actually reaching a decision, I asked to speak to Frank.

"He's not in. I'll have him call you when he shows up."

"That's okay. It's not important."

I went into the rest room and splashed cold water on my face, then rinsed my mouth. My skin felt tight, and my stomach was churning. With the clarity of hindsight I decided that I should have called Frank when Sheryl Ann showed up in my kitchen. Of course if I'd done that, she'd probably have bolted, and short of physically tackling her there wasn't much I could have done about it.

Maybe that's what she'd finally done—taken off again. Now that she'd learned I was the one the police had their eye on, she might have decided that a life incognito was preferable to one in prison on kidnapping charges. The thought didn't bring me much comfort, however. It only added anger—at both Sheryl Ann and myself—to the tumult of emotions I was already experiencing.

The assistant manager approached me as I left the rest room.

"Checkout time is noon," he said. "Should we keep your friend's room for another night?"

I gave a fleeting thought to my MasterCard bill, inching toward its limit. But I didn't see that I had a choice. "Please," I said. "And tell housekeeping not to touch it."

His lips pinched in disapproval. "Not even fresh towels?"

"Right."

"Most of our guests are pleased with our service."

"I'm sure it's lovely," I said, turning to leave. "But it's important that *nobody* goes into her room."

"You mean . . ." It had been slow coming, but finally he understood. "You think that there may have been . . . foul play?"

I didn't want to scare him out of cooperating. "It's a possibility," I said.

"Oh dear."

Outside, the air was cool and fresh. A welcome relief from the stale, closed interior of the hotel. I hoped it would clear my head as well as my lungs.

Think. I had to think. But I was having trouble focusing. I seemed to do fine rehashing past events, especially with the benefit of 20/20 hindsight. Whenever I tried to look forward, however, I hit a wall. Where had Sheryl Ann gone, and why? And how was I going to explain my own involvement in her disappearance?

I was too nervous to work, too keyed up to go home. So I drove to Sharon's instead.

"Hey, this is a surprise," she said, grinning. And then her face fell. "Or did we set something up and I forgot? I'm beginning to worry about this brain of mine. It's like a sieve. I've been meaning to get some of that ginkgo supplement, but I keep forgetting." She laughed lamely at her own joke.

I followed her inside where "Love the One You're With" was blasting through the loudspeakers. "You didn't forget," I yelled over the music. "I'm just at loose ends."

She hit the stereo remote, and the volume dropped to a more comfortable level. "Is it Foley still, or something else?" She kicked Kyle's Rollerblades to the side with her foot so I wouldn't stumble on them. "You want something to drink?"

"Are you speaking coffee or wine?" With Sharon you can never tell.

She grinned. "Whatever suits your fancy."

"Coffee." I slipped onto one of the leather stools at Sharon's island counter. Given the way I felt, if I started drinking I might never stop.

Sharon put on a pot of water. "You didn't answer my first question. Is it Foley again?"

"No. I mean, not exactly."

Suddenly the idea of visiting Sharon seemed inane. What was I going to tell her? That I'd seen Sheryl Ann, paid for her motel room, and now she was missing? Words like *aiding and abetting* and *obstruction of justice* floated through my mind, although I thought—and I certainly hoped—that they didn't technically apply. Nonetheless, for Sharon's sake, I thought the less she knew about it the better.

"Is it Michael, then?" she asked. "Are you still worried that he doesn't believe you?"

I shook my head. "I think he still has his doubts, but that's only natural in light of his training."

Sharon stopped what she was doing and turned to face me. "It's not one of the kids, is it?"

"No." I stood up. "Actually, I think I'll pass on the coffee. I've got to run."

"But you just got here."

"I know. I can't stay though. I . . . I was in the neighborhood and just thought I'd drop by and say hello." I grabbed my purse and darted for the door.

"Kate, if something's wrong—"

"No, nothing is wrong." I laughed nervously. "More wrong than it's been, I mean. It's just that . . . I guess the tension is getting to me."

"You want a Valium? I've got practically a full prescription."

"I think I'll pass." Or swallow the whole bottle, I added silently in a touch of black humor. "Thanks though."

Sharon was my closest friend. If I couldn't talk to her,

I had no one to talk to. No one except Michael, who I couldn't reach.

I didn't know if I was angrier at Sheryl Ann or myself.

In order that the morning wouldn't end up a complete waste, I stopped by the cleaners to pick up my black wool jumper and then Safeway for fresh crab, one of Michael's favorites.

The house still smelled of the waffles and syrup from breakfast when I returned. It was not an aroma that played well on my nervous stomach.

As I dropped my keys on the hallway table, I heard a faint click from somewhere at the rear of the house. The hairs on the back of my neck stood on end.

I stopped and listened. Nothing but the pounding of my heart and the hum of the refrigerator. The front door had been locked when I came home, and the house looked untouched. My imagination, I decided. Or the wind.

I laid the jumper over the arm of the sofa and went to put the crab away. As I shut the refrigerator door, I noticed that the "to do" list I keep by the phone had fallen onto floor. Had I knocked it off earlier that morning?

Probably.

But I knew I'd never rest until I checked the house for signs of an intruder.

Opening the back door, I called Max from the yard and wiped the mud from his feet before letting him inside. Given the way he'd practically ignored Sheryl Ann's uninvited entrance, I had my doubts about his usefulness, but I figured there might be an intimidation factor in seventy pounds of canine energy.

Then I picked up the phone and called Sharon.

"I heard a noise when I came home," I told her. "It's probably nothing, but I'm going to check the house. If I don't call you back in five minutes, call 9-1-1."

I considered taking a knife, then decided I'd never use it. Instead, I grabbed the fireplace poker, which seemed somehow more user-friendly.

"Anyone there?" I called, moving down the hallway.

Silence.

"Sheryl Ann?"

More silence.

I inspected the rooms one by one, peering in back of open doors and inside closets. I even checked behind the shower curtain. The house was clear.

I called Sharon from the bedroom phone and told her everything was in order. But I couldn't shake the feeling that it wasn't.

Sheryl Ann's disappearance weighed on my mind for the remainder of the day. Several times I thought of trying to reach Frank, and each time I held off. Having waited this long, wouldn't I be better off unburdening myself to Michael?

Sharon called late in the afternoon. "Just checking. You've been acting strange all day. Are you okay?"

"I'm fine."

She hesitated. "Kate, if there's anything I can do . . ."

A car pulled into the driveway. I watched Frank step from the driver's side and start up the walkway. "Oops, looks like I've got company. Frank is here."

"Why?" The question was laden with suspicion.

"It's nothing. I called him earlier. Actually, I called Michael and only asked if Frank was in. I didn't leave a message, but I guess this is an example of the personal service the department is trying to encourage."

"Michael probably asked him to keep an eye on you."

"Maybe. There's the bell. I have to run."

Since I knew from experience that Frank wasn't fond of dog drool, I held Max by the collar with one hand while I opened the door with the other.

"Hi," I said. "I didn't expect a return phone call, much less a personal visit. Come on in. Just let me put the dog in the other room."

Frank headed for the living room while I shoved Max into the laundry room.

"Can I get you some coffee or soda?"

"No, thanks." His tone was unusually terse.

When I returned, Frank was sitting at one end of the couch, arms resting on his knees. Although I'd decided to wait to talk to Michael, now that Frank was here I couldn't very well say, "Forget it." I took a seat in the chair opposite him, wondering where to begin.

He saved me the trouble. "Sheryl Ann Martin is dead," he said.

32

On some level I'd been expecting it, but the news still hit like a wrecking ball to the chest.

"When? How?"

"Last night. Trauma from a fall." Frank leaned forward, arms resting on his knees. "It was near the old railroad trestle. A woman walking her dog spotted the body this morning in the creekbed."

I winced at the vision of Sheryl Ann's broken body sprawled on the jagged rocks that lay at the bottom of the ravine. As the shock passed, a terrible sadness took hold, pressing against my skin from inside. "Was she . . . was her death an accident?"

"At this point, it's not clear what happened." Frank cleared his throat. "She had your phone number in her pocket, along with a key to the Snuggle Inn. Your name is on the bill."

I couldn't tell how much he knew, but there was no point being evasive. Whatever he didn't know, he'd find out soon enough.

"She was here last night," I told him, fighting the quaver in my voice. "Here at the house. She showed up out of the blue."

He nodded, silently, his eyes focused on my face.

"She wanted to stay here." I could almost hear Sheryl Ann's voice. *You'll let me stay won't you? Please, Kate. I'm scared.* I pushed the memory from my mind and looked at Frank. "I didn't think it was right to let her spend the night in the house."

"You should have called me."

"I know. But Sheryl Ann was sick. She needed a good night's sleep."

"So you paid for her room at the motel." Frank's tone was neutral, but he threw me a sharp, curious look.

"We were going to contact you today." Not the absolute truth—we were going to wait for Michael—but close enough. "When I went to pick her up this morning, she was gone."

Frank ran his thumb across his lower lip.

"She didn't kill Bobby," I added.

He regarded me silently. It was hard to tell what he was thinking. Finally, he asked, "Was this the first time you'd talked with her since you escaped?"

I nodded.

"What time did you drop her at the motel last night?"

"About nine-thirty. Why?"

"Did you stop anywhere first?"

"The grocery."

He raised an eyebrow.

"Sheryl Ann wanted to pick up some snacks."

"Alcohol?"

I shook my head. "Cookies and chips."

Frank tapped his fingers against his thigh, as though he were playing scales on a minipiano. "Were you drinking before you took her to the motel?"

"We had a little bourbon, but that was earlier in the

evening." Along with the sorrow, I was beginning to feel a niggle of worry. "Why do you ask?"

Again, he ignored the question. "Did you come directly home?"

"Yes."

"And you didn't go out again?"

"No, I didn't. What's this about anyway?" I rocked forward. "You don't think that *I* had anything to do with her death?"

It was almost the same response I'd given Foley only a couple of weeks earlier, an irony that wasn't lost on me. I'd been counting on Sheryl Ann's reappearance to set things right. Last night I'd thought we were finally approaching the end of this nightmare. And here I was now, in worse trouble than before.

"You just admitted to being the last person to see her alive," Frank said.

"One of the last." I didn't like the way he used *admitted*.

"That's where we often begin an investigation."

"So you *do* think she was murdered."

He stopped his tapping, and sighed. "The honest truth is, I'm not sure what to think."

That made two of us.

"It's possible it was an accident," Frank continued. "There was a quart of rum smashed on the rocks next to her."

"Where would she get rum?"

He shrugged. "There's a convenience store at the corner and a bar a couple of blocks away." After a moment's pause, he continued. "Guess I'm having trouble understanding why she came to you in the first place. You, of all people."

"She thought I would help her. That we'd go to the

police together. I'd make it clear that Bobby was responsible for the kidnapping.''

He looked skeptical.

I thought about trying to explain further, but I wasn't sure what I could add. From an objective perspective, it *did* seem odd that Sheryl Ann would expect the woman she'd kidnapped to befriend her. But having been there, I wasn't surprised.

Frank traced the welting of the couch cushion with his palm. ''Did she leave anything here?''

''Like what?''

He made a *who-knows* gesture. ''We'd like a complete inventory of her personal effects.''

''She didn't have any. At least not with her.''

''None?''

''Well, she had her purse, and some ratty clothes she'd picked up from a secondhand store. We threw the clothes in the garbage.''

He seemed to consider this for a moment; then he asked, ''What did she tell you about Bobby's murder?''

''That she'd gone out and when she came back, he was dead.''

''And Tully's body?''

''She didn't check. But she did say there was a scent in the room that was vaguely familiar. Like ginger ale.''

He squinted at me. ''Like ginger ale?''

''That's how she described it.''

''Did she have any ideas about who killed him?''

''None.''

Frank bit his lower lip. ''Did Sheryl Ann give any more indication about what she and Bobby were up to?''

''I told you that already. They were trying to cover up Tully's death.''

He hesitated. "I'd like us to be on same team, here."
I nodded.

The muscle along Frank's jawline twitched. "You're not holding out on me, are you?"

"Why would I be holding out?"

"You tell me." He waited a moment, then rose to leave. "You think of anything else, be sure to let me know."

33

The phone rang just as Frank was leaving. Through the static and crackling I could barely make out Michael's voice.

"I'm so glad to hear from you," I told him. After the morning's events, I felt as though I'd been thrown a lifeline.

"Mean . . . are happy . . . ?" He sounded like he was talking in a wind tunnel.

"Where are you calling from?"

"The plane."

"Pretty fancy." This was a first for me, talking to someone calling from a plane. I pictured our words, as scattered as they were, drifting through the atmosphere like apple blossoms in spring. "Are you still over Texas?"

"I'm still *in* Texas. The plane has been sitting on the runway for close to an hour . . . say it will be another hour at least. They're waiting for a replacement . . ."

The reception cut in and out, leaving me to mentally fill the gaps. Not quite the cutting-edge technology I'd imagined.

"I've been wanting to talk to you," I told him. "There've been some new developments in—"

"I can't hear you," Michael said. "Can you speak louder?"

"There have been—" A loud burst of static rattled in my ear.

"What?"

"Never mind," I said, deciding it was neither the time nor place to tell him about Sheryl Ann. "I'll talk to you later this evening."

"Assuming . . . flies."

I pressed the phone harder against my ear and shouted. "Have a safe trip. I've missed you."

In response, I got more static and a dial tone.

Libby and I shared the cracked crab, although we set aside some choice sections for Michael for when he got home. Anna had a grilled cheese sandwich.

It was a quiet dinner. Libby's mind was on her history paper, still in its formative stages despite being due the next day. Anna was coming down with a cold, which I assured myself she couldn't possibly have picked up from Sheryl Ann. My own energy had been sapped by worry and the steady flow of questions and elusive half answers that peppered my brain.

I didn't for one minute believe that Sheryl Ann had fallen to her death by accident. In the first place, she had no reason to go out. She was sick, she was tired, and she was looking forward to spending the night somewhere warm and dry for a change. The rum made no sense either. If she'd wanted a drink, she could have picked something up when we stopped for provisions.

On the other hand, who had reason to kill her?

Frank suspected that I did. My skin grew clammy at the memory of our conversation.

I was clearing the table when I thought of another possibility. Had Sheryl Ann taken her own life? She was a young woman given to impulsive, often irrational, behavior. And she was in a heap of trouble. Maybe I'd been less supportive than she'd hoped. Or maybe the gathering clouds of the judicial system had loomed too darkly on the horizon.

The possibility that her death might be a suicide set off a new wave of sorrow and self-blame. There were so many things I could have done differently.

Finally, I asked Libby if she'd mind keeping an eye on Anna while I went out for a bit. I was hoping the night clerk at the motel might be able to clarify a few things.

"Don't open the door for anyone," I told her. "And keep the phone close at hand."

I expected her to bristle at my caution, but instead she nodded gravely.

The lobby of the Snuggle Inn was empty. The young man behind the desk looked bored, but brightened considerably upon seeing me.

"Good evening, ma'am. Do you have a reservation?" He apparently didn't recognize me from the previous night.

"I'm not looking for a room. I want to talk to you. Were you the only clerk working last night?"

He nodded warily, the way Anna does when she's not sure if she's done something wrong.

"A friend of mine was staying in room 217. I was here when she checked in, remember?"

I could tell by the expression on his face that he didn't. "You do look familiar, but—"

"I'm interested in knowing if you saw my friend again

after she checked in. She's about my height. She was wearing jeans and a red turtleneck."

"I'm afraid we have so many guests . . ." He paused for a second and his eyes grew bright. "Wait. That's the lady who died, right?"

"Right."

"I heard all about it when I got to work." His voice was pitched with excitement until it dawned on him we were talking about someone I'd called a friend. In a considerably more subdued tone, he added, "I'm sorry for your loss."

"Did you see her go out last night?"

He shook his head. "Like I told the police, I didn't see a thing."

"Did anyone come to the desk asking for her?"

Another headshake.

There'd been only an outside chance he'd seen her leave, but my disappointment was nonetheless profound.

"Only time I saw her at all," he continued, "was when she asked for an envelope and stamp."

I'd turned away, and now I turned back. "She was mailing a letter?"

He nodded. "She wanted to know the pickup schedule. I told her we kept the letters here at the desk until the mailman made his delivery, usually not until the afternoon. There's a mailbox at the corner that gets an early-morning pickup. I suggested she might want to drop it there if she was worried about timing. Funny thing was, it almost seemed she wanted the letter *not* to go out too early. She asked me twice if I was sure the mailman wouldn't come before nine."

I felt a ripple of excitement. "Did you see who the letter was addressed to?"

He shook his head. "She handed it to me, and I put it in the box of outgoing mail. I didn't even look at the front of the envelope."

"Thick? Thin? Heavy?"

"Not thick, but maybe a bit heavier than usual. She only put a single stamp on it."

I thanked him and started to leave, then thought to ask about the room. Now that the police were involved I saw no reason to keep incurring charges. "Has the account for the room been closed? It's on my card."

He clicked a sequence of keyboard keys and checked the computer screen. "Yup, closed out a little after one today. As I understand it, the police came by and searched the place, then released the room." He smiled. "If they'd come an hour earlier, you'd have saved yourself another night's charge."

Michael didn't get home until almost ten. His shirt was rumpled and his eyes bloodshot from the stuffy air inside the plane. He gave me a quick hug, then went off to change out of his travel clothes. It was clear that he was exhausted and grumpy.

Much as I hated to add to his aggravations, I thought it better he hear the news from me than find out about Sheryl Ann's death tomorrow at work.

When he'd traded slacks for jeans, he grabbed the leftover crab and a bottle of Anchor Steam from the fridge. I poured myself a glass of wine and joined him at the table.

"God, airline food is bad," Michael said. "A stale roll with some tasteless gray meat inside, and they call that dinner. This was after we'd been cramped into microseats with a limited supply of fresh air while the plane sat on the damn runway for three hours. Next time I'm bringing my own rations.''

Like Sheryl Ann stocking up for her night in the motel. I felt the shadow of her death over my shoulder.

"I can make you an omelette or something."

"This is fine. I'm more frustrated than hungry at this point." He uncapped the beer. "How were things on the home front?"

I gave a noncommittal shrug. "You didn't happen to call in today, did you?"

"No. Why?" Michael was digging crabmeat from a piece of claw and didn't look up.

I took a sip of wine. "Well, there've been some developments."

I paused for another sip, then plunged in, hitting the high points first. Then I went back and filled in the when and where, and what I knew of the why and how. By then, I'd spent enough time agonizing over Sheryl Ann's death that I was able to talk about it without choking up.

Michael stopped eating and listened attentively, opening his mouth on occasion to speak, then closing it again without uttering a sound.

"I'm not sure that Frank knows about the letter," I said in conclusion.

Michael frowned. "Sheryl Ann came *here*? And you let her *in*?" He'd latched on to the very part of the story I'd tried to gloss over, and his displeasure was apparent.

"She let herself in," I told him.

He looked at me as if I'd sprouted a third eye. "She was here what, three or four hours, and you simply opened the house to her? Are you out of your mind?"

"It wasn't like that."

"You fed her dinner, gave her your own clothes, let her take a shower in *our* bathroom."

"You don't understand."

"Why didn't you call the police?"

"I thought about it, but who was I going to call? Besides, she might have run if I'd tried calling them."

"You might have tried while she was in the shower."

I looked at him, then away. "I guess I could have."

Michael held the icy beer bottle against his forehead, as though fending off a headache. "She could have killed you."

"She wasn't going to hurt me. She wanted my help."

"Lucky for you." The sarcasm was thick enough to cut with a knife.

"Not so lucky for her, though."

"What do you mean?"

"If I'd called the police, she might still be alive."

Michael's anger softened. "Kate, you've got to stop blaming yourself for everything that has happened to Sheryl Ann."

His sudden reversal surprised me. "You were railing against me a minute ago."

"Because I was worried about *you.* Sheryl Ann's death is not your fault."

"But on some level it is. If I'd never stopped to help her in the first place—"

"She might have been killed along with Bobby. Or maybe she'd have succeeded in running away with Bobby and been killed while crossing the street." Michael sighed. "You are not master of anyone's destiny, Kate. Not even your own."

"I know." Not that knowing eased the sorrow any. I touched his arm in a gesture of gratitude.

Michael covered my hand with his own and squeezed it gently before draining what was left of his beer. "Now that you've successfully deflected my anger—"

"That wasn't my intention."

He gave me a weary smile and rocked back in his chair. "So what's the story on her death?"

"Frank says he doesn't know what to think, but he's leaning toward its being an accident." I hadn't mentioned the glimmer of suspicion that had surfaced when he was questioning me, and I decided now was not the time to bring it up.

"Seems like an odd coincidence," Michael said.

I nodded and took a calming breath. "There's also the possibility she took her own life. The letter might actually have been a suicide note."

He tore bits of paper from the Anchor Steam label. "Why would she kill herself if she was innocent? And why would she come all the way back home to do it?"

"She came back because she was tired of hiding. She was going to go to the police, and she wanted me to go with her, as a reference, so to speak. But she was worried about what would happen, especially if no one believed her story. Maybe she changed her mind."

"In that case, she could have simply gone back into hiding."

As a rule, people who took their own lives weren't thinking logically. But I had to admit, Sheryl Ann hadn't seemed despondent.

"We'll probably never see the letter in any case. Did the night clerk happen to notice who it was addressed to?"

"He says he didn't."

Michael made a fist, compressing the bits of beer label

in his palm. "There's another angle to this, you know. If Sheryl Ann didn't kill Bobby, then whoever did is still out there. He might be responsible for Sheryl Ann's death."

The question was, who, besides me, knew she was staying at the motel? I thought of Sheryl Ann's second call. Who had she telephoned?

34

"Accidental death?" Michael was incredulous. He'd sought Frank out first thing that morning, sure that Kate must have been mistaken.

"You have a problem with that?"

Michael leaned on Frank's desk, supporting his weight on his palms. "Sheryl Ann was the one person who could support Kate's story about what happened in Idaho. She mysteriously winds up dead, and that doesn't raise a red flag for you?"

Frank rocked back in his chair, stretching the distance between them. "I didn't say we'd made a final determination—only that accidental death is a strong possibility. That's what I told her brother, too. He called me this morning looking for details."

"Stepbrother."

"Whatever. I hope he's not going to be one of these pain-in-the-ass relatives who's out to make trouble."

"What makes you think he might be?"

"Just a feeling I got. Like Sheryl Ann's death is the only case we got going." Frank pressed his palms together and stared blankly off into space. "He was full of questions, kept asking about signs of a struggle, that sort of thing."

"See, he doesn't think it's an accident either."

"He doesn't know shit. Hasn't seen her in years. *I* know what we've got on her death, and there's nothing there pointing to foul play."

"Yet."

Frank groaned. "I'm not exactly new to this line of work, you know."

"Besides, the timing—"

"I know, but sometimes that's the way things are." Frank pushed back from his desk. "The woman was apparently drunk as a skunk."

"That's another thing that doesn't make sense," Michael said, following Frank into the lunchroom.

Frank shrugged. "Makes sense to me. Kate tells her to take some cough syrup and go to bed. But Sheryl Ann is nervous, scared, lonely. There's nothing on TV, so she heads for the corner convenience store and buys a bottle."

"Except that no one can remember seeing her."

"The guy behind the cash register is a space cadet. He wouldn'ta remembered if ET had come in."

"It's too pat," Michael insisted. "There's been a multistate search for this woman and now suddenly she's dead. That strikes me as a strange coincidence."

"A coincidence, yes." Frank took his time pouring a mug of heavy black liquid from the coffeepot. "And a lucky one for Kate."

"Lucky?"

His eyes locked on Michael's. "You assume Sheryl Ann's version of events would have been the same as Kate's. That might not be how it went."

"What do you mean?"

Frank took a sip of coffee. "Her story might have been different, is all."

At first Michael wasn't sure he'd understood correctly. "Are you implying that *Kate* might have killed Sheryl Ann?"

"Just looking at all the possibilities."

"That's absurd, and you know it."

Frank frowned into his cup for a moment, then lifted his gaze and regarded Michael coolly. "I don't *know* anything. And neither, I might add, do you."

"You're wrong there." Michael could feel the heat of his anger prickle under his skin.

Frank leaned back against the counter. "How'd it go with Li Chen's brother?" He spoke amicably, seemingly oblivious to their verbal sparring.

Reining in his anger, Michael turned back. "No new leads and nothing to put a fire under the ones we've got."

"Sorry to hear it."

"Yeah. I keep coming back to the nephew, Jason Liao, but nothing sticks to him. The brother couldn't add anything except 'the kid wouldn't hurt his uncle.' "

"Hey, don't feel bad," Frank said. "You know the captain didn't really expect results. The only reason he sent you down there was the PR factor."

Michael frowned. "How's that?"

"The victim is a double header—an old man and a Chink. Lots of room for good press. The captain's gotta make like the department's busting its butt, right?"

"Some of us," Michael said, no longer hiding his irritation, "make an effort to do just that."

* * *

Michael rolled his shoulders, trying to ease the tension that clamped his muscles like a vise. He turned his head to the left, to the right. Nothing helped. It seemed like his whole world was spinning out of control.

He put in a call to Foley first. Michael wanted to be sure he heard Sheryl Ann's explanation about how Bobby's blood got on the jacket. Michael also worried that Foley would view Kate's role in Sheryl Ann sudden reappearance with skepticism, and he wasn't confident that Frank would have tempered that view.

Foley wasn't available, so Michael left a lengthy voice message, as well as a request for a return call. Then he turned his mind to the larger questions.

Sheryl Ann and Bobby—both dead. A fluke?

Life was sometimes stranger than fiction—no getting around that. And fifteen years as a cop had taught Michael not to let first impressions cloud an investigation. Still, he'd put money on the two deaths being connected.

Did that mean Kate might also be a target?

He pulled Sheryl Ann's file and took it to an interview room where he could read without interruption. The file was thin, as was often the case with a new investigation. If the coroner ruled the death accidental, it would stay that way. If not, Kate's name would show up on the list of suspects.

Again.

Michael reached for a yellow pad of paper and began summarizing what he knew. Thinking with his fingers, he called it. Sometimes his scrawlings were illegible, even to himself, but the very act of putting words on paper helped him focus.

Conventional wisdom had it that you started with those

closest to the victim. Lovers, family, and friends—in that order.

For Bobby's death, this put Kim Romano, the spurned girlfriend, front and center. Michael jotted her name on the notepad, then traced over the *K* again while he pondered the possibility. Though her grief at the funeral had seemed genuine, she'd shown anger as well. On paper, a clear suspect. But in his gut, it didn't feel right.

Michael rubbed his chin and cast the net wider. Rudy Harrington's relationship with his stepson left a lot to be desired, and resentment was an age-old motive for murder. Not to mention the fact that life would no doubt be easier for him if Bobby was out of the picture. But how did Harrington figure in Sheryl Ann's death? Bobby's mother was a more likely candidate there. She'd made no secret of the fact that she blamed Sheryl Ann for being a bad influence.

And what about Bobby's circle of acquaintances? Michael made a note to review the investigation file again. Off the top of his head, though, he thought it would be a dead end. Bobby hadn't had a lot of friends, but there'd been no one ready to pick a fight with him either.

There was less information on Sheryl Ann. Although the focus of the early interviews had been on locating her, the responses painted a picture of a likable, if somewhat flaky, woman.

Except that she'd been cheating on her husband. Could one of Tully's friends have taken it on himself to mete out justice? It would be unusual for friendship to rise, or fall, to quite that level.

As for family, Sheryl Ann was estranged from what little she had left. Or was she? Michael recalled a father stricken with cancer and wanting to mend fences with his errant daughter. And Kate had said her stepbrother had been looking for her, too.

But even if some tangled family feud was behind Sheryl Ann's death, what possible motive could they have for killing Bobby?

Unless the answer was none.

Michael sat up straighter, drawn by something so obvious he'd looked right past it. What if Bobby Lake had simply been in the wrong place at the wrong time? Caught in the cross fire so to speak. Was it possible that Sheryl Ann was the target all along?

He was just beginning to play with the idea, to wend his way through the possibilities, and the ramifications, when Gina entered the room without knocking and shut the door behind her.

Michael looked up, started to say he was busy.

She put her finger against her lips in a stage whisper. "Shh, don't say anything." And then she slipped her arms from her blazer and began to unbutton the teal silk blouse beneath.

"What are you doing?" Michael had intended outrage, but the words came out as more of a croak. He was afraid that a raised voice might attract attention.

Gina's eyes danced with playfulness. "What does it look like I'm doing?" She had the blouse completely undone by then, and Michael could see that she wasn't wearing a bra. She parted the soft fabric, exposing her breasts.

"As nice as you imagined?" she asked.

For a moment Michael was too astonished to speak. Astonished, and to be honest, a little mesmerized. Whatever else she might be, Gina was a beautiful girl. She started to approach.

Reflexively, Michael stepped back. His skin felt hot.

Dampness tickled the back of his neck. Glancing toward the two-way mirror, he looked in vain to see if there was movement on the other side. God, he hoped not.

"Don't be embarrassed," she said. "I understand what you're going through. I think it's sweet."

"Please." Michael's mouth was so dry he had trouble speaking. "You've got this all wrong, Gina. I've tried to explain to you, and you refuse to listen. I am not interested in a romantic—"

She silenced him by kissing her finger and touching it gently to his lips. "Shh. Don't worry about it. I understand."

Before he could gather his thoughts, she'd thrown her blazer over her blouse and was gone.

35

As word of Sheryl Ann's death spread, I was once again the focus of media attention. Actually, not so much the focus this time, as a source. My kidnapping and Bobby's murder had made for great drama on the nightly news. Sheryl Ann's death was the latest installment, and I was the person with the inside scoop. Or so the press thought.

Several reporters had called the previous evening, and another early this morning. I'd dismissed them all with a polite but firm "I'm not talking to the press. Please don't call me again." Usually that was all it took.

Then Anna, peeking through the curtains as we were ready to leave for school, spotted a newsman waiting by the curb.

"It's not a cable truck either," she said. "I can tell it's news reporters because of the big antenna on the roof." Her voice was a mixture of knowing sophistication and wariness.

"They only want to ask questions," I reassured her. "And we don't have to answer. We can pretend they aren't even there."

"I don't like them," Anna whimpered, stepping back from the window. "They're like pigeons."

"Pigeons?"

"Those birds that fly in your face and grab your food."

Our urban picnic in Justin Herman Plaza this last fall had terrified Anna, and not without reason. San Francisco is home to the nation's most abundant—and aggressive—pigeon population. Sensing Anna's defenselessness, the birds had chosen to pick on her, and had ended up with most of her lunch.

"Well, I guess they are a little like pigeons," I said. "Only they're hungry for information instead of food."

"I wish they'd stay away."

Silently, I agreed. As a mother, however, I've learned to sound brave even when I'm not feeling it. I reached for the car keys and slipped my purse over my arm. "Their questions are for me, honey. They won't hurt you."

Hand in hand, we left the house and marched to the car with determined strides. I avoided making eye contact with either of the two men waiting near the street.

"Mrs. Austen," one of them called to me. "I'm Scott Griffith from Channel 7 News. Could I take a minute of your time?"

I walked on.

He trotted alongside of me. "Is it true that Sheryl Ann Martin, the woman you claimed kidnapped you two weeks ago, was staying at a local motel at your expense?"

"No comment," I told him, shoving my free hand into my pocket so he wouldn't see me shaking. "Now please leave us alone."

"Is it true the police regard you as a potential suspect in her death?"

I kept my eyes straight ahead and picked up the pace.

"Why would you befriend her after what she did?"

Opening the car door for Anna, I bustled her inside.
The man stood beside me. "And why did you give
Sheryl Ann some of your own clothing?"

I checked Anna's seat belt.

"Was it meant to be a disguise?"

I slammed the car door and turned to face him. "Leave
me alone."

"Does this mean you have something to hide?"

With a pounding heart, I got into the driver's seat
and locked the doors before starting the engine. Anna's
pigeon analogy, I thought irritably, was close to the mark.

Several blocks later, I was still steaming. A disguise?
The guy was off his rocker. What kind of disguise was
jeans and a turtleneck? And then it registered. My red
turtleneck. My *A Woman's Place Is in the House, and the
Senate* sweatshirt. Might someone have mistaken Sheryl
Ann for me? We did have similar builds. In the dark, that
might be enough.

Instead of dropping Anna off by the flagpole, I walked
her all the way to the classroom. Then I drove to Pete's
Cafe for a latte and a croissant. I was reluctant to head
home, and too keyed up to work.

I was a possible suspect, a potential victim, and a definite media target. A choke hold of emotions made it
difficult to breathe. I felt weak and cold and afraid.

I'd been trying to do the right thing all along, but
somehow it always turned against me. Even Michael. He
wanted to help me—I knew that; but he couldn't help
feeling irritated, too.

As I licked the last drift of creamy foam from the inside
of my cup, it dawned on me that I was never going to

get my life back until this whole mess was resolved. I could sit around calming my nerves with croissants until that happened, or I could make an effort to move things along. Given the five pounds I'd gained in the last few weeks, not to mention the gloomy state of my psyche, the choice was fairly obvious.

Less clear was what to do about it.

Sheryl Ann's coworkers had given me the name of a friend, Darla. I didn't know her last name, but I did know that she was a manicurist at the nail shop in the Walnut Ridge Mall. Seemed as good a place to start as any.

I don't get to the mall all that often, and when I do it's usually to dash into a single store for something mundane like sheets or underwear. On the occasions that I trek the full length of both floors, I'm always astounded at the changes. Shops seem to come and go, like sets on a stage.

In my quest for Darla, I discovered that the cheese-and-sausage place was now an accessories store. The shoe shop had been replaced by a bath shop, and the upscale sporting goods shop where I'd bought Michael a tennis racket for his last birthday was currently selling items for closet and office organization.

I hadn't remembered any nail shops, but now I discovered two.

I tried the Nail Shoppe first. It was glitzy in an ultra-modern, but not very inviting, way. There was a black lacquer reception counter inside the doorway, empty. The room was likewise empty, except for three young women, also in black, huddled at the back, giggling. Finally, one of them looked up.

"Can I help you?"

"I'm looking for Darla."

"Who's Darla?" She looked to her companions for help.

"There's no one here by that name?" I asked.

Three neon-shade heads shook from side to side.

"Sorry. I must have the wrong shop."

My second stop, Nails by Design, seemingly appealed to an older, more affluent, clientele. The lighting was soft, the decor an enticing muted green and peach. The receptionist, a fortyish woman of Mideastern descent, who I suspected might also be the owner, kept watch over the operation from an antique Louis XIV desk.

"I'm looking for Darla," I said again.

She tapped a coffee mocha nail against her flawlessly powdered cheek. "Do you have an appointment?"

"No, I just wanted—"

She called to a dark-haired woman who was bent over the hands of a client in workout wear. "Can you take a walk-in, Darla?"

"What are you wanting?" Darla asked, addressing me. "Silk wrap, overlay, acrylic?"

"A manicure," I answered meekly. Not that I'd started out wanting even that. I'd had a manicure only once in my life, when I was in high school. The choices then were much simpler—clear, pink, or red.

"Hot paraffin?" Darla asked.

I shook my head. "Just a manicure."

"Yeah, I can do it soon as I'm done here. Give me fifteen minutes, okay? And let Miriam know if you want the spa chair."

A spa chair? I didn't even ask; I knew it would cost extra.

I wandered the mall while Darla finished with her client. I was beginning to understand why my nails looked so ordinary. I never spent more than five minutes on them.

This was a fact not lost on Darla. "You don't get manicures regularly, do you?" she asked, looking at my hands.

"Not really."

She dunked my fingers into a bowl of warm water. "So what's the occasion?"

"Actually, I just wanted to talk to you. You were a friend of Sheryl Ann Martin's, right?"

She looked up and her eyes narrowed. "How'd you know that?"

I'd used the past tense without thinking and now found myself in a quandary. "You know she's dead?"

Darla gave a cautious nod. "You're a policeman, uh, woman. Is that it?"

"No, I'm the woman she kidnapped."

"You're the one?" Darla's wary expression gave way to astonishment. "You must be glad she's dead."

I shook my head. "I know this must be hard to understand, but I liked Sheryl Ann. There's not any part of me that's happy to see her dead."

Darla removed my left hand from the water and dried it.

"She paid me a surprise visit the night she was killed," I continued. "I was the one who took her to the motel." Credentials established, I moved on. "You *were* a friend of hers, weren't you? I got your name from some women she worked with."

Darla nodded. "Well, sort of friends. Dick—that's my boyfriend—and Tully are friends." She swallowed. "Were friends, I guess. If he's really dead."

"You don't think he is?"

She shrugged. "Dick and Jack Clevenger—he's another guy in the band—they're not so sure."

"Any reason?"

"I don't know—it's Clevenger mostly. He keeps bad-mouthing Tully. And he's been bugging me about whether I've heard from Sheryl Ann. Like he's blaming her."

"For what?"

"For taking off, I guess. He thinks Tully cheated him. Anyway, we got to be friends through the guys. But I wouldn't say we were, like, close friends."

"Do you know who her close friends were?"

"I don't think she had any. Sheryl Ann was fun to hang around with, but there was a sadness there, too. Kind of like she was drifting, never really connecting. That's why she stuck with Tully, I think. Because it was easier than leaving."

"Stuck with." I hesitated. "I know he hit her once—is that what you mean?"

"Did he? I didn't know about that. It wasn't so much that he was mean to her, just that he was kind of a flake. A nice flake, but I don't know that I'd want to be married to him." She laughed. " 'Course, I don't know that I want to be married to Dick either."

"Can you think of anyone who would have reason to harm her?"

Darla's eyebrows arched. "You don't think it was an accident?"

"I don't know why she would be outside on a rainy night. When I left her, she was exhausted and sick."

"She wasn't much of an outdoors person anyway. Wouldn't walk any farther than she had to. And no, I can't think of anyone who'd want to harm her. But when she told me she and Tully were taking some time off—''

I interrupted. "What? You talked to her? When?"

"She called from some nowhere town in Idaho, asked me to take in the mail and pick up the newspapers. She sounded odd. Said they were headed to an even more nowhere town called Whitehall. At the time, I thought maybe she and Tully had had a big fight. Now, well, I don't know what to think."

"Do you remember what she said?"

"Just that they'd decided to get away for a bit. I know she'd been worried about Tully. He'd been real down recently."

"Any idea why?"

Darla lowered her voice. "Money. He had some debts to pay off. I think he owed even more than he let on."

I had the feeling we weren't talking student loans or even MasterCard.

"I overheard Dick and Clevenger talking about it just last week. Clevenger was trying to help Tully get some extra money. There was some business deal or something. Then Tully took off, or that's what we all thought at the time. Well, Clevenger went ballistic. I guess he figured he'd gone out on a limb for Tully, and then Tully had let him down somehow."

"What kind of business deal?"

She shook her head. "To tell you the truth, I always thought there was something kinda shady about the whole thing. I mean, they never talked about it openly, but we all knew." Darla reached for a clean towel. "What color do you want?"

"I don't know. Something subtle."

"How about a clear pink? Just a little color and gloss."

"Sounds good."

She shook the bottle before uncapping it. "I think that's why she called Clevenger the other night from the hotel."

"Who called Clevenger?"

"Sheryl Ann. She didn't leave much of a message. Just a 'Hi, it's me. I'll try again tomorrow.' "

The mystery call she'd made from the motel? I leaned forward as though we were exchanging secrets. "Did she say *where* she was?"

"No, but Clevenger has caller ID. He told us she was in town."

36

Standing at the sink in the men's room, Michael splashed cold water on his face, then wet a paper towel and ran it across the back of his neck. Today was the day. He was going to speak to Gina before things got out of hand. With a pointed laugh, he looked closely at himself in the mirror. Hell, they were already out of hand. The real issue was what to do about it.

Once he brought the matter to the captain's attention, it would be out of his control. Gina would lose her position with the department and probably wind up with a permanent mark on her record.

If the captain took Michael's report seriously, that is. There was a chance, maybe even a good chance, that he'd see Michael as creating an issue out of nothing. Captain Greyson was of the old school. To his mind, women, particularly young women, were delicate souls in need of masculine direction and protection.

Either way, Michael thought glumly, the story was bound to work its way through the station accompanied by twitters of locker room humor. He'd bear the brunt of it, but Gina would come in for her fair share of smirks and guffaws.

He tossed the damp paper towel into the trash, then took another for his hands. For everyone involved, the whole thing would be better dealt with privately. Gina wasn't stupid. Nor, Michael thought, was she psychotic. She was simply young and misguided and maybe a little lonely.

Perhaps by trying not to hurt her feelings, he'd inadvertently encouraged her. Maybe there'd even been some ambivalence on his part. When an attractive woman throws herself at your feet, it's hard not to feel the tug of temptation. Especially given the tensions at home.

Surely if he and Gina sat down now and talked it through, they could set things straight.

And he'd do it before the day's end. But first he wanted to get up to speed on Sheryl Ann's death.

Grabbing the notes he'd jotted while reviewing her file, Michael put in a call to Les Oliver, the responding uniformed officer.

"I've got a few minutes right now," Oliver said. "You want to meet me at the creek where the body was found?"

"Thanks."

"No problem. I hope you know you can count on me to keep my mouth shut."

"I appreciate it." Poking around in another detective's case was tricky business, especially when the other detective was Frank Bowen.

In theory, the department worked as a unit. They shared information and bolstered each other's investigations because they shared a common goal—getting criminals off the street.

But theory didn't take human nature into account. The reality was that a case "belonged" to the detective assigned to it. If he wanted help, he'd ask for it. If he didn't ask, you didn't offer. And you especially didn't go behind his back and start sniffing around on your own.

Michael didn't see that he had much choice, however. Kate was in trouble, more trouble than she realized, and it wasn't going to end until this matter with Bobby and Sheryl Ann was resolved.

Les Oliver was waiting for him when Michael pulled off Rudgear Road onto the shoulder near the creek. The spot was a couple of blocks off the main drag, at the edge of a residential area. There were no houses directly facing the creek at that point, just a narrow stretch of shrubbery, but the houses on Hope Lane were less than a hundred yards away.

"Don't know that this will help you much," Oliver said. "I'm happy to do what I can, though."

"Thanks."

"I guess this one's a little too close to home for you." Oliver hoisted his pants around his substantial midsection.

Michael grunted a noncommittal response. The last thing he wanted was to get into a detailed discussion about Kate.

"Come on. I'll show you where the body was found." Oliver led the way toward the creek. "Anything in particular you're looking for?"

"Frank Bowen is leaning toward accidental death. Was that your impression?"

Oliver scratched a fleshy cheek. "Just looking at the body and all, I'd say it could go either way. But you start looking at the bigger picture, he's probably right. She'd been drinking pretty heavily—"

"You referring to the bottle of rum?"

"Well, that, plus we got a call that night. A neighbor reporting a drunk woman prowling the street. Description matches the deceased."

Michael hadn't known about the call. "You have the neighbor's name?"

"Uh-uh. An anonymous 'concerned citizen.' Plus there was no sign of a struggle. Nothing obvious anyway." Oliver pointed to an outcropping of rocks some fifteen feet below. "That's where she fell."

"Facedown?"

"More on her side."

"And you think she came off the bridge?" Hope Lane jogged a bit to the north when it reached Rudgear and then spanned the creek.

"Given the placement of the body, that would be my guess."

"How about possible witnesses? Isn't this a popular spot with some of the homeless?"

Oliver laughed. "Not on a wet winter night. They got a lot of better options."

"Anything on the bridge that might shed light on what happened?'

Oliver shook his head. "Afraid not."

"And up here on the bank?" Michael looked at the area where they were standing. Hard dirt and rock sprinkled with pine needles.

"Only thing of note at all is there." Again Oliver pointed. "The edge of the bank. See how the soil has crumbled away? Doesn't mean much one way or the other though."

Michael had to agree. "Thanks for your help," he said.

"Wish there was more I could tell you."

They headed back to the road. "Who else was out here besides you and Frank?"

"A second patrol unit, couple of people from the coroner's office, forensics—the usual. Oh, and Bill Williams was here for a bit."

"What was he doing here?" Williams was another detective on the force. A new man who'd only been with Walnut Hills a couple of months.

Oliver shrugged. "I think he pulled the assignment first, but then with the victim being one of Frank's cases, Frank took over."

Department politics again, and now Michael was muddying the waters even further. "Well, thanks again."

Back in his car, Michael scribbled a few thoughts in his notebook. Follow up on the call from the concerned citizen, check to see if any fingerprints had been lifted from the shards of the rum bottle. If Frank hadn't already talked with other guests at the motel, that needed to be done.

He'd see what he could do about phone records, too, although that would be tough without a court order. Even with an order, getting a dump of incoming calls would be nearly impossible because of the cost involved. Anything high-tech and expensive got pulled out only for the biggest cases. Which this wasn't. In fact, it wasn't officially even a homicide case.

Michael tapped his fingers on the steering wheel. Without a witness or solid physical evidence, it would be tough sledding. They'd be stuck looking for motive—a wide-open field as a starting place.

He stopped his finger tapping. Hadn't Dick Arnold, the saxophone player in Tully's band, mentioned that Sheryl Ann had called his girlfriend from Idaho? At the time Michael had been excited to discover evidence that Sheryl Ann had in fact *been* in Idaho. Now he focused on the fact of the call itself. You didn't call someone and ask her to take in your mail and newspapers unless she was a friend.

Michael used his cell phone to call Arnold and got an answering machine. He left a message, then headed back to the station.

Michael was standing at the watercooler when Janet asked him if he had a couple of minutes to spend with Sheryl Ann's brother.

"He says he had an appointment with Frank," she explained. "But Frank's not around."

Typical. Frank seemed to have mastered the art of sidestepping responsibility. Normally, Michael would have been irritated, but today he saw it as an opportunity to get information firsthand.

"Sure," he told Janet. "Bring him back."

Michael mentally ran through the short list of things he knew about Clay Potter.

He lived in Bakersfield and was married. Michael remembered the wife's displeasure at Kate's call to their home. And Potter had been in Walnut Hills not long ago looking for Sheryl Ann.

This, despite the fact they hadn't been in touch for years. If memory served him right, she'd run away from home not long after her father and his mother had married, and she hadn't been in contact with any of the family since.

Frank was worried that Potter was shaping up to be a pain in the ass, which probably explained why Frank had conveniently missed today's appointment. That Potter might also be able to shed some light on the investigation was something that had seemingly slipped Frank's mind.

Seeing Potter approach, Michael rose from his desk and introduced himself.

Clay Potter was tall and bony, with a protruding Adam's apple and receding chin. In his mid-thirties, he already had a shiny dome fringed with clipped brown hair. After shaking hands, he stood awkwardly until Michael gestured to a chair.

"I know I have the right time," Potter said. "I had an appointment scheduled with the officer in charge."

Michael nodded. "He's been unavoidably detained. I'm familiar with the case, however, and I'm happy to help. Can I get you some coffee or a soda?"

"No. I just want to get this over with."

"I understand. I'm sorry about Ms. Martin's death."

"It was certainly a shock." Potter took a breath, clearly fighting his emotions.

"Were you close?"

"No." Potter cleared his throat. "I hardly knew her. I was out of college already when her father married my mother. Sheryl Ann left home not long after that. I haven't seen her since." Yet he was shaken, that much was clear.

"You've come to make arrangements for her body, right?"

He nodded. "And for some answers." Potter cleared his throat again. "Detective Bowen said it looked like her death was an accident."

"That's his best guess at the moment. The coroner's report isn't final yet."

Potter shifted uneasily in his chair. Despite the suit and pressed shirt, there was something unpolished about him, as though he were ill at ease outside of his familiar milieu.

"What will that show?" he asked.

"A number of things are possible. The preliminary report shows trauma to the head and body, but we don't know if that's the actual cause of death. Nor has it been determined if the trauma is the result of her fall or something else in addition."

"You mean, whether she was hit over the head first?"

Maybe not so unpolished, after all, Michael thought. "Right. With luck, the coroner will be able to tell if she was alive when she fell, if there were signs of a struggle— that sort of thing."

Potter nodded, absorbing the information. "But so far, nothing has shown up to make them think it was anything but an accident?"

Michael hesitated, wondering if he dared give voice to his own doubts. Finally, he decided against it. "Nothing so far."

Potter relaxed. So much for Frank's worries that the guy was going to be all over them for dropping the ball. To the contrary, he seemed relieved. An observation that Michael noted with interest.

"You were looking for Sheryl Ann prior to her death," Michael said. "You were at the house, spoke with her neighbors. Why the sudden interest in a stepsister you barely knew?"

Potter twisted again, his long frame angled on the edge of his seat. He offered a self-conscious smile. "I thought you might ask that."

Michael waited for him to continue.

"Sheryl Ann's father has terminal cancer," Potter began. "They haven't spoken in years. I gather they didn't get along even when she was still living at home. Then with the tragedy of his first wife's death and his remarriage to my mother, well, things went from bad to worse. Sheryl Ann blamed him and he blamed Sheryl Ann. My mother, I'm sorry to say, probably contributed to it. Now that he's facing his own death . . . well, before that actually, he began to feel the loss. He wanted to mend fences, so to speak. These last few years he's talked about her more and more. Finally, he asked me to help find her."

Too late, Michael thought sadly.

"He wanted to make a provision for her in his will," Potter continued, rubbing his knee.

"What kind of provision?"

"A lump-sum inheritance for sure. Maybe even a share of the business."

Heavy-equipment leasing or some such thing, Michael recalled. Not a business Sheryl Ann would have embraced hands on. "What kind of money are we talking about here?"

"He hadn't worked out the details, but there'd be a couple hundred thousand straight out. The business would be on top of that."

Involuntarily, Michael rocked forward. Money and motive—how many times had he seen that combination? "Who inherits now?"

"I'll get most of it, I guess. Eventually, anyway." Potter was taking his time, answering carefully. "My mother will be well provided for during her lifetime; then what's left will come to me. I'll inherit the business, as well. I've been working with my stepfather since right after their marriage."

Under the desk, Michael tapped his fingers against his knee. He wanted to go slowly. So far Potter seemed oblivious to the fact that he'd just painted himself as a possible suspect. Michael wasn't eager to change that.

"You and your stepfather get along fairly well, I take it."

"Remarkably." There was that smile again, a sort of self-deprecating apology for being. "My mother is a strong woman. Some might even say controlling." He paused. "My wife is a lot like her. They're very close, in fact. The men in the family, the two of us, have found strength in unity, so to speak."

"It must have irked you that he wanted to bring Sheryl Ann back into his life. She'd be getting a portion of your inheritance, after all."

A spark of something—fear? worry?—flickered in Potter's eyes, but his expression didn't change. He shook his head. "No, it didn't bother me," he said.

Michael brushed a loose paper clip to the side of his desk. How hard should he push the guy? This wasn't an interrogation. Wasn't even an official inquiry. But Potter was hiding something.

"Let's not play games," Michael said.

"It's the truth. My stepfather and I have a good relationship. Nothing was going to change that."

"But the money—"

"You sound like my wife," Potter said irritably. "There are more important things in life than money."

Michael sat back. Maybe that explained the wife's displeasure with Kate's call. She was the one with her eye on the money. "I take it she wasn't happy that you were looking for Sheryl Ann."

Potter seemed to realize he'd given away more than he'd intended. "It wasn't her decision," he said, sitting up straighter. "Now, if we can talk about the procedure for releasing the body . . ."

Half an hour later, when he'd gone over the paperwork with Potter and sent him on his way, Michael put in another call to Dick Arnold. Still no answer.

He started for the Snuggle Inn to see what he could learn there. Halfway to the motel, he remembered that he had the name and number of Arnold's girlfriend in his desk. He turned and headed back.

Flipping open his file notes, he found where he'd written down Darla Quick's name and address. Michael was congratulating himself on his turn of good luck when he noticed the red rose and accompanying note on his desk.

> *I'm thinking of you, too. Always.*
> *Love,*
> *G.*

37

Rain hammered the car roof as I sat in the mall parking lot admiring my nails and rehashing my conversation with Darla.

Had Sheryl Ann been mixed up in the moneymaking scheme Tully and Clevenger had concocted? Grabbing my umbrella, I headed back into the mall to find a pay phone and, more important, a phone book.

There were five Clevengers listed, but no Jack, John, or initial *J*. I looked up the number for the Hideaway next and deposited my thirty-five cents.

I got the answering machine. Partway through the message, the phone picked up.

"So what dy'a think?" asked the male voice on the other end.

I hesitated. I had many thoughts, though I was fairly certain none would be of interest to the man who'd posed the question. "I'm looking for Jack Clevenger," I said after a moment.

"Sorry. I thought you were someone else. Clevenger isn't here right now."

Though I'd hoped he would be, I hadn't really expected it. "Could you give me his number?"

"Might be better if you left a message."

"It's important," I said. "Could I speak to the owner?"

"This is Rudy Harrington. I am the owner."

"Ah." Bobby's stepfather. I didn't want to use my real name. With great effort, I drew on my dwindling reserves of perkiness. "My name is Katherine Sommers, and I'm trying to reach Mr. Clevenger about hiring the band."

"Hiring?" Harrington sounded like I'd woken him from a deep sleep.

"They play for hire, don't they? I'm having a party and I'd like—"

"You can leave a message." Harrington's tone was curt. "I'll see that he gets it."

I knew when to cut my losses. "Thank you. Tell him I'd like to speak with him as soon as possible."

I took the back way home from the mall. In the name of freeway improvement, CalTrans had made a two-year mess of traffic near the main Walnut Hills interchange. With the rain and wind, I had the feeling things would be at a standstill. Besides, the back road, which wound through the few remaining orchards and pockets of open space, was far more peaceful—and peace was something I could certainly use.

I pulled out of the parking lot in front of a beige panel truck. When I turned west, the truck did, too. I gave a fleeting thought to the notion that I was being tailed by reporters, before dismissing it as more egocentric than plausible. A small segment of my life might well be news-worthy, but in the scheme of things, I wasn't exactly hot property.

Another possibility, of course, was that I was being followed, but not by reporters. I hadn't forgotten the horror of being attacked in my driveway. Never far from my mind, too, was the possibility that Sheryl Ann was dead because someone had mistaken her for me.

To quiet my growing anxiety, I tried to turn my thoughts to the beauty of the countryside, which glistened with rain. The hills were a lush velvety green and the deciduous trees, though still bare, were swelling with spring buds. Wildflowers had begun popping up here and there, not in the profusion that would follow in the months to come, but enough to signal a change in season.

As I approached the train tracks, I glanced in the rearview mirror and saw the same panel truck some distance back. Or maybe it was a similar truck.

Where the road split, I detoured north to stop by my favorite roadside market. The proprietor, Mara, greeted me with a smile.

"Did you come all the way out here on a day like this just to buy bread and lemons?" she asked when I got to the checkstand. She was dressed in a down parka and rang up my purchases with gloved hands.

"I was in the neighborhood. And the bread alone would be worth the trip."

She laughed. "I think they must sneak some addictive chemical into it. Once people start, they keep buying."

"So that explains it."

She bagged my purchases and handed them to me. "I was sorry to see in the paper this morning that your troubles haven't ended. I am saying a prayer for you."

"Thanks. I can use all the help I can get."

Half a mile down the road, I again noticed the panel truck. Panic swelled in my chest, making it difficult to breathe.

I sped up. So did the truck.

There's nothing to worry about, I told myself. It was broad daylight, even if it was gray and wet. And I wasn't in some deserted warehouse district. There were people around, although in truth there weren't many actually out on the road.

I locked the doors.

All I had to do, I reminded myself, was drive into town where there was plenty of activity. Or to the police station, which was even better.

By the time I pulled into the police lot, the truck was nowhere to be seen. I felt foolish, like a child who imagines monsters behind every piece of furniture. But not foolish enough to head home just yet.

Inside, I looked for Michael, who wasn't at his desk.

Frank spotted me and walked over. "How's it going, Kate?"

"Okay, I guess. Have you seen Michael?"

"He was here just a minute ago. Probably in the rest room or something."

"Maybe he's getting water for this rose." I sniffed the perfectly formed bud that was lying on his desk amid the papers and empty coffee cups. "It's lovely."

Frank tapped the back of Michael's chair with his palm. "You know, I've been meaning to ask—"

His words were cut off by Michael's return. As I expected, his face registered alarm.

"Kate. What are you doing here? Is something wrong?" Michael took my arm with what struck me more as policelike authority than affection.

"Uh, not really. At least, I hope not." I brushed his cheek playfully with the rose. "This is beautiful. Where'd you get it?"

Frank's gaze met Michael's, then slipped away. He

rocked back on his heels. "Catch you later," he said to neither of us in particular, and wandered off.

Michael took the rose from my hand, his expression stiff. "I interviewed a new witness in a car-theft case. His wife grows them."

"She grew this?" Even I knew that you did not grow long-stemmed roses in the backyard.

Michael tossed the rose back onto his desk. "I wish I had time for coffee or something . . ." His hand was still on my upper arm, propelling me toward the door.

I decided this was not the time to mention my fears about the beige van.

As we neared the front entrance, a pretty young woman with straight, shoulder-length hair coming from the other direction winked at him.

"You must be Kate," she said, holding out a hand by way of introduction. "I'm Gina." She was a little taller than me, with the fresh, smooth skin of youth.

"Pleased to meet you."

"Frank's looking for you," Michael said sharply. "You'd better find him before he leaves." With his thumb digging into my upper arm, he dragged me through the door and outside.

"Sounds like you're having a rough day," I told him.

"I'm busy is all. Sorry I don't have more time right now."

"That's okay. I just thought I'd drop by and say hello."

He planted a quick kiss on my forehead. "Glad you did."

I pulled my jacket tight against the cold. It was obvious that he wasn't glad at all.

38

Michael swallowed two Motrin, then popped a third for good measure. He felt as though someone had placed a steel band around his head and was twisting it tighter and tighter. Kate's visit couldn't have come at a worse time.

He'd handled it badly, too, and he felt terrible about that. He'd try to make it up to her this evening. In the meantime, he needed to deal with Gina.

Michael's eyes followed her as she crossed the room to the copier. He'd been watching for a moment when he could find her alone. This seemed as good as any.

She had her back to him, humming softly under her breath, but she must have heard him approach because she turned to greet him with a smile.

" 'These magic moments,' " she began singing, softly enough that only he could hear.

"Gina, we need to talk."

So discreetly did Gina brush a hand against his thigh, it took Michael a moment to recognize what she'd done. "I know we do."

"And you need to listen because so far you aren't—" Michael paused as Frank passed behind them.

This wasn't going to work. Not here. Michael waited until Frank was out of earshot, then said, "Let's grab a cup of coffee at the bagel shop. It'll be easier to talk if we aren't constantly interrupted."

"Sure. Just let me get my jacket."

During the block-long walk to the bagel shop, Gina made several attempts at small talk, which Michael ignored. She huddled close as they stood in line to order, smiling up at him with a flirtatious twinkle in her eye. He ended up paying for her latte because Gina made no attempt to pay for it herself. As their knees brushed under the table, he realized that coming out to talk was probably not such a good idea after all.

He took a sip of coffee, wondering where to begin. Certainly not by humiliating her or making accusations.

"I'm not really sure how this all began," he said, "and I apologize if I misled you, but somehow this ... this thing between us has gotten out of hand."

She smiled. "It does seem to be snowballing."

Christ, he'd managed to give her the wrong impression again. Time to stop mincing words. "I'm not interested in a relationship with you, Gina. Not a romantic relationship."

She dipped her finger into the foamed milk and licked it. "I know you're feeling guilty. You're attracted to me even though you think you shouldn't be. That's nothing to be ashamed of."

"But that's just my point: I'm *not* attracted to you."

She arched her eyebrows playfully. "Really?" Then, with seriousness, added, "I understand what you're going through. In fact, I admire your principles. With Kate's troubles and all, you feel especially loyal."

"It's not loyalty, Gina. It's love."

She seemed to consider this while she sipped her latte. "Maybe you do love her. There are different kinds of love, after all. But you obviously have feelings for me, too. I know it's a difficult situation, but we'll find a way. I'm patient." She smiled again, reached across the table and put her hand on his. "And I'm not asking for the moon, you know."

Michael pulled his hand free. Maybe she was really nuts. Wacko. In that case, nothing he said was going to make a difference.

"Listen, and listen carefully. Please." Michael leaned across the table. "You're an attractive young woman with a good head on her shoulders. You've got a lot going for you. But there is nothing between us, Gina. You need to stop this . . . this pursuing me the way you are."

"*I* need to stop?" She gave him that look again, only this time the playfulness was considerably subdued.

"Yes, you do."

"Funny, I'd have said it was the other way around."

"What do you mean?"

"Weren't you the one who touched my cheek, who traced the curve of my neck and told me you found it sensuous?"

A flash of memory brought him up short. Michael had forgotten the part about her neck. Or maybe he'd suffered selective amnesia. The possibility that there was more he'd conveniently overlooked frightened him.

Michael tried to explain. "The night that you, Frank, Dan, and I went out for drinks—I was feeling lonely, I guess, and a little angry at Kate. I probably drank more than I should have—and I said things I wouldn't have under different circumstances."

"You were listening to your heart."

He shook his head, although at some level there was undoubtedly a degree of truth to what she'd said. "Certainly you are mature enough to understand that people sometimes do and say things they later regret."

"In a moment of weakness, you mean?"

"I suppose. Anyway, it was wrong. I'm sorry that I gave you a mistaken impression. That was never my intention."

"It wasn't just that evening," she said after a moment. "Ever since I started working with you, I knew. The other guys kept their distance, but you'd come by and say hello, ask if I had any questions."

All in the name of goodwill, Michael thought glumly. And look what it had unleashed.

"And the past few weeks . . ." she continued, offering him a sultry smile. "Well, you've made your feelings clear." Her eyes locked on to his. "Very clear."

Michael gripped his coffee cup tightly with both hands. He leveled his gaze at her. "Apparently, I haven't made them clear enough."

"Oh, I'd say you have."

"You've got it wrong, Gina. I am not interested in you, I am not attracted to you, and I'm becoming increasingly annoyed with your refusal to understand that. I don't know how much clearer I can make it."

Confusion and something else, maybe anger, crossed her face. "Do you get a kick out of this? Leading me on and then pushing me away. Is it some kind of ego trip with you?"

"I wasn't leading you on," Michael barked. "You've twisted everything around to fuel some adolescent fantasy—"

"Look who's talking!"

Now he'd managed to insult her, which was the very

thing he'd been trying to avoid. He'd also raised a few curious stares. "I'm sorry," he said, backtracking. "I didn't mean—"

Leaning across the table, she cut him off. "Yes, you did. I've tried to understand where you're coming from, to let you have it both ways; but I have feelings, too, you know. Maybe for you it's all a game. It's not like that for me. You've taken hold of my heart, Michael, and now you want to stick pins in it."

The raw emotion in her tone, and on her face, made him catch his breath. "No, Gina, that's not what I want. It was never my intention to hurt you."

She shoved back her chair and stood facing him. Her cheeks were wet with tears, but what caused her eyes to glisten was anger rather than sorrow.

"Good," she said hotly, "because I don't take pain well." And she stomped out, leaving the rest of her coffee untouched.

A few of the patrons were staring at him openly but most pretended to be otherwise occupied. He was sure they'd all caught the last few exchanges, if not more. He could only hope none of Kate's friends were among them.

39

The good news was that I didn't see a single panel truck between the police station and home. It did not, however, compensate for the brush-off I'd received from Michael. That hurt so much I couldn't think about it without feeling shaky.

Gathering the day's mail, weighted as usual with catalogues and commercial pitches, I opened the door, then gave the house a quick check before stepping inside. Everything looked to be as I'd left it. I put the kettle on for coffee and checked the answering machine. Two reporters and a hang-up.

I was starting back to the kitchen when I noticed a fax had come in. No doubt another advertisement. Every step forward in technology seemed to bring new avenues for unsolicited junk.

But the minute I lifted the paper from the tray, I knew this was something different. It was a short note, typed in cursive script.

They say the wife is always the last to know.
And you aren't even his wife.

My hand was quaking. No signature, no originating phone number. Just those two sentences. Yet I felt as though a slimy three-headed monster had invaded my home and wrapped itself around me.

From the kitchen came the sizzling sound of water boiling onto the burner. I raced to turn the kettle off, then sat at the table, stupefied. My body seemed to be made of Jell-O.

Was it true? Was Michael having an affair? It would certainly explain his recent behavior, and the rose on his desk. Until today, I'd been willing to write off the distracted demeanor and sleepless nights to his concern about me. Now, I felt like an idiot.

I was also hurt and terribly afraid. I loved Michael. Loved what we had together. With sudden clarity, I realized what a burden I'd become to him. How difficult I'd made things at work. How much of my energy had been focused on myself of late.

As had become my habit in times of crisis, I picked up the phone and called Sharon.

"I have a problem," I told her.

"I hate to break it to you, Kate, but you've got more than one. You're the queen of problems."

"This isn't funny."

"Sorry." She turned serious. "What is it?"

My gaze fell again to the fax and I felt tears threaten. "Can you come over? I'd rather not go into it over the phone."

"The gutter man is here, and I've got a dentist appointment at two. How about we meet for coffee after that?"

I wasn't sure I'd be able to swallow a sip, but I need her company. "Okay."

"What the hell, I'll cancel the dentist," Sharon said after a moment. "And who cares about gutters?"

"Later this afternoon is fine."

"You're sure?" She paused.

"Absolutely."

"Okay. The Granary at three?"

"See you then."

For the next two hours I watched the clock and wandered aimlessly from room to room; then I stuffed the fax into my purse and went to meet Sharon.

"You think *what?*" Sharon's reaction was about what I expected. What my own would have been in her shoes.

"Michael's been so distracted lately," I said. "He's not himself at all. I thought it was because of this stuff with my being abducted and Bobby's murder. But that isn't it."

"You don't know that."

"It makes sense, though. Things between us began to change even before Bobby and Sheryl Ann came into the picture. I talked to you about it. Remember?"

Sharon dipped the tip of her biscotti in coffee. "Lots of couples go through periods like that. It doesn't mean one of them is having an affair, for God's sake."

"You're forgetting the fax." I waved the paper in front of her face for emphasis. "And the rose on his desk this morning."

"I don't see why you're so willing to accept that as—"

"Because it fits—that's why." I threw myself back against the chair. "How could I have been so blind? It's just like with Andy. You'd have thought I'd learn."

"That's why you're overacting, Kate. Because of Andy. But it's *not* the same."

My ex-husband, Andy, had calmly announced over breakfast one morning that he'd quit his job, was taking half our meager savings and heading off for Europe to "find himself." I shouldn't take it personally, he explained. It was simply that domestic life had lost its allure. And the Italian model he'd hooked up with in Switzerland had obviously helped him forget the banality of being a husband and father.

"Maybe not exactly the same," I said, staring into my coffee mug. "But rejection is rejection."

"Kate, you're being a jerk. Michael is not having an affair."

"How would you know?"

"Because I know Michael."

"Maybe you only *think* you know him. I would have said the same thing myself not so long ago."

Sharon sighed. "Before you go flying off the handle, at least see what he has to say. The two of you need to sit down and talk this through."

"I don't know; I was thinking maybe I should hire a private investigator first, before I confront—"

"I said *talk*, not confront." She reached across the table for my hand. "Kate, you've been under a tremendous amount of stress. It's understandable that you'd be easily upset. But I have to tell you, I think you're close to losing control."

There was a draft in the restaurant, and I pulled my sweater tighter across my chest for warmth. "You may be right about losing it. But the fax—"

"There are a lot of weirdos out there. And your name has been in the news for a couple of weeks."

She had a point. "You think this is some kind of practical joke?"

"A mean-spirited one. I wouldn't give it any credence until you've talked with Michael."

Easy to say, but hard to do. My mind had a mind of its own.

Sharon finished her coffee and biscotti. I pushed my cup away, still two-thirds full.

We exited the restaurant into a torrent of rain. "Wouldn't you know it?" Sharon said. "I leave my umbrella in the car, and now it's pouring."

"We can share mine. I'll walk you to your car."

"I'm in that little alley along the back."

We huddled under my umbrella and rounded the block to the narrow street behind the restaurant. At the far end, two men were standing close, deep in conversation.

"There's Frank Bowen," I told her, steering us around a puddle. "Maybe I should ask *him* about Michael."

"I wouldn't advise it," Sharon muttered.

I rolled my eyes. "I was joking. You think I'd air my dirty laundry in public like that? Especially since Michael and Frank aren't exactly buddy-buddy."

Sharon turned to look at the two men again. "In case you're interested, that man he's talking to is Rudy Harrington, Bobby Lake's father."

I looked again. Harrington was heavyset, a bit shorter than Frank. He had dark hair and a fleshy face. He looked nothing like Bobby. But then, he was Bobby's stepfather, so there wouldn't be a resemblance.

Frank looked up and saw me. Or I thought he saw me. When I waved, he turned his back toward us.

"Doesn't look like they want to be disturbed," I said.

"I wonder if there's been some new development in Bobby's murder case."

Or maybe Frank was keeping an eye on me as a possible suspect.

We reached Sharon's car and I held the umbrella while she climbed inside.

"Thanks for listening, Sharon. And for the advice. I hope you're right."

"I'm willing to bet on it," she said.

I wished I felt as confident.

40

People without children can give their emotions free reign. Feel like making love before dinner? Go for it. You're in a pissy mood? Let those accusations fly.

But when children enter the picture, scheduling becomes an issue. Even serious, rational discussions require advance planning. Not that I was any too sure I was going to be rational about it.

I sent Libby and Anna out for the evening, paying Libby twice the going baby-sitter rate to ensure her cooperation. I also set the table and had dinner in the oven by the time Michael arrived home. That way there'd be no last-minute preparations to get in our way.

I rehearsed what I wanted to say and how I wanted to say it. Calmly, rationally. My insides felt like they'd been through a meat grinder, but I wasn't going to give him the satisfaction of knowing that.

I fully intended to hold off discussing the fax until we'd had a glass of wine and unwound a bit. Instead, I hit him with it the minute he walked through the door. Michael had brought me flowers—a beautiful bouquet of roses that only made me more suspicious. I didn't even thank him.

"Who's the woman?" I demanded, tossing the flowers onto the floor.

"The woman?" Michael's expression hadn't been particularly cheerful to begin with, and now it was downright pained.

"Don't play stupid with me."

"I'm not—"

"The least you could do is admit it." Angrily, I handed him the fax. "Guess this explains why you were in such a hurry to hustle me out of your office this afternoon."

"I wasn't—"

"Don't give me that. You couldn't wait to be rid of me."

Michael grabbed the fax. His face was impassive, but I could see a pulse flutter in his jaw. "When did you get this?"

"It was waiting this afternoon when I got home."

"What time?"

"What does it matter?" My wrath had burned itself out, and a forlorn loneliness had taken its place. "Is it true?" I asked. "Are you having an affair?"

Michael reread the fax. His face was pale, and his jaw continued to twitch. But he didn't rush to proclaim his innocence.

"You're involved with someone, aren't you?"

"Goddamn it." Michael tossed the fax on the table. "No, Kate, I am not having an affair."

The words were right, but not the tone. I felt my throat tighten. "There's a *but* in there, isn't there? You're not having an affair, *but . . .*"

His mouth was tight. "This is not the way I wanted to tell you."

His words were like slivers of ice thrust into my chest. "Tell me what?"

"Let's sit down and talk about this, okay."

I snapped at him. "Don't patronize me. Just tell me what's going on."

"It's complicated."

First Andy and now Michael. *Dumping Kate* was becoming a national pastime.

"Maybe we should sit down," Michael said.

He sat at one end of the couch, I perched on the other. Our regular places, but both of us were so stiff that nothing about it felt familiar.

Michael pressed his fingertips together, studying them. Then he looked up. "There's no truth to the fax, Kate. I am not having an affair. I am not involved with anyone but you." He paused. "At least not willingly. But there's a woman at work, a girl really—"

"What's her name?" My throat was so dry I could barely form the words.

He hesitated. "Gina Nelson."

My stomach clenched. *Gina.* The woman who'd introduced herself to me this afternoon. The name Michael had inadvertently dropped some weeks back, then denied mentioning.

"She's a criminal justice student at the college," he explained.

A younger woman. Pretty, bright-eyed, and perky.

"She's developed some strange infatuation with me. I have to admit that at first it was kind of flattering. But then it . . ." He ran his tongue over his lower lip. "It makes me very uncomfortable."

"The rose on your desk was from her?"

He nodded.

A young woman with a crush, or a two-way flirtation? "What other things does she do?"

Michael looked away. "Little stuff. Notes, coming up to me at odd moments." An embarrassed silence. "Telling me we're meant for each other."

"And you don't encourage her?"

He shook his head.

"Why didn't you just tell her to stop?"

"I've tried to talk to her, but she doesn't want to listen. Then this afternoon after you left, I tried again, more forcefully. I laid it on the line. Now I think she's angry." His tone was pained. I knew Michael well enough to see that he was genuinely upset.

I felt the pounding in my chest begin to subside. He wasn't having an affair. There was no *other woman*, not in the sense I was worried about. "Have you reported this?"

"No. I should have. That's clear now, but I kept thinking she'd get over it." He sounded miserable. "Now I'm afraid I've made things worse."

"Why didn't you tell me before this?" Even if there wasn't another woman, it still hurt to know he hadn't been open with me.

"I don't know," Michael said. "In the beginning I didn't think it was worth mentioning. Especially because things were a little strained between us." He punctuated the remark with a tentative smile. "And I didn't want to worry you. Then there was this whole thing with your abduction and Bobby's murder. Somehow the timing never seemed right."

"So you were just going to keep quiet about it? Forever?"

"I guess I'm not used to sharing what's bothering me. Part of that is the cop's way of keeping the job contained.

But part of that is probably me, too." Michael reached for my hand. "I worry you'll think less of me."

"Think less of you for sharing what you're feeling?"

He nodded. "You'll learn that I'm not always in control."

I smiled. "Of course not. You're human."

"But still—"

"Michael, that's what love is about. Not pretending."

"I know. I'm learning." He pulled me to his end of the couch and circled my shoulder with his arm. "Anyway, that's the story. I'm not having an affair. You are the only woman in my life, and in my heart. And I'm worried sick about where this is going."

I nestled against the familiar contours of Michael's body and relaxed for the first time all day. "You think it was Gina who sent this fax?"

"It sounds like something she might do. But the timing doesn't make sense. Seems to me she'd have been more likely to send it *after* our conversation."

"Maybe there's a Linda Tripp in her life."

His laugh was hollow. "God, I hope not."

"You're telling me the truth, aren't you? I couldn't bear it if you lied to me."

"I wouldn't lie to you, Kate." He turned to face me. "Especially not about something as important as this."

Michael's lips brushed my cheeks. I thought of the dinner in the oven and remembered that, for once, we were free to ignore it.

"If you ever get tired of me," I said, pulling his hand across my chest, "I want you to tell me. I'd rather know than worry like I have been."

"It's not going to happen, Kate. I—"

The front door flew open. I sat up as Anna charged into the room, followed by Libby.

"I threw up," Anna announced.

Libby shot me an apologetic look. "I didn't think you'd want me to take her to the movies if she wasn't feeling well."

"No, of course not."

Michael turned away and, as unobtrusively as possible, began tucking in his shirt, which had come loose in the snuggling.

I felt Anna's forehead. It was warm, and her eyes looked glassy. "Let's take your temperature and get you to bed," I told her.

As I left the room, I gave Michael an apologetic smile, which he returned with warmth and understanding.

Libby trailed after me. "I didn't know if she was really sick."

"It feels like she has a slight fever."

"I'm sorry." Libby tugged at the zipper of her jacket. "I know you and Michael wanted some time alone."

Her tone was hesitant. I couldn't tell if she was afraid I'd be mad or was worried that Michael and I were having problems. Maybe both.

I gave her a hug. "You did just the right thing. I'm glad you brought Anna home, and everything is fine here."

Some Tylenol for her fever, a story to settle her in, and Anna was sound asleep. Michael was putting the finishing touches on the salad when I returned to the kitchen.

"How is she?" he asked.

"Asleep, for now. I'll check on her in a bit. With luck, she'll be her usual bouncing self by morning." I wrapped my arms around his waist. "Too bad they couldn't have given us another ten minutes."

He laughed. "Ten minutes? What did you have in mind, the express stop?"

I poked him in the ribs. "Don't push your luck, mister."

"I think I already have," he replied soberly.

We were halfway through dinner when Michael, with offhand nonchalance, asked, "What was your take on Darla Quick?"

I put down my fork and swallowed. "How'd you know I spoke with Darla?"

"I'm a cop. Investigating suspicious deaths is what I do. And since Darla was a friend of Sheryl Ann's, I talked with her."

I swallowed again, this time out of nervousness. "When?"

"This afternoon." He smiled. "Not long after you did."

The smile was reassuring. He wasn't mad. "What do you mean, 'investigating?' Isn't this Frank's case?"

Michael nodded. "But I have a vested interest in seeing it solved. And quickly." He paused. "Your name keeps popping up, Kate."

"I'm not happy about that either."

Michael speared a wedge of avocado from the salad. "That's why I'm staying involved, though with Frank it's tricky. I have to be doubly careful not to step on his toes."

"Why don't you like him?"

"I'm not sure *liking* is the point." Michael was silent a moment. "It's not something I can easily put my fingers on. I guess what it comes down to is that he's a bit too taken with his own power and importance."

It was, in my experience, a description that fit a good number of men. Frank was a bit rough around the edges, like some of the fraternity boys I'd known in college, but I'd always found him easy company.

"And he's lazy," Michael added. "He cuts corners, always looking for a quick fix. Maybe more than that." Michael seemed ready to elaborate, then apparently changed his mind. "Anyway, I want you off the hook."

"Likewise."

"I want Bobby Lake's killer found," he continued. "I want to know what happened to Tully's body. And I want to know if Sheryl Ann's death was an accident."

I looked him in the eye. "It wasn't. I'm sure of it. Like Darla said, Sheryl Ann didn't even like the outdoors. She wouldn't have gone for a walk on a rainy night."

"Darla knew Sheryl Ann fairly well?"

"I thought you talked to her yourself."

Michael nodded. "What else did she tell you?"

I set my fork on the table. "Tully was in debt big-time. He needed cash, and he needed it badly, as in yesterday. Sheryl Ann told me the same thing."

"Sounds reasonable. Apparently, he was quite a gambler."

"Darla also said that Tully and Clevenger were involved in some moneymaking scheme. She thought it might have been illegal, or at least something that pushed the edges. Do you suppose Sheryl Ann could have been part of it?"

"What do you think?"

"She never talked like she was." Then again, it wasn't easy to get a straight story out of Sheryl Ann. "Darla told me Clevenger had been asking about Sheryl Ann, *and* that he'd gotten a phone call from her the night she died. He has caller ID, so he knew where to find her."

Michael leaned forward, pulled on the lobe of his left ear. "It hit me this afternoon that the killer may have been after Sheryl Ann all along, and Bobby's death was just peripheral. If it turns out Clevenger was in Idaho at the time . . ."

"He would have known Sheryl Ann was there because of her call to Darla." I felt a surge of excitement. "What did you learn from Darla?"

He eyed me with amusement. "Not as much as you did."

"Really?"

"People sometimes clam up around law-enforcement types, even those of us who are gentle, sensitive, and compassionate. Which is why, *on occasion*"—he patted my hand to underscore the limited parameters—"it's nice to have your input."

"Is that a compliment?"

"The genuine article." His fingers found mine and nestled around them. "Just remember the caveats."

The day had begun so abysmally, and now here we were, a team again. It felt incredibly good.

I was up early the next morning, filled with a kind of energy and enthusiasm I hadn't known for weeks. It was all going to work out.

Anna was feeling better, so I sent her off to school, then went for a walk and ended up jogging instead. A high-stepping, aerobic jog that brought a glow to my cheeks. Then I took a long, hot shower and began working on the paper collage that had stymied me earlier.

A little before noon I heard the mail truck making its way around the neighborhood, and I went to empty the box. Bills and junk mail for the most part, a bank statement, and a letter hand addressed to me—from the Snuggle Inn.

Above the logo, Sheryl Ann had inked in her own name.

41

Clutching Sheryl Ann's letter in my hand, I was reminded of the time several years ago when I'd accidentally replayed an old phone message from a friend who had since died. There was something haunting and unreal about it.

Finally, I tore open the envelope and pulled out a single sheet of paper. A small metal key fell to the floor. It looked as though it might fit a commercial storage locker of the sort you found at airports and public pools.

I ignored the key and turned to the note.

> *Kate—if this reaches you it means either I've screwed up (again) or that I'm in trouble (again).*
>
> *The man at the desk says the mail isn't picked up till after ten, so if all goes well I can retrieve the letter tomorrow morning before it's mailed. If not, well, that's why you're reading this, isn't it?*
>
> *I didn't tell you before, but I think Tully was in trouble. Maybe I'm just paranoid (having the police on your tail will do that—are you sure turning myself in is the right thing to do?), but I'm scared. And I think the key may be the key. (Ha,ha. Key, key, get it?) The key was in Tully's*

pocket when he died. I have no idea what it's for, but when
he came home that day he was saying something about "key
to happiness." And like I said, I'm scared.

My throat hurts, my head aches and I'm not thinking
clearly. But I feel like you're my friend (even though you
probably don't think of me that way), and I'm so grateful
to you for helping me. I really wanted to stay at your house,
but I guess I can understand why you didn't want me to.

> *Your buddy (ha ha),*
> *Sheryl Ann*

P.S. I've decided the ginger smell must be aftershave or
cologne. For some reason it makes me think of the opening
song the band usually played.

My first reading of the note was so clouded with emotion that the words didn't register. It wasn't until I'd
taken a deep breath and read through again, slowly, that
I began to understand what she was telling me.

I picked up the key and examined it. The only marking
was a series of numbers. Numbers that probably identified
the locker. But nothing that indicated *where* the locker
might be. Mentally, I began going through the options.
Oakland airport? That was closer but the San Francisco
airport was much larger. Bus terminal? Train station?
Maybe a gym or pool. The longer I thought about it, the
more numerous the possibilities. Still, the key was more
than we'd had before.

My skin tingled with excitement. I tried calling Michael.
He wasn't available. Frank was, and I almost asked to
speak with him instead, until I remembered what Michael
had said last night. If Frank was the sort of cop who

wanted easy solutions, he wasn't going to wear out any shoe leather looking for the right locker. Especially when it wasn't clear that the key had any bearing on Sheryl Ann's death.

I checked the clock. Three hours before I picked Anna up from school. Enough time to check a few places myself.

Oakland International Airport is far more user-friendly than its counterpart in San Francisco. Parking is easy, and there are only two terminals, a short walk from each other. The key from Tully's pocket was similar to the ones that fit lockers in the first terminal, but not identical. I checked the numbers anyway, just to be sure. They didn't correspond.

My experience was the same at the Southwest Airlines terminal. As I scanned the concourse, hoping for an additional bank of lockers, I noticed a man leaning against a nearby wall, reading the newspaper. Unremarkable except for the fact that I was reasonably sure I'd seen him in the first terminal I'd checked, as well. He wasn't wearing a blue windbreaker, but he had the same unruly dark hair and sallow complexion as the man Sharon and I had seen at the reservoir and outside Anna's school.

My heart rate picked up. Perspiration gathered on my forehead. Was my imagination running wild? With all that had happened, I wouldn't be surprised. Still, I wasn't taking chances. If it was the same man, that made three times I'd seen him in the last few days.

I started toward the main entrance, then stopped at the ATM machine and glanced back. The man was no longer standing where he had been, and I didn't see him in the oncoming throng of passengers. To be safe, I stopped at an airport shop and bought a pack of gum. Still no sign of the man.

Looking over my shoulder, I scurried to the car and locked the doors behind me. Slowly, the knot in my stomach began to relax.

Before calling it a day, I tried the AmTrak station, the bus station, and the Walnut Hills Airfield—all to no avail.

Having run through the obvious possibilities, I was feeling discouraged. The odds of finding the correct locker seemed formidable. I suspected they would appear equally so to the police, who, despite considerable resources, would be reduced to the same trial-and-error approach I'd tried.

At least they had extra manpower to assign to the search—assuming they wanted to.

I had the terrible feeling they wouldn't be interested.

42

Michael spent the morning in court on an unrelated case and didn't get to the station until noon. Gina wasn't at her desk. From the looks of it, she hadn't been in at all that day. He breathed a sigh of relief.

At least things were out in the open now with Kate. He felt good about that. Sorry about the way it had happened, but happy that he'd finally been forced to tell her. Something he should have done when this whole thing started.

And Kate had gotten some useful information from Darla. He was happy about that, too. Clearly, it was time he paid another visit to Jack Clevenger.

Janet called to him as he headed to his desk. "There's a call for you. Adam O'Neil. You want to take it?"

Michael ran the name through the data bank in his head. O'Neil. It was familiar but he couldn't place it.

"About a stolen BMW," Janet added.

Right, his neighbor's son-in-law. A good-deed follow-up to a stolen car. Just what he didn't need at the moment. He had a full plate already, but nodded. "I'll pick it up at my desk."

"Sorry to bother you," Adam began.

"Not a problem. But I don't have anything new to report."

"That's not why I'm calling. I mean, it is, only I have something for you."

"How's that?"

"This guy down the street by the name of Charlie Guff. He's got a fancy new Porsche, mag wheels and all. He usually parks it in the garage, but his wife had the garage filled with rummage sale stuff, so last night he parked the car on the street."

"If it was stolen, he needs to file a report with the patrol officer."

"No, that's just it. It wasn't stolen. Guff happened to look out the window and see someone messing with his car. He chased the guy away, but he got a look at him first. You think maybe it's the same one who took my car?"

Michael leaned an elbow on his desk. "Hard to say. Unfortunately, car theft is not uncommon."

"You want to talk to him, he's home right now."

Michael pressed his knuckles to his forehead and groaned silently.

"I told him I'd give you a call. I'd sure like to catch that creep who drove off with my car."

Reluctantly, Michael took Guff's name and number. Between Sheryl Ann's death and his troubles with Gina, an auto theft wasn't high priority. On the other hand, this was a problem he could easily tackle.

"I'll try to get out there today," Michael said.

"Thanks. Maybe this is the break you need. I certainly hope so."

"That makes two of us." Michael grabbed the notes he'd taken yesterday when he was going through Sheryl

Ann's file. He had a full afternoon, but fifteen minutes spent talking to Guff wasn't going to set him back.

He was reaching for his jacket when Frank gestured to him from across the room. "I wanted to thank you for taking that interview with Sheryl Ann Martin's brother the other day. I plumb forgot about it."

"Not a problem. The guy's not looking to make waves, though. In fact, he seemed relieved that we're not calling her death suspicious."

"That's good to hear."

"You're still looking at the possibility it is, aren't you?"

"Of course." Frank's voice lacked conviction.

"Because the guy looks an awful lot like a suspect himself." Michael recounted the highlights of his conversation with Clay Potter, then paused. "Kate said she saw you talking with Rudy Harrington yesterday. Is there a new development I haven't heard about?"

"No." Frank paused, his expression guarded. "Just routine follow-through."

Michael felt a tremor of uneasiness. What was Frank not telling him? He started to push for more information, but Janet appeared just then and stood next to Michael.

"Sorry to interrupt, but it's the same guy. He said to tell you Charlie Guff is expecting you."

"Who's Guff?" Frank asked.

"A guy who saw a prowler hanging around his shiny new Porsche. He lives down the street from our neighbor's son-in-law, who had his new BMW ripped off a week or so ago."

Frank squinted at him. "You working auto detail now?"

"I'm working at being the good neighbor. I talked with their son-in-law as a favor, and now it looks like I'm in up to my eyeballs."

"Happens that way, doesn't it?" Frank chewed on his lower lip a moment. "Did Guff get a good look at the guy?"

"I won't know till I talk to him. Why?"

Frank shrugged. "Just curious."

"My guess is it's more like 'young, dark, medium build.' The sort of generic description that's no help at all."

Charlie Guff opened the door before Michael had a chance to ring the bell. He was a ruddy-faced man, thick around the middle, with a bristle of curly gray hair.

"Hey, good of you to come out so quickly. Adam must have a pipeline straight to police central." He laughed with good-old-boy humor. "Come on in. Can I get you anything?"

"No, thanks." Michael took a seat in the den where Guff had set up a home office. The electronics, Michael noted with envy, were all top of the line. "Mr. O'Neil tells me you saw someone casing the neighborhood last night, and your car in particular."

"Right. About two o'clock. I work at night sometimes. My brain cells kick into gear about the time most folks are heading for bed. I happened to look out the window, and I saw this guy sizing up my Porsche."

Guff scooted his chair closer to Michael. "You have to understand I don't usually leave it out on the street. I'm not that stupid. Plus I know Adam just had his car ripped off. But the church is having this rummage sale, and my wife said they could—"

Michael interrupted. "Adam told me. What I'm interested in is what you saw. Why do you think the guy had his eye on your car?"

"He was standing next to it, up close." Guff's voice

exploded with remembered indignation. "He had a wire or something in his hand. If I'd been a minute later, I bet he'd have been in the car and gone."

"What did you do when you saw him?"

"I went outside and yelled at him, which I realize now was pretty stupid. The guy could have shot me, or pulled a knife. But right then, I was mad. Mad as hell."

"Did you get a good look at him?"

"Damn right I did. The streetlight's directly overhead. You'd think that would be something of a deterrent, wouldn't you? But these young punks think they're invincible."

"He was young?" Michael asked. That was usually the case.

"Early twenties I'd say. Shorter than me, so maybe 5'6". Slight build. Dark hair, shaved on the sides. Oriental, Asian, whatever the PC term of the moment is. And he had one of those little chin beards. Like a goatee— only just the tip of his chin."

"Anything else? How about distinguishing marks, that sort of thing."

Guff scowled as he delved into his memory for detail. "His lower lip was pierced right here." Guff pointed to a spot on his own face. "Looked like a diamond stud."

Michael had been taking notes, but he stopped now and looked up. "You sure about that?"

"Absolutely. I just bought my wife a pair of diamond earrings, so I've got my eye tuned to stuff like that. It was a good-sized diamond, too, if it was real. How'd a punk kid get that kind of money? I ask you. Stealing cars, right?"

"You think you'd recognize him if you saw him again?"

"Pretty sure I would."

Michael could feel the tingle of excitement across his shoulders, but he didn't want to get his hopes up. There were lots of kids with pierced body parts these days, even lots of Asian kids with skimpy goatees. But in light of Guff's description, he was certainly going to pay Jason Liao another visit.

Although it was close to 2:00 P.M. when Michael pounded on the door, Liao appeared sleepy-eyed, and his hair was in tufts like he'd just woken up.

"Hey, man." Liao blinked at the light of day. "What are you doing here?"

"I came to see you." Michael stepped inside without waiting to be invited. The apartment was messy with food wrappers, beer bottles, and assorted articles of clothing, but it was furnished with a leather sofa and chairs, a big-screen television, and a state-of-the-art sound system. Jason lived well.

"I already told you. I don't know nothing about my uncle's death."

"Yeah, I remember."

Liao picked up a pack of cigarettes from the couch and lit one. Taking a long drag, he blew smoke in Michael's direction.

"What time did you get in last night?" Michael asked.

"Last night?" It clearly hadn't been a question he expected. "I dunno. Late."

"Before three?"

"I didn't check the clock."

"Where were you?"

"Out." He rubbed his eyes. "With friends."

"Which friends?" Michael asked. "Give me some names."

Liao sneered. "Tom, Dick, and Harry."

"Last names?"

"I don't know their last names. We're, like, casual."

"Sure." Michael stepped closer. "I'd say you're, like, lying."

"Since when is it against the law to be out at night, huh? I don't have to tell you nothin'."

"A gentleman over on Pine Manor says he saw you nosing around his car last night. That's the same area where a BMW disappeared last week. You know anything about that?"

There was a flicker of alarm in Liao's eyes. Michael was sure of it. But Jason shook his head. "Hey, man, I got my own car. Don't need no yuppy BMW."

"That so?" Michael pulled a camera out of his pocket and snapped a picture.

"Hey, what are you doing?"

"Just a little token of remembrance, Jason. I have a whole scrapbook full of friends I don't want to forget."

Michael was back at his desk, rolling a pen between his palms and trying to figure out how to proceed with Liao, when the captain buzzed him.

"I'd like to see you in my office," Greyson said stiffly. "Now."

Alarm spiked in Michael's chest. Was there fresh evidence against Kate?

No, there couldn't be. Or could there? Michael remembered Frank's uneasiness earlier when he'd asked if there were any new developments. He pushed the thought away. Maybe the captain had gotten wind of Michael's unofficial investigation. Not good, but nothing he couldn't handle. Wouldn't be the first time Michael found himself on the receiving end of a tongue-lashing.

But there was something about Greyson's manner that made Michael's gut clench. Whatever the captain wanted, it wasn't routine.

Greyson's office was no bigger than Michael's, but it had a window. Michael hadn't even had an office until he moved from San Francisco to Walnut Hills, so he wasn't complaining. Still, he could never enter the tiny space without thinking what a difference a window made.

"Close the door," Greyson said, without looking up. When he did finally raise his eyes in greeting, Michael could see that his expression was troubled.

"Gina Nelson came to see me this afternoon," Greyson said.

Michael felt the words fall upon him like a long, dark shadow. He swallowed. His mouth was dry as cotton. "What did she want?"

"She's filed a sexual harassment complaint. She claims you made suggestive remarks, improper advances, and that you used your position in the department to pressure her in ways that made her uncomfortable."

For a moment, Michael was too stunned to speak. He rocked back in his chair, shaking his head. "What? That's not true."

"It's not up to me to take sides," Greyson said. "A complaint has been filed. We have to follow procedure."

"But what she told you is totally not true. In fact, it's the other way around. She developed an infatuation for me. She's been finding excuses, trumping up situations for us to be alone."

Greyson was quiet a moment; then he said simply, "Don't do this, Michael."

"Don't do what?"

"This pointing the finger back at her."

"I'm telling you the truth." Michael was outraged. "If anything, she's been harassing me."

Greyson rubbed his temples. "I know you've been under a lot of pressure lately, maybe you and Gina had a . . . a fling or something. I'm not suggesting it's all as one-sided as she makes it sound, but you are her superior. It's up to you to use good judgment and set an example."

"Whoa, stop. Listen to me. You've got this wrong. We did not have a fling. We did not have any kind of relationship, period. I tried to be friendly, and she misinterpreted it. I've explained that to her. I've told her repeatedly that there is nothing between us and never will be. That's what all this is about. She's angry, or hurt, or maybe just plain crazy."

Greyson eyed Michael critically, his bushy brows still as sleeping caterpillars. "She showed me some of your notes."

"My what? I never wrote her any notes." Michael tried to remember if he'd *ever* written Gina anything. Certainly nothing personal. Nothing that could be construed as suggestive.

"The one, for example, where you made reference to the, uh, provocative unfolding of a pink rosebud." Greyson was clearly embarrassed. He kept his eyes focused on a spot to the left of the door.

Michael looked at him in disbelief. "Not possible. I never said anything like that. Never! She's delusional."

"I saw the note, Michael."

"Was it my handwriting?"

"It was typed. But it was signed with the initial M, exactly the way you sign your memos."

Michael shook his head. "Whatever you saw, it didn't come from me. I swear to it."

"So you deny there's any substance to her complaint?"

"Damn right I do."

"I'm sorry it's come to this, Michael. I realized that the timing is particularly bad." Greyson hesitated. "But my hands are tied. I'm going to have to place you on administrative leave until this can be sorted out."

"You can't do that!"

"I can. I have to, in fact, though it pains me to do so. I'll make every effort to see that this is handled as expeditiously as possible."

Michael opened his mouth to protest further but Greyson silenced him with his hand.

"Don't dig yourself in deeper than you already are."

43

Something was wrong. It was obvious to me the minute Michael walked through the door. His mouth was grim, his expression tight. He managed to look angry and forlorn at the same time.

"What is it?" I asked, going to him. "Something about Sheryl Ann?"

He shook his head, looked at me. "I've been put on administrative leave."

"You've been . . . Whatever for?"

Without answering, he headed for the bedroom, where he flung his jacket angrily on the floor. He sat on the bed and punched the mattress with his fist.

"Michael, what happened? Is it because of me?" First Bobby's death and now Sheryl Ann's. Without meaning to, I'd put him in a terrible position at work.

He sighed heavily. "It's not you, Kate. It's Gina."

"Gina?"

"She's filed a harassment complaint."

I felt a flutter in my chest. "I thought she was the one—"

"She was." His tone was bitter.

"Then how could—"

"She claims I've been sending her love notes, flowers, hints of my affection. *And* that I threatened to influence her evaluation if she didn't cooperate."

Dumbfounded, I sat on the bed next to Michael. A niggle of doubt stirred beneath my breastbone. "But that's not what happened. Is it?"

"No, that's not what happened." He took my hands and looked me level in the eye. "Kate, what I told you was the truth. Gina's story is pure fabrication. It's so far off the mark, she's got to be making it up intentionally."

"Why would she do that?"

He shook his head. "Beats me."

"So it's your word against hers?"

He hesitated. "Worse than that. She has some notes—"

"What notes?" My chest felt ready to explode.

He held up a hand. "I didn't send them. They're typed and signed with an initial only. They could have come from anyone. My sneaking suspicion is that she sent them herself, but how am I going to prove that?"

"Greyson knows you. So do your fellow officers. They must know—"

Michael shook his head. "It won't hold water, Kate."

"She can't make these wild accusations stick."

"Even if I'm vindicated in the end, it's going to be a messy business getting there."

"But that's so unfair!"

He nodded, then dropped his head to his hands. "Yeah." The word was a short stab of sound carried on a wave of despair, and I felt helpless in the face of it.

"It will work out, Michael. The men on the force know you and respect you."

I hugged him and massaged his shoulders with the palm of my hand.

"I deal with people every day," he said finally. "People who break laws, bend laws, thumb their noses at morality. I see humankind at its worst. Why, then, do I continue to assume that most people are decent? Why does it surprise me that she would stoop to something like this?"

"It's because *you're* decent. You're one of the most decent human beings I know. Others understand that, too. It will work out, Michael. I know it will."

He sighed. "I wish I had your confidence."

Later that evening, I found him in the den watching a basketball game on television. Rather, the television was on, but Michael was staring out the darkened window.

"What does administrative leave mean exactly?" I asked, sitting beside him. "Are you still free to work on police matters?"

He gave me a quizzical look.

"This is bad timing, I know, but . . ." I handed him Sheryl Ann's letter. "It came in the mail today."

When Michael had finished reading the note, he looked up. "It doesn't sound like she was planning on killing herself, does it?"

"No. Doesn't sound like she was ready to head out for a walk in the rain, either."

He flipped off the television and read the note again. "This ginger aftershave she's talking about—that's the scent she noticed in the cabin after Bobby was killed?"

"Right. And she associated it with the band. That points to Clevenger. Only it doesn't sound like Sheryl Ann was part of whatever they were up to."

"I wonder what's in the locker this key fits."

I told him about my search that afternoon. "I didn't have a chance to check the San Francisco airport."

"You'd have wasted your time. Their lockers are electronically keyed. Put in your money, punch a code, and when you come back, you punch the code again. Very few of the major airports use keys anymore."

"Still, that leaves hundreds of places that might have lockers. Can Frank put some men on checking them?"

Michael held the key in his palm as if weighing it. "Until the coroner says otherwise, Frank is treating Sheryl Ann's death as accidental. I doubt if he'll do anything with the key but file it somewhere."

"But if Tully and Clevenger were involved in something illegal . . ."

Michael nodded. He was silent for a moment. "That's why we're going to hold on to the key for a bit and see if we can find the locker ourselves."

"Won't that make things worse for you with the department?"

"Not if it all works out right in the end." Michael pressed his fingers against his forehead. "I think I'll pay Jack Clevenger a visit tomorrow."

44

Michael bent against the bitter wind and made a dash for the main entrance of Clevenger's town house complex. It was one of the many housing developments that had sprung up in the eastern half of town during the last decade. What they lacked in charm and spaciousness, they made up for, Michael supposed, by being halfway affordable.

He walked past the pool, deserted on this cold February day, and rang Clevenger's bell. A loud barking erupted from inside. Michael was ready to ring a second time when he heard footsteps and an "Okay, boy, I hear ya" addressed, he guessed, to the dog.

A moment later, Clevenger opened the door. His affable, good-to-see-you expression was wiped clean the minute he saw Michael. The black Lab, however, showed no such disappointment. He sniffed Michael's hand and circled his legs.

Clevenger scowled. "What do you want?"

"I'd like to talk with you."

"About what?"

"Maybe if I came in—"

He shook his head. "Sorry. The place is a mess."

An excuse so phony even its delivery rang false, but Michael would only aggravate Clevenger by pushing the matter. He stepped closer, hoping for a whiff of ginger. What he got instead was the stench of stale tobacco.

"It's about Sheryl Ann and Tully," Michael said.

"Like I told you last time, I don't know where Tully went to, and all I know about Sheryl Ann is what I read in the papers."

"You didn't talk to her in the last couple of days?"

Clevenger's expression took on a layer of wariness. "Why would I?"

"Darla Quick said you were asking about her."

"Just trying to be sociable."

"Is that why Sheryl Ann called you the night she was killed?"

The muscle in Clevenger's jaw twitched. "Where'd you hear that?"

"Darla."

He sighed. "Then you know I never actually talked to Sheryl Ann. She left a message is all."

"You didn't try to call her back?"

"It was pretty late by the time I got the message."

"But you knew she was staying at the Snuggle Inn."

"So?"

Michael patted the dog's head, wishing they were having this conversation somewhere else. The doorway was not conducive to small talk or to broaching a subject indirectly. Besides, Michael was afraid Clevenger would close the door in his face if he pushed too hard.

He chose his words carefully. "I understand you and Tully were in business together."

"We were part of a band."

Michael nodded. "I mean the other business."

Clevenger's eyes narrowed. "What other business?"

"Tully was hard-up for money; you were helping him out."

"Yeah, sort of. Wasn't really a business."

"I'd like to hear about it."

Clevenger didn't respond immediately. When he did, the hostility in his voice was thick enough to cut. "You got a real question, ask it. Otherwise, I got things to do."

Michael smiled as though he hadn't heard. "What's the dog's name?"

"Cody."

Michael snapped his fingers, calling the dog, and then began rubbing behind the dog's ears. Cody sat at Michael's feet, head cocked for optimal scratching.

"If you want to play hardball," Michael said, "we'll do it your way. It will be a whole lot easier for everyone, yourself included, if you cooperate with us." He was no longer part of the *us*, but Clevenger had no way of knowing that.

"Why should I?"

"We've got three suspicious deaths—Tully, Bobby, and Sheryl Ann. You knew all three people."

"Coincidence."

"I don't think so."

"You've got no proof of anything."

"Tully owed you money. When he disappeared, you thought he and Sheryl Ann had skipped out. You were angry. Then Sheryl Ann called Darla from Idaho. Suddenly you knew where to find them."

"You think I killed Bobby, you're crazy."

"What about Sheryl Ann?" Michael asked. "According to Darla, you've shown unusual interest in finding her."

Clevenger was agitated. "I got nothing to say to you. Come here, Cody." He grabbed the dog by his collar.

As Clevenger's right hand yanked the dog inside, Michael caught a glimpse of scabs on Clevenger's lower right arm, just above the wrist.

Michael felt as though he'd been punched in the chest. "What happened to your arm?"

Clevenger looked startled. He slammed the door in Michael's face.

Michael stepped back. Scabs in the very place Kate remembered gouging her attacker.

Michael experienced the familiar quickened tempo of his pulse. The excitement of feeling he was on the right path.

What he needed now was the ammunition to corner Clevenger.

Michael started his search with the Greyhound station. Sheryl Ann had said Tully was returning from a trip, and bus stations were more likely than airports to have the old-fashioned key lockers.

When the bus station turned up nothing, Michael tried the municipal airports, outlying train stations, and eventually community pools and local gyms. Again, with no luck. Kate had wanted to cancel her client appointments and come with him, but Michael had convinced her it wasn't necessary. Now he wished he'd encouraged her to come along just so he'd have some company. It was tedious work, made more wearisome by the fact that the key from Tully's pocket wasn't even the same shape as the ones he was finding in his search.

By five o'clock when he decided to call it a day, Michael had covered all of the obvious spots and a good number of the leading contenders. No luck anywhere. He was exhausted and discouraged.

"Did you talk to Clevenger? Did you find the locker?" Kate started firing questions at him the minute he walked in the door that evening.

Michael hung his coat over the doorknob. Kate's enthusiasm helped wipe away some of the exhaustion. He kissed her forehead. "Yes. No."

"Okay, sorry. Let me back up. What did Clevenger have to say?"

"Not much. He made it clear we're on opposite teams."

"That's good isn't it? If Clevenger were innocent, wouldn't he be more cooperative?"

Michael shrugged. "It can go either way."

"What about his aftershave lotion?"

"Definitely no gingerlike aroma in the air."

"Maybe he only uses it on special occasions."

Michael poured himself a glass of ice water from the refrigerator, then turned to Kate. "When the man attacked you in the driveway late last week, you thought you scratched his arm with the key, right?"

She nodded. "I'm sure I did."

"I saw scabs on Clevenger's right arm, above the wrist."

She looked confused for a moment, and then slowly the connection dawned. "You think he's the one who attacked me?"

"The physical description fits."

"But why?"

"Maybe he was trying to get information about where Sheryl Ann was."

Kate rubbed her arms. "Where was he when Bobby was killed?"

"I don't know yet, but I think we may be on to something with Clevenger. The key of Tully's, on the other hand, is getting us nowhere." Michael recounted his day's quest. "Even if we do find the right locker, we may be too late. Most places clean out their lockers on a regular basis."

Kate looked dismayed. "Then we'll never know."

"Maybe not about the key, but we'll find a way to nail Clevenger, even without it."

Michael was brushing his teeth and studying the deepening frown lines in his face when Kate burst into the bathroom later that evening.

"We've got to get to the bowling alley! It's only ten o'clock—there's still time."

He rinsed his mouth and wiped the dripping water from his chin. "You want to go bowling?"

She laughed, shook her head. "Tully was a bowler. He had trophies and everything. I bet they've got lockers there."

A part of him resisted. He was tired. He'd had enough lockers for one day, and Kate's logic aside, the chances of success were slim. "I'm about ready for bed."

"If you don't want to come with me, I'll go myself. I'll never be able to sleep until I know."

That did it. "Okay," he said, but not with her level of enthusiasm. "Give me five minutes to put on my shoes."

Her eyes twinkled. "I'll tell Libby to keep an eye on Anna."

*   *   *

The bowling alley was at least forty years old, and although it had been renovated one or twice, it was clearly a relic of a different era. Nonetheless, all of the lanes were busy, as was the bar.

"Look what we've been missing," Kate whispered. "Maybe we should get out more often. Join a bowling team."

"Very funny."

"I haven't been bowling since high school."

"Neither have I, and it suits me just fine."

Michael spotted a bank of lockers at the far end of the building, near the lanes occupied by a raucous group of high school kids. He palmed the key and said a silent prayer.

It was clear right off the bat that the key design was the same. So was the numerical sequence. Kate was ahead of him, already bending to read the numbers near the bottom.

"This is it," she said, barely able to contain her excitement. "I'm sure of it."

Michael crouched beside her. He inserted the key, held his breath, and turned it. The door opened.

Inside the locker was a black canvas gym bag. Michael pulled it out and opened it, revealing a stash of loose bills.

"How much?" Kate squeaked.

He zipped up the bag and stood, relieved to find that nobody seemed to be paying them the least attention. "Let's talk in the car."

They left the bowling alley at a deliberately casual pace, but once they were outside, Kate picked up the tempo and practically raced to the car.

"Is it real?" she asked the minute she was inside. She turned sideways in the seat, facing Michael.

He examined the money. "Looks to be real." The bills weren't new, and they weren't all the same denomination, though most were fifties and hundreds. Nor were they neatly packaged in stacks. They looked like the worn and crumpled bills of everyday commerce. Had to be several thousand dollars at least.

"Where do you think it came from?"

Michael shook his head. "I don't know. Robbery, drugs, Ponzi scheme . . ."

"From the looks of it," Kate said, "Tully's money worries were over."

"Except that he owed Clevenger. Besides, there's nothing that says this was his to keep."

"Wow, no wonder Clevenger was angry when Tully disappeared."

Michael was silent.

"What now?" Kate asked.

It was the same question Michael had been asking himself. If he turned the money in, he'd have to explain why he was working a case when he'd been suspended. But he couldn't *not* report finding it either.

For once, Michael was thankful that Frank wasn't a stickler for following rules to the letter.

45

I slept intermittently, kept awake as much by Michael's tossing and turning as my own winding thoughts. Twice, he got out of bed and rambled around the house. The first time, I dozed lightly until I felt him crawl back into bed next to me, bringing with him the frigid night air. The second time, I followed him into the kitchen.

"What's wrong?" I asked.

"Nothing."

"Michael—"

"I'm having trouble sleeping is all. Sorry if I woke you." He opened the refrigerator. "I think I'll heat some cider. Do you want some?"

"Maybe a taste."

He poured cider into a saucepan, then added a strip of lemon peel and spices.

I slipped my arms around him. "Michael, tell me what's bothering you." It was clear something was. He was usually asleep the minute his head hit the pillow, and he stayed asleep even in the face of teenage and canine commotion. "Is it what's happening at work, with Gina?"

He shrugged.

"What is it then?"

"I told you, nothing."

"Doesn't feel like *nothing.*"

"Nothing important." He turned and kissed my forehead. "We're together, Kate—that's what's important. You're safe, and we're nearing the end of this nightmare."

"You really think so?"

"Absolutely. Frank wants this wrapped up as much as we do."

Michael had called him as soon as we'd returned home from the bowling alley. Under normal circumstances, he'd have bypassed Frank and gone directly to Captain Greyson, but being on administrative leave limited his options. Ironically, the very thing that irked Michael—Frank's willingness to bend rules and procedures—in this instance played to his benefit.

"He's going to run a check on Jack Clevenger," Michael continued, extracting himself from my arms to get the cups. "He's also looking into Tully's activities before his death. Something will turn up."

The pungent scent of warm, spiced cider permeated the kitchen. Michael handed me a cup, and I held it in both hands, savoring the warmth. I was reminded that only a few days earlier Sheryl Ann had been sitting across the table from me. Sorrow swelled in my chest at the memory. At least we were close to catching her killer. That was some consolation.

I took a sip of cider. "You think the money was part of whatever Tully and Clevenger were up to?"

"That's my first guess."

"And you think that Clevenger killed Sheryl Ann looking for it?"

Michael took a minute before answering. "He knew she was at the motel."

"But why kill her? I don't think she knew what he and Tully were involved in."

"Maybe not. It looks like he wasn't taking any chances, though."

We sipped our cider in silence. My thoughts drifted to Michael, who was uncharacteristically edgy this evening.

Finally, I reached for his hand. "It's this case that's got you worried? Not something about us?"

He turned his hand so that our palms met. "Not about us, Kate. I promise."

"Things will work out—both with this case and at work."

His smile was tinged with resignation. "One way or another. The timing is just so bad. I don't like having to turn to Frank for help. It rankles."

"I know it does. But as you said yourself, he wants this case wrapped up, too."

"It needs to be wrapped up the right way," Michael muttered. "I feel like I'm between a rock and a hard place."

I went back to bed, leaving Michael to a second cup of cider. I was asleep almost instantly. The next thing I knew, Michael was gently shaking me awake. The clock read 8:00, and the gray light of morning showed through the window.

I sat up, blinked at the clock to make sure I was reading it right. "My God, why did you let me sleep so late? The kids will be late for school."

"It's okay." Michael was fully dressed and slipping into his jacket. "I'm giving Libby a ride to school, and Anna wasn't feeling well, so I said she could stay home today. That's okay, isn't it? You didn't have anything marked on the calendar."

I lay back against the pillow. "That's fine. I just hope she hasn't got a major bug, what with her throwing up the other day."

"She says her head hurts."

"If this keeps up, I'll take her to the doctor."

"I've got stuff to do," Michael said. "I'll give you a call later this afternoon."

"Where are you going?"

"There are a couple of things I want to check." He sounded deliberately vague.

"Are you taking the money?"

"Frank thought we should wait a bit before logging it into evidence. Fewer questions that way."

I smiled. "You aren't afraid I'll go on a shopping spree with it?"

"That's not my biggest worry, no." He frowned. "It should have been logged into evidence right away, though. I hope Frank has covered the right bases."

"But we don't know that it's connected to a crime."

Michael kissed my forehead. "Let's just hope that Anna doesn't decide to search out the pudding cups." He'd stashed money in the closet with our earthquake supplies, safely buried beneath Costco-sized cartons of stew, fruit, cereal, and pudding. Although Anna had once helped herself to a week's worth of disaster dessert, it was the safest hiding place we could come up with.

I put my arms around his neck. "I love you," I told him.

"I love you, too."

* * *

Rain pounded the roof and lashed against the windows. It was a perfect day for staying indoors and indulging oneself. Anna and I decided to do just that.

We spent a leisurely morning enjoying the change of pace. She was sniffily and sleepy, but healthy enough to fill up on waffles and hot chocolate. Though I had plenty of work, I couldn't seem to gear up for it. I felt suspended in time, waiting. For what, I wasn't entirely sure, but I knew that between Frank and Michael something was bound to break soon.

Leaving the kitchen cleanup until later, I settled Anna in front of the television and stepped into a long, hot shower. The water pulsated against my shoulders, easing the tension and drowning my thoughts.

When I'd toweled off, I took my time rubbing lotion into my skin and playing with a new gray-green eyeliner, blending it with a tiny sponge the way I'd recently read about in a magazine. I was drying my hair when the doorbell rang.

"It's the UPS man," Anna called out. "He's got a package."

"Don't answer the door. I'll be there in a minute." Too late. I heard the door squeak as Anna opened it.

I slipped on my robe and knotted the sash. By the time I made it to the front hall, I could see the UPS man, package in hand, leaning into the hallway.

There was nothing distinguishing about his appearance—medium height, medium complexion, dark eyes, a watch cap on head—but I knew right away that something wasn't right.

As I hurried to Anna, I saw a vehicle parked in front of the house. Not the brown UPS truck but a beige van.

Dread exploded inside me.

The man mumbled the word "mother," and then, abruptly, he pulled the cap over his face and pushed his way inside. Another man, also masked, followed.

It happened so quickly, I had no time to react. The first man slapped a hand over my mouth and snapped my head back against his chest in a viselike grip. His thumb pressed against the hollow of my throat, cutting off my breathing.

My hands clawed the empty air. I twisted and kicked, struggling against his overpowering strength. All the while, my eyes were focused on Anna, who was struggling just as hard in the grip of the other man.

Don't you dare hurt her, I thought as panic flooded through me. Don't you hurt so much as a single hair on her head.

The man clutching Anna was the shorter and stockier of the two. He had stubby fingers with uneven, grease-blackened nails, and hairy hands that looked like they belonged in some B-grade monster movie. Behind the mask, his eyes were dark and cold.

He brought out a gun and held it against Anna's head. "You got the picture now?" His voice was low and gravelly. "You try *anything* and your little girl gets it."

Anna whimpered, a frightened-animal cry that started deep in her throat. Her eyes shone with panic. Her squirming and twisting intensified.

At the sight of the gun, I stopped struggling, afraid to even blink.

"Pffst." I formed the words in my throat, but with the hand tight against my mouth, talking was impossible.

Anna was still squirming frantically.

Max had stirred from his spot in the back bedroom

and approached the men, tail wagging. The taller man kicked at Max, who looked stunned. Then, dragging Anna, the man opened the door and booted Max outside into the rain.

Anna continued to flail.

I willed my body to go limp. "Pffst." I tried again.

Finally, the man's grasp relaxed.

I gulped for air. "It's okay, honey," I sputtered, addressing Anna. My voice was frantic rather than soothing. I tried a second time. "It's okay."

Mother lies, again. Even Anna would recognize that. There was nothing at all okay about the situation, but I was hoping she would take her cues from me. "He's got a gun, Anna. You can't fight someone with a gun."

Her eyes were wide. She looked at me, blinking away tears. But she stopped thrashing.

The man snickered. "A gun is always the trump card, kid. Remember that."

He dragged Anna across the hallway, nearer to where I was pinned by his companion. As he approached I caught a whiff of ginger-scented aftershave.

"What do you want?" My head was still locked against the taller man's chest so I couldn't get a good look at him.

"We want the bag," Hairy Hands said.

"What bag?"

"Don't play stupid, lady." The man who held me had a slight Brooklyn accent. "The one with the money."

"That's all you want?" My heart was racing. I couldn't take my eyes from the gun pressed to Anna's head. These men had killed twice already. Maybe more than that. Now they were going to kill us.

Brooklyn laughed. "That's enough, ain't it? We've

been trailing after that bag seems like forever. Tully shoulda known better.''

I agreed wholeheartedly. If not for Tully, none of us would be in this mess. "Where'd the money come from?" I asked, stalling for time to think.

"The tooth fairy."

"Is that why you killed Bobby and Sheryl Ann? For some ratty old money?"

His thumb found the hollow of my throat again. "Look lady, cut the Chatty-Cathy stuff and tell us where the money is. We got things to do."

Panic had turned my brain to mush. I needed a plan. There was no way they were going to let us go. I knew that. Even if I handed over the money. Our only hope was somehow to escape, but with a gun aimed at Anna, I couldn't take chances.

"Where . . . is . . . it?" He emphasized each word, his mouth close to my ear.

"In, in the storage room."

Hairy Hands nodded at his companion. "What are we waiting for, then?"

I was having trouble breathing. It felt as though my lungs had turned to stone. Once they had the money, they'd kill us.

"Let my daughter go," I pleaded. "I'll give you the money. Just let her go." I addressed Hairy Hands, since he was the one holding Anna. Also the only one of the two I could make visual contact with. His eyes were glassy.

"You're missing the message here, lady. We got the gun. We give the orders. Now let's get that bag."

"Please. She's only six." I could hear the desperation in my voice. I didn't like it.

Anna started to whimper again.

"Look, we can find the storage room ourselves, if that's the way you want it." He pressed the gun against Anna's flesh. I could see the soft dimpling of her skin beneath the cold, hard metal.

"No, wait! I'll show you where it is."

With my arms pinned behind my back, I led them to the rear of the house and showed them the closet.

"Open the door." He released one of my arms.

I pulled out the green plastic tub. "In there."

"Get it."

Nervously, my eyes on Anna, I pried off the lid. "The money's under the cans," I told them, moving the beef stew and cling peaches that were supposed to sustain us during an emergency. Here was an emergency of a different sort, and there were no hidden supplies to help me through it.

The man holding Anna began pawing through the bills, tossing them onto the floor. "Where's the rest of it?"

"The rest?"

"The money wasn't loose like this. It was in a bag. Where's the bag?"

Fear clouded my thinking. Surely they weren't interested in a canvas gym bag?

"Where is it?" he demanded.

"I . . . I . . ."

My captor wrenched my arm behind my back with such force, I cried out.

Anna watched in alarm.

"I don't know where it is," I cried. "I only know about the money."

An open palm struck the side of my face sharply, bringing tears to my eyes. "Don't play cute."

"It's the truth. I don't know were the bag is." I tried to think what Michael might have done with it. He wouldn't have thrown it away, but I had no idea where it was. The evidence room maybe. "It might be at the police station," I said in desperation.

In a flash, the hand moved to my face again, slapping the other cheek. "Nice try, but it won't work."

Anna began struggling. Hairy Hands pinched her upper arm so hard she yelped.

"Clevenger's got his money," I said. "What does he want the bag for? We'll buy him another one. We'll buy him a dozen."

"Hey, you hear that," the taller man said to his companion. "She thinks this money is Clevenger's." He laughed. "As if we'd hang out with a dumb shit like that."

"Doesn't matter what she thinks. Let's take them to the shop. Maybe they'll remember better with a little help."

Shop? Visions of hot embers and thumbscrews blinded me.

"I'd tell you if I knew," I screamed at him.

Another slap. He yanked me by the arm, dragging me down the hallway.

"Please don't hurt my little girl. Whatever you do to me, please—"

Out of the corner of my eye, I noticed the man raise his arm again, as if to strike another blow. I flinched. And then I saw that instead of an open palm, he held a hypodermic needle in his hand.

"No!" I twisted, trying to bite his arm.

There was a quick jab into my thigh.

"Who are you?" The cry rose up in my throat, but

already my mouth felt fuzzy. I muttered something that was indecipherable even to my own ears.

As consciousness faded, I focused on Anna. Tried to give her a reassuring smile. But my lips wouldn't cooperate. The look of terror in her eyes was the last thing I saw.

46

Michael was on the freeway, headed north. Rain pounded the windshield, limiting visibility. He yawned, shook his head to clear it. He felt as though he'd been up all night. Hell, for all intents and purposes, he had been. He'd probably managed no more than two hours of sleep total. And even that was fretful.

He hated being out of the loop. Hated feeling like a bystander to events that touched him so deeply. He itched to drop by the station, if for no other reason than to be there, to feel the pulse of a case moving forward.

But that would only make things worse. Administrative leave meant *leave, stay away*. If this mess with Gina had any chance of working out right, he'd have to play by the rules.

He ran a hand along the back of his neck, fighting the swell of panic that threatened to surface whenever he his thoughts ventured to Gina.

Christ, how had it happened, anyway? How could she so totally misinterpret his intentions?

First things first, he reminded himself. His mind was cluttered enough without worrying about what was going to happen with Gina.

The windows had begun to steam up. Michael turned on the defroster. Turned his mind back to the issue at hand. For the time being, he needed to focus his energy on Clevenger. And now that he'd spent the morning talking with the other band members, Michael had the feeling it was going to take all the energy he could give it.

None of the people he'd spoken with had been able, or willing, at any rate, to add to what Michael already knew. Michael had the impression it was a crowd that didn't have much use for the police in any shape or form. Only Dick Arnold, the sax player, seemed halfway cordial. His smooth baby face didn't exactly break into a smile when he saw Michael, but at least he'd remembered they'd met previously at the Hideaway.

Arnold was aware that Clevenger had been trying to help Tully out of a financial jam, but he didn't know any of the particulars.

"I know Clevenger lent him some money," Arnold had said. "But Jack's a smart guy. Wouldn't have done it if he wasn't confident he'd get it back."

"Because he trusted Tully?"

"Clevenger doesn't do things based on personal feelings. He must have known Tully was coming into some money."

"Any idea how?"

"Nope."

"You think it was on the up-and-up?"

Arnold shrugged.

"Could he have been dealing in stolen goods?"

Another shrug.

"How about drugs?"

A moment's hesitation.

"Look, I'm not aiming for a drug arrest here, just information. Does Clevenger do drugs?"

Arnold had refused to look him in the eye. "Let's just say he's got friends who do."

Drug dealing was certainly high on the list of possibilities, but it wasn't the only option. Could have been anything from counterfeiting to conspiracy. And everyone Michael had spoken to that morning agreed on one thing—Jack Clevenger had been in town the entire weekend that Bobby Lake was murdered. That one niggling detail bothered Michael, like a fly on a quiet summer afternoon.

He stopped at a QuickStop for his third cup of coffee, and called Frank from the pay phone near the men's room.

"Anything?"

"Not yet."

"Did you look?" Michael's tone had an edge of nastiness, which he hadn't intended.

"Hey, don't get all huffy on me. I'm not the one with the departmental cloud over his head, remember."

Michael bit back his irritation. "This is important. If we can tie Clevenger to both Sheryl Ann's and Bobby's deaths—"

"Right, but we can't do it by pulling a rabbit out of the hat. Jack Clevenger's got no record. There are no whispers about him on the street. If he lent Tully money, it was strictly between the two of them. And we certainly can't go after a guy for helping a friend."

"He's got a scab on his hand. The very spot where Kate gouged her attacker."

"I'm not saying you're off base, Michael. I'm saying we've got certain procedures—"

"Maybe I should talk to him again."

"That's the very thing you *shouldn't* do."

"But if it's going to—"

"Look, I know it's tough for you right now." Frank's voice held genuine sympathy. "I've got a handle on things, okay? The best thing you can do right now is stay out of it."

"You're making this case a priority, aren't you?"

"I'd like all this to end as much as you would." There was a weariness to Frank's tone that caught Michael by surprise. "If we can nail Clevenger, we'll do it. I'm going to pay him a visit myself, this afternoon."

"Tell him we found the money. Maybe that will shake him up. Let on you know more than you do."

"I know how to handle an interview," Frank said testily.

"I wasn't implying you didn't. Speaking of the money, when do you figure to log it in?" Michael was glad he didn't have to answer to the captain just yet, but he wasn't as comfortable about playing loose with the rules as Frank was.

"Soon. If we can make the case first, it will set the right tone."

Maybe, Michael thought. But the longer they waited, the more there would be to explain.

When he finished talking with Frank, Michael called Kate. No answer. Anna must not have been so sick after all, unless Kate had taken her to the doctor's.

Michael used the rest room, then found himself drawn again to the bank of pay phones. The telephone had become his lifeline. The only way to keep his fingers on the pulse of activity that, until yesterday, had been as vital to him as his own heart.

It was against his better judgment, but he did it anyway.

"Hi, Janet. Any messages?"

"Michael? How are you doing?"

"Surviving."

"Don't worry. You'll be back before you know it. Such nonsense. Making a mountain out of a dust speck."

She didn't, he noticed, rush to defend his innocence. But he didn't blame her. How could anyone from outside know what the truth was when the two people directly involved couldn't recognize it?

"Anything important going on there?" he asked.

"I probably shouldn't tell you this, but Gina was in Greyson's office all morning. She's been sitting at her desk like a zombie ever since. She does *not* look like a woman delighting in victory."

"She's crazy. Who can tell what she's thinking?"

"I don't know about crazy. I've talked with her. She's pretty upset."

"I never—"

"I'm not accusing you, Michael. I'm saying she has her reasons."

Maybe calling in wasn't such a good idea after all. "Anything else?"

"Just a message from one of the uniformed officers, Les Oliver. Did he reach you?"

"When?"

"He called about an hour ago. I gave him your home phone number."

"Did he leave a number where he could be reached?"

Michael reached into his pocket for his notebook and jotted down the number. Then he cleared the line and deposited another thirty-five cents.

"Hey, I'm glad you called," Oliver said. "I'd just about given up hope."

"What's up?"

"I picked up Jason Liao this morning."

"What for?"

"Car theft."

"I suspected as much. I've had my eye on him in connection with a homicide too."

"Yeah, he told me. See, that's the interesting thing. He's been talking his head off."

"Saying what?"

"I think you'd better hear that for yourself."

"Where are you?"

"St. Mary's Church, near the BART station."

"A church?"

"I happened to know there was a room here where we could talk without interruption."

The room was in a separate building at the back of the church. A cluster of classrooms, from the looks of it.

Jason Liao was handcuffed, his hands in front of him. He looked up when Michael entered.

"I didn't kill him," Liao said. "I know you think I did, but I didn't."

Michael glanced at Les Oliver.

"Tell him what you told me," Oliver said.

"I'm going to get some kind of deal here, aren't I? Cooperating with the police and all."

"Let's hear what you've got; then we can talk deals." Michael pulled out a chair and straddled it, facing Liao.

"You want to know who killed my uncle, right?"

Several sarcastic responses came to mind. Michael swallowed them and nodded instead.

Liao licked his lips. "I'm pretty sure it was a guy by the name of Carlo."

"Last name?"

"I don't know that, but he works for Rudy."

"Rudy?"

"Rudy Harrington."

Michael looked at Les Oliver, who raised his eyebrows and nodded. Carlo the bartender. Rudy's longtime friend.

"Rudy knew your uncle?" Michael asked.

Liao shook his head. "My uncle found out what we were doing."

"And then?"

Liao's gaze settled on his feet. "He was going to go to the authorities . . . so they killed him. I was afraid they'd do that. That's why I kept having those parties, so I'd have an alibi."

"They? I thought you said it was Carlo."

"Yeah, but Carlo don't do nothin' without Rudy telling him to."

Michael's mind was working fast and furiously to fill the gaps, but there were too many. "You said your uncle found out what you were doing."

Liao nodded.

"What *were* you doing?"

Liao was silent. He continued staring at the floor.

"He's part of a car-theft ring," Oliver explained. "Just like you thought."

Only Michael had never in his wildest dreams connected the car thefts with Rudy Harrington. "What's Harrington's involvement?"

Liao looked up. "It's his operation. I just grab the cars. He's got a garage where they strip them."

"You steal cars, and Rudy's team turns them into parts?"

"Faster than you'd believe, too. It's an amazing thing to watch." The statement was delivered with an overtone of admiration.

"I gather it's a big operation," Oliver said to Michael.

Liao shifted in his chair. "It's not like anyone gets hurt by it," he argued. "Insurance covers the car. So maybe it's a little hassle, but the guy gets a new one eventually. It's what you call a win-win situation."

"And where do you suppose the insurance companies get *their* money?" Michael wasn't expecting an answer, and he didn't get one. He didn't waste any effort explaining.

"You're saying Harrington is responsible for your uncle's death?" A discomfiting thought tugged at Michael's mind, but didn't stay long enough to take form.

Liao nodded, his face registering, for the first time, a hint of sorrow. "Wasn't supposed to happen that way. The old man shouldn'a gone poking into my business."

"So now it's your uncle's fault he got killed?"

"No." Liao's mouth trembled. "No, wasn't his fault at all. It's my fault."

"Compounded by the fact that you kept quiet about it." Michael made no effort to hide his disgust. "Was stealing cars so important to you that you were willing to let your uncle's killer go free?"

Liao shook his head. "Rudy said not to worry—he had it covered."

"Meaning?"

"I don't know exactly, but Rudy told me to forget it ever happened. So that's what I did. He's got connections. You don't mess with someone like that."

Les Oliver rocked forward onto his toes and addressed Liao. "Tell him the rest."

"You mean about the money? Every couple of weeks Rudy goes over to this bar he owns with a gym bag full of cash—"

Michael was on his feet so fast the chair toppled to the floor. "A gym bag? What color?"

"Black. Why?"

"How big?"

"I dunno. A gym bag."

"Don't go anywhere," Michael said. "I'll be right back."

Both Liao and Oliver gave him an odd look. Michael dashed to his car and pulled the canvas gym bag from his trunk where he'd stashed it with some thought of forcing Frank to log it into evidence.

"Like this?" he said, thrusting the bag in front of Liao.

Liao looked at it. "Yeah, like that."

So it wasn't Clevenger's money that Tully had run off with. It was Harrington's. And Harrington happened to be Bobby's stepfather.

Michael's mind sparked with unconnected thoughts, like fireflies on a summer evening. Here, there, and over here again. He struggled to contain them. Surely, all of this was not coincidence.

Cursing himself, he wadded the gym bag into a ball, bending the stiff cardboard at the bottom. If he hadn't been so preoccupied with worry about Kate, maybe he'd have gotten to the bottom of this sooner.

Angrily, he tossed the bag onto the table. A blue computer disk slipped from inside and slid across the surface.

With it was a simple white business card. Michael recognized it instantly.

47

Michael raced for home with one hand on the horn, slowing at red lights only long enough to check for cross traffic. Let her be out shopping, he prayed silently. Or at the pediatrician's. Just let her be safe.

But she wasn't. He could feel it in his bones.

And when he saw Max, who was never outside except on a leash, charging up the street to greet him, Michael's heart turned to ice. The disarray inside the house only confirmed what he knew.

Drawers had been emptied, furniture overturned, closets emptied. He checked the earthquake supplies. The money was gone, as he suspected. But it wasn't the money they'd been after. Not really. It was the disk.

Cold dread seeped through his skin, into his veins, permeating his whole body. He felt as though he'd risen from the dead.

At least he hadn't arrived home to find bodies. Or blood. That left him a gossamer strand of hope, and he was clinging to it with all his might.

Harrington and his men had taken Sheryl Ann to the creek. Whether they'd killed her there or elsewhere, he wasn't sure. But it had been nighttime then. This was broad daylight. Would that make a difference?

The phone rang.

Michael jumped, picked it up on the first ring. Then held his breath.

"Good, you're finally home." The voice on the other end was male and familiar. Rudy Harrington? Michael couldn't be sure.

"Who is this?" he asked.

"Not important. But I've got something you want."

"What's that?" Through sheer determination, Michael managed to sound calm, even casual.

A humorless laugh. "I think you know the answer. And you have something I want."

"The computer disk?"

"You found it, then. That will make the drop easier."

"If you want it back, you'll have to release Kate and Anna."

The caller continued as though he hadn't heard. "Take the disk to the library. There's a book there called *The Joy of Being Your Own Boss*. Stick the disk inside and leave. Don't bring anyone. Don't alert anyone. Don't get any ideas about copying the disk, either."

Michael's mind was racing.

"You listening?"

"Yeah. When do you want me at the library?"

"Now."

"And then?"

"Guess you'll have to wait and find out."

"Will you let Kate and Anna go?"

The voice on the other end snickered. "Listen, Stone. You don't have much choice here, do you?"

"Wait." His throat was so tight he was having trouble speaking. "How do I know they're still alive?"

"They are."

"Nuh-uh. I need proof. If they're dead, I have no reason to cooperate with you."

There were muffled voices, as though a hand had been placed over the mouthpiece. Michael could feel the sweat trickling down his sides. Finally, the voice was clear again.

"We're only doing this once, so listen up."

There was more shuffling on the other end, and then he heard a woman's voice, faint and confused. But definitely Kate's.

"What?" Her speech was slurred. She was addressing one of her captors. "You know my name. It's Kate . . . Kate Au . . . ouch, what do you want? I don't know what you want me to say."

"Kate? Can you hear me?" Michael yelled into the phone. He didn't know whether they were holding the receiver to her ear or not.

"What? Michael?" She was talking more clearly into the phone now. "Where are you?"

And then there was more shuffling. The man's voice returned. "See you in an hour," he said, and hung up.

48

My head felt like a basketball. A basketball stuffed with dry cotton. And it hurt. I giggled. A basketball being dribbled down the court.

It hurt more when I moved, but the dirt floor underneath me was hard and uncomfortable, making it difficult to stay in one position for long. A basketball . . .

Stop, I told myself.

A basketball with a mouth. I giggled again. A talking basketball.

"Mommy."

Suddenly the fog lifted, and I was awake. My head still throbbed and my body still ached, but it was *my* head. *My* body. I rolled over and peered through the dim light of the windowless interior.

"Anna? Are you all right?"

"Mommy?"

"I'm right here, honey." My throat was parched, but gradually my brain was clearing as the effects of the drug wore off.

"Mommy, where are we?"

Someplace dark and dank. Small. A shed maybe? I could make out a thin sliver of light through one of the wallboards. "I'm not sure, honey. Those men brought us here. I think it must be some kind of barn or something."

As my eyes adjusted, I could see a shadowy form lying about three feet away. Anna squiggled toward me like a worm.

"Are they gone?" she asked.

"I don't know." I listened for conversation or movement outside the shed. I heard nothing but a dog barking in the distance. Still, I dropped my voice to a whisper. "Are you okay, honey?"

"My head hurts. And I'm scared."

"Me too, sweetheart." Terrified in fact.

"I'm tied up. My hands and feet."

"Can you scoot behind me? Let's see if I can untie your hands."

Anna was young and agile. She managed to push herself along the dirt floor so that our backs were touching. My hands found hers and I gave them a tight, reassuring squeeze before I began to work on the rope that knotted her wrists. When her hands were free at last, she untied mine. Then I hugged her to my chest as if the power of my embrace could carry us to safety.

"My shoulder hurts," Anna said. "And I'm thirsty."

"I'm sorry, honey. Try not to think about it."

My eyes were now fully adjusted to the dim interior. The room was about seven feet wide and half again as long. Light seeped through the cracks on three sides of the room, leading me to believe that the fourth, the one with the door, was shared with another structure. Greasy rags and empty soda cans were heaped in one corner, a couple of old tires in another.

I walked the perimeter, exploring with my hands as well as my eyes. There was a single door, latched from the other side. The wallboards were weathered and cracked, but strong enough that they withstood my attempts to pry them loose.

I did manage to break off the rotten end of one board, near the base. I dropped immediately to my knees and peered out. Weeds and a wooden fence. That was all I could see.

A hard knot of fear lodged in my chest. We were trapped. Prisoners awaiting our execution. I swallowed to clear the sour taste that rose in my throat.

Anna peeked through the hole, then stuck her head through. "How are we going to get away?" she asked, pulling back inside.

Not *will* we get away, but *how*. Her innocence brought tears to my eyes. Her faith in me filled me with renewed determination.

How? That was the question I needed to concentrate on. There had to be a way out. For Anna's sake if no other. I wasn't going to let them kill her.

Anna brushed the dirt from her cheek. "If I were a baby, I could crawl through that hole. Or if Max were here, he could dig his way out."

Dig. That just might work. I'd tried to enlarge the hole by breaking off more of the board, but I hadn't thought to widen it by digging below.

"We're going to pretend we're Max," I told her.

We each took a soda can and began scooping dirt. We worked fast, and largely in silence, tossing loose dirt to the side like gophers. We were lucky the dirt was damp and soft. The hole grew rapidly.

Anna tested it twice, and on the third try she squeezed through.

"See if there's a way into the shed," I told her. "But be careful. If you see anyone, come right back."

I'd gone over the plan with her while we were digging, as well as what I imagined the layout of the structure might be. If she could find a way inside the main building, she might be able to open the door to our small prison. Unless it was locked.

The thought of sending my six-year-old daughter out alone into the unknown frightened me so much I felt sick, but the idea of staying put and waiting for the men to return frightened me even more. I said a silent prayer for her safety as I watched her small red sweater slip out of sight.

Please, Lord, be with her and keep her safe. I prayed to a god I wasn't even sure existed. Tried my best to forget that in spite of the many different gods we humans honored, bad things still happened to innocent children.

I barely breathed, so carefully was I listening for indications of Anna's progress. Meanwhile, my mind resonated with imagined sounds of all that could go wrong. The growl of a snarling dog. A gruff "gotcha." A child's terrified scream.

The agony of waiting was almost unbearable. It seemed an eternity, but by my watch, less than five minutes had passed when, finally, I heard the squeak of metal hinges and then scuffling of feet. I held my breath.

"Mommy?" Anna's voice was faint through the thickness of the wooden door.

"I'm here, Anna." I could see the handle turn, but the door didn't budge.

"Can you open the door, sweetie?"

"I'm trying. It's stuck."

My heart dropped. Locked was more like it. Tears of frustration filled my eyes.

But at least Anna was free. I needed to send her away before the men returned. "What's out there?" I asked. "Do you have any idea where we are?"

"It's just a building. Like a barn, only newer. Inside it looks like a big garage. A lot of old car parts and stuff."

"What's around the building?"

"There's a road in front, and a big hill behind us."

"Are there any houses around?"

"I can't see any." She was quiet a moment; then in a burst of excitement, she added, "There's a latch. It's up high on the door. That's why it won't open!"

More scraping.

"Anna? Can you reach the latch?"

"Just a minute."

"What are you doing?"

"I'm getting things to stand on."

"Be careful." The seconds passed slowly, agonizing. Finally, I heard a snap. I pushed against the door, and it gave slightly.

"Wait," Anna said. "I have to move the tires away."

And then she was in my arms. Tears of joy streamed down my cheeks. We'd managed to free ourselves!

Anna's description had been apt. We were standing in what looked like a commercial garage. There was a wall of tools and several large pieces of equipment I didn't recognize.

"Let's get out of here." I took her hand and started for the open door. The gray afternoon sky had never looked so appealing.

Before we'd taken more than a couple of steps, a

shadow fell across the rectangle of light that filtered through the doorway.

Someone was outside.

I put my finger to my lips, directing silence, then motioned for Anna to return to the little room at the back. While she crept toward the rear, the way I'd come just moments earlier, I looked around for something to use as a weapon. A three-foot length of pipe was the best I could do.

But I had the element of surprise in my favor. All I had to do was use it.

I hid behind one of the larger pieces of equipment. It didn't fully conceal me, but with in the poor interior light, I was hoping it would be several seconds before whoever it was saw me.

The dull tread of boots on bare ground grew closer. When I heard a twig snap just outside the open doorway, I raised the pipe, ready to swing.

Then stopped just in time. "Michael! How did you get here?"

He swung around, gun poised and aimed directly at my chest. For an instant he didn't move; then the tension drained from his stance. "Jesus. Kate?" He holstered the gun.

I dropped the pipe and ran for his arms. My body was shaking uncontrollably. A moment ago I'd been ready to swing with enough force to crush a skull, and now I could hardly stand up under my own power.

Michael held me tight. "You're all right?"

"How did you know we were here?"

"It's a long story. Where's Anna?"

I started to gesture toward the back room, when I saw another figure in the doorway.

"I see you brought reinforcements."

Michael turned abruptly.

"Keep your hands in the air," Frank said. He had a gun aimed in our direction.

49

I knew in an instant. Frank wasn't backup; he was the enemy.

"Easy now," he said to Michael. "Take your gun and slide it across the floor."

Michael did as instructed.

My stomach turned queasy with the knowledge that we were trapped. I thought of Anna hidden out of sight, and willed her to keep silent.

Frank retrieved Michael's gun and stuck it in his waistband.

"I had a feeling you'd pull something like this." Frank was addressing Michael. He didn't even look at me. "I told Rudy there was no way you'd go for that library drop."

Michael held his hands at shoulder level, his posture almost relaxed. If he was surprised to find himself staring down the barrel of a fellow officer's gun, he didn't show it.

"Why did you do it?" Michael asked. "Li Chen, Bobby Lake, and Sheryl Ann Martin. That's three murders. I hope they're giving you a big cut."

Frank looked tired. "Murder wasn't part of the plan."

"What was the plan?"

"Cars. Just cars."

We were standing with our backs to the northern side of the building. I fought the urge to glance toward the room where Anna was hiding, and kept my eyes focused on Frank instead. If she stayed quiet, maybe he'd never think to look for her.

Frank wiped a palm on his pant leg. "I stumbled onto their operation about a year ago. Rudy offered me a . . . a retainer to keep things from getting too hot."

"A payoff, in other words."

"Not everyone's as high-and-mighty as you." Frank's voice was taut with anger. "Plenty of cops do stuff like this all the time. You know that. Wasn't like I was letting child molesters go free or anything."

Michael nodded. "Just killers."

"I told you it started out as cars."

"It's become a lot more."

"I didn't know what lengths they'd go to. By the time I realized, it was too late. Rudy had tapes of me taking payoffs. He threatened to send them to every television station in the area unless I made sure things went the right way."

"Made sure they got away with murder, you mean."

"Li Chen was an old man," Frank said, almost apologetically. "He wouldn't have lived more than a couple of years anyway. All I had to do was make sure there was no hard evidence pointing to Harrington or his buddy Carlo."

"How do you justify Bobby and Sheryl Ann? They had more than a couple of years ahead of them."

A rustling sound came from the tiny room where Anna

was hiding. My heart stopped. I didn't dare look at Michael.

Frank appeared not to notice. "It isn't like you think," he insisted. "I didn't know for sure until this morning that Harrington was behind Sheryl Ann's death. With Bobby, I had my suspicions, but, again, I didn't know anything for sure at the time. That's the way I wanted it. The way I'd have liked to have kept it. But Rudy needed more favors."

With my mind focused on Anna, I'd been only half-listening to what Frank was saying. Bobby's name caught my attention, however. "Rudy killed Bobby? Bobby was his stepson."

Frank looked at me for the first time. His gaze was flat and devoid of warmth. He bore little resemblance to the man I'd joked with at barbecues and holiday parties over the past few years.

"It was Carlo and Rudy together," he explained. "They were looking for Tully. Sheryl Ann told people she and Tully had taken off for a vacation. Rudy was expecting to find Tully. He didn't even know Bobby was involved."

"But when he discovered Bobby at the cabin . . ." My mind screamed in protest. "How could he shoot his own stepson?"

Frank shrugged. "They said Bobby was being difficult."

I felt cold inside. Like ice. If Rudy hadn't balked at killing his own stepson, he'd never spare Anna.

Michael shifted his weight. "What kind of favors did Rudy want?"

"Little stuff. Mostly he wanted the computer disk back."

"So you helped him look for Tully?"

Frank shook his head. "He knew Tully was dead. Rudy

and Carlo are the ones who took his body. Didn't make sense to me, but they thought the fewer connections there were, the better. They didn't ask for big favors, just information now and then. And that I keep an eye on Kate."

I felt somehow defiled. "Why me?"

"Rudy felt sure you and Sheryl Ann were in it together, and that you knew where the disk was."

"All those panel trucks I saw—that was you?"

Frank shook his head. "Carlo. He carried out the actual surveillance. I suspect that's how he knew where Sheryl Ann was staying."

I swallowed against the dryness in my throat. Sheryl Ann had come to me for help. Instead, she'd walked into plain sight of a man who was looking for her.

"Why did they have to kill her?" I wailed.

"They tried to get her to tell them where the disk was."

"But she didn't *know* where it was."

Frank shrugged. "But by then she knew Rudy and Carlo were involved."

"So what now?" Michael asked. "You preparing to add more murders to your scorecard?"

"It's not what I want, you know." He hunched his shoulders and managed to sound aggrieved.

I'd been listening intently for sounds from the back room. I was prepared to throw myself into a spasm of coughing to cover any noise, but luckily Anna was holding still.

A car pulled to a stop outside. Michael tensed.

"Frank, please. Listen to me." I started forward, remembered the gun, and stopped. "We're friends, remember? You've had dinner at my house. You're a good man. You made a mistake, got in deeper than you meant to, but underneath you're a good man."

The sound of footsteps grew nearer.

"It's not too late," Michael added. "You can still do the right thing."

Frank wavered for just an instant; then Rudy Harrington appeared at the door.

He walked over to Michael and spat at his feet. "You picked the wrong man to mess with."

"You didn't honestly believe I'd race over to the library with the disk, did you?"

Harrington's face grew flushed. "You got it with you?"

"It's in a safe place."

"Where?"

"If you want it back, you'll have to release Kate."

"You still don't get it, do you?" Harrington laughed with the smugness of a boy pulling wings off a fly. His eyes scanned the garage. "Hey, where's the kid?"

Time ground to a halt. I felt a cold, crushing weight in my heart.

"What kid?" Frank asked.

"The girl. What kid do you think?"

Frank squinted at Harrington. "You drugged Anna, too?"

"She's still sleeping," I said quickly, and more loudly than was necessary. "With children, drugs take longer to wear off."

"Best let her sleep," Michael added. "One less person to keep track of for the moment."

Rudy pulled out his own gun and aimed it at us. "Go check on her," he told Frank. "She's in the storage room at the back."

Please, Anna, pretend like you're asleep. Just lie down, put your hands behind your back as though they're tied, and close your eyes.

She had to have been listening, and Anna was a savvy six-year-old. I prayed that she'd taken my hint.

As Frank stepped into the back room, I felt my lungs close down, as though all the air had been squeezed from them. I thought I might faint.

He emerged a few seconds later. "Yeah, she's still asleep."

I sucked in a great, calming breath. *Thank you, God. And thank you, Anna, for listening to me.*

"Start with the mother," Rudy said.

Frank spun around. "What do you mean?"

"Kill her."

"Now?"

Rudy nodded.

"You harm Kate in any way," Michael said hotly, "and I'll never tell you where the disk is. Your only chance of getting it back is to let Kate and Anna go."

Rudy laughed. "Go ahead, Frank."

Frank leveled his gun at me, holding it with both hands.

"Please, Frank." I tried to meet his eyes, but he wouldn't let me. "Please, don't do this."

"Turn around, Kate. Walk over to the far wall."

Panic slammed against my chest. "You're a good person, Frank. You can't do this."

"Move."

I stepped backward.

Rudy kept his gun aimed at Michael. "This is your last chance. Tell me where the disk is, or your girlfriend gets it in the back of the head."

"This is *your* last chance," Michael said. "If you let Kate and Anna go, I'll get you the disk. Otherwise, it will wind up on the captain's desk in about one hour. Along with a full explanation."

Rudy scoffed. "Frank will make sure the captain never sees it. He's got an interest in keeping his name in the clear as much as I do." He turned. "Don't you, Frank?"

With Frank's gun pointed directly at me, I inched toward the wall. I refused to turn my back on him. In the far distance, I heard the wail of sirens. I felt a ray of hope, then recognized the sound. Fire trucks, not police.

"I'm sorry, Kate," Frank said. "Very sorry."

Suddenly Frank swung to the right and fired at Rudy. Rudy gaped, openmouthed like a goldfish. Rudy's gun discharged, and Michael crumpled to the floor. Then Rudy sank to the floor, too.

With a scream, I rushed to Michael.

His face was contorted with pain. He took a breath. "Get Rudy's gun."

I couldn't move.

"I'm going to be okay, Kate. It's just my leg. It hurts like bloody hell, but I'll live. Now get the gun."

I looked around for Frank. He was gone.

"Do it, Kate."

Like a sleepwalker, I approached Rudy. He lay on his stomach, the gun in his outstretched right hand. A pool of blood was forming under him.

I hesitated.

"The gun," Michael said.

Holding my breath, I pried the still warm weapon from Rudy's fingers. A slight gurgle escaped from his lips.

Outside, the screech of sirens grew louder. I took off

my sweater and handed it to Michael along with Rudy's gun. "You sure you're okay? I've got to check on Anna."

He nodded.

But before I'd gotten to my feet, she was there, standing in the front doorway. And behind her were a half a dozen firemen in turnout gear.

50

"The fire department?" Sharon shielded her eyes from the sunlight peeking through the clouds, and laughed.

"Yep." I'd given her a quick account of the whole story while we were waiting for the dismissal bell to ring. Now, because we still had a few more minutes, she was coming back for details.

"That must have been a sight," she said.

Anna had indeed called the fire department. She'd sneaked out the hole at the back of the shed and run to Michael's car, where she used the cell phone to call 9-1-1. Luckily, she was able to see the street sign from the vantage point of the car.

"Why not the police?" Sharon asked.

"She heard someone on television once joke that if you want a quick response, better to yell *fire* than *get me the police*."

"Well, it worked."

"It might not have except that Frank had a change of heart at the last minute."

As I said his name, I felt a pang of sadness. Two days after he'd held a gun on us, Frank's car had gone over the cliff along a rugged section of the coastal highway. A witness said that he was driving at an excessive speed and appeared to head for the cliff deliberately. We'll never know.

I can't forgive him for his part in the nightmare I lived, but neither can I forget that he saved my life. I'm still not exactly sure why he did. Maybe, as I'd told him that day, he was, at heart, a good person.

Sharon hunched her shoulders against the chill. "Is Michael okay?"

"He's going to be hobbling around on crutches for a while, but the doctor thinks that with some physical therapy, he should have full use of his leg."

"He's lucky the bullet hit where it did."

"Very lucky." I flashed on the moment he'd been hit, when I was frozen in place with fear that he'd been killed. It was a memory I wanted to push away, but I had a feeling it would be a long time before I could.

"He's back on duty, too," I added. "That stuff with the college student, Gina, was a misunderstanding."

"You mean like, he's from Mars, she's from Venus?"

"A bit more than that. Frank was behind most of it. He wrote the captain a note explaining it all before he . . . before he died. Apparently, Frank kept telling Gina that Michael was interested in her. He sent her suggestive notes and signed Michael's name. We think he was the one who sent me the fax as well. Gina took it from there."

Sharon's eyes widened. "Why?"

"He wanted to distract Michael. It seems Michael was beginning to get wind of police misconduct and was looking at Frank in connection with it. The closer Michael got to discovering what was going on, the more desperate Frank became."

"Geesh, and you kept telling me Frank was a nice guy."

"He clearly wasn't that, but I don't think he set out to hurt anyone. Most of his trouble came from covering up."

"And from getting mixed up with Rudy Harrington. Now there's a creepy guy."

I agreed.

"So that guy from the band, Clevenger, he wasn't involved in any of this?"

"Only peripherally," I explained. "Tully was running heroin for him from Mexico. When Tully disappeared, Clevenger assumed he'd appropriated the drugs for himself and run off with Sheryl Ann. Clevenger was livid. He was out of the pocket money he'd advanced Tully, *and* he faced an angry contact who was expecting the shipment. It was Clevenger who attacked me in the driveway, desperate to locate the drugs."

"So where was the stuff?" Sharon asked.

"With Tully."

"He was carrying it around?"

"He swallowed it. A couple of condoms' worth."

"Yuck."

That was my feeling, too. "If only he'd stuck to drugs, none of this would have happened. But when he saw the bag of money, I guess he couldn't let the opportunity pass. Apparently, he had no idea the computer disk was even in the bag."

"The guy was a magnet for bad luck, wasn't he?"

"Compounded by bad judgment."

Sharon stepped back to let an au pair pushing a stroller by. "What was on the disk that made it so important, anyway?"

"Rudy's records for the auto-theft business. Money laundering, payoffs to Frank—there was enough there to put him away even without the murder charges."

The bell rang. Anna was first out the door. She raced to where we were standing, waving a sheet of paper.

"Guess what? I'm famous. Lauren's grandmother read about what happened all the way out in Fremont! My name was even in the paper."

Fremont was only about thirty miles from Walnut Hills, but to Anna it might as well have been France. Or the moon.

With dramatic hyperbole, Sharon's face registered awe. "I've never known anyone famous before. What's more, you're famous for being clever and brave. Those are very admirable qualities."

Anna beamed. "All the kids wanted to hear what happened, too. And there was a big fight to see who would sit next to me at lunch."

Kyle shuffled out a minute after Anna.

"Hey, sport," Sharon said, greeting her son.

Kyle glared at her. "How come *we* never get kidnapped?"

She rolled her eyes. "Because so far we've been lucky." Sharon turned to me. "Bobby and Sheryl Ann weren't part of any of what was going on, right? I mean, they weren't wise to Tully or Clevenger?"

"Right. I'm not even sure Bobby's punch is what killed Tully. It could have been the heroin. And Sheryl Ann . . ." I stopped, hearing her voice in my mind as I often did. I shook my head. "So senseless, all of it."

Sharon gave me a hug. "Well, I'm glad it worked out for you. For purely selfish reasons among others." She grinned. "If it hadn't, I'd have had to find someone else to help me with the PTA Talent Show."

"Wait a minute. Who said anything about my helping with the talent show?"

But Sharon had already taken Kyle's hand and headed for her car.

51

Michael propped his crutches against the file cabinet and slid into the chair at his desk. He was so glad to be back it was all he could do to refrain from hollering with joy. Hell, he was glad to be alive, period. There was nothing like looking down the barrel of a loaded gun to make you appreciate life.

Carlo was behind bars; Rudy was in the morgue. They had signed confessions for the deaths of Li Chen, Bobby Lake, and Sheryl Ann Martin. Carlo hadn't wasted any time cutting a deal. Life in prison had far greater appeal than death.

Michael was writing up his final notes on the cases when Janet buzzed him.

"Clay Potter on the line," she said.

Sheryl Ann's stepbrother. Michael picked up. "Stone here."

"You're the officer I talked to a few days ago when I was in Walnut Hills?"

"Right."

"Well, uhm, I heard about what happened. It was on the news."

Michael mumbled a form of acknowledgment.

"And I just wanted to be sure I heard right. Sheryl Ann's death wasn't an accident?"

"No. She was murdered." That was sometimes harder for relatives to hear than that a family member had died accidentally, but if Potter had been listening to the news, he surely knew already.

"And you've got the man who did it?"

"There were two of them. One is dead. The other has confessed. They followed her to the motel and drugged her, trying to learn where the money her husband had stolen was hidden. Then they pushed her off the bridge. I suspect she had enough drugs in her that she didn't feel anything." Small consolation, but sometimes it helped.

"What about the neighbor who reported seeing a drunk woman?"

"Trumped up by the men who killed her. They wanted us to think it was an accident."

Potter was silent.

"You sound like you have some doubts," Michael said. He hoped the guy wasn't ready to confess, himself. Two confessions and they'd have a hard time making either one stick. A defense lawyer's dream.

Potter sighed. "No, I just wanted to be sure. My wife was out of town that night, and, well, she and my mother were adamant that Sheryl Ann shouldn't get any of the inheritance. I just worried, you know, that . . ."

"The man who killed her is in jail. He was able to give us details only the killer would know."

"Thank you." Potter's voice was almost inaudible.

Michael hung up the phone shaking his head. What was the guy doing married to a woman he suspected of murder?

The voice inside his head stopped him. Hadn't he

come close to the same thing? No, Michael assured himself, he hadn't. He'd never really doubted Kate. Not in the same way.

He looked up and saw Gina eyeing him furtively from across the room. She lowered her gaze the minute he glanced over, but when he hobbled into the coffee room later that morning, she followed.

She stood at the door and didn't approach. Her gaze was directed somewhere near his feet.

"I wanted you to know I'm sorry. I didn't cause trouble intentionally."

"I know."

Gina bit her lower lip. "Frank told me that you'd confided in him, said . . . stuff about me. And the notes were so . . . Oh, God, I feel like such a fool."

"He manipulated you, Gina. Don't blame yourself. He lied to you and used you."

She nodded, still not looking at him. "I guess there was probably some wishful thinking on my part, too." She paused. "You were so kind to me. I thought you liked me."

"I do like you, Gina. As a friend. And I'm happy to continue working with you here at the station."

She looked at him, finally, and smiled. "Thank you. Kate is a lucky woman."

Not half as lucky as I am, Michael thought.

Epilogue

Spring has finally arrived. Winter monotones have given way to a blaze of color. Tulips and daffodils dance in the breeze, and everywhere I look are flowering trees, a profusion of delicate pink and white mixed with traces of brilliant, leafing green.

I breathe deeply, filling my lungs with the sweet scent of jasmine and alyssum. The sun's warmth grazes my skin with its healing touch.

Shielding my eyes against the afternoon brightness, I watch Michael and Anna tossing a softball in the front yard. Because of his exuberant participation earlier, Max has been temporarily banished to the house at Anna's request.

"Ready?" Anna says.

Michael cups his palms, making a target of them. "Aim for my hands."

She squints her eyes and aims, but the throw is wide to the left. Michael totters after it, favoring his right leg. The wound is mostly healed, but the leg muscle remains stiff, making his gait uneven. It's barely noticeable when he walks, and the doctor says that with continued physical therapy it will improve further.

My eyes follow Michael as he retrieves the ball from beneath the dogwood. Despite the limp he moves with the easy confidence of a man who's comfortable in his own skin. He turns and says something to Anna that sets off ripples of laughter between them. Overhead, the mockingbird joins in with a chorus of her own.

Such simple pleasures make me almost giddy with happiness. I savor the moment. Store it away in my memory for a rainy day.

Libby calls from the house. "Kate, have you seen my Spanish book?"

"No," I tell her. "I haven't."

"Check next to the television," Michael says. He tosses the ball to Anna, who catches and then drops it. "I think I saw it there yesterday."

"*¿Donde el bano?*" Anna yells. Under Libby's tutelage, she has picked up a strange collection of Spanish phrases.

A beige van drives past the house. Anna freezes, one arm in the air ready to throw. Her face is painted with apprehension.

"It's okay, Anna. The bad men are gone. Forever."

It takes a moment, but gradually she relaxes. She throws the ball again. This time it lands right in Michael's hands.

"Good throw, Anna."

"I'm going to make popcorn," Libby says. "Anyone want some?"

"Me!" Anna is off in a flash, her slender limbs a portrait of energy in motion.

"Heads up," Michael says, tossing me the ball. He joins me near the steps a minute later and brushes his hand against my back. "A penny for your thoughts."

"I was just thinking how happy I am. And how close it came to being terribly different."

He nods. "You can't dwell on what might have happened, though. It will make you crazy."

"I don't dwell on it," I tell him. "But I can't forget it, either."

"No," Michael says gravely. He moves his hand lightly over the small of my back. "Neither can I. And that makes what we have all the sweeter."

Then he turns and gives me a smile. A sunshine smile that lights his eyes and causes a flutter deep within my chest. I am, indeed, a lucky woman.